I0699671

What If We Met In A Bookstore

What If We Met In A Bookstore

The Breezewood Chapters

Book One

Callie McLay

To Alena and Kate. This book is for you. And to mom, for teaching me how to write and hold a pencil correctly, even though I still hold it wrong.

Contents

One

BRIAR

I 'm not fond of early mornings. Don't get me wrong, I like breakfast and warm sunshine and being awake and alive, but I don't enjoy the feeling of dragging my eyes open from a deep dream. I'd rather stay in bed and return to my dreams where reality seems more alive than when I'm awake. It's in my dreams that I have adventures. I'm invisible, I can fly, and I can hold my breath underwater for hours. And sometimes, I dream of him. He's holding my hand or holding a door open for me with a soft smile. I get lost in his eyes and there's a moment or two where I think it's real. But it isn't real. None of it is, and I know it never can be. Too bad I have to wake up.

I roll over to silence the alarm on my phone, the "Narnia Lullaby" melody forcing me awake rather than lulling me back to sleep. I yawn, rubbing my eyes while checking for notifications on the screen. Nothing important. Just a few junk emails and a

Goodreads update from friends. I set my phone face down in the covers and stare blankly at the ceiling. Sunshine glows in speckles across my textured wall, hinting of a clear day.

I heave a tired sigh. With a snap decision, I take the morning head on. I debated last night after reading until midnight to set my alarm to nine a.m. rather than six-thirty but here I am, awake at dawn. Getting up early means I can get a latte at the shop down the road, then spend the rest of the late morning and afternoon browsing the book and thrift stores. It has been a while since I had the time to do that. Why not get an early start?

Gold and pink blush across the sky as I stagger into the kitchen wearing my blue flannel pjs. Chilly fall air presses in around the house, the trees outside just beginning to turn colors. I yawn again, smiling through my tired eyes.

Mornings on the coast of Alaska are my absolute favorite. Waking up just minutes from the ocean with mountains off in the distance and some behind you is serenely comforting. I pull my eyes from the window and put a sourdough bagel in the toaster.

I turn on the light above the kitchen table and pull a chair out, a hollow scraping sound of wood against cold tile assaulting my ears. As is typical of me during the morning, I have the nagging feeling that I'm forgetting something important. I glance at the calendar, a horrid squeezing feeling in my gut. My fears are instantly relieved. The calendar is blank. I don't have classes anymore. My summer class ended a couple of weeks ago and I decided to quit college, forgoing registering for fall semester. I breathe a sigh of relief. Freedom at last. No more deadlines to worry about. Just immense chunks of time for reading, painting, and writing. I grin to myself, beginning to fill the tea kettle. My mind wanders as I set it on the stove to boil.

Writing and art at university was enjoyable when I was there. Even so, I didn't want the debt that came with staying long-term and decided coming home was the better option. Plus, I had no desire to teach any of my skills. What was the point in going to college if you didn't have a plan or the money? Staying home sounded far more agreeable. Besides, Mom and Dad didn't mind and were glad to have me house sit for them while they were gone on vacation. I also knew they secretly wanted me to stay home. It gave them more time to pour into me and help me figure out my life—something I secretly wanted as well.

My bagel pops, and I shuffle to grab the cream cheese from the fridge. Libby, my elegant tabby cat, darts from the living room and curls around my legs, purring like a charter boat off the Homer Spit. Her whiskers tickle my ankles, and I side step, bending to pet her ears.

"You just want cheese," I say and put a dab on my pointer finger. She licks it off appreciatively, continuing her motorboat purr. I pull a ceramic mug from the cupboard and set a chai tea sachet in the bottom. The tea kettle whines, and I pour the hot water over the aromatic leaves in a lazy, drawn-out motion. I make the resolution to down this cup of tea before I leave, hoping it will be enough to warm my insides as I walk to the coffee shop. Spicy steam teases my nose as I finish pouring the last of the water and set the kettle back on the stove.

I set my steaming mug on the table next to my plated bagel then jog upstairs to change. As I pull out an olive knit sweater and some navy blue jeans, I reminisce about my job from a few summers ago before I'd left for college—the old bookstore off Main Street. The piles and piles of dusty books, some old, some new, always greeted me with open arms. They'd beckoned with ink-stained, papery fingers, drawing me into portals that were difficult to get out of. I hardly ever wanted to leave work. Such memories led me to try applying there again. I'd called the owner earlier in the week, hoping to get my job back, but the bookstore couldn't afford to keep another person staffed. Sad. I remember the owner's words after he explained why he couldn't rehire me.

"Sales are down. The age of reading hardcopy books just isn't as popular as it used to be. I had a couple in here the other day drop off several large boxes of books. Said they were decluttering. When I asked why, they mentioned they could have thousands of books on their device in ebook format and save tons of space. No use arguing with them. They gave the store a bunch of free books."

I'd politely let him know I understood the situation. Part of me actually died just thinking about people packing up their books in exchange for digital ones. I couldn't imagine doing that with mine. You would have to be completely crazy to do something like that.

With the bookstore job out of the question, I had to consider other options. But right now, I really don't want to. Not just yet. I need to sort through some things and figure out what I want to do with my life.

I run a quick brush through my rust-colored hair, piling and pinning it on top of my head in a quick messy bun. I squint my hazel eyes goofily in the mirror, my version of saying "good enough." I snatch an empty book bag from my bedroom hook and set my phone and wallet inside. My heart thrums with morning excitement as I rush down the stairs, three cats now trailing behind me. Herbert, a fat tuxedo cat, trots to the water dish next to the fridge. Libby mews softly as I plop into my chair to chug my tea and down my bagel. Scout, my sister's striped orange cat, ducks under the table and settles at my feet, waiting for handouts. I scarf my breakfast, the toasted sour bread combining deliciously with the smooth cream cheese. I'm lucky none of the cats decided to help themselves while I was absent. I finish my meal by dousing my taste buds in spiced chai then head for my coat.

I lock the front door behind me and take a deep breath. The rich earthy air hints of mystery and adventure, something I've always admired about cold mornings full of sunshine. Even if the clouds are slowly rolling in and threatening to take over the clear day, I love the atmosphere. There's just something about tea, sweaters, cold mornings and coffee shops as your destination. I'm such a romantic, I know.

Walking to the coffee shop takes about twelve minutes, and I cross the road without any trouble. This early in the morning, there aren't many people out and about. I catch a glimpse of Kachemak Bay to my right as I make my way towards Main Street. The coffee shop is only a few buildings down the road. As I turn into the parking lot, I smile, noticing only two cars in the drive. The coffee shop and the old bookshop share a building. The businesses nest in a tall castle-like wooden structure with walkway porches that wrap around the exterior at ground level. While each business is separated and has their own doors and interior walls, the mashup is unique and every visit feels like a warm hug. The bookshop isn't open yet, but the coffee shop is, its bright yellow OPEN sign blinking. I traverse the creaky front steps and push into the welcoming wooden doors. An herby chocolate smell greets me, and I take another deep breath. The barista behind the counter smiles, and I nod politely, scanning the chalkboard menu. There isn't anyone else here except for me, the barista, and maybe another worker back in the kitchen.

"I'll have an eight ounce latte please." The girl behind the counter nods and selects an option silently on the iPad screen.

"Will that be all?"

"Yes, please." I fumble for my wallet, pulling it from my bag and handing her a few bills. When my latte is in my hands, in a real glass mug, I settle by the window in a worn leather seat. The bay is obscured by trees and other buildings but the road of mainstreet and the parking lot is visible. I take in the flash of an occasional car passing by or the coasting of a seagull.

As I take a swig of the foamy latte, a little bead of froth coating my upper lip, I nearly inhale the drink in panic as I spot a figure lumber across the parking lot. I cough, setting my latte down with a start.

He's here. Of all places. I thought he moved out of state! The boyish grin, freckles, and short honey-brown hair are exactly as they were last time. Only, there's a bit of facial hair now. Oh no. He's walking towards the coffee shop. He's coming in? My stomach squeezes, fluttering in panic. I lick the foam off my lip.

The door chimes and I turn away, hiding my face behind my latte mug. There's a brief interaction between him and the barista, then silence. I steal a glance over the rim of my cup. His back is to me, and I hear him list off a few drinks moments later. An eight ounce hot chocolate with whipped cream and a sixteen ounce americano. At least he didn't order any fru-fru coffees. Wait. Who's the hot chocolate for? Him or someone else? I hide my face again with the latte cup as he turns in my direction. I take much larger gulps than normal. Who drinks their latte like this? I'm losing it. All in the name of trying not to be noticed. I lower the cup to the table in front of me as I spot him at the far end of the room, looking at a few paintings along the wall.

I watch cautiously, curious. Most people who come into a coffee shop look at their phone while they wait for their drink. But not him. He's studying the pictures on the walls, and he's giving each piece of art an ample amount of time. A part of me wishes I had some of my art in here. I have tons of sketches and paintings at home, but I've never put the work into having them displayed. Maybe if my art was in here, he'd look at it longer than the others? I blush and push those thoughts away. Get it together, Briar. He threw you away. He doesn't like you. He told you himself. Stop imagining what-if scenarios. Move on.

I take another sip, my mind fighting a torrent of resurfacing emotions. When I look up, I notice he's back at the counter retrieving his drinks. Then he's gone. I watch him walk back across the parking lot, my nerves calming with every step he takes. Did he see me? He's walking faster than before. Either way, the distance between us is good. I don't know what I would have done had I known for sure he'd seen and recognized me.

When he disappears down the road, I stare into the remains of my drink. Peter West was here, and now he's not. I look towards the paintings then back at my drink. It was all a blur. I marvel at how quickly a soul can leave a space and change the atmosphere. Moments ago, heat flared over my skin in his presence. Now, cold creeps over me like icy waves slapping wooden docks. Part of me wishes I could bottle such emotional power, capture a part of someone I care for and pull it out at any moment to relive their beauty and every conversation we've ever had. But that isn't possible, and it shocks me to be thinking like this, especially about him. Do I still *care* for Peter? He's been my biggest crush to date, and even though I'd had my heart nearly broken by him and my imaginary future with him shoved far away, I still feel *something*. My head says move on, turn the page, but my feelings say, *I cannot*. But feelings get me in trouble. I've known that ever since I could function in society. Just because you feel something doesn't mean it is the right thing to do. Feelings sometimes lie.

I'd had a real crush on him for five years, and about three years ago, I'd given in to my feelings. I messaged him after debating for hours, even days, asking him if he thought of me as a friend or as something more. My cheeks heat with the memory of my boldness. Why did I ever do that? I was immature, obviously.

He responded to my message in what seemed like ages, though it was probably only a minute. The little text bubble popped open before my eyes with the words: *I only ever thought of you as a friend.*

Oh, and there was a smiley face emoji attached to it too.

I'd responded with an 'okay, thanks for understanding. Just wanted to make sure I didn't hurt any feelings,' then I left the message app fast. I could never look him full in the eyes after that. I avoided him, and to this day, I haven't really seen him. Too much embarrassment floods me when he's around. I know he's avoided me too. He said he didn't like me and that's it.

But part of me wondered, and still wonders, if he was telling the truth. What about our past? He'd given me plenty of smiles and fleeting looks growing up through school. I thought for certain all those meant he didn't think of me as 'just a friend'. But he's a fool if that's true. I gave him the full opportunity to admit his feelings and he denied it. He must really *not* like me. I cringe in my seat. Seventeen-year-old me was a mess. Now, twenty-year-old me is still a mess. I'm still thinking about this guy. The lyrics of "Think of Me" from *Phantom of The Opera* play through my mind briefly. Has he thought of me since my bout of immature boldness? Does he remember me at all?

Stop it. I can't go down this road. Peter made it perfectly clear before college that he wasn't interested in me. I need to move on and believe him. Better yet, I need to remove myself from ever seeing him again. I gulp the rest of my latte and return my cup to the counter. Maybe it was best to just go back home and not risk running into him again.

"Thank you, it was delicious," I say. Then I'm out the door, heading in the opposite direction of Peter. If I still care about him, I need to respect him and leave him alone. I'm a grown adult who can get over childhood crushes and move on with her life. That is, I'm going to try.

Two

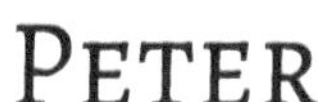

PETER

There's a part of me that wishes I could go back in time. So many mistakes, so many blunders. I could fix them all. The times when I embarrassed myself or the places where I didn't speak up when I knew I should have. I could have avoided so many regrets. But then there's the other part of me that doesn't wish it.

I have from good sources that mistakes are what make us into better people. Sure, I wish I hadn't made the mistakes in the first place, but if I hadn't made them, would I appreciate much of what I do and who I am now?

For example, in middle school, my mom and friends made me apply for the spring talent show. My mom was forcing me to take piano and cello lessons at the time, and while I was a decent player, I hated performing. I still do to an extent.

I did the talent show anyway and made it through without too many hiccups. However, the entrant after me was a fantastic musician. They went to my school and I know they started playing violin and piano around the same time I took up my own instruments. But they were way better. Like, *way* better. I was so embarrassed. Not embarrassed because they were better, embarrassed that I had slacked off. I hardly practiced and complained most of the time about what I had to do. My mom always gave me the same answer.

"You don't have to do it Peter. You *get* to do it. There's a huge difference. I'm making you do it now because you lack the motivation. You'll thank me when you're older."

Boy, was she right.

Through my life though, I've discovered that mistakes make you realize where you are lacking in a certain area. I like to find mistakes, learn from them, and try harder. It isn't easy, but it's always worth it.

That's why I'm where I am today. Back in Homer, Alaska. I never thought I would have the courage to come back here long term. Not after the biggest mistake of my life.

When I left for Colorado after graduation, I made plans to continue my education online and work part time logging and doing construction. However, I never got my associates. Online classes went to a halt after the first semester. Instead, I met someone who gave me the coolest job ever.

August Heaverly. He's probably my best friend back in Colorado and for good reason too. He got me free training as an escape room designer by helping him work on the local escape rooms. I went to my first escape room as an attendee and beat the record time. August offered me the chance to learn how to design the games and puzzles. I readily accepted and left my college degree behind. While I learned to design escape rooms, I also worked part-time hauling logs and doing all the manly stuff girls like, but it didn't really matter because the only girl that mattered to me wasn't there. And it was the biggest mistake of my life that separated us.

I never told anyone my story. Only August knows bits and pieces. When I was in the middle of puzzling out a clue I'd devised and my eyes rolled to one side or my mouth quirked, he'd punch me kindly in the shoulder.

"I don't know what's stopping you. If you like her, go talk to her."

"It's not that easy, August. She doesn't like me. We haven't talked in three years. *Three years*."

"Makes no difference. If you still have a crush on her after all this time, you'll go to her. If it's real."

"It's real. I mean, I'm just not ready to go yet. I want to, but I'm scared. Is it weird to tell someone who doesn't like you back that you like them?"

"Do you know for sure that she doesn't like you back?" August's voice was low and gravely but kind and understanding. He was in his fifties and had the shiniest black and gray hair I've ever seen.

"Well, not exactly."

"Then no, it isn't weird. If no one ever says anything, feelings continue to burn and headspace is booked. What's that term they use nowadays... This thought is living rent free in my head?"

"Yeah. She's living rent free in my head. When I'm not thinking about music or work or puzzles, she's all I can think about."

"Then go make her a part of your life. I'll still be here when you get back. I even have a job for you." August grinned. I looked at him closely and my eyes narrowed. As the puzzlemaster for our area and often an actor in the rooms, August had this *look*. Everyone who had ever been to his escape rooms knew the look quite well. One eyebrow slightly lower than the other, (or maybe it's one higher than the other) a dimple in his left cheek, and a squint of both eyes. Everyone held their breath when they saw the look. It meant there was about to be a plot twist in the narrative and the puzzles were about to get puzzlier. He gave the same look then and I knew he was about to drop something on me.

"Don't tell me you..."

"I got an offer from one of my supervisors. The escape room brand I'm running here is looking to expand. They want to open a branch in Alaska but they need a designer to set it up. If you're interested, I was thinking of recommending you for the job."

"You're joking." I hadn't expected that.

"Am not. The requirements are simple enough. I think you'll pass just fine."

"Requirements?" My voice squeaked a little, my tongue completely dry. I was thrilled. Beyond thrilled. I'd been trying for years to get hired on as a designer, but August said it wasn't up to him. The supervisors and uppity ups of the brand decided who represented them, and they decided it personally. If August was telling the truth, which he was by the look on his face, then all I'd worked for would finally come to fruition. I could be an escape room designer and get paid for it.

"The requirements are simple. Build an escape room in a month's time showing off all your unique puzzling skills. When the month is up, the supervisors, my bosses, will show up to assess the first trial run. You will have to recruit your own volunteers to test out the room at the time of the showing. If they like what they see, you're hired."

"I... I don't believe it. For real? This is for real?" My hands were in my hair, gripping my skull with excitement. I'd been working on ideas for my own escape room and filled a few journals with diagrams and descriptions. Many of my puzzles included musical equations which I wove with a few other of my interests. Now, I could bring these ideas to life.

"If you accept, you'll have to move back to Alaska. I would imagine the designers want the official room to be in Anchorage if you get hired on, but as for your test project, you can go back home if you'd like." The smirk in August's voice pulled me from my excitement momentarily.

"You want me to build it in Homer?"

"Why not? You're familiar with the town. Maybe you can incorporate some of it into your room. Since the room will be catering to Alaskans or those visiting Alaska, adding a touch of the state knowledge into the room might tickle a few brains. It would also tickle the supervisor's brains. You know what I mean?"

"Yeah, I do, but you're playing a different game. Actually, two different games. One is telling me to pick up this opportunity for my dream job and the other is telling me to go talk to *her*." I saw right through August on this one. He thought he was so smart. I swear, if he could have, he would've called her up right now and told her I wanted to talk with her. This is part of the reason I never told him but I still have her number in my phone.

"You always were good at puzzles."

"August, I can't talk to her. Not yet, but you are right. I should go back home. It has been a while and it would be good to be in a familiar place to use all my ideas. Plus, my family misses me." I said all this with a sigh and a chuckle.

"So you accept? I'll email my bosses right away." August grabbed his phone from his pocket, finger poised to type up a response. I nodded eagerly.

"Yes. I accept."

My acceptance was what started this whole thing. I'm back in Homer, once again reunited with the place I know best. The salty air and the low-flying gulls combined with the most artistic atmosphere for miles is wonderfully calming. There are colorful murals along buildings and little shops overflowing with knick knacks and paintings. The same feeling I had growing up about this place returns like a warm hug amidst a brisk wind.

I've only been here a few days, but already I've settled in with my mom, dad, and sister. Once again, I occupy my old room. I'm surprised my family didn't turn it into an office or something. They were all glad to have me back, and after I'd told them everything over the phone before flying here, they were over the moon.

Now, after catching up with everyone, I was set on beginning my project. Creating an escape room required money and a... well, a room. But it had to be big enough and in a public space to host a crowd of volunteers. I called around earlier this morning to ask local businesses about hosting such a thing and made a few connections. I even listed some potential sponsors to help me fund the project after it was completed. One potential host wanted to meet up to discuss the project before lunch and I readily agreed.

I scribble down some ideas for pitching the project in my notebook before leaving the house. My sister lets me borrow her car, so I park at one of the small shops down Main Street. I'm early. It's only seven-fifteen and my meeting isn't until seven-forty-five. Coffee sounds nice. I toss a look at my sister's car and clench the keys in my hand. Why drive when the coffee shop is a few hundred feet away? I head towards the coffee house that's attached to a bookstore. It's a pleasant building with its warm wooden siding and angled roof. Looking at it reminds me of the feeling of visiting a beloved grandparents' home and being shown childhood treasures. Excitement mixed with nostalgia.

The cold fall air pulls and pushes the trees along the building while a warm glow emits from the windows. As I step into the shop, my taste buds perk up. Bitter smooth coffee is on my mind. I acknowledge the smiling barista and give the menu a glance. I already know what I want. A sixteen ounce americano and an eight ounce hot chocolate with whip; my little sister's favorite.

After I make the order, I step into the gallery room where artwork adorns the walls. Each wall is updated every week with something new. I slide my eyes over the melancholy portrait of a moose in a sailor's outfit. Typical Homer art. The ocean permeates everything as well as the beautiful state it surrounds. Dark blue and gray colors with hints of gold make up the piece. The entire thing is hand-drawn with colored pencils. Impressive. Each stroke is about as small as the lines on my fingers. The artist's initials are signed in golden pen in the corner. I don't recognize them and move to the next framed piece.

A round art in the center of a rectangular frame depicts a black bear eating blueberries, his pink tongue peeking out of the foliage. I smile. Creative. This one was drawn with ink and maybe some sort of marker. The bear's expression makes him look both hungry and innocent. It's a piece my sister would hang in her room if she had it.

I'm pulled away from the art as I hear a soft shuffle in the corner and the barista calls out my drinks. I turn back towards the counter, and find I'm not the only customer in the shop. A girl sits neatly in the corner by the window, a shiny glass mug against her lips. Rusty hair is piled messily on her head, and she wears a soft olive green sweater. My face goes instantly red at the sight of her. I shuffle quickly to the front and accept the drinks.

"Thank you." I smile at the barista and turn towards the door. My pulse quickens, and I step quickly off the wooden porch. Gravel crunches beneath my shoes as I carry both drinks across the parking lot. Each step is awkward because I know, instinctively, she's watching me from that window. My blood is hotter than espresso at the thought of her watching me leave. The worst part of it is that I have absolutely no idea what she could be thinking. I'm an idiot coward who can't even turn around and wave. It's too late now. That would be really weird considering how far I've walked already. I clench my lips tight, forcing myself to walk as normally as possible. Pretend you didn't see her.

I make it back to my sister's car with the coffee and cocoa, my heart still racing. I look behind me, a small part of me wishing I'd see her again, walking towards me. But no, absolutely not. I would probably die if that happened. I'm not ready to face her.

I set my sister's drink in the middle console then relock the car. I take a sip of coffee and stroll into a new shop across the street. It's seven-thirty-five, but I don't care. I try to discard the image of her in my mind, attempting to focus on the meeting at hand. But it isn't working out. I don't want to get rid of the image. She's the same Briar Verlice I used to notice while in school. She almost always sat alone and was immersed in a sketch at her desk or lost in the pages of a tome heavier than her lunch bag.

Briar would look at me sometimes and smile. I'd smile, too, but then look away. I'm sure most people probably understand the feeling. All your emotions are going so wild you think that everyone in the room is looking at you and knows exactly what you're thinking. That's what it felt like everytime I caught Briar's eyes. Like fire and ice and paranoid whispers. We talked a few times, friendly and normal, but ever since my mistake, I avoided her. Even though I liked her. And by golly, I still like her. My head throbs. I'm so glad August isn't here.

I chug some more coffee and push open the door to the small shop. Wildlife paintings and glass statues are staged around the room and I notice a man is leaning against the front counter reading, his glasses perched on his nose. He stands straighter and closes the book. I can't help but notice that it's a copy of *Redwall* by Brian Jaques.

"Hi, I'm Andrew. You must be Peter?"

"Yes. Nice to meet you." I recognize him but can't remember why or from where.

"A pleasure." Andrew smiles, his glasses reflecting the light streaming in from the windows. He's tall and has brown, graying hair with some wrinkles along his jaw.

"You mentioned being willing to host or sponsor an escape room?"

"Yes. I'm quite interested. That's, in hosting it. I'm afraid I can't offer any financial support, but I would love to be a host."

"That's great." I'm serious. Already, someone was willing to host a public event in their space and we've barely talked.

"In fact, I think this opportunity will probably be my last resort in keeping my shop alive." He looks at me with hopeful eyes. I glance around. The quaint building we stand in is quite obviously an art gallery... Not exactly the place to host an escape room. Too many valuables and breakable objects.

"You own this place?"

"Oh, no. My friends own this. I was over here retrieving some old books that they found on a trip. I own the book store down the street." He motions to the left.

"The bookstore next to the coffee shop?" *Didn't Briar used to work there?* That's why he's so familiar. He was her boss. A twinge of excitement grows in my gut. Maybe I'll get to see her again, this time with the courage to talk to her.

"Yes. Come on. I'll retrieve these books and then we can meet in the shop. I don't open till ten, so we have plenty of time to chat till I need to deal with customers." I nod, pulling my notebook from a deep pocket. I flip it open to my pitch, scanning it before following Andrew to the back of the gallery. From what I remember, Andrew is an interesting man. He likes to work on something else while working on something else. He's a multi-tasker, and while it is slightly annoying, he can do it pretty well. He and Briar got along decently. Both of them read like crazy.

As I follow Andrew into the back, I take a deep breath. Leaving Homer to pursue a career three years ago had been my cover story, when in reality, I was just running from embarrassment and mistakes. Now, I'm coming to terms with the fact that I'm probably going to have to face those mistakes and embarrassments. If Briar still works at the bookstore, we'll be seeing each other whether we like it or not.

Three

BRIAR

Libby curls lazily in my lap while I hover an oatmeal chocolate chip cookie close to my lips. My sage highlighter squeaks. *Little Men* by Louisa May Alcott is balanced on my lap while I carefully drop crumbs away from the pages. Even though I've read this book numerous times, annotating my favorite parts seems to bring me closer to the characters and the world they live in. Plus, I'm able to garner so many interesting descriptions for my own future writing projects.

The small clock in the corner of the room ticks, the only repetitive sound in the house besides my cat's warm purr. Outside the house, dark moody clouds roll in off the bay. I glance to my left and see my empty tea mug. I'm inclined to get up and start another brew, but I'm cozily pinned to the chair by paper, cookie crumbs, and warm fur. I remember doing homework as a kid and complaining to my mom that I couldn't do my math because of the cat. Libby always made a point to get right in the middle of what I was doing. She would often curl herself directly on top of my math book and I made no effort to move her, glad for the obstruction of my vision of geometry equations.

The afternoon flits by, and soon the sound of smattering rain hits the house. Libby stretches in my lap, repositioning herself and slumbering on. Scout and Herbert are each curled up in their own places on the loveseat near the window. Wind begins to whine around the yard, and water droplets plaster themselves against the glass. I stare towards the bay, my eyes zoning out. My mind wanders to this morning's events and my heart beat picks up. I close my book. I can feel my pulse in my fingers, and I frown. Peter should be the furthest thing from my mind but he keeps showing up, and all I can see is him looking at art along walls or walking across parking lots with warm drinks. *Oh, Briar, get your thoughts together*. I do, for the most part. I reopen my book and stare down at the page.

"Love is a flower that grows in any soil, works its sweet miracles undaunted by autumn frost or winter snow, blooming fair and fragrant all the year, and blessing those who give and those who receive."

This quote stands out to me, and I sigh, shutting the book. Is this love that I feel then? It has simmered beneath my skin for many seasons and flares up even warmer whenever I see Peter. My mom would tell me it is not love but infatuation. But if both are similar, how do I distinguish between the two? I make the effort to close off my mind to any more thoughts and feelings of romance and the like. I gently slide Libby into my seat and walk to the kitchen, book and highlighter now on the side table by my chair.

While my tea brews, I stare out the kitchen window into the swirling storm. Gold-tinged leaves drip and dance in the torment, the bay roiling in the distance. Every blade of grass is now anointed with a droplet of what I imagine to be fairy gems or magic potions. Somewhere outside, there's probably a hidden pool where nymphs dance and collect the rain. I can imagine selkies and mermaids singing in the storm, swimming close to the docks, only to disappear when someone comes near.

There's something extremely romantic about the rain, and I can't help but imagine stories and fairytales woven into this reality. I take a sip of my honeyed tea and glance at the clock. It's four-fifteen. I toss a look at my book on the side table and swallow some tea. Should I go read some more or write on my story for a bit?

Libby jolts straight up from sleep, letting out a lazy meow. At the same time, a delayed tap collides against the front door, interrupting my thoughts. I set my tea down abruptly. I never answer the door with someone unknown outside when I'm home alone, and today is no exception. I tiptoe to the side window and draw the curtain up slightly. There's no one there. Frowning, I look again, but no one is in sight. I brave the door handle and draw the entry open.

Situated neatly on the rug outside is a forest green envelope sealed with a fancy letter B stamped in silver wax. Part of the envelope is wet as if soaked by rain. A gust of wind blows a lone white feather across the doorstep and into the bushes. I pay it no mind as I wrinkle my brow at the envelope. What on earth? I've never received gifts in such fashion before and my family is out of town. Who knocks on the door in a storm and leaves presents? It isn't my birthday or anything. I study the envelope from the doorway and decide it looks innocent and safe enough to bring inside. I do so and lock the door with a click. Libby laps water from the bowl by the fridge and Herbert and Scout haven't budged from their places.

My toes are snug and warm in my hand-knit olive socks as I enter the kitchen, my fingers trembling slightly. Brows furrowed and heart pounding, I quickly pull open the envelope, careful to not rip the sopping wet corner. Inside is a cream piece of paper inscribed in black ink. I unfold it and read:

Please, send help immediately. I'm not sure who to ask, but whoever finds this, just know that there is danger....W...n..........

The ink runs together, the last few sentences and letters of the note too broken and blurred to make out what it says. I lower the paper. My mouth goes dry. A cryptic note? A cry for help? I shiver and set the paper on the table and skirt the kitchen. I quickly retreat to the loveseat with Herbert and Scout and settle between them, their furry bodies acting as shields to the eeriness that has now wormed its way into the house. Who brought the message? Is this a threat of some kind? A warning? Or a cry for help? I shiver again, burying one of my hands into Herbert's fur for comfort.

The rain has slowed outside, but the wind is still blowing like mad. Herbert yawns and uncurls. He looks at me with slits for eyes, and I give his nose a gentle pet. He yawns again then leaps off the sofa, headed for the food and water bowl. Oh, to be a cat and sleep and eat and have no worries. I sigh, my mind still spinning from the note.

I reach for my phone off the arm of the couch and open it to find a jumble of notifications. A few more Goodreads notifications as well as an email from a blog I used to follow. The email subject catches my eye.

Subject: Discussion Thread- Homer Conspiracies & Disappearances

Body: There are 206 new posts on this thread. Link to blog here.

Annoyed, I swipe it away, not wanting to read through all the suppositions and lies. I stand up from the couch, carrying my phone with me. I make sure all the doors and windows of the house are locked, then I call Mom.

My phone buzzes as the number connects.

"Hi, Mom. How is vacation?"

"It's great! We spent the day hanging out with Grandma and Grandpa at the beach. How's everything going there?"

"It's going okay, except, I just got a note on the porch with a strange message." I tell my mom the details of what happened and what the note said that I could read, and I hear dad on the other end asking for more info. Mom repeats everything to him. There's a muffle as the phone is passed to Dad.

"Hey, sweetie, just stay inside. I'll let one of my friends know what's going on and ask him to keep an eye on the house. Are you locking doors?"

"Always. Thanks, Dad. Just wanted to let you guys know in case something happens. I'll be safe." I hear my mom in the background say something along the lines of *"I don't like that at all. She should have someone stay with her."*

"Hey, kiddo. Do what you think you need to do to stay safe. If you want one of your friends to come stay with you or if you need to go stay with them, it's up to you. I trust you to make your own decisions."

"Thanks, Dad. I'll let you know what I decide."

"Love you."

"Love you, too, Dad. Bye." I hang up and scroll through my notifications to distract myself. Spotify tells me I have new podcast episodes to listen to and my Goodreads friends liked my highlights from *Little Men.* I close my phone, nothing seeming to distract me from what I found on the doorstep.

My life has turned into a cozy mystery, and with the way I overthink, I'm scared it will soon end up in the murder mystery section. If that's going to happen, it must be well-thought-out and someone had better write it down when it's all said and done. Also, get it in all the bookstores and tourist shops in Homer. Put this small town on the map, even more than it already is. At least something in my life could be categorized as interesting.

I squirm and shake my head. What have my thoughts come to? I'm thinking about murder and nothing threatening has even happened.

With that in mind, I control my fears and insecurities. Yeah. You know what? I'm not going to be afraid. I'm going to leave this house as if that note never happened. I'll go spend the rest of my day doing something I enjoy. Browsing the bookstore for my next great read.

I find my wool jacket and loosen my hair from my bun till it's free and wavy. If it's raining and windy outside, I'm taking it head on, *Pride and Prejudice* style. With my phone and wallet in my pocket and a book bag on my arm, I face the winds of coastal Alaska. Instantly, raindrops pelt my face and my hair whips around my shoulders. I really should take my car, but that isn't romantic at all. While I don't have a dress or someone like Caroline Bingley to make the remark about how my hem is six inches deep in mud, I will arrive with wet socks and muddy lace-up boots that rival even Elizabeth's attire. I don't even care if anyone sees me. I don't mind if Andrew, the bookshop keeper, sees me. He knows me well enough that he's used to my visits and whirlwind entrances. He was my boss once after all. Plus, the bookstore is big enough and full enough, too, that if I wind down the right path of books, I might never be found.

The walk to the bookstore is extremely wet, and I narrowly miss a filthy splash from a taxi driving through a puddle. When I reach the entrance to the shop, I look behind me out of caution. If the someone who gave me the note was still around, they probably saw me leave my house. If they followed me, they would have to be somewhere nearby to see exactly where I went. I wait, almost willing someone to drive by or walk into view so I could at least speculate on who they might be. No one does, and I'm both relieved and disappointed.

Andrew greets me with a nod and smile, his eyes barely glancing up from the book he's reading. He's almost always reading or talking with a customer. He sits on a small, worn leather stool, and all around him are extremely rare copies of books—piles and piles of gold foil covers in original leather. To the left of his desk are counters with books beneath glass; copies so old they cost several thousand dollars. I barely make it a few steps past his desk and he is alert, almost as if he forgot to tell me something.

"Oh, Briar, I wanted to let you know we'll be turning the upstairs room in the next couple of weeks into an escape room. I'll be needing a lot of the books organized up there into correct piles. We'll be closing off upstairs starting tomorrow. Would you be interested in helping? I have a guy helping transform it."

"Wait, you're closing the shop?"

"Just upstairs, and only temporarily."

"What gave you the idea to turn the upstairs into an escape room?"

"Sales are down. Each year it gets worse. The only thing keeping this place afloat is the attached airbnb above the coffee shop. I thought it might attract more people to the bookstore if we had the escape room here."

"But why an escape room? Why not a book club or a book raffle or something?"

"I read mystery novels and I've always been intrigued with the idea of building your own mysteries. Aka, escape rooms. Hosting something that involves puzzles and requires some book knowledge has been on my bucket list for ages. I couldn't resist when a young man reached out to ask about support and a building."

"Huh. I'm intrigued." I secretly want to be the one to help save the shop but it appears someone else beat me to it with an idea. If it was me, I'd publish a fiction novel about this place, hoping to draw a crowd to the shop by marketing it to tourists and young adults. Maybe, just maybe, I'd do it one day.

"I'll pay you to help organize. Are you interested?"

"Of course. I'd love to help. But I thought this place was... you know... running into the ground?"

"It's not that bad, yet. Right now, this is an investment. If this escape room guy can craft this place into a unique stop and book sales go up, it will all be worth it."

"What time do you need me here by tomorrow?" I can't bear to see this place die so I almost turn down the money, but I know Andrew won't let me. Excitement pounds in my chest cavity. I might have a job here after all.

"Would nine-thirty a.m. be okay?"

"I'll be here."

"Excellent. Thank you, Briar." Andrew smiles then goes back to his book. I depart, heading for the stairs. I beam a wide grin all the way up and melt into a corridor of tomes near a window. The heady scent of old paper and leather is so welcoming. As I scan the shelves and spines upon spines, I barely notice where I'm walking. I turn a corner in the maze and bump into someone blocking the path, their back to me. They turn around and lock eyes with me, their fingers lightly brushing the pages of the book they're holding.

I hold in a gasp and take a step backwards. Their gentle voice resonates in the corridor and in my head, bringing back memories from many years ago.

"Hello, Briar."

Four

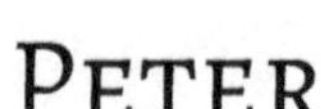

Peter

After Andrew showed me the upper room of the bookstore and we'd talked about what was to be left undisturbed, I rushed back to my car and drove home. Anna's hot chocolate was still warm and the whipped cream was surprisingly still intact, if a little melty. I delivered it with flourish into her waiting hands.

"For the sweetest sister around."

Her soft blue eyes sparkle in amusement as she takes the gift. "Awww, Peter you shouldn't have."

"Well, you did let me use your car." I give her a wry smile.

"You're my older brother, *and* I knew you would be a responsible driver."

"Regardless, the hot chocolate is for you, just because."

"Thank you." She beams up at me and takes a sip of the sweet drink. At seventeen, Anna looks just like my mom did when she was younger. The faded pictures on the walls of my parents' home as teenagers stare back at me, and it's as if my mom stepped out of the picture frame. Anna says it could be the same for me as I look a lot like my dad, just a little taller.

"Tell Mom I'll be drafting emails for sponsors upstairs." I swirl the remainders of my americano in my right hand.

"Will do. How did your meeting go?"

"Really well. I think I have a room. Now for the financial side of it all so I can get to work."

"That's great. Let me know when I can get a tour before anyone else." She winks and smiles. As I head up the stairs, my back still to her, I mumble something about her being a spoiled younger sibling. She hears and guffaws in mock annoyance. I rush up the rest of the stairs, giggling like a child. It's a running joke between us to tease the other one as we go up the stairs, and then run for our lives and hide. Normally, we try and chuck a pillow at the one running, but I hear Anna laughing as she leaves the house. No pillow today.

I enter my old room and slide into a chair at my desk. A *2Cellos* album poster adorns one wall, a memory of the first live concert I ever attended while medals from middle school soccer games and spelling bees remind me of past success. My laptop is dark but open. I boot it up, setting my drink onto the desk. The window overlooking my workspace lets in gray, moody light, and I shiver slightly. It's set to be a rainy day by the looks of the clouds, and my bedroom temperature almost confirms the fact. I stand and grab a navy blue sweater from my closet then settle back into my chair to type in my password: 0!musicaltalent. I smirk, remembering the day I made the password. It was the day when I decided to give playing my cello my all. I wish now I had brought it back with me from Colorado, but I didn't like the idea of forking over another four hundred dollars for my instrument to ride next to me on the plane.

When my computer hums to life, I guide my mouse to my email and begin sorting through unopened ones. One of the emails stands out from the rest, and I frown, opening it. The subject line catches me off guard. I quickly read the lines then sit back heavily in my chair, one hand plowing through my light hair.

Subject: Discussion Thread- Homer Conspiracies & Disappearances

Body: There are 206 new posts on this thread. Link to blog here.

I want to delete the email. Seeing it reminds me of my foolishness. I close it, dread weaving its way through my spine.

Briar happened three years ago. I let her go to college without telling her how I really felt about her. In fact, I told her a lie. I told her I only thought of her as a friend. I was scared and wasn't ready to commit to anything. I liked her, I still do, but I didn't know what I wanted then. I also let some of my friends in school encourage me to not have anything to do with her because of what drama she was connected to. That and they said she would distract me from my career. I don't know why I listened to them, but I did.

Pushing the conspiracy blog from my mind, I open a new draft email. I type in a few of the email addresses I'd found from researching potential sponsors and set to work. When I finish up the emails, I attach a graphic I made last night to each message—a picture of my escape room logo with some musical and Alaskan elements. I hit send and push them out to various businesses. With that done, I reopen the conspiracy email. I don't know how long I sit there, but at some point, my mom knocks on my door. I break my concentration.

"Come in." I scoot away from my computer and swivel my chair towards the door.

"Hey, you hungry? I made tomato soup and toasted cheese. Your sister had to go to work and Dad gets off at five, so I just made some for us."

"I am actually. That sounds great." Mom steps into my room, soup and sandwich already in hand. She knew I'd say yes. She sets it down on my desk and gives me a quick hug.

"Anna told me you got a room for your project. That's great. Any big plans?"

"Lots of plans. I think I've underestimated just how much work goes into this, but I have most of my ideas jotted down. I just need to build them once I get the sponsorship funds."

"I can't wait to hear all about it. When Dad gets home, tell him what you told me."

"I will. Thanks for lunch, Mom." I look at my sandwich then smile at my mom.

"You're welcome, son." She shuts the door behind her with a soft click.

I spoon up a mouthful of soup and sigh contentedly as the rich hot tomato flavor slides down my throat. I break off a piece of my toasted cheese sandwich and swirl it in the soup, setting it on my tongue. Nothing like hot soup on a cold day. As I eat, I turn back to my inbox.

Curious, I reopen the conspiracy email and follow the link to the blog. Some random local decided to read into things after a strange incident that happened six years ago involving Briar and the police. As a result, this blog emerged along with a huge following of teenagers and people who liked to distract themselves with mysteries. I hate to say it but I was sucked into it for a time. Nothing major, just started believing some of the things that were said and not really questioning them.

I open the most recent thread and scroll to the newest post.

New Post: Share all the weird happenings from the past month. Let's make some connections to the big disappearance incident.

Comments:

User51: I've seen plenty in my long life but as far as weird goes in the past month, I saw a black suv pick up three unidentified individuals from behind the ferry building at dusk on October 12th. The ferry isn't even open right now. Thought it was odd. Maybe connected? 25 likes ~ 45 dislikes

Sherlock007: Anyone can connect anything to a strange occurrence if they want it to, but if it's actually connected is a completely different story. My advice would be to follow the vehicle and see where it goes to get better evidence. But even that is sketchy and might have you end up on this thread as a strange occurrence. 60 likes ~10 dislikes

Harlowedoyle_2.0: Not to make this more of a mess, but has anyone actually gone and talked to the girl who disappeared in the past few *months? Chances are you could learn a lot from going to the actual source. *shrugging emoji* 62 likes ~5 dislikes*

Arcticthunder25: Some people have in the past but we always get the same answer. She fell asleep in the bookstore. Somehow the police couldn't find her despite looking there. Seems to me like the police are probably in on this and covering something up. I think there's more to the story than everyone is letting on. 100 likes ~ 20 dislikes

I back out of the post and comment threads, unwilling to read anymore. It's all just steering into nonsense. Assumption after assumption backed up with zero evidence. I close out of the link entirely.

I shake my head, resting my chin on my hands, just staring at all my read emails. When my eyes begin to bug out, I shut my computer. There's an audible pelting of rain against my window as the wind sends the water sideways. I look at the clock on my wall. It's been hours since I first came upstairs. My lunch is long finished and now my brain is as melted as the cheese on my sandwich was. I get up and start to carry my dishes out my bedroom door. An notification sound comes from my sister's bedroom at the end of the hall. I stop in my tracks and turn towards her door. Another ding, and I'm certain it's her phone. Did she accidentally leave it here on her way to work? I make the executive decision to check, and sure enough, her phone is on her charger next to her bed. I don't even mean to snoop, but the notifications hadn't disappeared from her screen yet. When I walk in, all it takes is a glance; I know what it says.

> *J. M. : Don't forget about the meeting today at 7. We'll be at the lighthouse.*

> *J.M. : Bring your notes.*

I back out of Anna's room, confused. Anna works at the bakery in town. What meeting is she going to during work hours that was at the lighthouse? And what notes? Not to mention the lighthouse was on the spit, not downtown where her work was.

I amble slowly downstairs and set the dishes by the sink. Mom is at the table, carefully handwriting recipe cards and thank you cards with a calligraphy pen.

"Thank you for lunch, Mom." She glances at me, pen in midair.

"You're welcome." I'm quiet a moment before I decide to bring up my sister.

"Did Anna mention going to a meeting tonight at seven for work?"

"No, she didn't. Why?" Mom dips her pen in an ink jar and continues pulling the stylus across delicate cards.

"Well, she left her phone here and I happened to read a notification on her screen mentioning something about a meeting. It was from someone named J.M. Know anything?"

"I don't. I suppose you can call the bakery and let her know she left her phone."

"I was thinking about that," I say, scratching my head.

"She'll probably need it. I'm not sure what kind of errands she had planned after work. She gets off at nine." Mom begins to hum softly to herself in between conversation breaks.

"Hmm. Okay, thanks. I think I'll drop it off for her."

"Mmhmm. That's nice." Mom's attention zones out then in on her project, each stroke of her pen pulling her further away from my voice. I step out of the room and don my coat and make sure to grab Anna's phone before leaving. Anna took her car which means I have to walk. And it's raining. Hard.

I haven't been in weather like this for a long time. It's a sweet-smelling rain but icy cold. I'm confident I'll be soaked by the time I even cross the street. I did not think to bring my raincoat with me from Colorado, so my simple fall breaker is going to have to do.

I step out into the wild storm, wind pulling at my sleeves and rain already rolling off my hood. Anna's phone is tucked safely into my back pocket, and I steer myself towards a cluster of trees that line my family's neighborhood road. Everything is a tumbling mess, but it's beautiful. Homer is unique, and I know of no better place to find rugged beauty than in this coastal town. I pass by Main Street on my way through town, hoping to go down the next road and cut through the trail in the woods by the library to get to the bakery.

As I do so, I see someone walking briskly towards the bookshop, their rusty hair loose and wet. My stomach does a flip flop and I recognize them immediately. Briar. I continue walking and pass Main Street quickly, my head swimming. Knowing Briar, she was probably headed to the bookshop. In school, I had some courage to at least ask if she wanted to join my team during sports or see if she was interested in entering the local art competition with my sister. It seems the older I get the less courage I have to talk to girls.

Before I know it, I'm at the steps of the bakery, and I give the little free library at my left a gracious nod. I love my town. There are free libraries all over, and they brighten up even the dingiest of roads. When I step inside, my mouth waters. Even though I recently had lunch, the scent of warm pastry and rich chocolate mousse overtakes me. I glance at the chalkboard menu, the signature method of product display in Homer.

I pull Anna's phone from my pocket and step up to the counter. A lady in a black apron greets me, her teal-tipped dreadlocks and large, silver hoop earrings pair with a name tag that reads Margo.

"What can I get you today?" Margo asks. Her smile and tone of voice tells me she's one of the outgoing employees that probably keeps everyone on their toes.

"I'm here for Anna. I'm her brother," I say, looking towards the kitchen. I spot my sister rolling a mound of dough in the back. She hears her name, and her eyes flicker to mine. There's a quick blink and intake of breath, a moment of unfamiliar panic in her features, and then it's gone as she comes out to face me.

"Peter," is all she says.

"You left your phone at home. Mom said you'd probably need it."

"Yes, thank you," she says, holding out her hand. I notice the front of her apron and extended arm is covered in flour. Margo laughs.

"You two look so alike. I figured you were siblings the moment I saw you walk through the door."

"We get that a lot," I say as I set Anna's phone into her hand. There is a moment of calm that coats my sister's face as she slips the device into her side pocket. I've been her brother too long to know that she is indeed hiding something, and it bothers me, twisting my heart.

"Thanks, Margo. I can help him with his order," Anna says a little too sweetly. Margo sidesteps and disappears into the kitchen, and I hear her telling the other employees how much Anna and I look alike. "Do you want anything?"

"I didn't plan on it, but now that I'm here, I think I'll take a raspberry galette and... an explanation on what you're doing later this evening?"

Anna blinks, taken aback. "What do you mean? I work till nine."

"That's what I thought but wanted to double check. Figured we could watch a movie or something." I shrug, trying to act innocent.

"I'll get you your raspberry galette. On the house," she says, paying for it with her employee discount before I can protest. "Anything else?" I shake my head.

"No, I think that will be it." She nods, and I wait while she bags my pastry from under the smooth glass counter. She hands it to me in a crinkly brown bag with a wad of napkins. A bit of flour brushes off onto my sleeve. "Thanks for the dessert and the extra flour," I say, trying to bring that sparkle back into her eyes that I saw earlier this morning. It doesn't return.

"You're welcome," she says, frowning at the flour dusting on her arms. I can tell she's nervous at the way she taps her fingers on the counter, so I take that as my cue. I smile and leave, a churning unease in my stomach. Something is going on with Anna, and I can't help but think about the text on her phone. Call it family intuition. She's my sister and I'll protect her with my life. If she's hiding something from my family, especially if it's leaving work to go somewhere she didn't tell us, I'm going to find out what it is.

And finding out what it is means I'm going to the lighthouse tonight. And if Anna shows up, there's going to be a lot of conversation and Dad is going to hear all about it. I'm going to have to play what people call a reverse *Uno* card and do whatever it takes to keep my family out of danger.

Five

BRIAR

J oel Moore. I haven't seen him since high school, and he's now a whole head taller than me. He and Peter were best friends growing up, and I know they talked about me. But I never heard what they said.

Curly brown hair, green eyes, and a white button up shirt. I didn't expect to see him here. Not after all this time. What was he doing in Homer and at the bookstore? I guess I thought the same about Peter, yet he still showed up. I squeeze my fingers into my palm as I take him in. I'm sure my cheeks are blooming red, but I try not to think about it too much.

"What are you doing in town?" I finally ask. He smiles, the corners of his eyes crinkling in genuineness.

"I moved back to Alaska a year ago. Homer seemed like a good place to come for Thanksgiving."

"Oh, that sounds nice. Is your family still around?" I'm curious because the last time I saw them was when I graduated, and a lot could happen in three years. His parents were really nice. And rich.

"Yep. They still live up on the hill and invited me to stay at their house for the holidays this year."

"Do you live locally or somewhere else?"

"I live in Fairbanks actually. My job had me move up here and, well, I wish I could live in Homer, but that would be a long commute."

"Yeah, no kidding." I squirm as silence stretches between us. Joel closes the book he was reading and hugs it against his side. There's a quirky pull to his mouth, and I know in an instant he's trying to break the awkwardness. He is much better at conversation than I am.

"Do you come here often? It's a fantastic place." He gives the bookshop shelves a staredown, and I follow his gaze across the many unorganized piles. It's a literal treasure trove.

"Quite often. It's my favorite place to unwind. I'm pretty sure I've spent most of my paychecks here. Not a bad place to spend your money though." I instantly cringe. Why did I mention money?

"No, indeed." Joel shoves a hand in his pocket and turns towards the classic section. "See anything you like over here?"

"Oh, lots. What do you like to read?" I'm almost positive he'll say something along the lines of *I don't, I just like the pictures*, but he doesn't.

"Mostly suspense or nonfiction, but I've taken a liking to the classics, specifically the *Odyssey* and even some poems by Tennyson."

In school, Joel was always the sports type of guy, not the reading kind. I scan his features to see if he's pulling my leg, but the kind set of his eyebrows and gentle smile looks sincere. If he changed tastes, it looks good on him.

"I never thought you were into books. Is this a recent thing?" It has to be. He was always working out and winning state wrestling or soccer tournaments. When did he pick up reading?

"Sort of. I mean, I read when I could during school, but I was always so distracted, you know? Now, I have more time as my job allows me to read. It's pretty nice." Ah, so he has an office job. Not the type of job I see him working, but again, reading looks good on him.

"Sounds like you work at a bookstore too," I say.

"Naw... It isn't as fun as that." He moves, and a curl of hair sweeps across his forehead. "Is that what you still do?"

"No. Actually, kind of." I pause, standing on my tiptoes for a moment then slowly settling back down. Why is it so awkward to talk to him? There's nothing between us. At least, right now. My mouth runs on before I even have time to really think. "I used to work here before college, but due to financial reasons, the shop can't really hire me. However, as of a few minutes ago, it sounds like I'll have it back for a little while." I try not to stare too long at his curly hair and the freckles on his nose as I wait for a reply, so I glance at the book under his arm. The cover is my favorite color of blue.

"How wonderful,"Joel says, his grin larger than ever. I flicker my eyes up to his and smile back, my fingers squeezing into my palms even harder. This is so awkward.

He unhugs the book at his side and grasps it in both hands. "Well, I suppose I should let you get back to digging for buried treasure. I have some errands to run." I nod in response, unsure of what to say. He's smiling so big that I can't read what he's thinking. "I'll see you later, Briar."

"Bye," I say kindly. He passes by and threads out of the maze and down the stairs. I breathe an internal sigh, glad the confrontation is over. We have a small history, Joel and I, and it's embarrassing for both of us.

Little did I know that all through school, Joel had the biggest crush on me. I was oblivious and completely caught off guard when he cornered me at work in this bookstore. Flashback to five years ago when he asked me out and I had to turn him down. I didn't like him in that way, and the pain I caused him just by simply saying no was evident afterwards. Even behind all his smiles from today, I know he remembers the moment. It's awkward to say the least. Even though I've never thought of him in that way, I still feel silly when he's around, knowing he wanted to pursue me at one time. I won't even try to guess what he's thinking now, but if I had to, he's probably just as nervous as me after running into each other.

I try to push the past away, now set on scanning the shelves for treasures. I begin by reading the titles along the bottom shelves.

Every time I come to the bookstore, I have a mission. I look for books with pretty covers, familiar author's names, or titles that draw me in. Then I read the back or the inside left flap for a description. If it sucks me in, I make a pile in my arms and continue hunting. On rare occasions, I find myself reading a book I've found and without realizing it, an hour could have gone by.

Andrew, the store owner, always knows when I'm upstairs reading because the floor doesn't creak in so long. I've stayed past closing time on multiple occasions. Andrew has had to come find me once or twice, and even though I was embarrassed to have to be gently led out of the shop, I secretly liked being one of the bookstore's biggest fans. I know Andrew secretly likes it too.

This time, however, I'm not going to stay past closing if I can help it. I'm here to unwind, lose myself in a book, and forget the strangeness of today's events, all while making it home in time to watch an episode of *Road To Avonlea* before bed. I'm on the second season, and the whole series is just a warm hug.

I turn a corner in one of the many shelved aisles and spot a teal book with silver foil jutting out of place. I haven't seen it in the shop before, but that doesn't mean it's new. Each time I come to the shop, there are always special books I've missed.

My fingers pull out the shiny book from between the others, and it slides into my hands, winking at me like a jewel. The teal leather is worn, but the foil cover is bright and new-looking. *A Study on Fairies.* The title is fitting for the color and design of the book. I open it, and my eyes go wide with delight. There's a beautiful illustration set into the inside of the cover. A delicate scroll of flowers and vining leaves wind around a portrait of a fairy. She wears a cobweb dress covered in dewdrops. The painting itself has tiny flecks of foil on it which makes the water on her skirt look actually wet. I hold the book tighter, afraid to let it go.

After looking at the painting for a few moments more, I peruse the rest of the pages and am thrilled to find a whole collection of fairy stories, apparent sightings, myths, and even more illustrations. As I turn through the pages, a slip of paper flutters to the floor, landing on my shoe. I kneel to pick it up. The paper is cream-colored and thin, black ink bleeding through. I close the book and tuck it underneath my arm so I can read the note.

I don't trust our ruler. Darkness seems to permeate the castle each year and his mercy is waning. Please send anyone willing to help confront the darkness.

I'm confused. The note doesn't appear to be written to anyone in particular. But after studying it more closely, I recognize the handwriting and the paper. The note from the mysterious green envelope at my house was written on the same type of paper. The handwriting matches. My burning cheeks from earlier are now pale and cold. I don't even have to look at them to know. I turn my head to make sure no one else is in sight. Who put this note here?

I'm instantly creeped out. Who's following me? And not only that, why? I try to think of who could be doing this, and immediately suspect Andrew because of the location and the book. He knows what kind of books I like and he knows I come here often, but that doesn't explain the other letter. Andrew couldn't have put the envelope on my doorstep earlier because he would have had to have been working at the shop. He is currently the only employee.

I think of Joel next. He was up here and he had been near the shelf where the book was. He knows I like to read and that I used to work here, and it is possible he remembers where I live. He knows more about me than Andrew does.

Whoever put the note in the book made a huge gamble that I would actually choose it and hold it just so, in hopes that the note would fall out. My note-leaving-stalker knows me too well it seems. I'm a sucker for any cover with foil lettering.

Suspects aside, the other thing to address is the why. Why send ambiguous notes to me?

I resolve to find out what is going on with all these odd riddles. And I'm going to find out tonight. I pull out my phone and dial up my cousin Jen's number. She's staying with me tonight, or I'm going over to her place. It's time I finally told her about my feelings and resolve about Peter and all that has happened. Maybe she can help me sort through these events. Maybe she can even help me figure out how to navigate these tangled emotions. In the end, we can watch *Road To Avonlea* together.

I select her profile in my contacts and pause a moment before hitting the call button. She's my favorite, and I'm surprised I haven't told her about all this sooner. The phone rings and I wait, betting my life she'll pick up on the last ring. Sure enough, she does.

"Hey! Sorry, I was transplanting some of my aloes and I had dirt all over my hands." I hear a sink running and a dog barking in the background.

"It's okay. Hi, cousin."

"Hi. What's up?"

"I was wondering if you wanted to come to my house and spend the night tonight? There's been some... unusual activity around and I would rather not be home alone."

"Oh, curious. So you decided to bring me into the fray? What's going on?"

"No need to freak out, but I've been getting strange notes and one was on the doorstep. I can explain it all now or when you get here?"

"I'm free tonight and tomorrow I don't have to be home till noon. You can explain when I get there."

"Okay. Dinner at seven?"

"It's a plan. I'll bring snacks."

"Great. See you later, Jen."

She hangs up and I'm back in the bookstore with my thoughts. I walk to the back of the store, closer to the window in the children's section. Old fairy tales and children's classics line the floor beneath the window along with weathered copies of *Nancy Drew*. I read lots of those yellow-covered books growing up, so it's no surprise why my thoughts keep drifting towards possible crimes surrounding my circumstances.

I browse the shelves a bit longer but only end up with the foil fairy book at the front counter. Andrew's eyebrows raise as I set the tome before him.

"This is a nice copy. Where'd you find it?"

"Near the classics. You don't recognize it?"

"I forget which books come into the shop. I sort through so many and people move books around sometimes." He opens the cover and scans the interior page, searching for a price. There isn't one. "Hmmm odd. I must have missed labeling this one."

"Give it the value it deserves. It's a nice copy," I'm buying it because it is a gorgeous copy but also because it's connected to the note.

"Fifteen?"

"Fair enough." I pull a twenty from my wallet and he begins to count change. After he hands me some bills, I bring up the note.

"You don't happen to know where this note came from do you? I found it in the book." I withdraw the note and Andrew focuses on the writing.

"No I don't. Interesting. Sometimes books come into the shop with old bookmarks and letters or receipts inside. I always miss a few. Looks like you found a treasure and maybe a mystery."

"Maybe. Thanks." I tuck the note into my pocket and heft the book back into my arms.

"Sure thing. Have a nice evening, Briar. Oh, and see you tomorrow morning?"

"Yes, I'll be here."

"Excellent. Cheers!" He goes back to his book, glasses balanced on his nose. I push out the front door and step back into the rain.

There's a pot of creamy potato soup on the stove and hot biscuits on the table when Jen arrives. I'm already hanging up my linen apron as she knocks. All three cats follow me to the door and crowd my feet as I open it. Jen is a bundle of joy and squeals in delight. She's wearing octopus Xtratufs and a neon peach raincoat. Sandy-colored hair escapes her two french braids. She leans in for a big hug, the straps of her green overnight bag against my cheek.

"It seems like it's been forever since I've seen you! When was the last time exactly?" She withdraws and smiles down at my furry processional.

"A few weeks ago at least. I'm sorry we haven't done anything sooner." I invite her inside, and the cats make way as she enters.

"Oh, don't worry about that. We are together now, and I want to hear all about these mysterious happenings."

"We can talk about it all over dinner." I lock the door and take Jen's coat.

"Something smells delicious. Oh, biscuits?" She wanders into the kitchen, and I laugh as Scout bounds ahead of her and hops up on one of the chairs, waiting to be handed his own biscuit.

"It's a soup kind of day, and biscuits are a must with soup. I have rhubarb butter or raspberry jam."

"Rhubarb butter please." Jen plops into a chair and leans over to pet Libby who begins to put on her best begging face. After the hot creamy soup is ladled and the butter has melted on the biscuits, I tell Jen all about the day's events and my feelings. She's on her second bowl of soup as she listens, and I know some of her biscuit has made it into a furry tummy. There's a pause as I finish explaining my past with Peter, and then it's her turn to talk.

"Briar, I can't believe you never said anything. I could have told you ages ago if he liked you or not."

"Really? He's so confusing. I didn't want to make things weird, and I just wanted it all to disappear without drama if it wasn't anything."

"I'm drama?" She quirks an eyebrow, and I let out a low laugh.

"You know what I mean."

"Well, I can tell you right now if he was into you at one point. Have any memories you can share?"

"There's one, but it is by far the most confusing of them."

My mind turns back three years to when Peter and I graduated. I remember standing at the podium, giving my speech and looking out over the crowd of parents and students and teachers, thanking them for the years I'd had learning among them. I remember locking eyes briefly with Peter as he stood in the crowd. He'd given me a soft smile, one that speaks a thousand words in the moment, but after it's gone, you aren't sure if it actually happened. After I stepped down from the podium and a few other students spoke, it was Peter's turn. He'd said something witty that made everyone laugh as he approached the mic, but I don't remember what he said because all I could recall was the end of his thank you speech.

"In every person's life, there is a door. A door to a future that is wholly unknown. But each door leads to a unique adventure, and right now, I'm embarking on just that. I don't know exactly where I'm going or even where I'll end up, but that's okay. It's all an adventure, and I'm so grateful I gotta kick it off with all my friends, family, and teachers. Thank you."

He looked at me as he said the word 'friends', and I couldn't help but smile in return. He wasn't just accidentally looking at me. He meant to. But that's when moments like that ended. We never saw each other again after graduation, not till today. After my embarrassing text to him and the nearly unbelievable reply that evening after graduation, it's like we never knew each other.

I relay the memory and my thoughts to Jen, and she brews on it for a moment.

"Something else must have happened that night that distanced us. Peter is shy but not *that* shy," I say. My instincts tell me he was only ever being nice but my mind says that friends don't give each other looks across the room that feel like fire.

"Yeah... Everything is telling me he likes you but not talking to you for three years and telling you he only thought of you as a friend is conflicting. It's like he was playing with you, but that doesn't seem like Peter, considering I know his sister a little." Jen finishes the last of her soup, and I lean my head into my hands.

"I didn't realize you knew Anna. I was never in her circle of friends. What's she like?"

"Confident, sporty, and I know she works at the bakery. She's quite a bit different than Peter, but from the times I've chatted with her, I know they get along. Not sure how close they are though considering Peter has been out of state for several years."

"I'm sure she's nice." I sigh. "We don't have to talk about boys the whole time, you know. Frankly, I wish we didn't. I don't want to waste any more energy on it. I want to talk about this mystery."

"Sure thing. And yes, I've been thinking about that the whole time. It's so weird you're getting notes."

"I don't know why."

"You said you brought home the book you found the second note in, right?"

"Yeah, it's over here." I get up from the table and grab my book bag off the entry hook. Jen oohs at the cover as I set the book before her.

"Oh, nice. Do you think there could be any clues inside the book?"

"I didn't even think about it. I've been too busy thinking about who could have put the note there."

"May I?" Jen asks, motioning to the book.

"Oh, of course. Please, look all you want." I give her full access to the tome, and she begins on the first page.

"Looks like a book you'd pick up. Whoever they are, you fell for their trap."

"I know." I move my foot towards Herbert who curls into a ball at my approach. I rub his large belly with my toes, and he purrs happily. "Would you like any tea? I have chaga chai and fireweed earl grey."

"Anything chai would be excellent," Jen says, turning pages one at a time.

"It shall be done." I put the kettle on to boil then pack up the rest of the soup and biscuits. As I set out cups, I glance over at Jen. Her oval face is pinched in thought as she lands on a particular page.

"What color of paper did you say the note was made of?" A hint of unease coats her voice.

"Cream. Why?" I walk over to the table. She just stares at the page, and I glance down. There's a sheet of cream-colored paper nestled tightly against the spine. Jen pulls the paper out of the book and holds it up, turning it over. Together, we study the words that are carefully inked in an elegant scroll. The letters seem far too pretty for such a chilling and strange message.

Already I've seen the teeth of monsters sink into one of my comrades. Peter will be missed. The darkness on our land is growing. I don't have a plan and can only hope and wait for someone. Someone who can talk sense into those in command. I hope this letter finds this individual. In any event, I hope all darkness is lifted and truth and light will reign supreme.

"How very odd." The mention of the name Peter sends bolts of ice through my mind. This is all too strange.

"Briar, do you think that whoever is leaving these notes is playing a game of some kind?" Jen's voice is almost a whisper. I close my eyes and nod. I know she's referencing the conspiracy blog. It is possible. Other than the time an opossum, who is not native to

Alaska, ran free in the streets of Homer and made the news several times over, I'm pinned as one of my small town's most exciting news stories. It's highly possible someone from a conspiracy blog is leaving me strange notes and trying to work something up for likes.

"Briar, what are you going to do?" Jen's voice shakes, her face pinched. My own fingers tremble and I swallow, throat dry. I don't know what to do. All I know is I don't want to remember. I don't want to relive that stressful day under the noses of the police or the scrutiny of my town's eyes. I don't want to recount the looks I got from my classmates when I told them the truth. No one seemed to believe me except for the police and my family. Peter said he believed, but I know he had doubts.

"I'm not sure, but I know that I don't want to be the talk of the town again." I open my eyes and stare at the page. It's strange enough that I'm desperate for answers. I'm also scared, my inner thoughts leaning towards the worst possible outcomes. Why did the letter mention the name Peter? And why did it make it out to seem as if this Peter had been hurt and worse?

"Is there anyone you can talk to? Anyone you suspect?" Jen's voices is calm and caring, but the edges of her voice and the wideness of her eyes tells me she's creeped out.

"Andrew said he didn't know. The only other person I suspect is Joel. He was at the shop yesterday."

"Do you have his phone number?"

"I don't." I get up for the kettle and carefully pour our tea. Slowly, I sit back down, the steam billowing across the rim of my cup like sea fog. Jen frowns, sliding a hand over the wrinkled note, not even noticing the cup I'd set before her.

"But you have Peter's." I nod. I never deleted it. You could say I haven't moved on from him one hundred percent.

"Yah, but I don't want to call him. That would be weird." A blush threatens to crawl up my neck so I turn away from Jen briefly, wondering what else I should say.

"But what if something has happened to him?" Concern coats her voice and it pulls me back to face her.

"What if nothing has happened? I'd be calling him for no reason. Plus, I saw him this morning, remember? He was fine."

"Then you could just ask if he's been getting weird notes. No harm. Plus ask him for Joel's number." Jen glances down at the note again then back to me. I know she wants me to mend my relationship with Peter but I'm not sure it's a good idea. If he wanted to talk with me, he would.

"Jen, I don't think I'm ready to call him, even if it is to get Joel's number." I'm scared to call. Scared of what he'll think but also scared about what he might say. Would he even answer? Would he ignore me?

"You've already gotten three notes from someone. It's weird enough that you got them, let alone the name Peter being in one of them. Don't you think you should at least ask if he's responsible?" I contemplate her words. How serious are these notes anyway? If this is all a big joke and no harm is involved, will simply ignoring them and forgetting about it make them stop? But what if there is harm, something crafted up by someone wanting attention for selfish reasons? In this day and age, anyone seems to do anything for attention. I set a hand to my forehead, rubbing it back and forth as if the action will give me the answers I seek. I thought I had convinced myself that I should move on from Peter but I suppose I can break my own rules when someone's life may be in danger. Whether it's mine, I can't say, but if it is anyone else's, I certainly don't want to be at the center of the drama and partially responsible. The truth matters to me. I stand up straight.

"Jen, if I've moved on from someone, is it entirely normal to call that someone for informational purposes?" She thinks about it for a moment then grins.

"Uh..yeah that's acceptable." I sigh. Jen has a special way of making scary things seem light-hearted and not a big deal. I'm still not entirely convinced, but she's making me at least consider it. After a few moments of tea sipping and forehead scratching, I set my cup down with a clatter. I may regret this but my love of mysteries and thriller novels catapults me into a decision.

"Then, I suppose I could call him, just to ask if he knows anything about this." Jen claps her hands together a couple times then that's the last I hear about Peter for the rest of the evening. We make our migration to the living room shortly after and before long, the familiar red streets of Avonlea collect us in a cozy hug. I'll attempt to call Peter tomorrow, if only to find out once and for all what's going on.

Six

Peter

The lighthouse. It's an old building with white wooden siding, red trim, and a metal roof. It used to be in working condition but was decommissioned and turned into a hotel. When the owners retired, it was boarded up and abandoned. In the past three years however, the lighthouse was updated and from all appearances, turned into a privately owned home.

Tonight, there are five cars in the driveway, and the lights are on inside. I park my dad's car farther down the spit and walk towards the building. Evening is coming on, and while it still stays light out, I can feel the twilight chill rolling in off the water.

When I reach the parking lot, I shake my head. Anna's car is parked in with the group. She gave my family the impression that she would be at work till nine. It's six fifty-eight, and she's not at work. As far as I'm aware, the owners of the bakery in town do not own the lighthouse, so there should be no connection between the two. I wrinkle my brow and head towards the first window I see around the back. There are large rocks packed neatly around the base of the lighthouse, and I balance on one to peek inside the window.

I've never looked inside the lighthouse before, but now that I am, I wish I'd done it sooner. From what I can see, the front door opens up into a wide, spacious room. There are curved book-shelves lining the walls that I assume go all the way around and touch the ceiling. A spiral staircase offers one route up for easy access to books and a few steps extend to the left and lead down into a sitting area.

Couches are nestled together in a circle on a large, burgundy and gold rug. A coffee table and group of young adults with stacks of paper, notebooks, and pens fill the center. I shy away from the window at the sight of people but slowly return and watch from my vantage point. Because there are steps from the front door that lead down into the sitting area, I am looking down on the group. I can't hear anything, but I can see everyone. I can even watch when someone comes through the front door.

Anna and another gal are chatting and comparing notes, and three guys are doing the same. I try to study their notebooks but I'm too far away and the words are too small. My heart thuds as tires and gravel crunch. Someone else is pulling up and parking. A car door shuts, and I inch back from the window. The front door opens. A guy in a gray hoodie enters, and the whole room looks up at the same time. Muffled talking begins, and pens and paper are set down. I almost dismiss the new guy as he's welcomed by the rest, but when he takes off his hood, my jaw goes slack. Joel Moore. My best friend from high school. We haven't talked or seen each other in ages, but I know it's him. The same smile and curly hair. I watch Anna as Joel descends the stairs into the sitting area. She stands and waits with the other girl as Joel sits down in an armchair. The other guys get on their knees and start showing Joel their notebooks. The girls nod and listen, and Joel sits still, a hand under his chin. He says something to the girls and they disperse.

One girl steps out of view of the window, and Anna begins to ascend the spiral stairs. I become fixated on Joel as he stands from the chair and leans over the coffee table to point at some words on a notebook. He talks and the rest of the group patiently listens. Before I have time to move, I'm met with Anna's shocked expression, her eyes wide with horror. Dang it. I forgot about the spiral staircase. The steps follow along the curve of the wall right beneath the window I'm looking through. From the angle I'm at, I can only see Anna's face as she passes by the window. It's too late to retreat now. She knows I'm here. With little warning, my phone beeps and there's a text from Anna. I know it's an angry one.

Meet me outside. Now.

I see her pass by the window and disappear from view. I withdraw from my spying place. Soon, she's on my side of the lighthouse and her arms are crossed. Her pinched brows and straight lips tell me she's furious.

"Peter, what do you think you're doing here?"

"I'm watching out for you, sister. What are you doing here? Aren't you supposed to be at work?"

"I am at work." Her blonde hair is down and curled nicely. It wasn't like that this morning. There's even a touch of makeup on her face that looks great. That also wasn't there this morning.

"You told Mom you get off work at nine. Last I knew, you worked at the bakery. Remember? The bakery you were at this morning where you served me a pastry? It was delicious by the way."

"I still work at the bakery, but I have other work." She clenches her teeth then gives up as I continue to stare at her. She closes her eyes and rubs a hand across her face.

"Anna, what are you doing here? Why didn't you tell Mom or Dad or me about this?"

"What is *this*, Peter? Am I doing something illegal?" Her hands settle on her hips. She begins shifting her weight to mostly one foot then to another.

"I don't know, are you?"

"No, I'm not."

"Then why didn't you tell any of your family?"

"Because. I'm not allowed to," she says, her voice becoming shaky. She glances away then back into my eyes.

"Not allowed? Are you serious? What bakery forbids you from telling your family where you're at?"

"This isn't connected to the bakery. This is a different job." She glances at the lighthouse then to the ground. I know the look. Guilt.

"Anna, you better tell me right now what is going on or Dad is going to be here in fifteen minutes flat to take you home." Even though I have my dad's car at the moment, he'd find a way to get here.

"No! You can't tell him." Her eyes go wide, and I see fear in them. Fear I've never seen before.

"Then tell me, right now." I make my tone serious, and my eyes bore into hers. She better tell me the truth.

"Okay. Okay. Just, ugh. You snoop! You read my texts, didn't you?"

"Not on purpose, but yes," I admit. She takes a deep breath and swallows. The hesitancy in her manner is so thick I feel my own heart racing at what she's about to say. How bad of a situation is she in? Just when I think she's going to answer my question, she throws me for a loop.

"I have to show you Peter. I can't just tell you. Come on." She grabs my hand and pulls me with her. I wrench my hand away and stop in my tracks.

"Where are you taking me?"

"Inside. I have to tell you inside. I can't tell you without letting the others know."

"Anna..."

"Just listen Peter. It's... It's so important."The pleading and desperation in her eyes make me immediately capitulate. It is so unlike Anna to beg me for something like that. In most situations, she would come tell me herself. Something must be really wrong for her to keep a secret like this, especially from Mom and Dad. I'm at her heels in an instant, dread hollowing out my gut.

When we walk through the front of the lighthouse, the group in the sitting area goes quiet. They all look up, and Joel stands to his feet.

"He was snooping around outside. Sorry," Anna says. I watch Joel grimace as I make eye contact with him. There is no fond exclamation of reunion, and though I know he recognizes me, he doesn't let on to any of the others that he does.

"Does he know?" Joel asks. A few of the other teens whisper. Notebooks close.

"No, but he's not going to back down till he does. Otherwise, my parents will get involved," Anna says. Joel's jaw hardens.

"Then we'll have to have him in. Can't take the risk."

Anna nods and gives me a weak smile as I glance her way.

"What's going on?" I ask, my body going rigid with the tenseness of the room. Joel is a different person since I saw him last. Up close, he's practically the same except taller and more muscular. But his demeanor is not the Joel I know.

"Just do what he says, Peter," Anna puts gently. She brushes past me and files down the steps to go stand by the other girl.

"Joel Moore," I say. Heads turn as his name spills from my lips and Joel's eyes narrow briefly.

"Peter," he responds, not even bothering to use my last name.

"What have you been up to lately?" Whatever Anna needs to show me, it better happen quickly because I'm not about to make small talk forever.

"Nothing worth mentioning."

"Well, you better mention it because I need to know what in the world you are doing here that involves my sister." Red faced, I stare into Joel's eyes with scorching intensity. Joel catches on and stands up straighter.

"Listen, Peter. You were never supposed to get involved, at least, not like this. Anna wasn't either, but now that you are both here, you have to follow along."

"I'm not following along with anything."

"Peter..." Anna exhales from across the room, and I can hear the embarrassment in her voice.

"Trust me. After I tell you all I know, you'll be following along. But you have to be smart about it."

"Just tell me already!" Dad and Mom are going to hear about every single word, and I don't care what Joel says. If Anna is in some kind of danger... If Joel or anyone has done anything... I grow sick with the possibilities. Anna is my closest friend. Even closer than Joel ever was.

Though I'm hopping mad, I take a moment to observe my surroundings. I'm still up on the steps by the front door and am facing the stairway that leads down into the sitting area. Now that I'm inside, I can see everything that was obscured from the window. There are bookshelves on all the walls stretching up into the top of the tower. Where the stairs disappear to, there is an upper floor.

The inside of the lighthouse is so unlike what I thought it would be. It's hard to imagine this place as a working lighthouse or even a hotel. Now, it looks like a library and some cool clubhouse. A really cool clubhouse. For an instant, I try to imagine moving my escape room to this building. It would be amazing.

Joel snaps his fingers and points at the stairway that leads up inside the tower. Two of the guys begin gathering notes while the remaining guy heads towards me. He gives me a once over then passes by and heads up the steps. Recognition spikes in my brain. Everyone in this room... I've talked to them before.

"We'll be heading upstairs. It's safer there to discuss things," Joel says. My brows nearly leap off my face.

"Safer? What are you afraid of?" I give Anna a warning look.

"Peter, just listen okay?" Anna approaches, and she's clearly embarrassed by the flush on her cheeks. The other girl follows and sighs as she passes me by. Pretty soon, it's just Joel and me at the bottom of the spiral staircase.

"Peter, this is important. I promise you will want to hear this."

"Not till we sort out what's happened between us." I cross my arms and don't budge. Joel lets out his breath and rubs a hand through his curly hair.

"What do you mean?"

"The moment you saw me today... Where did our friendship go?"

"People change. We grow up and move away. Things are never the same." He doesn't meet my eyes when he says those words.

"That may be so, but that doesn't mean we forget the past. What about all the fun we had in high school? Where did those memories go?"

"Peter, I didn't forget any of that. I'm sorry I've been a terrible friend, but there's been a lot on my mind lately that blocks out parts of my brain. It's hard to focus on the fondness of the past when the present and future are in a tangle."

"What's going on, Joel? Why is Anna involved?"

"Come upstairs and I'll tell you everything and I mean everything." His eyes dart to the door and windows. Mine do, too, and then back to him. He's afraid. A chill creeps up my spine and I swallow.

"Fine. But it better be quick. I have to let my family know where Anna and I are soon."

"It won't take long." Joel turns and locks the lighthouse door. I wait for him to lead me up the stairs before taking the first step.

The upper room of the lighthouse is the exact opposite of what I thought it would be. Instead of a large signal light in the center of the room, there's a rectangle table. The table is covered in notebooks and surrounded by eight chairs. All around there are windows, but blackout curtains have been drawn across them. I can only see a crack of light between some, but it's fading fast. A small chandelier hangs over the table and casts a warm glow over our serious faces.

The floor is scuffed, old, and bare. The entire room smells of salt and dust. While the downstairs had been furnished, the upstairs is bland in comparison. But there's still interest here. I can tell that secrets have been spilled in this room before. Whatever club my sister is a part of, this is where they've discussed their deepest.

The door at the top of the stairs is secured by Joel, and now all seven of us are locked in this room together. Though I'm still mad and the tiniest bit scared, I'm intrigued and excited. It isn't everyday you get caught up in a secret meeting in a library lighthouse with your sister and high school best friend.

"Anna, can I have your notes please?" Joel asks, extending his hand.

"Sure thing." She reaches into the pile of books on the table and hands Joel one.

"You can take a seat," Joel says, his eyebrows scrunching together as he reads quickly over Anna's notes. The chairs skid back on the wood and the whole upper floor shakes a little. My stomach grows queasy at the awkwardness and tenseness of the moment.

I'm soon slid a clipboard with names printed down the front. A pen rolls to me.

"What's this for?" I ask.

"You must sign it in order to hear what we are about to tell you. It's a non-disclosure agreement."

"Are you serious?" I look at Anna and she avoids my eyes.

"Sign it, and we'll tell you everything."

"And if I don't?"

"We'll send you on your way. No information."

"I don't believe it. Why'd you risk bringing me up here anyway?"

"Because I believe you'll sign it," Joel says. Anna keeps her head down but looks up when I don't respond for a few moments.

Anna, Joel, Naomi, Orin, Cedric, Samuel. The names are all signed in cursive and I can feel my hand itching to sign my own. I want to know what this is all about.

As I look over all the faces and read their names, something finally clicks. Everyone in this group I recognize, now that I've seen them up close. Besides Anna, we all went to the same high school together. I was only super close with Joel and didn't hang out with hardly any of them except for Briar. But it's strange that it's taken me this long to recognize them. Three years isn't long enough to forget about your high school classmates. While the realization is surprising and strange, I shove it aside momentarily to get to the bottom of this situation.

"What happens if I tell someone about this meeting after I've signed the paper?"

"Then your family might get hurt," Joel says quietly. Anna cringes when I sit straight up in my chair, the floor shaking in my abruptness.

"Are you threatening my family?" I squeeze my fingers into fists. Joel tilts his chin upwards and looks me dead in the eyes.

"I would never hurt your family. It's not me you have to worry about. This is why we are meeting like this." I glance over the group's faces. All of them have a faint look of fear mixed with tiredness. Anna especially. I cave, not wanting to put up with anymore dodged questions. I grab the clipboard and scribble my name onto the paper. One of the boys, Orin, who's at my left, slides the clipboard in front of Joel. "Thank you, Peter. I knew you'd sign," Joel says calmly, setting the clipboard into his lap.

"Better start talking," I say, sitting back down.

The only other girl in the room, Naomi, clears her throat. She's naturally tan and sports shoulder-length, wavy, brown hair, pink lip gloss, and gold sea star earrings. Now that I recognize her, not much has changed. She was often involved in drama club and was into fashion during school.

"This group exists because there has been *strange* activity going on in Homer over the past few years but especially these last few months." Naomi glances at Orin who nods in agreement.

Orin pulls thick-rimmed navy glasses off his face and rubs a hand through short, black hair. "I've seen weird stuff too. I work for the city and am outside a lot, especially during the summer and fall. The number of strange things I've seen has gone up in the past three years. And get this, most of them have been on Main Street."

"What kind of strange things?" I lean closer to the table as Orin and Naomi look at Joel.

"Things that would put all of us in mental centers if we let the world know."

"Please be specific." I'm normally a patient person, but when it comes to my family and their safety, patience takes a back seat sometimes.

"Anna?" Joel ushers a hand to her and she nods. I blink, waiting.

"The bakery is a little ways off Main Street, but it is pretty close to it. Since beginning to work there, I've noticed things. Or rather, have been asked things that don't make a lot of sense."

"Tell him about last week," Joel says.

Anna nods slowly, licking her lips in nervousness. "I was closing up the shop last week and a man, who looked to be homeless by the way he dressed, came into the shop just before I could lock the door. Thankfully I wasn't alone, but my coworkers were in the back so they didn't see or really hear what happened. He came to the counter and wouldn't meet my eyes. While looking at the floor, he asked me if I had been anywhere interesting recently."

"What does that mean?" My forehead continues to wrinkle as she continues.

"Yes. I was utterly confused at first. All I could respond with was that Homer was interesting enough for me. He kept staring at the floor then mumbled some things I didn't understand. Finally he left and that was the last time I ever saw him."

"But not the last time you heard from him," Joel adds.

"Well, no..." Anna trails off.

"What do you mean? Has this random guy been harassing you?"

"Harassing? No. Nothing violent. Just strange. I've gotten two notes in green envelopes left on my car. I can't help but think they are from the same guy."

My mind reels at her words. Anna has been receiving messages? What did they say?

"Anna isn't the only one getting these messages. I've received a few on the windshield of my car. Naomi has once, and the others have all been witnesses of this homeless character we believe is responsible for them. He's followed a few of us but hasn't approached us personally."

"What are these messages saying? I mean, if it's just a random homeless guy writing letters, that can't be any stranger than a lot of people in Homer. No offense." I chuckle dryly. Joel smirks a little but it disappears quickly.

"Anna has taken account of all the messages we've all collectively received. I'll let you read them." Joel hands me a yellow-paged notebook, the one Anna gave him earlier. Anna then slides a stack of green envelopes stamped in silver wax next to me. I glance at them briefly then begin to read the first three messages written down on the notebook.

Anna: October 28th, Message: I know many of you hate us but I kindly ask for your help. I do this under the ruler's nose.

Naomi: October 29th, Message: If anyone is reading this, know that I need help. Please, send for anyone to aid me in the overcoming of darkness.

Joel: October 20th, Message: I've sent over ten of these messages. If you cannot help me, please find someone who can.

"What in the world?" I lay the notebook flat and lean back in my chair. "Anna, why didn't you tell any of us about this, Mom, Dad and me?"

"Because, Peter, Mom and Dad wouldn't believe me, and you weren't supposed to find out and—"

"Excuse me?"

"Peter. Let her talk," Joel cuts me off sharply. I huff out a breath and sit farther back in my chair.

"You'll call me a liar, Peter, but I'm telling you because I need you. We need you." Anna stands up and walks over to one of the blackout curtains then touches something along the edge of the fabric. The chandelier dims and the blackout curtain lights up like a movie screen. I glance at Samuel, a blond athletic guy, remembering him as the techy kid from school. He has a portable movie projector in his hands, and I watch his fingers press play on the top of the machine. There's no sound, but the footage that appears is absolutely nostalgic.

Our old high school classroom. It's just as I remembered it. A dirty whiteboard with our teacher's name in the top left corner, grungy gray carpet, and a shelf of textbooks.

Whoever was filming this zoomed in on the front three desks. Briar, Joel, and myself are huddled around what looks like a piece of paper. Orin and Naomi are in view, too, and they are also leaning in around us to look. The camera jerks briefly, catching a frame of the filmer. Sam's one of a kind watch meets the lens, detailing him as the director of this film. Then the camera steadies and begins to pan down over the shoulders of the huddle. Strange. Briar is writing something on the piece of paper, but when her pencil touches the paper, nothing has been written. She's writing, but the video camera isn't picking it up.

"Do you remember this, Peter?" Anna asks. I contemplate for a moment and slowly nod.

"Vaguely. Was Briar writing a story? I don't really remember it, but I think that's what it was."

"Yes. She was. And she showed it only to all of you in this room, according to Sam's video. But I also heard the story. From you, Peter. You told me pieces of the story that evening."

"I did?"

"Yes. All of us know parts of the beginning, middle, and end. Or at least, we did." Anna motions for Sam to turn off the projector and then the lights are undimmed. Anna returns to her chair. "The video we just showed you is strange because all of you should remember that Briar did indeed write something down on that piece of paper. But the video camera didn't pick anything up. My theory is that whatever was being written down was only meant to be seen in person."

"I'm lost. What are you saying?"

"Peter, whatever that story was, whatever book it was from, it's all magic. Don't you remember the news a while ago?"

I'm startled that Anna would use the word *magic* to describe a possible blurry video job, but everyone else in the room is dead serious in their expressions. I turn back time to what Anna is referring to as the *news*. Headlines stream in front of my mind's eye as I recall the day of a possible kidnapping.

FIFTEEN-YEAR-OLD GIRL MISSING. REPORT ANY SIGHTINGS TO HOMER POLICE DEPARTMENT.

That had been the scariest day of my life and for Briar's family's lives. Briar had gone missing all day, and we couldn't find her anywhere. No one could. But I finally did. At the bookstore. She claims she was at the shop the entire time and fell asleep while reading. But friends, family, and I searched the entire place. We couldn't find her. The police searched. Andrew searched. And when she mysteriously emerged from the shop, I was fortunately there still looking for her.

That was a crazy day. The interrogations that happened were long and drawn out. Briar had insisted she had been asleep while the rest of us swore she wasn't in the bookshop. It was never fully solved, and to my knowledge, Briar still believes she fell asleep and dreamt strange dreams. I think she knocked herself out by accident and came in the back door. All in all, I didn't really care what had happened, as long as she was safe. Thank God she was. But none of this makes sense compared with the video Anna just showed.

"What does Briar disappearing have to do with the old vid?"

"It's intricately connected. Because, well, we finally know where Briar went."

"What? Where?" I look at Joel. His hands are folded and his chin is resting on them as if he's been waiting for this moment his entire life.

"We believe Briar accidentally entered a different world via the bookstore. Ha, we don't believe it. We *know* it. All of us, including Anna, have been there ourselves," Joel says.

"You've got to be kidding me. Are you serious?" My mouth is wide open, and I watch Anna sigh as if she knew this would be my reaction. But she's absolutely serious. They all are.

"We have to show you, Peter. We know you wouldn't believe us just by telling you. We'll take you there tomorrow if you'd like," Anna says.

Joel speaks before I can utter another word. "The story Briar wrote down on that piece of paper in high school is an excerpt from a book of myths about the same world that we are referencing. Only those who've read a certain passage of this book and are in the bookstore can enter. We think Briar is the one who opened the portal to this realm. Only by accident."

"But that's not even the craziest part," Orin adds. "That weird guy that's been wandering around, our number one suspect for the notes, we think he's also from this world."

Silence.

Actually, silence isn't the word I'd use to describe the space between talking right now. My ears are literally ringing with insanity. I want to dial up my dad's number right now and have him sort out this mess, but part of me knows that this isn't all nonsense. There's a nugget of truth here, and I'm willing to wait a little longer to find it out.

Seven

BRIAR

When morning breaks and Jen leaves, my mind flickers back in time. I distinctly recall going to the bookstore at age fifteen and reading a peculiar book. During my time there, I had the most vivid dream. I was walking in a forest I'd never been in before. Blue sky, so much green, and rocky land surrounded by the scent of fresh rain.

When I found myself back in the store, I learned that the entire town had been in a panic looking for me, as if I had been kidnapped or something. They said they had been looking for hours. Peter and my family especially. I must have slept for such a long time because evening was approaching when I stepped out of the store. I gave everyone quite a scare and even had to go to the police station and clear up the mess. It was so embarrassing having the whole town's attention for a bit, but it died down soon after.

I find myself at the table again, looking at the mysterious notes. My cellphone is clutched in my hand and I relax momentarily as Libby purrs against my leg, but my shoulders tense up when I think about calling Peter. I'm still taking in the reality of the messages and what they could mean.

With the appearance of the envelopes, I can't help but think someone remembers the incident from years ago and wants to stir up trouble. While it's hard for me to fully grasp, I highly suspect one of my high school classmates is responsible. I have a small inkling it could be Peter sending them but if not him, anyone in this town could be a part of this. I suck in a breath, remembering my interaction with Joel yesterday. He's on my top list of suspects, and I want Peter to know that. I'll call him and let him know what's going on, tell him about the notes, and warn him in case he's in any danger. In this day and age, there are so many crazy people, and it's better to be safe than sorry. But whatever is going on, I don't want people to think I'm the crazy one.

These messages bring back some of the memories. Memories of me pleading to my family and the police that I had never left the store. Memories of Peter being concerned for me and saying he believed what I said. And memories of being so absorbed in the book I was reading that day that I fell asleep and had beautiful dreams.

These are the awakened memories that lead me to believe that someone is playing a huge joke. I know I'm not crazy. But some of my classmates and many others in Homer didn't believe my story. Some far-out locals even went on to start blogs and conspiracy threads about how the police and I were involved in some drug trafficking ring and that my disappearance and news story was a cover up for other things going on. Of course it's ridiculous and no one had any real proof to make it a hit story or anything. But there were some in our town who actually believed it, or at least, didn't believe me and said I disappeared for some dark purpose.

I always wondered if Peter ever truly believed me. He hung out with Joel, and Joel hung out with the few other classmates who didn't see eye to eye with me. When graduation came and went, I had the feeling that some of the classmates had talked Peter into forgetting about me and what I said. Did Peter tell me he believed me to make me feel better or had he actually meant what he said? I never tried to push for the truth, but I still wonder if what happened that day when I was fifteen caused something to grow between us.

A few days after the incident, I remember writing down a few plot points of the story I had read in the bookstore. The book had been so peculiar and beautiful I had wanted to write down some things to use in stories of my own. Well, one thing led to another, and soon some of my classmates were reading over my shoulder. Peter's desk was next to mine, and I could feel his eyes on my paper. Sam, one of the nerdy kids, was playing around with his new video cam recorder and videoed me and my plot point sheet. A few others poked fun at me and brought up my disappearance again, saying what a liar I was. I ignored them and kept writing. I remember that day because Peter and Joel never said anything against me. But they never said anything in favor of me either in front of everyone.

I withdraw from my memories and sit straighter in my chair. I swipe with my thumb on my phone and find Peter's contact. I haven't used it since the night after graduation, and my hand shakes a little. What will he think, me calling him out of the blue? I think I'll faint if he answers, or at the very least, any words I have will dry up the moment I hear his voice. I'm naturally introverted, and anyone who relates knows that phone calls are in the top ten list of fears. Maybe I should just text him. I begin to type out a message:

> *Hey Peter, this is Briar Verlice. I have something to tell you and I…*

I stare down at what I just wrote, and my face pulses with heat. What am I doing? I can't send this. Not after what I sent him last time! I quickly erase the message and lay my head onto the table. Do I have to call him? I think of all the reasons why Jen said I should and why I said I should. She told me to tell her how it goes, and while I had said yes, a part of me wants to just forget it and have someone else check on Peter and ask if he knows what's going on.

As I sit in the quiet of the morning, the wheels of my mind turn for the umpteenth time. Somewhere within my introverted self is a courage that wants to come out. I tap into it and hit the call button next to Peter's name before I chicken out. As soon as I do, my heart begins to pound. I shakily bring the phone to my ear and wait. The dial up continues, and my knuckles turn cold. Then the dreaded sound. I hear the phone scratch on the other side and I know he's answering it.

"Hello?" The voice on the other end has me taken aback. It isn't Peter's voice. It's a girl's voice. I scramble for words.

"Hi, this is Briar. I'm looking for Peter?"

"Oh... He's not available right now. Can I take a message?"

"I... uh... I was just wondering if he was okay?" Dumb. So dumb. Why couldn't I have phrased that better?

"Yes, he's okay." There's an awkward silence. Who is the voice on the other end?

"May I ask who I'm speaking to?" I want to know who has Peter's phone.

"His sister, Anna." Relief floods me. It's just his sister.

"Okay, thank you. I was just concerned is all. Thanks."

"Yeah, sure thing."

"Goodbye."

"Bye."

I quickly hang up and practically hurl the phone away from me. Cold calls are the worst. I cover my head with my hands and retreat from the table. At least Peter is okay.

I shoot a look at the clock on the wall and groan. It's nine-twenty. I completely forgot about helping Andrew out at the bookstore! I race for my jacket and book bag while sweeping my hair in an updo with a claw clip. Libby, Scout, and Herbert follow me to the front door, and I give them each a pet on the head before whirling out.

I stumble through the door of the book shop, the creak of the hinges alerting Andrew of my presence. The clock behind Andrew's desk says I'm five minutes past nine-thirty, and I cringe.

"Sorry I'm late."

"You're on time for me. I was running a bit late myself, and didn't get here till nine-twenty."

"That's a relief." I sigh. Andrew smiles then squints at his watch.

"I'll consider you clocked in." I stand straighter, taking in the scent of the books. Andrew motions with a hand. "Follow me and I'll show you what to do."

When he leads me upstairs, I find the room already in a state of chaos. Well, more than it already is. But I welcome this kind of chaos. As a bookdragon, I find heaps and piles of books absolutely charming.

"When does the escape room guy start working on the puzzles?"

"He was going to stop by sometime today and take some more measurements. If anyone comes upstairs during the day, it will be me or him. I'm closing it off to customers till everything is built."

"All right."

I follow Andrew all the way to the back of the room. There are a few shelves that have been completely emptied, all the books shoved up against another bookcase.

"I want you to empty all the shelves in the room and then re-stack them with books by size and color. If they become full with a certain color, begin on another shelf right across from the other. For example, red books in a stack along the left wall and red books in a stack along the right wall. Does that make sense?"

"Yes, it does. But, won't all your organization by authors be completely undone?"

"Yes, but it will be worth it for the project."

"How long would you like me to work for?"

"How long can you stay?" Andrew slides his glasses down his nose a little as he smiles.

"All day I suppose. I didn't have anything else planned."

"Excellent." He slides the glasses back up and laces his fingers together across his middle. "I'll be downstairs manning the counter. Holler if you need anything."

"Will do."

Andrew leaves, and I remove my jacket and set my book back down by the window. There's so much work to do. Taking all the books off the shelves and stacking them in piles is going to take forever. There's barely any room in the maze. I'm fairly certain this is going to take more than a whole day to complete.

If I had spoken all this out loud, it might sound like complaining, but I'm actually thrilled. I have permission to take loads of books off the shelves and go through them. It has been something I've wanted to do at every bookstore.

I hum a tune from *How To Train Your Dragon* while I begin emptying the first shelf next to the window. As I pull books off, the scent of dust and old leather gets stronger. I make a pile at my feet and sort by color and size, careful to leave some room for walking.

I check my phone and see that it's already ten. The store is open now.

I adjust my speed, and by eleven, I have four shelves emptied with stacks along the floor in neat, color-coordinated piles. I've heard the downstairs door creak several times and voices, indicative of customers.

I begin organizing the piles, and before twelve, I have fully shelved all the red, blue, and green books that I can fit. It looks fantastic, but I've hardly made a dent in the piles.

"Briar, how's it going?"Andrew's steady footsteps reverberate up the stairs. The scent of butter, cheese, bacon and basil draws me from my work, and I turn to see Andrew carrying a sandwich.

"You didn't have to do that."

"Since I'm friends with the owner of the coffee shop next door, It was simple enough to bring you some lunch. I have tea downstairs too. Chai?"

"Yes please." I take the sandwich and nearly drool.

"I'll be right back."

Blueberry, basil, bacon, and cheese sandwich. I could cry. I take a bite and lean against a shelf, grateful for the hearty lunch. Tart berry, salty bacon, aromatic basil, and creamy cheese. What's not to love? When Andrew returns with the tea, I'm halfway done with the sandwich.

"This is amazing... Thank you."

"You're welcome. Oh, careful, this is hot." He hands me the chai, and I accept it with my free hand. "What you've done so far is great. If you can finish one wall today and then another wall another day, whatever is leftover from the sorting, we'll haul out and find a place for it downstairs."

"Are you taking out all the shelves in the center of the room?"

"That's the plan. We want it to be a big, open room with books surrounding it on all sides. We'll move a table in here eventually."

"This project continues to intrigue me the more I learn about it."

"I'm excited for it. Let's hope it's enough to keep the store open," Andrew says hopefully.

"I'm sure it will do great." I take a sip of the tea then set it on an empty shelf.

"I'll let you get back to it. Shop closes at six but you can stay till eight as I'll be doing paperwork and catalog stuff."

I nod and with a few more bites and another gulp of tea, I'm back at it.

When it's three pm, I'm at the final shelf along the left wall, the side where the stairs emerge. I didn't realize this last shelf was double stacked. As I pull books off and set them on the floor, my fingers close over a certain weathered cover, leather and gilded. There is no title on the spine or the cover, so I turn it over in my hands. I open its pages and my memory renews. The story comes back to me as I flip through it. My mind lights up in recognition. This is the book I read in the fall when I was fifteen, the day all the crazy stuff happened. I linger on a few sentences within the book then shut it and slip it into my book bag. I can't believe I never bought it after I read it that one time. I thought for sure I did though. Regardless, I'm buying it today.

As I begin to pull the last of the books off the shelf and stack the sorted ones, my fingers tingle and I sway in place, my head like a helium balloon. I step away from the shelf and walk towards where I set my tea. As I reach for my cup, the bookstore begins to fade like some immersive dream.

I can't believe it. I'm dreaming again, except it feels completely and factually real. I'm back in the forest glade from years ago.

The sun is shining, the trees are basically whispering to each other by the way the wind is pulling on their branches, and I'm standing on thick moss. I pull my hand back to my body, my tea no longer in front of me. I pause, taking in the scene. As I listen, I begin to notice more. There's a strange watery sucking noise behind me and I turn, afraid of what I'll see.

Instead of something frightening, there's a perfect circle cut from the branches of the trees. My first thought is a portal of some kind because I can see the bookstore through the center of it. As I walk towards the round gate, the sound intensifies. I know what's happening but I'm too late by the time I reach it. The bookstore disappears and the sound is gone. All I can see through the cut out trees is the rest of the forest beyond. I'm stuck in this nightmare. Did I pass out in the bookstore? Whatever it is, I need to wake up soon. Andrew's not going to appreciate me sleeping on the job. What if that escape room guy also finds me passed out on the floor? I groan, embarrassed already.

I turn from the empty portal and look past the glade. Rocks covered in moss lay here and there, sunshine peeking out from the trees over a hundred feet away at an angle. I walk towards the light, curious what the view might be. A dream as vivid as this one? I blame it entirely on that incredible sandwich.

I pass between pink-tinged birches, their bark as flaky as the croissants sold in the coffee shop. A bird flutters and sings overhead, and I spot a mouse scrambling into a hole at the base of a spruce. When I reach the edge of the forest, I stand impressed at the landscape before me. I'm on a mountain, and the trees end at the line of a great cliff. Mountains are stacked in the distance, and I look to the right and the left and see more mountain faces that plunge into a green valley. The sun is setting, the light a warm gold while casting deep shadows. I kick a loose stone over the edge and watch it tumble to the forest below. It hits the side of the mountain face with an echoing crack and drops below the green. As the stone's echo fades, the air is replaced with faint rustling trees and soft hissing grasses.

I step back and follow the sunlight, circling to the right of the drop off. I weave between more trees, and soon I'm face to face with the sun.

I take a deep breath, strangely at peace. Even though I need to wake up from this dream, I take the moment and enjoy the realism. I've missed sunshine like this. Fall in Homer is usually wet and chilly, and we don't often get the sun so warm like this till late spring.

I stand at the cliff edge until the light has almost faded, my rusty hair loosening from my claw clip. I pull it out and shake my head, combing through it with my fingers. I hold the clip firmly in my hands and stare into the green valley.

I need to wake up. From past dreams, I've always been able to wake from an adrenaline rush of some kind. Especially if it's induced from heights. I back up, preparing for a running start that scares me half to death. But I can't stay in this beautiful dream for much longer. I race towards the edge, my eyes closed, then I propel myself as far as I can. My eyes open and I can't help but scream. I plummet, and my vision turns blurry. The ground is approaching fast, and all I can hear is the wind and my scream. The treetops are about to overtake me when something catches me out of the sky and I lose my balance. I'm on my back and instead of falling down, rushing sideways.

"You don't have wings, you know, and suicide isn't recommended for someone as pretty as you," says a masculine, mischievous voice. I frown and sit up awkwardly, nearly pitching over the side of... a bird? Mottled gray and white feathers are splayed out, and I'm resting at the shoulder of the avian creature. We're coasting through the air at a great speed, a flap occurring every so often. My eyes roam up to a man seated confidently aboard the bird. I rotate so my feet are pointed towards the front of the creature and I get a better view of the one who had spoken. "What were you doing jumping off a cliff anyways?" he asks. I don't answer, still too stunned to speak. I'm a little perturbed now that my dreams are intricate enough to negate my plans.

"I wanted to hit the ground so I'd wake up from this peculiar dream," I say. The man looks at me with raised eyebrows. His features age him to be around twenty-five with an athletic build, caramel-colored hair, and big, brown eyes. I study his face for a few moments, but it must be too long because he looks away with a smirk.

"I'm no dream, but I'll take the compliment," he says.

I scrunch my face in embarrassment and shake my head. "No, no, I mean, this whole thing. Oh, never mind." I'm being utterly ridiculous, explaining myself to my subconscious, but it feels so real. I pull myself to my feet, extending my hands to keep balance. The bird's round head is connected to a snowy white body with flecks of gray and black. When the bird turns its head, I catch a glimpse of its massive eyes. We're on an owl and it is huge. Enough to hold two or three people.

"Before you decide to jump again, can I at least get your name?" the man asks without looking at me.

"Briar," I say. The owl takes a swoop left, skimming the treetops. I grab onto a leather strap that's fashioned for a handle or foot rest around the bird's middle as we descend through a hole in the canopy and land gracefully on the mossy floor.

"Mine's Wystan."

"And your owl?" I ask, tilting my chin towards the bird's head.

"This here's Auriol. He's been my pal for the past three years."

"I see." I beat my forehead with the palm of my free hand. *Wake up already.*

"You okay there?"

"I'm fine. I just.... need... to wake... up," I say through gritted teeth, slapping my face. Wystan gives me a concerned look then leaps from Auriol's back with precision.

"I'll give you a hand."

"I'm fine," I say again, letting go of the leather strap and sliding down the bird's back and tail. Auriol steps away and begins to preen while Wystan crosses his arms.

"I've never met a maiden who's so bent on ignoring me or Auriol. Most girls would swoon and jump at the chance to ride with a captain of the Breezewood night patrol."

"I don't swoon... nor do I jump at the chance to ride with any man on any mode of transportation."

"I do believe I've met a sprite. With hair as red as mushrooms and clothes as strange as they come. Where are you from anyway?"

"Home. I mean... Earth. Homer, Alaska." I look down at my blue jeans, knit sweater, and leather lace-up boots. Compared to him, he's the one who's dressed strangely. Thin gray armor covered in green moss and sprigs of grass here and there cover his chest and shoulders. There's a short sword at his hip and a crossbow on his back. His arms are bare, and he wears mottled brown and green breeches and leather boots similar to mine. Only the toes of his boots are covered in moss. He looks like something out of the animated movie *Epic,* only life size and not covered in leaves.

"Never heard of the place called Homer. But you must be a Worlder." Wystan chuckles, shaking his head. Auriol hoots softly, preening another wing.

"Of course you haven't. It's real and all this is... my imagination."

"I think you've fallen and hit your head."

"So do I," I say, glancing around the forest. It's warmer here, but the light is nearly gone. Soon, everything will be pitch black.

"Good. At least we agree on something. Why don't you come with me? You can stay in the castle tonight and maybe get a little rest. Perhaps you'll feel better in the morning." Wystan uncrosses his arms and extends a hand towards me.

"Yes... Yes, that would be nice." Falling asleep sounds agreeable, even in a dream. I've done it before, dreaming within a dream. All I can think of is the Christopher Nolan film *Inception*.

"It isn't far from here, and we can walk. Auriol has to hunt anyway."

I don't take his hand. Instead, I sweep my hair up in a new bun and secure it with my claw clip, miraculously still with me. Wystan drops his hand, a muscle tightening in his jaw. Maybe my lack of attention will discourage him. But he isn't dissuaded and instead offers a small bow.

"Miss Briar, the night is coming on and the forests are dangerous. Stay close as I lead to the safety of Breezewood Castle," he says.

Castle? I'm intrigued.

Auriol hoots again, and Wystan salutes the bird. The large owl then stretches out his great wings and lifts into the air with powerful flaps. He is completely silent leaving the canopy.

"Good old Auriol, off to catch his dinner. He eats about twenty mice a night, you know?"

"Twenty? Is that all?" I'm more than slightly amused as we begin to walk through the trees, the light fading fast.

"I suppose he could eat more, but he's keeping a lean body for battle."

"What do you battle?" I ask, not believing a word of this. My mind is creative, but that blueberry sandwich is going to get all the credit until proven otherwise. I've got to get out of here.

"Bears, beasts, and other people who pose a threat to my people's lands."

"Does Auriol eat people?" I'm horrified at the thought.

"He has never told me that, but I can assure you his diet consists mostly of mice and rabbits and bugs."

I don't ask for anything more, my mind reeling with the strangeness of my circumstances.

"Ah, we are here. One moment please while I get permission to enter," Wystan says. He steps away from me and passes between several trees before coming to stop before a wall of rock. Within the dimness, I make out the contour of a door set in the stone. Wystan knocks three times against the door, and after ten seconds, it moves with a heavy grating sound. Warm light spills from the opening along with the delicious smell of bread and cloves.

"Home already, Wystan? I thought you were going to help Auriol hunt this evening?" an old, haggard voice says from within the doorway.

"Plans have changed. I brought a visitor."

"A visitor? Not another fox I hope."

"Not a fox, but she's got hair as red as one," Wystan says with a chuckle. I approach the doorway, pretending I didn't hear his comment. As I step into the beam of light, the voice on the other side of the door becomes low and whispery.

"Wystan! You mischievous toad. You've brought a girl to Breezewood Castle?"

"Not just any girl. A sprite, I say. Look at her clothes," Wystan says.

I catch the features of the older man and watch as his eyes go from curious to hard. He's stooped and dressed in similar fashion to Wystan, except he wears a green cape and has no crossbow.

"Wystan, she's a Worlder..."

"Not one we need to worry about. If she was a dangerous Worlder, Finn, she'd have fancy gadgets and weapons. This isn't a weapon, is it?"

I guffaw as Wystan reaches for my claw clip and unclips it, my hair tumbling around my shoulders. He clips it open and shut twice like it's a crab pincer.

"Please give it back," I say, reaching for it. He hands it to me with a smirk. Finn shakes his head.

"She's a Worlder, all right. The clothes give it away. You know what the king does with Worlders, right Wystan?"

"The king doesn't have to know she's here. Look, we'll have her change her clothes and she can lay low for a while."

"I'm not staying here," I say, standing straighter.

"She can't stay outside alone," Wystan says, pleading with Finn. Finn's eyes soften as he looks at me and Wystan.

"Only for tonight, and then she needs to be taken back to wherever she came from."

"You really think the king is going to feed her to the wolves? How could she harm anyone?" Wystan motions to my slender frame and short stature.

"Feed me to the wolves?" I ask, ignoring his comments once again.

"The king has a thing for feeding Worlder's to the wolves. Doesn't like them too much," Wystan says fearlessly. At first I'm concerned, then an idea sparks in my mind. My cliff jumping might have failed, but if I can face this king who likes to feed strangers to wolves, maybe I'll finally wake up from this nightmare.

"Take me to your king."

Eight

PETER

Joel, Sam, Naomi, Orin, Cedric, and Anna all agreed to meet me at the bookstore later today and prove to me all the things they spilled last night. After the meeting, Anna and I drove home in our separate cars, me in dad's car since mine is still in Colorado. When we got home, we didn't say a word to Mom or Dad about what had happened. With my promise to Joel and the group in writing, my insides wriggled with shame when Mom and Dad asked how my work day went. The unanimous 'good' with little explanation tore me up. In time, I would tell them everything—all the secrets and the meetings and whatever else crazy happened. Anna gave me a wan smile as we parted ways on the path to our rooms. I know she didn't like keeping secrets from Mom and Dad either.

It's morning now, and I'm up early. I have things I need to get done, apart from forever watching over Anna's safety. Today is her day off, and I know she will be stuck at home helping Mom with projects, which takes a load off my mind. With Dad at work, I have to drive Anna's car into town today for my errands.

I start the car, my mouth full of crisp, honeyed toast. I glance at my notepad on the passenger seat where I've scribbled down several sponsor stores.

In my early time getting ready this morning, I curated each sponsor store a puzzle to incorporate into the escape room if they choose to go in on the project. While the bookstore will be the main sponsor, since the room will be in the literal building, I still need funds to get the items to build the secret rooms I have planned. My hope is that having the plans for each sponsor puzzle already drawn up will be just the thing to get them to accept. I need at least five stores to accept my offer in order for this escape room to become a reality.

The first store from the eleven on my list is the fabric and hardware store off the main road coming into Homer. Popular in Homer but not super well-known outside of our town, I count on them being willing to accept my offer. They just seem like the type of store who would support this kind of thing, considering they support lots of other local businesses and regularly promote fun things to do around town.

When I pull into the parking lot, my cell phone rings on the seat. I park and scan the caller ID. It's August. I quickly answer it.

"August! Hey, how's it going?"

"As good as could be expected, being as old as me," he chuckles. "What are you up to?"

"Doing errands. Why the phone call?"

"Wanted to check in and see how your escape room is going."

"So far so good, even though it's only been a few days."

"Time is precious in this business, especially when you're in the room, haha."

"I'm aware." I grin, picturing August's twinkling eyes. "I've actually already secured a room location and I'm visiting sponsor stores right now. When I'm ready to start building, I'll call you again, okay?"

"You're making quick work of it. I knew you'd be the one for the job."

"Well, nothing is certain yet but so far, everything is looking up."

"Well, that's great, Peter. Hey, what would you say your timeline is? I'm going to start up a report to keep track of what you do. My bosses will want a record."

"Oh, uh... Sure thing. If I get the money by the end of this week, I could start building Monday. I'll text you right before I pick up my tools, okay?"

"Perfect. I'll be in touch. Go get 'em, Peter." August's deep, gravelly laugh is the last thing I hear as he hangs up. It's joyful, and I'm left smiling. He's not really one for awkward goodbyes, and I love him for it. He's authentic and the best boss anyone could have.

I slip my phone into my pocket and gather my notebook and the copy of the logo I made for the escape room from in between pages. When I'm in the store, I wander around till I find an employee.

By the time the exchange is over and I'm back at the car, it's nine-thirty am. I try to be as quick as I can with my other stops around town, each proposal received with a similar if not the same answer. 'We'll get back with you tomorrow. This looks really great."

After a lunch break earlier in the day of ham and cheese panini sandwiches, time has passed and it's now five o'clock. I'm hopeful. Now with all eleven stores visited before they've closed, I know I need to hurry to the bookshop before they close. Andrew was expecting me to come take measurements. Not to mention, the whole crew of classmates and my sister are going to be there, too. I wonder what sort of story Anna is going to make up to tell our parents. Something about being impatient to see my project, I'll bet.

I zoom over to the store, my tape measure ready and notebook under my arm. When I step through the door, Andrew is behind the desk writing something down. The whole place smells of damp paper and dust, and I like it.

"Peter! Hello. Welcome."

"Hi, sorry I'm a bit later in the day. Had a bunch of sponsor errands to run."

"You're here now, and just in time. I have the upstairs room already getting started on rearranging. Should make your job a little easier, at least to visualize."

"That's great," I pause, hearing the engines of several cars pull up. "Oh, my sister and a few friends were going to come in and look around. They wanted to get an early look at the project. I hope you don't mind."

"Not at all. The more publicity, the better, I say. Maybe the rumors can begin about this place getting a little more interesting, huh?" He pushes his glass down to smile at me. I nod.

"Anything helps, I suppose." Footsteps trample into the bookshop, and I turn to see the whole troupe spill in.

"Anna, Joel, hello," Andrew says, recognizing them instantly.

"We came to look around. I know you close at six, so we'll try to leave before then."

"Take your time."

"I'll be back in a bit with any comments," I say as we all head up the stairs. Sam, Cedric, Naomi, and Orin follow along behind me as Joel and Anna lead the way.

"Oh, and I have a gal working on organizing upstairs. I told her you would be there sometime today," Andrew yells. I don't reply, expecting to see someone upstairs but there's no one immediately visible. I check around a few of the shelves as Anna whispers to me.

"Psss... This way. We'll have to make this quick. Orin and the rest of you, stand watch. Joel and I will take it from here."

"Roger that," Sam says, grabbing a book off the floor and pretending to read it while leaning up against a shelf at the top of the stairs. Naomi also grabs a book then begins to check for anyone else upstairs.

"I don't see anyone. Did Andrew say there was someone up here?"

"He said there was someone organizing up here."

"Coast is clear. They might be in the bathroom," Orin says after checking the maze a second time.

"Okay, Peter, this way," Anna directs. I follow, eyebrows scrunched.

"Shouldn't I get my measurements first? That's why I'm supposed to be up here."

"Hurry." Joel says, checking his watch. I take out my tape measure and begin measuring the lengths and widths of the bookshelves in the room. Cedric grabs the other end of the tape measure and stretches it across the room. I quickly scribble down the measurements.

"Okay, this will work for now."

"Good. Now, if we can just find it..." Anna begins looking around for something. She digs in a shelf and pulls out books. Joel looks around warily, and I see him make eye contact with Sam who nods stiffly. Anna begins to sigh, and her demeanor changes to one of frustration. "Where is it?" she huffs, her hands going to her hair.

"What are you looking for?"

"The book. *The* book. The one Briar was writing about that day at school from the vid. The one we should all know parts of."

"Why do you need it?"

"We don't exactly need it. I just want to make sure it's still here, that no one has bought it or stolen it."

"Why?"

"Because, Peter. Whoever reads one of the sentences in that book and says it in their mind or out loud, will open the portal that's in this store. It's attached to it. At least, that's what we've discovered so far." I look at Anna with a frown, still not quite believing her story. But she and everyone else is acting serious. Maybe I'm the one being silly.

"So, what if someone steals it or buys it? They can't exactly do anything if the portal is here, right?"

"Peter, that book is the key. Without it, no one can get to this other world. If I forget the key sentence, or if we all forget it, we have nothing else to remind us what it is. That book is the only thing that will keep the gate open. Removing it from the shop will have long- term consequences, especially since someone else could figure out what it does and hold all the power."

"Wait... Not only if we forget whatever this sentence is, if the book is out of the shop, then this gate closes down?"

"As far as we've tested, the book needs to stay in the bookstore for people on the other side to come here. If the book is outside of the shop, it only allows people to go through, but they can't return unless it is in the shop."

"I'm so confused," I say, looking between the rest of my class-mates.

"Hey, is this one of your guy's drinks?" Cedric says, picking up a paper coffee cup from off one of the shelves.

"No one had a drink when we came in," Joel says.

"Hey, someone's bag is here too." Cedric gets down on his knees and pulls up a two-handled book bag and looks inside.

"Whose is it?" Sam asks.

"It's not mine," Naomi pipes in.

"Guys, let's just find the book first. I can't have us going in then not being able to come back."

"Hey, there's a book in here as well as a wallet and a phone," Cedric says, pulling out a smartphone. I frown, stepping towards him.

"It probably belongs to the person Andrew said was organizing up here. We should just put it back." Cedric doesn't listen right away and lights up the lock screen. I stop in my tracks. The lock screen photo is of Briar holding a striped cat. I open my mouth, then close it.

"This looks like... That's Briar, isn't it?" Cedric asks, a small smirk at the edge of his lips.

I'm about to nod in agreement when Naomi adds in, "That is her," She looks down into the bag and gasps. "Anna, I found it!"

Anna whirls around from looking at shelves and clasps her hands together."Oh, hurrah! Okay, Joel, Peter, let's hurry. Naomi and the rest of you, you know what to do."

Naomi pulls out the book and hands it to Anna. Anna flips through the pages quickly then hands it back to Naomi.

I'm still shocked that this might be Briar's phone. It makes sense that she could be the one organizing for Andrew. She used to work here. But where is she? Joel clears his throat.

"I'm confident Briar is the one organizing. I saw her here yesterday, and she said she got her job back temporarily." I take note of that.

"Peter, repeat after me in your mind," Anna says, listing off a sentence that sounds oddly familiar. I nod and say the sentence several times in my own head. Anna smiles, then she and Joel look at each other hopefully. Are they waiting for something? I'm waiting for something, all right, and it had better be good because I feel completely ridiculous right now. All the other classmates are watching me, and I feel like a guinea pig.

"You have to wait exactly sixteen seconds after saying the sentence for the portal to appear. If you've said it, you'll be able to see it and walk through. If you don't know it or say it, you won't be able to see it or walk through," Anna says in a whisper. In a matter of seconds after she says that, I grow dizzy and there's a faint change in lighting near Cedric. I watch as he sidesteps whatever it is.

"Do you see it?" Anna turns to me excitedly. I don't see much of anything yet since my head is swimming.

"I'll walk through. He can see me disappear first," Joel turns and I watch as he steps past me and through a circle of light. I focus my eyes, blinking a few times till I see what Anna is referring to. It's like a round window looking into a forest. After Joel steps into it he continues to walk away.

"Come on, Peter." Anna takes my hand and pulls me with her. I don't wrench away this time and instead follow, letting her lead me to this unknown place. We step through, and instead of there instantly being what I can see through the other side, the bookstore is still here but it begins to fade. Little by little, the piles of books, my classmates, and the shelves disappear. Now, I'm in a forest and Anna and Joel are beside me.

"See, Peter? It's all real. We aren't making this up," Anna says. Her voice is soft and delicate as if she's trying not to startle me.

"And we still have your signature of which you've promised to not tell a soul about this," Joel says. Their voices seem distant to me, though. My mind is in overdrive. I'm still processing the impossible. When they first told me about this, I was certain they would all be fools today. Turns out it's me.

"Peter? Are you okay?" Anna tugs on my sleeve, and I blink, turning to look at her. She's staring up at me, a small smile on her lips. I know she wants me to say she's right and that I believe her. But I'm not ready to. Not till I can feel the trees and...

"Turn around, Peter. We have just a few more seconds before the portal closes," Joel says. I turn and see what he means. There's the round window of light again, making a watery sound. I can see the bookstore through it, and Orin is on the other side, waving gently. Cedric gets in the frame and quickly gives us the peace sign as the portal begins to close. It recedes into thin air, and then we are left with only forest. No one says anything for a long while. Only birds and rustling leaves fill the airwaves. I detach from Anna's side and move towards a birch tree, my hands itching to feel bark and branch while part of me screams for it to be nothing but air. I'm both thrilled and disappointed as my hands close over a real tree. I crumble part of the bark in my hands, the wind blowing it out of my palm.

"No way." Slight tears sting my eyes. I look back at Anna and Joel, then I take off running. I want to see this place, to see just how real it is. Where are we? How did all this come about? How did my classmates find out about all this and before me, for that matter?

"Peter! Wait up!" Anna yells.

"Peter, hold up. We have to tell you more!" I hear them yelling, but their voices catch on the wind and combined with how my heart is beating so hard, I can hardly bring myself to stop. This place is beautiful, and I want to explore. I race through the trees, and the more I run, the sparser they get. Pretty soon, I can see why and stop abruptly, grabbing onto a branch to catch my balance. I'm on the edge of a cliff, and the view pulls tears down my face. Anna and Joel stumble closely, their breathing short and heavy.

"Peter, you..." Anna stops as she sees my tears. I'm kind of crying, and while I'd normally be embarrassed by such a thing, I don't care in the moment. My emotions are on high and my brain's sense of reason and reality is messed up. Joel doesn't give me the time of day to explain myself and launches into a warning that lays heat.

"This place—it's not as safe and beautiful as it looks. Beyond the cliff, in that direction, is extremely dangerous. You can die here. The laws of physics still apply, for the most part. With that said, you can't wander off. I don't want to have to be the person to explain to your parents what happened to you. If something happens, I can't take the blame for your death. Things that happen here need to stay here."

"We should go back. I think you've seen enough to believe us. And time works differently here. We need to get back or Andrew is going to suspect something," Anna says, grabbing my hand again. I don't take my eyes from the view until Anna pulls me back towards the clearing and forest glade. Joel leads the way, confident, like he's been here a hundred times. I wonder how often he's really been here and for how long. If the only way in is through the bookshop, how has Andrew not suspected something?

We stop just before where the portal was, and Anna nudges me.

"We have to do the same thing again to open the portal. Think of the sentence and read it in your mind again."

I do so and I count sixteen seconds on the dot. The portal reappears, the bookshop once again visible. We step through after Joel does, and in a few moments, everything seems back to normal.

"How was it?" Cedric gives us a smile while chewing a piece of mint gum.

"He's still in shock," Joel says for me. I close my eyes and nod in agreement then rub my temples. My light-headedness is going away, but all I just experienced keeps replaying in my mind.

"Andrew closed the shop already, but he said we could stay a bit as he'll be here till eight," Naomi says, breaking my train of thought. Sam looks at his watch then at Joel. Joel nods. Whatever system they have in place to keep this whole thing a secret is kind of impressive. I still have so much to learn.

"Did he come up here?" Anna asks.

"No, we made sure he didn't. I went down and said it was taking a bit longer and we distracted him for a bit. No other customers."

"What about Briar?"

"Briar? Haven't seen her. Andrew said she was the one helping organize up here. I don't think he realizes she's not up here."

"Do you think?" Anna says, looking at the book in Naomi's hands then back to Joel.

"If she's in there, I don't like that she isn't back yet. We didn't see her," Joel says. I furrow my brows. Briar could be in there? I imagine her rusty hair and knit sweaters in that world. If I know her well enough and she hasn't changed much since highschool, she'd like it there.

"Okay, we need to hide the book better this time," Anna says.

"If Briar is in there, we need to make sure she can get back." Joel looks at me with tight brows. "Do you know which shelves will be staying and which will be getting moved?"

"As far as I know, the ones in the center of the room are going to be removed. The ones on the edges will be staying, but I'm not entirely sure which will be reorganized," I say, rubbing a hand through my hair. All my plans about this whole escape room thing are starting to tumble around. If people can get transported to this other world in this very room, how ethical would it be to have the escape room here? What if people accidentally go through if they are given access to the sentence Anna gave me? What sort of limitations does this whole thing have? If Joel or Anna don't call a meeting at the lighthouse in the next day or so, I will. All the secrets will be explained and all my questions answered. I'll make sure of it.

"I'll hide it behind the books that look the most organized I guess," Anna says.

"Cedric, watch the window." Joel tilts his head towards the far end of the room. Sam positions himself at the top of the stairs and Naomi and Orin busy themselves looking at books. I watch as Anna hides the book behind a row of red tomes on one of the shelves. It looks from all appearances that they have been organized like that.

"That should do it till tomorrow." Anna dusts her hands on her pants then looks at Joel. "We should go."

"What about Briar?" I ask. If she isn't here and she is supposed to be, then something is wrong. And the possibility of her being in that other world fills me with both dread and excitement.

"We can't really do anything about it yet, Peter. We need to leave now before Andrew gets suspicious. If she is missing and doesn't get back, I'd let Andrew call you..." Anna trails off. She blinks and looks at me.

"What?" I ask.

"Briar. She called your phone this morning. I answered it."

"She called me?" My mouth hangs open a little too far, and Anna notices. Her eyes slant a little in a tease and her lips tilt in a smile.

"Before you start complaining about me snooping on your phone, we are even now. Yes, she called. But it was really weird. She wanted to know if you were okay." Anna looks at Joel. He's deep in thought, and I get the feeling he's about to do something I won't like.

"Anna, take everyone out. Peter, you distract Andrew so he thinks I've left. Explain that if Briar doesn't come back tonight to have him call you. I don't want what happened years ago to happen again."

"Roger. Come on, Peter," Anna says.

"Wait, are you—?" I know what he's going to say.

"I'm going back in. If she's there, I need to make sure she's okay. It's dangerous there, and if she doesn't know what she's doing, something bad could happen. I'll bring her back safely and then she can sign with our group," Joel says.

I want to pipe up and say I should be the one to go look for her, but I don't have a good reason. I don't know what I'm doing or where to look or why Briar would even listen to me. Joel is obviously confident, but I don't like his plan. I hate to admit it, but I'm jealous. Jealous he's going back into the new world, and to save the girl I like. But since I truly care about Briar, I'm glad at least something is being done.

We all exit the upstairs, but not before I watch Joel disappear. I'm not crazy. There really is a portal in the old bookshop.

All my classmates quickly rush out the door while I engage Andrew in conversation. Anna says a quick goodbye, Briar's belongings on her arm, and Andrew waves, but his attention is on me.

"Was there a problem upstairs?" he asks. He scribbles on a pad of paper, and I notice that his writing is a flowy but disjointed cursive. It isn't the same handwriting on any of the notes the group showed me yesterday.

"Kind of. I finally got all the measurements and we were chatting for a bit. But I wanted to ask, where is Briar?" Andrew pushes his glasses down his nose as I finish.

"She was upstairs. Have you not seen her?"

"Not at all. If you don't see her in thirty minutes or so, call me. I'll get in touch with her family and make sure she's okay. Something could have come up and she may have had to leave."

"How strange... She normally says goodbye. But I will do that." His mouth is turned down slightly, a crease in his forehead. I nod, a bit grave and concerned myself.

"I'll be back later this week for final checks and will let you know about the sponsors."

"Thank you, Peter. I'm looking forward to it." Andrew is genuine and reaches across his desk to shake my hand. It's a firm handshake, but there's a tad bit of looseness at his fingers. My dad said you can tell a lot about a man by how they shake your hand. Andrew seems like a nice guy, but his handshake is a mystery to me.

I leave the shop as a new person. I've just experienced something that I've only seen in movies or books. It brings me back to my childhood when my mom read Anna and I *The Lion The Witch and The Wardrobe* by C.S. Lewis. Part of me always believed and wanted a place like Narnia to be real, but as I grew up, I realized how silly that was. But even still, the part of me *wanting* it to be real remained. Now, with my eyes wide open, I know that a place like Narnia exists. Maybe Lewis wrote Narnia to plant seeds of wonder and hope in us. Maybe Lewis himself traveled to this world. Regardless, I know that he and others were at least partially right. There's another world just waiting to be explored.

Nine

BRIAR

I had an inkling that the moment the words exited my mouth, Finn and Wystan would try and dissuade me from my request. I was right, but what I didn't expect was Wystan shutting the door behind us and dropping his voice to a low murmur.

"Briar, I may have been lighthearted earlier, but Finn is right. Our king is not one to be trifled with. A lady such as yourself will not fare well in the court of Breezewood. Worlders are vermin to the king."

"What's a Worlder?" I ask, genuinely curious. This dream keeps getting more and more detailed. Every moment that passes, I'm more impressed with the intricacy of the world I'm in. I've never had a dream like this, one with the right mixture of strange and believable.

With the door to the dark forest now closed, lights and delicious smells reach for my attention. Little rainbows are scattered across the gray stone walls of the mountain doorway I've entered. Crystal light fixtures in the patterns of leaves hold yellow candles. The flames flicker, causing the rainbows to dance in a gauzy, fairy-like way. The floor is smooth, polished stone that starts wide at the doorway then narrows into a hallway that turns a corner, farther into the mountain. The hall is lined with more candles and faint rainbows, the smell of bread, cloves, and warm beeswax growing stronger with each breath I take.

Wystan acknowledges me. "Anyone who is not from our world, someone from a civilization far more advanced than ours."

"Going to the king as a Worlder, especially in his house, is a sure death. Breezewood is dangerous for any stranger, but especially Worlders," Finn says, turning to look down the hall. His hands twitch and the way he keeps glancing behind betrays his thoughts. He's worried, but what about?

I'm half-listening to Wystan and Finn, half-focused on my surroundings. I want to take in all the details, torn between waking up and exploring this place.

When someone asks me what one of my favorite things to do is, depending on my mood, I'll tell them it's sleep. But in reality, my favorite thing to do is explore and go on adventures. Sleeping means dreaming, and I normally dream up all sorts of adventures. That's part of the reason why I like to read so much. Endless adventures without true risk. Except for the occasional emotional damage which is always a risk worth taking.

Now, presented with the chance to go on an adventure, I'm forced to make a decision. Try to wake up from this strange dream or preserve my sleep long enough to experience more in this place? I remember where I'm truly at once more, an image of me lying asleep in a pile of books in Andrew's bookshop. I grimace. I really need to wake up. The embarrassment of being found like that keeps my mind straight. At any rate, meeting this king will be an adventure. Being tossed to the wolves will be an adventure. I'll have an adventure, even as I'm on my way to wake up.

"My mind is made up. I would like to speak to your king." I take a step towards the hallway, eager to see more of the tunnels.

"Briar, it isn't safe!" Finn says, exasperated.

"Look, if all you want is a look at the king, I can get you that. But speaking to him, he'll waste no time in discovering who you are and demanding you be tossed to the wolves. You don't want that."

"This is all a mad dream. I want to be tossed to the wolves so I can wake up." I'm completely serious, and Wystan looks at me like I'm crazy. I've never had my subconscious argue with me like this before, and it's starting to scare me.

"Before you jump to thoughts of giving up on life, let me show you what you're up against. Maybe you'll change your mind about dying," Wystan says. He's ever the gentleman, which both annoys and pleases me, bowing and extending a hand down the hall. "This way, if you please."

I'm about to take the lead, but Finn brushes past us both, muttering something under his breath about petulant young people.

I follow Finn, Wystan at my heels. The winding hallway takes several turns, splitting off in other directions. I know without a guide, I would get lost in these tunnels. Our footsteps echo as we make our way deeper into the mountain. I expected the air to grow colder as we traverse deeper, but instead, it becomes warmer and the lovely smells become stronger. Pretty soon, the hallway ends and Finn stops, turning to look at me.

"From here on out, you can be seen and reported on by others. I leave Wystan as your protector, though a poor one he may be. Nice to meet you, Briar," Finn says in a rather distraught voice. He steps to the side to let me and Wystan pass him, and I nod gratefully.

"Thank you. Nice to meet you, too." Finn shuffles down the hall without looking back. Wystan grunts before grumbling,

"He's afraid you'll be dead by the end of the day and already blames it entirely on me."

I ignore him, not wanting to get into another explanation of why I seek an audience with wolves.

I shift my focus in front of me. There is an opening at the end of the hallway, and sounds of laughter bounce and reverberate in the air. I see the bars of an iron railing and I continue forward, eager to see what is over the edge. As I step out of the hall, my mouth slowly widens at the scene before me.

The hallway we exit is one of many, all in one ginormous circle surrounding a large, glossy floor. We are on a balcony looking down on this floor, and people are milling about in strange but beautiful clothes. The women wear long dresses of satin and velvet with wrist length sleeves. The fabrics are decorated with smooth green stones and woodland plants. Moss, white veiny twigs, leaves, and some pale purple flowers trim off many of their dresses. The men are adorned in neat gray suits, the same woodland accents pinned to their coats and shoulders. Some wear robes of silver trimmed with golden twig patterns. If I wasn't dreaming, I'd say they were fairy people though none sport wings.

Candles wink from the posts holding up the balcony, and all the walls appear to be made of gray stone. Laughter, soft rhythmic music and water are more audible now as I lean over the rail. There are tables of food and drinks, and I can smell the bread and cloves from earlier but it is much richer now. I look for the source of the water, and to my right on the balcony, a spring spills out of the stone wall. The water travels down the wall and across the balcony floor. I study the stream and see that a part of the floor slopes upwards, creating a small bridge over the stream that transforms into a waterfall. It spills down to the floor below and collects in a stone-tiled pool at the edge of the room.

I grab the intricate railing with both hands and turn to Wystan. "Where are we?" Heat pillows uncomfortably beneath my sweater and I adjust the collar, the wool just beginning to stick to my skin.

"You are at the heart of Breezewood. This is the kingdom common room."

There are a few people down below who glance our direction. Some begin to whisper, and one tips their head towards us. Wystan pulls me from the balcony edge till we are out of view. He looks me up and down, frowning. I stiffen as he places a hand on the small of my back. "If you come this way, I'll take you to get some new clothes. Then we can go see the throne room from a safe distance and decide whether or not you want to go through with your plan." I relax a bit as he guides me, gently, towards another doorway. He withdraws his hand as I step through. "Keep walking." His voice lowers and I obey without protest.

This new doorway leads to another hall much like the first, but it is wider and there are openings along the right side. I peek in the first doorway and find the floor partially carpeted in woven moss. I edge inside, hearing voices, but Wystan urges me on. When we get to the second opening, there is no carpet and I don't hear any voices.

"Go all the way inside, and when you meet with one of the women, tell them Wystan sent you to get proper clothes. When you are finished, meet me back in this hallway."

"Okay..." I say and step inside, Wystan's boots clicking away. I'm half-tempted to just follow him and see where he goes. I still want to explore. With the sight of so much interesting architecture, people, and the rather large owl from earlier, I'm intrigued. However, as I inspect the surroundings of this new room, I'm beginning to feel slightly claustrophobic.

A sheet of water, clear and smooth, flows from a slit in the ceiling into another slit in the floor. I catch my reflection in it and see that it is supposed to be a mirror. The walls inside this room are white stone, and there are candles suspended from several iron chandeliers, allowing generous light. There is a closed wooden door against the far wall, strapped with iron. It is a pretty space, but it is cramped and foreign. I'm not normally a claustrophobic person and will squeeze into most places without fear, but tunnels and caves and rock-solid walls with no windows or possibilities of getting out trigger me. The deeper I thread into these tunnels, the less likely I'll be able to find my own way back to the forest.

I shake my head. It's all a dream, I tell myself. It doesn't matter what happens. I'll wake up eventually and all this is made up in my mind. I try to remember that, even though all my other senses seem heightened to the point of reality. I'm just about to put my fingers into the flat sheet of water when the door behind me opens.

"Who are you?" a woman's voice rings out. Her eyes are wide with high arched brows complete with an open mouth. I can only assume her shock is because of my clothes. She's staring at my skinny jeans and sweater with distaste. I shrink back a little.

"Wystan sent me to get proper clothes," I explain, hoping I remembered everything he wanted me to say.

"Oh, Wystan sent you? Then you must be all right." Her demeanor changes and her face lights up. She's wearing a deep forest-green dress that looks to be of medium weight and not overly warm. It is simply cut with short sleeves and a rounded neckline. I relax, her face displaying kindness. "You must be a Worlder? We haven't seen one in quite a while. Don't you know it's dangerous to be here, especially in Breezewood?"

"I've been told multiple times," I say. I debate going down the hole of arguing with my subconscious about this entire world being a dream and that I'm just along for the ride, but I bite my tongue. There is little point in that when everyone here is stuck in whatever story I've created for them. I'll just follow along and make impulsive decisions along the way.

"My name is Tara. I can't do much about your striking hair, but I can disguise your Worlder clothes. Come, before someone sees you."

I follow Tara, noticing the hem of her dress is embroidered with copper thread in delicate leaves and flowers. She brings me to a new room much like the one we met in, but it is much larger. There are racks and stone tables covered in vibrant cloth. Blue, green, red, purple, and white dresses are in neat stacks or hanging from racks. Tara promptly chooses a heather green dress from a table and matches it against the sweater I'm wearing.

"Since you like green, this should do. Quickly, behind the changing screen." She hands me the dress, and I walk towards the screen she's indicated. The screen is in one corner of the room, made of woven willow branches and braided moss. I quickly change once behind the screen, pulling the dress on over my head. The instant it is on, I am no longer stuffy and overheated. The dress is soft and comfortable, and for the first time in a long while, I feel like a book character. I haven't worn a dress of this nature since I was probably five or six. I fold up my sweater and pants and bundle them in my arms. When I step out from behind the screen, Tara nods, pleased.

"Your hair will draw attention held up like that with whatever you are using. Best to let it down."

I reach a hand to my claw clip and let my hair fall. I shove the clip into the arm of my sweater and wrap it up tightly so it won't fall out. I glance down at my leather boots. Tara doesn't mention them, so I don't either.

"Thank you for the dress," is all I say. I don't know what else to add until I look at the clothes in my arms. I want to take them with me, wherever I am going, but remembering the dream I'm in, I know I won't need them. "Can I leave these here?"

"Of course," Tara says, reaching for my clothes. She pats my sweater and jeans with a hand then sets them on a chair, covering them with a dress. Somehow, my subconscious is revealing to me that I'd rather be in dresses than jeans, and I'm totally okay with that.

"Wystan said I need to meet him back in the hall. Can you show me the way back?" I'm not confident about where I'm going, and part of me wants to learn more about Tara. She seems like a maid in this place, but she's dressed so nicely and there's an air of familiarity about her. She has dark brown hair that is curled at the ends. It's partially braided up but with the rest free down her back. She has a long neck, long nose and tanned skin. Her big, brown eyes framed with dark lashes remind me of someone I used to go to school with.

"I will show you the way. Come."

⁂

When I'm reunited with Wystan back on the balcony, his eyebrows raise in approval at my change in appearance.

"Now you look like a maiden of Breezewood."

I feel like a lady in this dress, but I keep silent, not wanting to encourage whatever scenario Wystan is trying to conjure up with all his charm. I know when someone's trying to flirt their way into my good graces.

"You're risking her life. Why did you bring her into Breeze-wood?" Tara asks. Wystan's eyes flicker to hers and his jaw sets firmly.

"She could not stay out in the forest at night alone. Too many dangers."

"Even though some of the most dangerous of all live within our very walls?"

"Hush, Tara." Wystan glances behind, then his eyes fall to me. "She risks her own life. I am trying to show her sense."

"When she does not live to see the end of the day, don't come to me. I will not offer you any more help."

"Tara..."

Tara leaves. My subconscious is the epitome of drama.

"Take me to the king," I say, a bit disturbed with how emotional this dream is becoming. I've already been asleep long enough. It's time to wake up.

Wystan leads me down a new hallway, this time, actually leading in front of me. When we stop, we are at another balcony, overlooking a new room, this one smaller but much grander than the common room. Wystan motions quickly with a hand that we crouch. We hide behind a pillar, ready to spy upon the room.

A man in stone armor like Wystan's, though edged in copper instead of moss, is undoubtedly the king. There is a copper crown on his head, and he is standing in the center of the room talking with a group of men in long, navy-blue robes that touch the floor.

A sword sits on the king's hip, and his arms are crossed. From here, I can see that his face is deep in concentration.

"The king of Breezewood is a busy man. He oversees the protection of all the mountain people in our lands and keeps out those who wish to unearth us from our home. Not only does he protect us, he has the gift to provide for our well-being through the winter months," Wystan whispers into my ear.

"What do you mean, he provides? Are the winters cold?" I whisper back.

"The winters are quite cold. We also do not farm like other kingdoms do for winter storage. When our hands try to plant or water the earth for food, our crops die. We also can't hunt or purchase food already harvested for us to eat. But since so many factions outside our lands want us dead, they have refused to trade with us. That is why our king's provision is such a blessing."

"Is he magic or something?" I ask, knowing my subconscious a little too well.

"Not exactly. I wouldn't call it magic. He has the ability to sense prized minerals deep in the mountain which aids our miners in uncovering them."

"You eat gems?"

"In a way. The king turns them into food which we then can store for the winter."

The king's men below begin to disperse and Wystan quiets, standing with me slowly. We can't hear what the king says to the men, but soon there is a great commotion and someone is brought in before the king. Wystan's brow furrows, and he puts a finger to his lips. I peek out just enough behind the pillar to see what is going on.

Two guards with spears drag a man in by the elbows before the king. Some of the robed men edge closer to their ruler. I watch as the captive, held by the guards, struggles, his brown hair curly and messy.

"A Worlder, sire. He was found skirting the mountain edge."

"Leave me be. I can stand before your king on my own two feet." The king waves a hand and the guards release the captive.

"What have you to say for yourself, snooping on our lands?" There's an obvious tone of disgust in the king's voice. I find myself swallowing, not liking the attitude of this king.

"I was and still am looking for someone. A girl with red hair, not too tall. She is also a Worlder." the captive says. I gasp, and Wystan touches my shoulder to remind me to be quiet.

"We have not seen any Worlders here for some time. Now, since you tread far too close for our liking and we can't have you leaving and bringing information back to your home, you must be confined or disposed of," the king's jaw sets firmly, mind made up.

The captive stiffens and clenches his fists in defiance.

"Please, let me find my friend at least. Then you can do with me as you wish," he says. I know that voice. I know it. I crane my neck to see better and, without meaning to, lose my balance behind the pillar. Wystan grabs a hold of one of my arms and tries to pull me back behind the pillar, but it is too late and my free arm flails. It catches the attention of one of the robed men and he signals to the king. I'm visible now, and there is no point in hiding. I stay still, hoping I'll wake up at any moment. I don't.

"I make no promises, except to that of my own people. And my promise to them is to protect them and you are violating their safety." The king flickers his eyes up to me, and I hear Wystan groan behind me in defeat.

"I mean no harm. I have only come to your lands to seek my friend," the captive says. He turns, following the king's gaze up to me. His eyes widen and soften, then wrinkles appear on his forehead. I'm pleased to see him, but I frown. Why is Joel in my dream?

"There will be no more discussion of this now," the king says, turning to one of the robed men at his side—an advisor or servant of some kind.

"Briar..." Joel says, a tinge of relief in his voice. But I detect fear too, by the way his words drop and his eyes widen. He's dressed in a brown tunic and breeches that match the era of this dream. He doesn't look like the Joel I know with the clothes or the worried lines in his face.

"You know this man?" Wystan asks, a hint of surprise and, dare I say, jealousy in his voice.

"We were high school classmates," I say. Wystan looks confused.

"High school?"

"Nevermind." I retreat from the pillar and walk out into full view on the balcony. I want to run and jump off and float down to the floor. In all my past dreams, I've been able to fly in some way. Maybe I can in this one, just because. I'm about to do just that when Wystan reads my mind and steps in front of me before I can vault over the railing.

"Briar, don't do this. Stop trying to hurt yourself."

"I'm not. I'm just trying to wake up from this dream," I say, trying to push past him. I hear footsteps coming from the hallway we'd arrived through, and then I hear Joel's voice.

"Briar, this is no dream. You are in reality. This place is an extension of reality. You stepped through a portal in the bookstore to find this place."

I pause, digesting what I've just heard. Just as I thought, another part of my mind wants something so badly to be real that I've dreamed it up. I've always thought portals to other worlds would be my ticket to a new reality, a place of escape. Like *Narnia* or *Gateway to Fourline*. I've always wanted it to be real so it seems I've dreamed up my own friends to tell me my dreams are reality.

"I need to wake up," I say once more, ignoring Wystan and Joel's pleas. I hurl over the balcony just as guards rush from the doorway and descend upon my location.

Ten

PETER

I begin to worry. Briar and Joel haven't made any appearances yet. No one has contacted me except for Andrew to let me know that Briar didn't return to the shop. Anna looks at me from across the dinner table, her eyes clearly telling me to not say anything stupid. I chew silently. Dad and Mom chat about upcoming Thanksgiving plans and Anna interjects between bites. I should be paying more attention, or at least trying to be less obvious that my thoughts are elsewhere, but I can't help it. Anna gives me another knowing glare across the table then leads with a question designed to distract me.

"Are you making one of the pies this year, Peter, or will I be taking over?" There's a definite spark in Anna's eye as I'm pulled from my thoughts momentarily.

"Depends. Is there a contest this year or are we just divvying up cooking duties?"

"Oh, there is most definitely a contest," Dad quips. "Uncle T, Aunt Lucy, Grandpa, Grandma, and I will be judging. Mom said she'll make the pumpkin and pecan pies like always; however, it's up to you two and some of your cousins to battle it out with the apple pies."

"I'll gladly make both the pies if you won't. I've had practice," Anna says, smirking. I fork a meatball and push some salad around on my plate, considering.

"Just because you work at the bakery, you think you'll have an easy win this year?"

"I won the year before last, and with last year's loss, I'm even more determined to win this year," she says confidently. My heart squeezes, remembering I wasn't home for Thanksgiving last year or the year before. Maybe Anna's not only trying to distract me from the bookstore fantasy world, but she's also trying to bring me back into her world, hoping I don't leave again.

"Her pie crusts have improved quite a bit since then," Mom adds, smiling before taking a bite of salad.

"I'll make one of the pies. Can't have the cousins thinking I've given up on tradition by letting you bake my pie for me. Not to mention, they can't win again." I let the words slide easily over my tongue, glad I'm saying them. I'm extremely grateful for August giving me the work opportunity and suggesting I come home. He must have seen that I needed it, Briar or not.

"Hey." Anna shakes her fork at me, mildly offended. Clearly satisfied, she leans back in her chair. "Well, good. I was hoping for a challenge."

"The cousins don't stand a chance." I let the edges of a smile creep across my face, now thinking about the apple pie contest my sister and I hold with our cousins every year. This will be the eighth one, and fond memories from years prior resurface. I've won twice, Anna once, and a variety of cousins the other times. They are currently in the lead for the most family wins which we hope to change in the upcoming years.

My thoughts begin to turn more bittersweet as I recall the mirth and coziness of being with family and friends. I miss those times. I was able to fly into town for a few nights during the holidays the first year I was living in Colorado, but the times I missed, they instantly hit me in the gut. I'll never get that time back. I look at the smiling faces of my family and can't help but feel a sudden unsatiated ache as my thoughts drift to Briar.

What would it be like having her share in the fun traditions with my family? Would she even like my family and cousins if she were here? My hands and face grow warm at the bold idea of asking her to spend Thanksgiving with my family. If she returns from wherever she is, will I have the guts to confess my feelings to her and apologize for what I said and did years ago? I'm an idiot for holding out on her. I have a small inkling that Joel has feelings for her; at least, he did when we were in school but never made them clearly known. Though, neither did I. A part of me is scared that he'll beat me to her, and my brain is on overdrive thinking about all the what ifs. I squeeze my fork extra tight as I wrap pasta around it in a clockwise motion.

"What are your guy's plans for tomorrow? I know Anna doesn't have work and Dad will be home. Any ideas?" Mom turns to look at us. Amidst my imaginings and what ifs, I know I have to see Briar, to know if she's safe, even if it means explaining to Andrew what's going on. I turn to Mom.

"I may go help out at the bookstore," I blurt out. Anna looks at me, worriedly. She doesn't want Mom and Dad involved on account of what Joel has told her and the paper we've signed, but I ignore her look.

"All day?" Dad stops his fork midair.

"Maybe, I'm not sure yet," That was the truth. I don't know how long I'll be gone. Anna, reading between the lines, inclines her head to Dad.

"I would like to go with him if I can," Her hand trembles as she takes a sip from her glass. No word from Joel or Andrew mentioning Briar's return means they are still missing. I know she wants to go back and help look for them, too.

Was what I saw earlier today even real? I'm having second thoughts when Anna squeaks forward in her chair. "Peter and I kinda had a class reunion today. At least, his classmates. We all met up at the bookstore and talked while Peter got measurements for the escape room. I think they are all wanting to hang out again. It was fun getting to talk with everyone."

"Really? How many of your classmates?" Mom asks. I swallow another bite of meatball before answering.

"There were five of my high school classmates. It was interesting, getting to see them again. Some of them still live around here."

"I haven't had a class reunion since my tenth year after high school. I can't even begin to imagine how much each of us have changed since that reunion," Dad says, chuckling.

"This little reunion wasn't exactly planned, and it's only been three years since high school. Not that long, but it feels like ages. I hardly recognized some of them," I say. Anna grips her napkin tightly, and I wonder what I'm saying that's causing her to worry so much.

"What ever happened to that Verlice girl, Briar? Is she still around?" Mom's lips betray her reasons for bringing it up. While it's an innocent question, I know she remembers how much Joel and Briar and I hung out at school. I don't try and encourage anything, afraid Anna will explode with anxiety. I want to tell them everything, but now, with a taste of this huge secret, I can see why Joel made me sign that paper. If Mom and Dad knew, what would they say?

"She's still around. I saw her the other day, but I didn't see her yesterday." That was also the truth.

"Well, if you see her, tell her I said hi to her folks," Mom says. I nod, eager for this conversation to end. Anna wipes the corners of her mouth with her napkin after taking a sip of water.

"You know, Peter, I think we should go camping," Anna proclaims. My eyebrows raise.

"Camping? Tonight? Or tomorrow?" I don't even have to ask, knowing this camping trip is a total excuse to steal away into the bookstore and beyond.

"Tomorrow. We can pack tonight."

"Camping, Anna, but it's so rainy out," Mom deters, looking out the kitchen window.

"I know... It's just, well, Peter is my only brother, and we haven't gone camping in so long. Once he's a famous escape room designer, I probably won't see much of him." Anna looks at me with an admiring smile, one I know is genuine, but I can also see right through it. She lies to Mom and Dad easily because she's had practice, and I despise it. I want to shatter her lies but I still don't know what all the risks are if I do. Anna and Joel still haven't given me all my answers. So much for Joel promising to tell me everything. Now he's traipsing around in another world, looking for Briar.

"I'm not against you two having a sibling camping trip, but why all the sudden?"

"I'm just itching to get out of the house for a day or two," Anna smiles, setting her fork down.

Mom frowns. "Am I that boring?"

"No, Mom, that isn't it at all. I like being home, but I like having adventures every now and then," Anna patches quickly. Adventures, all right. If only Mom knew. Dad eyes me.

"What about you Peter? You want to go camping too?" I swivel to look at Anna. She's practically willing me to agree with her idea. I contemplate the suggestion, thinking over my sponsor list and the timeframe I gave them. I don't want to miss any of their calls, but for the sake of Briar, I think I'll survive.

"Camping sounds fun. Sure."

Dad nods at my answer."Okay. You guys can go. You just need to let Mom and I know where you'll be camping and when to expect you back so that if anything happens, we'll know where to look."

"Will do," Anna says, now eating her food much quicker. I shift uncomfortably in my seat.

"I guess we are on our own, babe, though a date does sound nice," Mom says, smiling up at my dad.

"So, where are we going, Anna?" I scrape the last of my spaghetti into my mouth and wait for her answer, the warm wool of my socks unusually itchy in the drawn out silence. She swallows a bite of food then sets her fork down.

"I don't know. Maybe East End Beach?"

❧❧❧❧❧❧ ❦❦❦❦❦❦

Anna and I drive towards town early the next morning. Like, five-thirty a.m. early. Mom and Dad thought we were crazy, but when Anna told them I would protect her and we wouldn't do stupid stuff, they let us go our own way. I mean, I'm twenty-one, so Dad wasn't worried about me as much as he was about Anna. She is his only daughter, after all.

I take a right turn and pull onto Main Street. I know nothing is open, but Anna mentions the bakery, so we head in that direction.

"Want a sweet start to camping snack?" she asks when we park in front of the building.

"Are we actually going camping? Or was that a cover-up so Mom and Dad wouldn't worry about us if we are gone overnight somewhere?"

"We will go camping. Chill out, Peter." She opens her car door and I follow, lured by her confidence and the promise of a sweet breakfast.

Anna knocks, and we are let in when one of her coworkers recognizes her. We leave the bakery moments later with drip coffees and cream-filled maple doughnuts. I'm halfway done with my doughnut by the time we reach the car, and Anna smirks.

"Tasty much?"

"Much." I reach for napkins, and she hands me a wad. We sip and eat in silence for a bit before I set my coffee in a cup holder and confront her.

"So, how do we get into the bookstore and, you know, go to that other world without Andrew getting suspicious when he never sees us leave the store, if we happen to stay overnight? Do we tell him?"

"No! Joel said not to tell anyone, remember?"

"Hey, I'm trying to be logical here. Orin and Naomi and the others can't just hang out there all the time and watch our backs."

"They do it quite often. Andrew is accustomed to us spending many hours in the shop. We try to buy stuff frequently to keep him from being suspicious, and one of us tries to keep him chatting for a bit so he never comes up to check and see if some of us are gone."

"So, what if Joel is in there right now, and he's out of the portal? Won't Andrew find him in there and be really suspicious as to why he is in the shop when it was locked? He'll think he broke in."

"Joel is smarter than that. He knows what time it is in this world and in the other. He'll make sure to come through during the day sometime when the hours are open."

"Still, if someone sees him just appear, not to mention Briar, too, then that could be bad." How did Joel know what time it was? Did he have a watch?

"Look, it wasn't a perfect plan, but we didn't expect Briar to go and get herself lost in Breezewood." Anna says it with a tone partially dipped in acid. I'm taken aback, curious what she has against Briar and that I'm finally given a name of this new world.

"I'm sure Briar didn't realize what she was doing. I'm pretty sure it has happened once before and you were only ten then."

"Look, I know most of the details from Joel and what you've said, but I still don't trust her," Anna says, taking a large gulp of coffee and a rather aggressive bite of doughnut. Her blonde hair is held up in a messy bun and she's wearing a green rain jacket. I study her, watching as she avoids my gaze. I don't want to assume, but my seventeen-year-old sis sounds jealous, and I don't have to think hard to know who's all involved. I don't press the issue.

"I think I need Joel's phone number. And the rest of the group's. If we are going back in, we need to communicate with them about what's going on. And I'm a part of this group now anyways,"

"Here," Anna says through a mouthful of doughnut. She pulls out her phone and another cell phone that is not hers. I accept the unknown one and wait for an explanation.

"Joel handed me his phone and wallet before he went through. He didn't want them to be accidentally confiscated by anyone on the other side." She reaches back into her coat pocket and pulls out a wallet.

"There are other people on the other side, in that world?" I'm intrigued. I take the wallet from her hand and look it over, identifying it as Joel's.

"Yes. Lots. Whole kingdoms full. And some of them are not friendly." Anna opens up her phone and scrolls through her contacts. I stew on all the info I've just been fed. They are mere morsels, but they carry traces of the whole secret. I decide to push Anna for more info while she busies herself with sending me contacts.

"So, this world is called Breezewood, there are other people there, and Joel can tell the time it is there and here at the same time?"

"Yes to all three," Anna says, not elaborating.

"What kinds of people? People from earth? Or unique people that are native to that world?"

"Both, and by kinds of people, I would say they are very unique. Their own cultures, politics, religion, currency, etcetera," Anna says. I frown, frustrated. My phone begins to ding, and after five notifications, I know I have all their numbers in my phone.

"Look, Anna, you are going to have to give me more information than that. Joel promised."

"I know he did," she says, a drop of acid still lingering on her words. She sighs then turns to look at me, setting her own coffee cup down. "Joel can tell the time in both worlds because Sam made him a special watch that keeps track of both times. Oh, and before I forget, we all have a special encrypted group chat. I'll make sure to send you an invite link to that." She looks down at her nails which are perfectly clean and painted a pale, robin-egg blue.

"You can send me the link later. Right now, I want answers. True ones. No lying to me, Anna. I mean it." Her head snaps up and she catches my eyes, hers watering. My brow furrows. *She's... crying?*

"I won't lie to you ever again, Peter. I promise." She wipes her eyes with the edge of her finger then puts on a smile, sighing and facing me square again. "Whatever you want to know, I'm an open book."

I hesitate, seeing the emotion still in her face. I know there's a wall of tears and a tidal wave of fear and past disappointments on the edge of overflowing, and I know I can break through her mask of confidence with a few well-placed words. But I don't want to miss this opportunity to hear the truth she's willing to tell. We can talk about all the stuff that's beneath her facade of sass as soon as I know what kind of danger we are all in.

"Tell me how you first met up with Joel and the others. How did you all find out about the portal? Surely the big news story and the tale from highschool that Briar wrote out wasn't enough to transport you all to this new realm. What actually happened?"

Anna licks her lips, ready to tell her truths when a pair of hands slaps on her window, palms pressed against the glass. We leap in our seats, the sound and shadow of the figure outside the car causing my heart to flutter unhealthily. Anna leans backwards towards me, and I put a protective arm over her shoulder. My left hand drops Joel's phone and wallet to my seat and I reach for my pocket knife. The man outside of Anna's window doesn't do anything to try to break in, but he's muttering something and I can't understand it.

"That's him. That's the homeless guy who came to the bakery last week," Anna says in a raspy, high-pitched voice. Her heartbeat is just as wild as mine beneath my hand, and I pull her closer. Whatever this guy wants, he better back away from our car and ask nicely, because after that scare, I'm in no mood to roll down any windows or open any doors. Then, I freeze in my seat as the man lifts his hands off the window. I wait, my body tense for whatever he has coming next.

Eleven

BRIAR

Instead of jolting awake and finding myself back in the bookstore, I am instead crumpled in an embarrassing heap upon the floor. My ears ring and my ankles cry out, severely stressed from the fifteen-foot drop I've just experienced. Worried voices and echoing footsteps barrage my ears, and all I can think about is why I'm not awake and back in the bookstore. My vision blurs as I try to sit up. When I reach out with an arm to steady myself, my head pounds with a sudden pain and I falter, sliding my free hand to my temple.

"Briar, are you okay?" someone asks. Through my disorienting haze, I recognize the voice as Joel's. I squeeze my eyes shut then reopen them, my vision clearing.

"She is clearly insane," says another voice. The voice of the king. I'm about to respond when strong hands and arms pull me to my feet and draw me towards the voice. I blink as he stares at me down his nose, a toothy sneer growing. "She has the fiery hair, as you said. I commend you for your honesty."

I hear Joel shift on his feet and I turn to see several guards escorting Wystan to the circle. "Your Majesty, I..."

"We will talk about your punishment later, Captain. For now, prepare the kingdom for the nighttime routines. Harvest begins tomorrow, and there is much work to be done."

"Yes, Your Majesty." Wystan dips his head in a low bow and glances my direction, worry creased between his brows. I don't know what to say as he and a few others exit the room through a doorway under the balcony. So much for him helping me.

"Now, to get to the bottom of this. Why are you, a Worlder, in Breezewood? What business do you have here?" The king gestures to me then folds his arms across his chest, waiting for me to answer. I lick my lips and pause, now aware I am being held up by two guards. I squirm and pull my arms out from their grips even though my ankles ache.

"This sounds insane, but I promise that I am in my right mind. I am asleep, Your Highness, and all of this is a dream."

His eyebrows raise at my words and I realize that there is nothing I can say that will make him believe me. Why do I even bother?

Joel clears his throat. "Your Majesty, she has stumbled through the portal by accident and believes she has fallen asleep. She does not realize that all of this is real."

"No one enters through a portal by accident. They have to deliberately come here."

"She's never been here before."

"Preposterous."

"Briar, have you ever been to Breezewood before?" Joel asks, his attention now on me instead of the king.

"I... I've had a similar dream before, but no. This is my first time," I say, believing he means this fortress and not the forest glade. I look down at my dress and study the intricate threads and feel of the fabric. I hone in on my sorry ankles and squeeze and un-squeeze my hands. The pain feels real. What if what Joel is saying is true?

"Your Majesty, I will take her away from here. We will not trespass on your lands again."

"There's a sure way to make sure neither of you will trespass on my lands again. The wolves are always hungry at night, and Worlders are their favorite."

"Your Majesty, I beg of you!" Joel instantly drops to his knees and clasps his hands together, pleading. I've never seen him do anything like this, and my eyebrows shoot up in surprise. "I'll do anything. Please, just send her away from Breezewood. Her family and friends on the other side of the realm will be worried. If you must, keep me instead."

The king's sneer disappears and is slowly replaced with a flat look of indifference. But then a gleam enters his eye.

"I suppose she can find her own way back home, but under one condition." The king reaches with his right hand to a set of rings upon his left. He carefully twists a pearl from a ring and extends it to me. "You will accept this truth pearl and promise to never again return to Breezewood, unless you bring the key back to me."

I look at the pearl balanced neatly between his fingers. What key? What is he talking about?

"Place the pearl beneath your tongue. It will absorb the truth, and upon your return, if you choose to return, the pearl will keep your tongue from lying. It will in turn protect my kingdom, for then I will know if you are a spy."

I look at Joel, his eyes wary, but he does not forbid me to take the pearl. I slide it into my own fingers, pausing. Place it beneath my tongue?

"Place it beneath your tongue or you both go to the wolves!" the king says, his hands reaching for a dagger at his belt. I comply and pop the pearl into my mouth, below my tongue. Instantly, part of the pearl dissolves and adheres to my flesh. Half of a pearl is now fixed in my mouth. I want to pull it out, but I'm afraid of what the king will do with that dagger.

The king smiles then looks over at Joel.

"She's an obedient one, but the wolves can have you in her place."

I hold back a cry. Joel's face, now ashen, bows his head in gratitude. My insides scream. "You can't feed him to the wolves! He... he's saving me! Do you not see how honorable he is? Does your kingdom not uphold honorable men?" The words fly from my lips before I can think fully. One of my poorer traits, unfortunately. I clamp my mouth shut and catch Joel looking at me with curiosity and sadness. A small upturn of his lips tells me he's grateful for my defense, even if it is poorly thought out.

"Honor among *our* people of course, but Worlders do not get that honor. Not anymore." The king makes a quick motion with his hands, and the guards once again clamp down on my arms and drag me towards the door. Two others grab Joel and pull him in the opposite direction. The king watches, saying something to one of his advisors with a bored expression, as if he deals with this sort of thing on a regular occasion.

"No! Wait! Please, I don't know my way back!"

I struggle, twisting, nearly tripping on my skirt as I try to crane my neck to catch one last look at Joel. He's doing the same and says as loudly as he can, "Follow the light, Briar. Follow it home!"

Crash. Doors shut, and I'm in a dim hallway, accompanied against my will.

"Walk and you will be outside shortly," one guard says in a monotone voice.

But I don't want to be outside. I want to wake up. I want to be sure Joel is okay. I want to be home again. Tears sting my eyes, and the onset of emotion surprises me. I don't remember the last time I've cried in a dream. *Is* this a dream?

I comply with their desire for me to walk peacefully, knowing any resistance will only make it harder for me to come up with a good plan. I glance at one of my captors, the man at my right, taking in his height. He's several heads taller which makes me feel extra small and alone in this bizarre world. Upon passing a light along the walls, I suck in a breath at a glimmer that dances across the man's neck for an instant. It's as if a small piece of him is made of glass or something else reflective. He turns to glare at me, and I look away, peering forward as if I have seen nothing. I glance to my left as we pass by another set of lights and find that the man at my left has the same thing occur, only it is along his jawline. I crinkle my brow and bite down on my tongue, feeling the pearl. This place just keeps getting weirder.

I'm soon before the same door I'd come through with Wystan upon first entering Breezewood. Finn is at the entrance, his mouth and eyes round at the sight of me. The door is cracked open, but Finn opens it wider and salutes the two guards. They nod and turn to leave us, their boots echoing down the glossy hallway. They must trust Finn to turn me out according to the king's wishes.

"You yet live, Miss Briar?" Finn asks softly, his white eyebrows reminding me of snow-capped mountains. I nod slowly, stepping towards the open door.

"Yes, but my friend Joel... He's taken my place to be fed to the wolves." I turn to stare out into the dark forest. I'm on the threshold of the opening and momentarily, in a bath of warm light. I shiver as a breeze of cool air washes over me.

"Ahh, the young Worlder who entered after you." Finn shakes his head sadly. His wrinkly hands grip the latch to the door and he opens it a tad wider. I turn to him, not yet wanting to leave.

"He came to rescue me, but the king..."

"The king shows no mercy to Worlders. It is a miracle he is letting you free." Finn cuts me off. I search his face, but he doesn't look me in the eyes.

"He's releasing me, but there's a condition." I open my mouth and reveal the pearl. Finn's eyes flood with concern and then he makes eye contact.

"He gave you a... truth pearl?" He's familiar with them then?

"To make sure I'm not a spy, I guess, though I'm innocent. This is just a terrible nightmare."

"Best leave this place then, deary, and never come back." Finn's voice shakes a little. "I'm afraid you must or we'll both pay the consequences."

"But Joel..." I reach out a hand to the door as Finn begins to close it.

"He'll be dead by midnight. Best forget about him. There is nothing you can do." He says it with such confidence that I don't have the words to fire back. My heart is still beating fast and the realism of this dream is exhausting me. He pushes the door till just his head is visible.

"I don't know my own way back," I say. I gaze up into the night sky, aware now that stars and a sliver of moon fill it.

"I do not know where your home is, but I will say it's farther up the mountain. We are forbidden to cross over the cliff and leave Breezewood lands." Finn points into darkness, and I see the faint outline of a tall, dark shape above the trees. I recall the cliff I'd leapt from earlier in the evening and swallow a lump of fear. Climb the cliff, in the dark?

"Thanks," I say with no enthusiasm. I run my tongue over the pearl, just to be sure it's still there and that I didn't imagine it. I clamp my lips shut and step out of the doorway, defeated. The stone door closes with a solid grating sound. Soon, I am alone with the forest, my arms hugging my middle to preserve warmth.

I remember what Joel said about following the light, but follow it where? Stars glint and moonlight washes over nearly everything in multiple directions. Maybe he meant to follow the moon and its light? It is over the place Finn pointed out. I nod to myself. *Yeah, Briar, that's your best bet. Better get on with it before some guard finds out you haven't left yet.*

The direction of the cliff is unfamiliar to me even though Wystan and I had flown from it and landed in the forest before walking to the Breezewood entrance. The land looks foreign in the dark. Even back in my hometown, walking from my backyard to the front yard at night feels unnerving and strange. I try not to think about all the creatures that could be watching me from the shadows, nor the possible cause for the stick I just heard snap a few yards away. I try to calm my thoughts as I pick my way through the woods, being careful to choose paths that have the most light. Before I can reroute myself, my thoughts drift to Joel and his sacrifice for me. Wolves. The king is going to feed him to the wolves. Are those wolves out here? Are they wild? That was one thing I had never confirmed. For all I know, I could be being fed to the wolves right now.

As if on cue, another twig snaps and the sound of stones against other stones hits my ears. I jump, hugging my arms tighter to myself and pressing on, ignoring the barrage of screams in my mind. Screams I want to let out. *Keep walking, Briar. This is a dream, remember?*

I step into a patch of moonlight and take a moment to orient myself, panic beginning to escalate in my lungs and legs. I want to run and hide, to be safe. I'm about to dash for the next path between trees when I hear the whoosh of branches and the thud of something heavy behind me. I freeze, unable to bring myself to look. I close my eyes, praying for this nightmare to end.

"Briar, hurry. Get on!" A voice. A kind, familiar voice. Wystan. I turn around then, relief shocking my limbs. I almost trip on my skirt as I propel towards Wystan. I step across crunchy leaves, twigs, and spongy moss, not caring how loud I'm being.

"I'm so glad you're here," I say with trembling lips.

"No time, get on." Wystan beckons me to Auriol, the glorious silver-white owl. He holds out a hand to help me aboard. I step up and immediately slide my fingers beneath the great bird's feathers. "Hold tight." Wystan straddles the bird, the leather saddle holding his feet firmly in place as he makes a signal with his hand. Auriol coos and spreads his wings. I reach for the leather strap for support and steady myself as we take off into the air. My hair spreads out behind me and my dress ripples in the wind. Moonlight bounces off Auriols wings, and I'm partly inclined to enjoy this ride, but the tension in the air kills the idea.

"What's wrong?"

"The king doesn't know I'm helping you, and if he finds out, I'll get demoted or worse. But that's not all." Wystan looks over the side of Auriol, and I follow his gaze. In the glade below where we'd taken off, dark shapes dart out from the trees and walk in circles. I shiver, glancing up at Wystan.

"Wolves?" I ask. I can't make out the shapes, but it's a fair guess. Wolves are the only thing I've heard about so far that seem to be dangerous. That is, other than the king.

"No. Those aren't wolves. Those are Reachers." His hollow low tone makes my tongue go dry. I try to swallow but my teeth begin to chatter instead. The air is so cold, much colder than it has been in Homer during the night. But it's strange because the trees in this world are still fully leafed and green. Fall has not touched them despite the temperature.

"What are Reachers?" I brave asking, my teeth clattering together like china teacups. Wystan notices and answers quickly.

"They are creatures drawn heavily to precious stones. They descend from mountain caves and are formidable enemies as their fur is jagged rock and their teeth iron. They can only be killed with a diamond spear. The problem is, they like to eat your spear tips." He says it coldly, as if he's had experience with them and resents every moment of it.

I don't want to ask anymore, afraid of what else he might say, though I have questions, so many questions. My teeth chatter harder, and Auriol makes a quick turn that has me holding tighter to the leather handhold. "We are approaching the cliff you came from. I'm not allowed to cross over it, but I'll make an exception for you."

"Much obliged," I squeak. Auriol lands gracefully on the cliff edge, and Wystan slides off immediately and reaches for me. I extend a hand and allow him to guide me to the ground.

"Do you know how to get back?" he asks. I look at him, the moon lighting up his face. I see disappointment in his eyes, as if he's sorry to see me go. He's only known me for a few hours, and even then, he doesn't even know me. But he still has my hand and isn't letting it go. My cheeks heat and I open my mouth to respond, but nothing comes out. His eyes widen the moment my mouth opens.

"You didn't tell me you had a truth pearl. No wonder the Reachers were after you." Wystan's hand clamps harder onto mine. Auriol hoots deeply, concerned. "Nevermind. I know where you need to go, and I won't let you go alone." He pulls me in the opposite direction of the cliff edge, deeper into the forest. The crossbow is still across his back and he unslings it, locking a bolt into place. A glimmer on the tip makes me wonder if it's made of diamond.

"I thought you weren't allowed over here?" I ask, out of breath. I shiver as we stop. He lets go of my hand, my fingers growing cold again.

"I'm not, but I know more than I'm allowed to, or should." He's distracted, looking between trees in the moonlight before turning to me. "Whatever you were thinking about before you came to this place, think about it again. That's how you get back."

I can hardly think straight, let alone remember what I was thinking about moments before realizing I was in a dream. I'm trying to turn back my thoughts when great growls surround us. Wystan pulls me to him, his crossbow pointed in the direction of the danger.

"Now's the time to think about getting home!" he yells. Three dark shapes emerge from the trees and several more step into view between us and the path to Auriol. Jagged and scrawny, the creatures appear to be part-stone, part-wolf, and strangely, part-porcupine. Their fur is sharp and pointed, their eyes slits of silver, and when they move, their joints sound like stone against stone. Deep growls reverberate in their throats, as if their mouths are actual caves. In the faint light, I catch glimmers of something reflective on parts of their coats.

"They sense your pearl. And my weapons. Hurry, Briar." Wystan's voice is steady, but I hear the waver. I concentrate. What was I thinking about before I came here? I was in the bookstore cleaning up books. Books...

My memory jogs, and I recall reading snippets of books I found interesting as I organized. I put one in my book bag if I remember correctly.

The darkness tears apart in one section of the forest, light spilling from a familiar shape. The portal from earlier. I see the bookstore on the inside. My head swims. This can't be happening.

Reachers scatter to the side then regroup, most keeping their distance. A few snap and lunge, however, and we jump backwards.

"Go! Now, Briar!" Wystan yells. I hesitate, afraid I'll be chased, but then I make a break for it and leave Wystan's side to the shivering gateway. I step through and whip around to watch as a bolt leaves Wystan's crossbow, aimed for the closest Reacher. The portal slowly fades before my eyes and all the sounds from that world are immediately replaced with familiarity.

The faint creak of old wood and the downstairs clock tell me I really am where I think I am. Books are in their normal scattered places, and then I catch a hint of that lovely smell of old bookshop.

The only unfamiliar thing is that I'm in the dark. I've never been to the bookstore before when it's nighttime.

I'm scared to do it but, I make the decision to look down at my clothes. Lo and behold, I'm still wearing the green dress. Nothing makes sense to me anymore.

Twelve

PETER

Breath raspy and frantic, Anna and I wait while the man on the other side of the window slowly backs away, his hands in the air. He's still muttering things. Some words stand out from his frantic barrage. Words like: *key*, *safety*, *stop*, and *wolf*. Shaking his head, he turns to leave. As he walks away, I quickly start the car and Anna sits straight up in her seat.

"I've never been so scared in all my life," she says. "Actually, that's not true. Breezewood adventures scared me more."

"Let's go. It isn't safe to park when homeless people along the road start pulling stunts like that," I say through gritted teeth. Anna swallows.

"Agreed." I put the car in reverse and we're off, tires crunching gravel. To get out onto the main road, we have to pass this guy. He's walking, shoulders hunched, hands in his pockets. He doesn't make eye contact with us as we pass him, but he scans our car.

There's just something else about his demeanor that strikes me as odd. He isn't just walking, he's sliding his feet along the road with each step. If that was me and my mom were watching, she would have told me to pick up my feet, afraid of me ruining my shoes. But this guy continues to do it. I watch him in my side mirrors, and it isn't until then that he makes eye contact with me. Something about his stare sends shivers up my spine, and I look away, unnerved.

"How weird," Anna voices.

"Very. Was he this weird when he came into the bakery?"

"Not like this... I mean, his request was odd but, no, he wasn't acting like this. I wonder what's wrong." Anna looks back, concern and nervousness etched in her features. I stare straight ahead then risk a glance in my mirrors. He's still walking, but his head is down now. Step, slide. Step, slide. Step, slide. I turn the corner and he's out of view. We pull onto Main Street and head towards the bookstore.

"Look, if we are going to go in there, we need Andrew's permission. We can't just break in."

"But Joel—"

"I won't be doing that. If we think someone is in serious danger, we call for help. I'm not breaking laws with no proof we are willing to share to cover our case."

"You didn't seem to have a problem breaking our family 'law'," Anna mutters.

I freeze, squeezing the steering wheel tightly with both hands. I know she's referring to our family's number one rule and law in the house. No lies. I clear my throat. I want to retort back that she is one to talk, but I heard her apology from earlier. She's my sister, and I want her on my side right now. Division won't be helpful when lives are at stake. "Anna, I'm not breaking any family laws."

"But you told Dad we were going camping. We both know camping is a cover. You even asked me on the way here."

"I did say that and I asked you today for clarification, but you missed the conversation Dad and I had after you went to bed. I didn't tell any lies. Dad... knows."

Telling lies has never done me any good, and I'm not about to start now. Anna thinks this *camping* trip is under my family's noses, but I won't lie to them and I won't lie to her.

"You didn't..." Anna's mouth drops open in astonishment. "Joel will kill you."

Before I can respond, I turn the car into the bookstore parking lot and slam on the breaks, dread pooling into my gut. This early in the morning, the windows on the shop are never lit up like they are now. A Subaru is parked in the front by the door, and I watch as a shadow flickers past a pane of glass. I failed to notice if it was like this when we drove past earlier.

"Andrew's here?" Anna's voice raises. She clicks her seat belt off and starts fiddling with the car door.

"Hold on, let me park the car," I croak, pulling up next to Andrew's vehicle. As soon as my brake is on, Anna pulls at the handle.

"Peter, if Joel or Briar are in there right now, Andrew is gonna toast them."

"I know, I know. I'm coming!" I shove Joel's wallet and phone into my pocket and lock my car. Anna is at the bookstore door, tapping lightly. I let out a pent-up breath and watch in the dim light as steam dances before my eyes. Crisp, cold air bites my nose and fingertips.

I hear footsteps on the other side of the door. They grow louder, scuffing against the wood floor, and I anticipate the turn of the handle.

"Anna, Peter, what are you doing here?" Andrew's eyebrows crinkle in confusion.

"Can we come in? We need to talk to you," I say before Anna can make something up.

"It's really important," she interjects.

"I... I... guess, sure. Come in." Andrew holds open the door and we tread in. He locks the door behind us, and we swivel to face him.

"Why are you two here so early in the morning?" Anna and I look at each other. She swallows and nods to me. Andrew hasn't seen Briar or Joel yet by the way he's acting, so maybe there's a chance we can salvage this.

"You know how Briar went missing yesterday?"

"Yes? Has she returned? Has something happened?" Andrew's voice wavers and he reaches up to take off his glasses.

I quickly reassure him. "No no, she hasn't returned. We don't know where she is. But we think we know," I say carefully. Anna looks at me, frowning.

Andrew relaxes. "Thank you for the update. I've been worried about her. It's so strange to me that she would just up and disappear." He calmly puts his glasses back on.

"Strange," Anna agrees and presses her lips together in a straight line. She's trying so hard to tell me to shut up without actually saying it, but what am I supposed to do? The bookshop doesn't open until eleven and we are here at six am.

"We came to ask, to see, if she had returned or come back. We found her belongings upstairs and have them in a safe place. The fact that she left her phone and wallet concerns me."

"Don't you think we should call the police if she's missing?" Andrew scratches his chin.

"No!" Anna injects, then chuckles. "We would like to wait first. I'd hate to trouble the police again. Don't you remember what happened a few years ago?"

"I do, and that's what I'm worried about. It's Briar who's involved again. Don't you think it's a bit suspicious?" Andrew glances out the shop window then at me. I nod as he begins again. "I don't know her super well, and disappearing at my shop twice now is quite odd."

"I'm ninety-nine percent positive her disappearance is not connected to whatever you think it is," I say, remembering all the crazy blogs and threads that popped up after Briar's last disappearance. If Andrew was reading into those, he'd easily suspect Briar since her disappearance was odd. Those threads made so many wild speculations that half our town seemed convinced Briar was involved in some government drug trafficking ring. I know Briar better than most, and she would never do drugs or get near them. Never. But, again, I don't know what actually happened to her yesterday. I can't say for certain what she would do. We haven't been around each other for several years.

"I hope for the best, on her and our accounts," Andrew says, crossing his arms and glancing at his watch. I look at his watch, too, and catch the time. Ten after six. Would Joel and Briar come back later in the day when the shop was fully open, like Anna suggested?

"Do you mind if we, you know, look for any clues?" Anna asks, looking to me for approval. I almost roll my eyes. As if she needed my approval, considering her outgoing and sassy nature. I felt like I was always asking for hers.

"I suppose that's fine. Let me know if you find anything, though if we don't hear from her by tonight, one of us needs to call the authorities."

"Yes, sir, will do," I agree before Anna can protest. She clams up and then turns for the stairs.

"We'll look upstairs first if that's okay."

"By all means." Andrew gestures towards the stairs then runs a hand through his hair before putting his glasses back on.

Once Anna and I are upstairs, she immediately begins searching for the book. I skirt the room to look for any other clues, just in case there's something we missed.

"I'm going to send you the link now to that encrypted chat. The others need to know what's going on and to be prepared to help out in case something happens." Anna whips out her phone and begins typing. Two of my pockets buzz as both Joel's phone and my phone dings. I extract both from my coat and glance at the screens.

Anna's chat link shows up on my screen and on Joel's, a message from his parents.

"Uh oh." I squint, trying to make sense of the preview text.

"What?" Anna asks, stepping towards me. She glances at Joel's phone and frowns.

"I don't know the code to open his phone to read the text but it's from his dad."

"Here, let me do it." Anna slides her fingers across the screen and lighting fast types in a number code that I don't catch.

"How do you know his password?"

"I've watched him put it in, and we make it a habit to know each other's codes in case we need to erase info in an emergency."

"Erase info? Hold on."

"It isn't just me. All the others know too."

"No not that. Erasing. Why would you erase info?"

"Because, Peter. The existence of Breezewood is a dangerous secret. Erasing info to keep it out of the wrong hands is a necessary caution. Both our world and the one just beyond the portal are threats to each other's existence. Can you imagine if our world and governments got involved? There would be war, and Breezewood probably wouldn't win. We have guns and high-tech weapons. They have swords, arrows, and catapults." I look at Anna with my mouth partially hanging.

"Wait, they are a medieval world? Castles? Knights?"

"As far as we've discovered, but it's so much more than that. They don't just have those things. They also have magic, and I can't even begin to fully understand it."

"Magic?" I'm about to ask her more, but she's already reading Joel's text out loud in a low voice.

> *Hey, I know you said you'd be busy this week but if you can, will you call me so we can talk about Thanksgiving plans?*

"What should we say to him?"

"Probably best to say nothing." Anna says, handing me back Joel's phone. I open my own phone and click the link, finding myself in an encrypted chat app with Anna, Joel, and the rest of my classmates. Except for Briar. I make a mental note to add her to the chat as soon as she makes an appearance.

A text bubble pops up, just as I see Anna put her phone away. I scan the text.

> *Anna: Hey everyone, Joel and Briar still haven't made any appearances yet. Peter and I are at the bookstore right now. I know, I know, it's early, but we wanted to make sure to help cover for Joel and Briar if they happen to show up. So far, Andrew doesn't suspect too much and we'll keep the authorities out of this for as long as we can. We'll keep you posted and will let you know if we need back-up. Peter is now added to the chat fyi.*

"You know my classmates better than I do and you aren't even a legal adult yet."

"I turn eighteen in a month, Peter. It's not like I'm a child."

"No, but still. How did you get involved with them anyway? You never finished your story."

"Right, that." Anna taps her fingers together beneath her chin in a thoughtful pose, her blue nails glossy and elegant. She's so much like Mom I can't help but smile. How she looks when she thinks and when her back is turned, I sometimes think it's my mom.

"Start from the beginning. We have time."

"Okay. It began a few years ago. I was ten when Briar disappeared, but it wasn't until I was thirteen that weird stuff started happening. This was after you told me the story that Briar wrote about and of course what happened with her disappearance." Anna lowers her voice and looks me square in the face. "I never put the two together until I went on an outing with Mom and Grandma to this bookstore one summer. Mom and Grandma were downstairs looking through the cookbooks and I was upstairs sorting through the fiction when I thought about the story you had told me."

"The chances of that are so low. How did you just happen to think about it?" I say, quirking an eyebrow.

"To tell the truth, I was actually jealous at the time that you had such good friends at school and that I didn't have anyone close. I began to think about your friends, and you know how one's mind wanders from thought to thought? Well, one thing led to another, and pretty soon I was thinking about Briar and her weird connection to the bookstore. The story you told me kept running through my head, and one sentence in that story stuck out to me."

"Let me guess, the portal opened?"

"It did and scared me so bad, I thought I was hallucinating or the bookstore had some fancy tech."

"What did you do after that?"

"I was so scared that I went downstairs to find Mom and Grandma. I was going to tell them what I saw but as I took to the stairs, I looked back and the portal closed. I knew no one would believe me. I didn't fully believe myself."

"Why didn't you ever tell me?"

"I wanted to, but I thought you would make fun of me like Edmund made fun of Lucy when she found Narnia. I had no proof, and it wasn't like my seventeen-year-old brother would believe me. Not to mention, I didn't fully believe it. It happened so fast."

"I'm still having trouble believing yesterday," I add, scanning the books and place where I remember seeing the portal expand. "Now, how about telling me how you got involved in the group. When did you all put the pieces together?" Anna looks around cautiously then lowers her voice several pitches, inching closer to me.

"I started digging into the conspiracy blog. You know, the one that started when Briar disappeared? I found a thread and some of your classmates happened to be in it, though, I didn't find that out till later. I got interested in the blog after my experience, wondering if anyone else had even considered what happened to me as a possibility of Briar's disappearance. Lo and behold, some talked about it." Anna pauses, assessing me.

"And?" I coax, wanting to hear the rest.

"It seemed like a dead end reading through blog posts and comments until one day I asked mom if I could stop by the bookstore. Eager to see if what happened to me once could happen again. When I got to the shop, your classmates, Joel and the others were upstairs. I accidentally opened the portal again when I came up the stairs. They all saw it. I was immediately roped into their group and when they found out I was your younger sister, they were relieved."

"Relieved because they could force you into not sharing information with me or anyone else?"

"No, relieved that I wasn't just a random person. I had connections with you and you had connections with Briar. They had already worked out several of the pieces. They knew how to open the portal and had been in several times. They were the ones that took me through first."

"And what did you do there, the first time you went in?"

"Explored the cliff top for a bit. Joel and Naomi and Sam were the first to bring to my attention the consequences of there being such a place. We all resolved to keep it a secret and go only when the time was right. Eventually we all connected over the conspiracy blog and soon I had everyone's numbers. We shared what we knew and now, we're here."

"And life is just dandy and sunshine now?" Anna slants her eyes at my sarcastic joke.

"Nothing is exactly dandy about this. But you know the feeling. You want to go back, don't you? It's a thrill." I can't argue with her about that. That world, Breezewood, was vivid and beautiful. An adventure waiting to happen. I did want to go back.

"Everything okay up there?" Andrew calls from the bottom of the stairs.

"Yes," Anna pipes up, shooting me a scared look. Had Andrew heard anything we'd said?

"We haven't found anything. Want us to check downstairs?" I shoo Anna away to search for the book. Andrew's footsteps creak on the stairs.

"You can, but I never saw her come downstairs. She spent most of her time up here, far past lunchtime." Andrew crosses over to me. Anna nonchalantly scans the books. I know she won't get out *the book.* She only needs to check if it is still here.

"I'm worried about her but don't want to cause a fuss if she just went home or is at a friend's house. Her car isn't here so she probably walked, right?"

"Yes, she did walk. Did you contact her friends and family?" Andrew looks at me with squinting eyes. There's an uneasiness about him that I feel is unrelated to Briar. Whatever it is, I don't want to inflame it.

"Not yet. But I will."

"How about right now?" Andrew says, pulling out a phone. I arch a brow and step backwards, confused. Anna glances over at us, eyes widening slightly.

"I... I guess we should. Her family has a right to know that we are concerned for her."

"Indeed. I have her dad's phone number. Here," Andrew hands me his phone, Briar's dad's contact info pulled up. "Let him know the situation. I'm going to go grab a few boxes for some of these books."

I accept the phone and nod, pinching my lips tight. Andrew leaves down the stairs and I whip around to Anna.

"Something is wrong," she says quietly. Instantly, she walks over to me, typing a message up on her phone. "Hand me the car keys please." I hand them to her without hesitation, looking down at Andrew's phone in my hand. My finger hovers over the call button. What should I say? Ask where she might be? I don't want to freak anyone out and start a mess of things, especially when there's so much I don't know. My own phone dings, and Anna gives me a worried look. "As soon as I give the signal, we step through. No hesitation. Got it?"

"We can't just leave. Andrew…"

I hear footsteps coming up the stairs now. But there are two sets instead of one. Someone else is coming. Anna and I turn to see Andrew crest the stairs with someone at his elbows. Anna gasps and I stiffen. The man from the bakery. He's here, in the room with us.

"I found this gentleman at the door. He said he knows where Briar is."

"No way," Anna mutters. I step backwards, shielding her.

"No offense, but we had an altercation earlier. I don't think—"

His eyes dart to mine, and my mouth goes dry.

"Hear him out. He's an interesting fellow, but if he knows where Briar is, then we should listen. Where is she?" Andrew asks. The man is in a long dirty brown robe and his fidgety movements give me an uneasy feeling.

"Home." the man says rather forcefully all while squinting at me and Anna. I lock my jaw. How would he know where Briar was? Was he at her house?

"Oh, this is good news! Never mind, Peter, I'll take my phone now." I hand Andrew back his phone, my eyes never leaving the mysterious man before me. "Well, thank you both for your willingness to help look for her. But, I have errands to run and will need to close up the shop. If you'll please come back later after eleven, that would be excellent." Andrew looks relieved but his movements are a little nervous. Curious. He heads for the stairs, dipping out of sight.

"Lead the way," I say to the man before us. He grunts and turns. Instantly, I feel Anna tapping a finger against my back. One. Two. Three. Four. The countdown has begun. I say the sentence in my mind while still following the man. As soon as sixteen seconds go by, Anna and I turn for the portal that has stretched wide. Before the man can turn around and see us, we're through.

***

The forest is dark on the other side of the portal and incredibly cold. A moon shines and stars pepper the expanse, making the experience all the more ethereal feeling. The crunch of frosty leaves beneath my shoes and the tickle of wind at my ears sends a shiver over me. Trees rub shoulders and rustle in the twilight. Anna grabs my arm, breaking the moment.

"Don't go running off again, please?"

"I won't. Not when it's dark like this."

"Good." She drops my arm. Her blonde hair looks angelic in the moonlight, and her eyes glitter with excitement. "It's good to be back," she says as if it has been years since she returned.

"Why did we step through now? Andrew will wonder where we've gone. Our car is still parked at his shop."

"We had no other option. That robed man knew we had been in Breezewood before, and my sources tell me he's the one we've been looking for."

"What?" My heart speeds up at the memory of looking that man dead in the eyes. Whatever he was doing there at the shop was for a dark reason. I could sense it. Andrew seemed nervous which bothered me. What did Anna mean this guy was the one we've been looking for?

"Just so you know, I hid the car keys and messaged the group to let them know we were going through. They'll be back to pick up the car so it doesn't stay parked at the shop for too long."

"What is going on, Anna? How do you know that about him?" I reach up to pull at my hair. All the dodged questions and interruptions are driving me insane.

"That man knows something about Breezewood. I never caught it at first, but after seeing him again reminded me, and past clues settled into place." I nod, still puzzled. Before I can ask another question, she's answering it. "Look, Peter. This world, this place—it's far different from our world. The more you come here and the longer you stay, the more you long to return. Eventually, it gives you the sight to see if others have been in Breezewood when you travel back to the modern realm. Their eyes give off a blue glow when you look directly into them. It's something with the magic. It wears off eventually but only people who are from Breezewood or have been there recently can see the glow. Hence why you probably didn't notice it. "

"This is so sci-fi. How can you even see that? I didn't see that."

"You can only see it if you have been here long enough."

"How long have you been here?" I look her up and down, unnerved that she's been here enough to earn this... sight.

"Long enough to earn the trust of several people in this world. Orin, Cedric, Naomi, Sam, and Joel along with me."

I take in her words, knowing she has lied to mom and dad many times in the past few years that I have been gone. "What about this man? How do you know he was a danger to us?"

"I never noticed it until moments ago, but he bears the pearlescence of Breezewood's king, a mark given to protect Breezewood from double agent spies. It is under his tongue. He can tell no lie when in the presence of the one who put the pearl there, which happens to only be the king of Breezewood. That man getting close to us only allows him to gather more information about us. I have suspicions he is an informant for the Breezewood king."

"Okay, that's weird. And intriguing but I take it this king isn't a good king?"

"He despises Worlders, which is what you and I are as we were not born and raised in Breezewood, and he takes advantage of other kingdoms simply because they get in the way of his plans. Other than that, he is by other standards, a good king. He protects his people but is harsh with outsiders."

"Why do you come here? Why come back?" A chill creeps up my skin and I shiver, casting a look at the trees around us. They creak in the night air, giving me the urge to wrap and arm around my sister in a protective manner. I wait, listening to both her and the forest around me.

"Because. The Breezewood king is planning something. Rumors have it he wishes to send a force to our world; whether for good or evil, I can't say. Regardless, it's too risky for both worlds. Joel, the others, and I have been trying to protect both worlds from an invasion of some kind. But mostly, we return to search for Worlders who have stumbled their way through and wish to return home. Not to mention to visit the friends we have made in this place."

"I'm still wildly confused, but I'm here, in this place, with you. We are here to find Briar and Joel. Where do you think they would have gone?"

"If I know Joel well enough, he's afraid Briar got picked up by Breezewood Castle guards."

"So...we go to the castle?"

"We can't exactly do that. But I know someone who can. Come on, follow me." Anna slides through the forest with a confidence I've never seen in her before. Growing up, she'd always been afraid of the dark. But here she is now, leading me on an adventure through a wild and beautiful world to rescue our friends. What has happened to her since I've been gone?

We creep through the forest, Anna holding back branches from smacking my face until we reach the cliff edge. All is dark below, but the tops of trees catch some of the moonlight.

"Where are we going?"

"To get help and to get answers. Follow the cliff line and I'll lead you to a safe trail down." We hike to the edge until Anna pauses and crouches, feeling around in the dirt. She grasps a root then scoots towards the cliff edge.

"Anna, what are you doing?" I rasp, reaching out to steady her. I can't tell how far the drop is, but if it is anything like the cliff I looked over yesterday when we were here during the day, she's crazy.

"I've done this several times. The root is a handle until you drop to a shelf below the lip of the cliff. Then, we follow a small trail cut into the side. It leads safely down to the forest floor."

"If you say so, but it's so dark."

"We have three phones with us, but I'd rather not use them unless we have to. However, since this is your first time finding the path, use it."

I do so immediately, selecting the flashlight button on my screen. The ground illuminates before me and I can see more of the root Anna grasps. It is sturdy enough. "I'll follow you I guess. Show me how to do it."

"Roger that," she quips, then with a quick motion, she swings her legs and lets go of the root. I hear a gentle thud and a confirmation. "You coming?"

"Yes, I'm coming." I shove the phone, flashlight still on, into my pocket so I can grab the root with both hands. As soon as I do, a scream rips through the forest, and it's coming from the direction of the portal.

Thirteen

Briar

All my thoughts seem unreal, but I know I'm not hallucinating. I run soft green fabric between my fingers, memories of changing into the dress extremely vivid. I recall walking through stone hallways shimmering with rainbows. It all happened. I'm not crazy.

Moments ago, Wystan was fighting for our lives and I left Joel in a foreign place, supposedly to die. And now, I'm back. The dress is proof. I swallow, my throat raw and dry from breathing hard amidst the terror of ferocious creatures. Creatures of stone and nightmares. I blink away the images, forcing myself to take in the bookstore surroundings.

If I'm in the bookstore at night, that means I'm possibly locked inside. How long have I been gone? What time is it?

I don't know what I would say if Andrew found me like this, dressed in something so foreign to twenty-first century America. Homer, Alaska, even. Ehh... On second thought, it isn't too strange. Homer has some interesting fashion trends. If you know, you know.

Still, I've never been in the bookshop dressed like this before, especially at this hour. The shop isn't even open yet. I'm not sure which is more embarrassing—being caught inside a shop after hours or being seen in unusual medieval attire off the clock by your boss.

I think about going back into Breezewood, knowing I can escape the embarrassment of being found in the bookshop at this hour, but the reality beyond the portal is too frightening at the moment. Wystan risked his life to bring me back safely, and I won't shatter his sacrifice. Even Joel risked his life and is currently paying the price for it. I'm at a loss for words, still bewildered that two guys who hardly know me risked everything for me. I shiver, still chilled from the cold air beyond the portal. What can I do to repay them? How can I ever return the favor?

I should leave the shop and go home. Maybe no one noticed I've been gone? I did walk here after all. I remember that I left my phone, wallet, and bag somewhere in this room. I do a quick search and find no evidence. Never mind. I'll worry about it later. For now, I'll just leave this place. I can sort out my thoughts later in the company of my family's cats and a mug of hot tea.

I make my way down the stairs and turn the corner to the right, walking past the front counter. All I hear is the slight groan of old wood bearing hundreds of books as I tip-toe across the floor. I peek behind the counter. Good, Andrew isn't here.

I walk to the front door and turn the handle, preparing for my fears to come true. But they don't, and the handle turns. Hurrah!

I slip out the door and shut it behind me, checking the handle to be sure it's locked. Maybe my fears were unwarranted, seeing as most business doors are locked on the outside, not on the inside.

I pick up my full skirt and run across the parking lot. I must look like a total crazy lady right now, running through the night like this. I pray no one can see me and that everyone is asleep in bed.

The air is not nearly as cold here as the world beyond the portal's was, but my breath still hangs in the air like a cloud. My ears tingle with the bite of autumn and my fingertips begin to follow suit. I turn to look back at the bookstore, each window outlined in a faint edge of silver, a reflection from the streetlight at the edge of the lot.

I leave the parking area and cross into the bushes along main street, determined to not draw attention from any early morning drivers or night shift commuters. Without much warning, I hear the crunch of tires behind me. The golden beam of headlights smacks the side of my arm, and I veer off further into the bushes, out of view. A Subaru pulls into the bookstore parking lot, head-lights lighting up the entire front of the shop. I recognize the man who exits as Andrew, and my pulse quickens. Whew, that was a close one. With how dark it is and now with Andrew's arrival, I'm curious as to the exact time. I don't want to stick around long enough to find out here so I escape down the road towards my neighborhood. *Please just let me get home before anyone else I know almost runs into me.*

I stumble through the front door of my family's house, using the hidden house key to get in. My keys had been in my book bag that has now disappeared. *Just like your dignity,* I tell myself.

The cats greet me with a flurry of upright tails and meows. I give them each a quick pet and lock the door behind me, a sigh escaping my lips like steam from a kettle. I stand in the dark of the foyer, back to the door, reliving what I've just experienced. The cats weave between my legs, but their attempt to win me over for more pets doesn't work. I'm trapped in the reality of my adventures.

Joel's last words haunt me like a phantom, and I shiver, confused and afraid. *Follow the light,* he'd said. I'd done that and was thankfully saved. Had he hoped the moon would guide me back to the portal? I tighten my fists and clench my jaw, feeling the lump beneath my tongue. I freeze, running over the smooth, round object. I dash for the bathroom and turn on the light, mouth wide for inspection. It's there. The truth pearl the king gave me, or rather, forced upon me via threat of a dagger. My limbs tremble, and I hold in a whimper. This is all real. Never would I have believed something like this could actually happen, that worlds beyond my own actually existed and operated. I want to call my cousin and parents and tell them everything, but I don't have my phone. Wouldn't they all think I'm crazy anyway?

I study my face in the mirror, the dress, my hair. I don't look like I belong in Alaska anymore. I look like a princess, albeit a frightened and tired one. The cats have followed me into the bathroom, Libby leaping to the counter and purring right in my face, weaving in front of me. I succumb to her pleadings and scoop her up in my arms, turning off the bathroom light and crossing to the stairs.

I plop down on my bed, Libby now curling up in my lap. She acts like she's always belonged on a green skirt like this, the perfect pet of a royal. I can't help but chuckle as the other two cats make themselves comfortable on my bed, the room now a hum of purring. It's as if I never left.

My desk is still a mess of unfinished sketches and watercolor paintings from days before and the warm cream colored throw blanket I'd wadded up is still by my laundry hamper. Home is normal. To my delight, the patter of rain breaks through the purring, simply adding to the concert of my homecoming. I wonder if it will snow.

I finally catch the time on my alarm clock next to the bed. Five a.m. I've been gone for hours. It's strange that Andrew is at the shop so early when the building doesn't even open until ten. It's his business, though, so he can get there whenever he wants.

I distract myself from everything by changing out of the dress and into some comfier clothes: fleece-lined pajama pants and a cotton t-shirt. Determined to get some sleep before actual morning, I forgo thoughts of tea and snuggle into bed. The cats find creases and nooks in the covers and make themselves at home. I drift off, threads of real dreams beginning to form.

I wake up to the sound of someone knocking gently on my front door. I don't remember a single dream, and I sit up in bed, wide awake. I spy the time, nine am, and swing my legs out of the covers. The cats are nowhere to be seen.

The sun is up and the trees are golden and orange, leaves barely clinging on as I look out my window. I spy down to the front door. A group of people my age are clustered there, a black Nissan Xterra in the drive. What's going on? I don't move away from the window fast enough and one of the girl's spots me. Her eyes and mouth widen and she shakes the shoulders of one of the others.

I groan. Great, now they know someone is home.

"Briar! Thank God you are home. We need to talk with you," one shouts. I hurriedly dress, casting a glance at the pile of green fabric slung across my dresser on my way out. *Definitely all still real.*

When I open the front door, familiar but worried faces greet me. It takes me a moment, but when I finally recognize my high school classmates, the girl who spotted me first comes to the front.

"Briar, can we talk? Please? I know this is strange, but it's crucial that we speak with you."

"Naomi?" I pause, unsure. Then I nod, holding the door wider. "Orin, Cedric, Sam..." I say as each one steps through the door. They nod with a small smile. I close the door behind them then turn. It's awkward for a moment, everyone's eyes glancing around, fingers twitching and weight shifting from foot to foot, but Naomi breaks it with her get-it-done personality.

"This is really weird... but I need to, *we* need to talk. Mind if we sit down?"

"Oh, of course. I mean, no, I don't mind. Right this way." I step past them all and lead them to the sitting room. The cats finally make their appearance and perk up at the sight of visitors. Scout flicks his tale from his place on the sofa and Libby makes a show on the floor by curling on her side, begging for scratches. Herbert slides under the couch, waiting for a foot to edge near his hiding place so he can capture it.

The three boys sit first while Naomi waits for me to follow suit. She sits last and begins, her voice low but confident.

"I need to know where you were last night before I begin any of this. Hold nothing back. We are all ears."

Shocked by the strange question, I hesitate. "I was at the bookstore yesterday helping Andrew, the shop owner, organize the upstairs..." I trail off on the last part, a bit unnerved that four sets of eyes watch my every move as if they know what I'm thinking. "You look like you all know what I'm going to say." I knit my hands together in my lap, nervous. If they somehow know what I'm about to say, why should I be afraid of what they'll think?

"Because we are pretty sure we know, but we'd like to hear it first."

"I don't exactly know how it happened, but I think I went through a portal of some kind and had a crazy adventure." I wait for them to shake their heads in disbelief, but they don't. Instead, some of them smile, and Naomi looks relieved though there are a few worry lines in her face.

"That's what we suspected. Joel suspected it first. He went in to look for you. Did you see him?"

"I... I did see him." I'm not sure how to tell them that Joel saved my life and might be dead on account of me. Where to even begin...

"Okay, okay... There's a lot to catch you up on. First, we need you to sign this." A clipboard gets passed to me by Orin who quickly slides a pen out of his front shirt pocket.

"A confidentiality agreement?" I ask.

"Yes. All of us here have signed it. Including Joel," Orin says, nodding to the paper.

"Even Peter," Sam pipes up. My eyes snap to his. He's grinning, almost like he knew I would react. Is he being serious right now? Were my past thoughts in high school broadcasted to the world or something? A blush creeps up my neck but I ignore it and answer as calmly as possible.

"Oh? And what does Peter have to do with all this?"

"He's kinda... involved now with the whole portal thing. So is his sister, Anna," Cedric says nonchalantly. I click the pen several times.

"So, who all knows?" I'm confused, bouncing between this conversation while trying to read the agreement I'm supposed to sign. Naomi takes over.

"All of us in this room, Joel, Anna, Peter, and possibly two other people. One of them may be your boss and another is a possible homeless guy. Still not entirely sure, but that's all we have right now."

"Andrew knows?" I'm not convinced, and yet, how would he not know if there was a magical portal in his bookstore? How often did his customers just disappear? I've already done it twice now, by accident.

Naomi catches me up on Peter's involvement, the strange notes getting found by the people in our group, and the connection it all has to the book I read in high school and the key phrase that can send us to Breezewood. Mouth wide, I tip my head back, then shake it in disbelief. But I believe it. This *is* real. I've always wanted a portal to travel through to another world. Now, I've found one, and so have my friends. Well, they are about to be my friends whether they want to be or not, especially after I sign this agreement. But then I remember Joel and reality kicks in like a punch to the gut.

"Oh... You all are going to hate me." I grab the sofa arm.

"Hit us with it. What did you do?"

"I didn't mean to, but in my time through the portal, I got to enter Breezewood Castle and meet the king. And Joel got captured, taken in my place." The words spill off my tongue far too quickly, but my thoughts are pouring out in a rush.

"How did you—"

Naomi, standing to her feet, cuts Sam off. "Briar, open your mouth." Her tone is rigid. My whole body grows hot with embarrassment and dread. What have I done? I open my mouth and everyone gasps, looking from me, then to Naomi. Cedric gulps.

"You met the king and escaped, alive?"

"That's a truth pearl, Naomi. We can't send her back into Breezewood with that," Sam says, running a hand through his hair. Why do I get the feeling that I just screwed up a ton of stuff? *Maybe because you did, Briar...*

"I can see that. Well, what's done is done."

"Is there any way I can get rid of it? I didn't want it. The king basically forced me to take it. He said if I ever came back to Breezewood, he'd know if I was a spy or not because it will force me to tell the truth."

"Truth pearls don't work with just anyone though, right?" Orin asks aloud.

"Right, but as soon as she steps through the barrier to Breezewood, the pearl can make her tell the truth if the king touches her. Right now, it is absorbing information," Sam says.

I'm weirded out immensely but Naomi steers the conversation once more.

"Can you spend the day with us?" She crosses her arms. I shrink back in my seat, still holding the pen and clipboard, both objects feeling kind of like a sword and shield. Naomi is fierce when she wants something.

"I technically have work today, I think. But I'm not sure since my phone and stuff disappeared. Do any of you—"

"Here, Anna passed it off to me yesterday. We figured you went through the portal when you had simply vanished and left your stuff behind. Andrew was worried about you." Orin hands me my book bag, all my things still there, minus the book I had wanted to bring home to read. Don't think I'll be reading it anytime soon... Unless...

"That book. Is it still at the shop?"

"Yes. Anna said it was. She and Peter made an emergency jump to search for you and Joel after they were confronted by Andrew and the homeless riddle note dude," Cedric confirms, scratching his chin.

"We still don't know if he's the one responsible for the notes." Naomi says. Cedric shrugs. Notes?

"Wait, you guys know about the notes?"

"Yeah...how do you know about them?"

"Because, I got three of them." I snatch the notes from where I stashed them and present them before the group. Naomi looks them over and passes them around.

"Still doesn't make a lot of sense but these ones have some different info than ours. If this homeless riddle note man is responsible, then I have no idea what he is playing at." Everyone shakes their heads in bewilderment, notes soon set on the sofa like old news.

Samuel taps on a smart watch at his wrist, thoroughly engrossed in something. Naomi follows my eyes.

"Sam, what's up?"

"I'm pretty sure Anna and Peter accidentally took their phones through. Their location signal has disappeared, and it was at the bookshop a few hours ago. I should have checked it sooner."

"Great. Just great." Cedric hides his face in his hands. "We are trying to keep technology as far away from Breezewood as we can. Especially smartphones. Did someone forget to tell Peter that?"

"Hey, people make mistakes. Didn't Joel take his watch through?" Naomi turns to Sam with a raised eyebrow.

"Yeah, and his signal is dead too. Why do we even make these rules?" Sam grunts, tapping more forcefully now on his watch.

We all startle as the front door rattles, someone's knuckles knocking unnaturally loud against the wood. Scout leaps off the sofa and dashes to the kitchen under the table. Everyone looks at me.

"I promise I'm not expecting anyone," I say in a whisper. The door rattles again with a string of knocks. I swallow and rise from my seat. "I suppose I'll go answer it then."

Fourteen

Peter

The scream causes my head to snap up, alert. A zing of adrenaline makes me loosen my grip. I stand, reaching for my phone as I scan the edge of the cliff.

"Peter? Are you okay?" Anna's voice is soft and concerned.

"Yeah, but someone else isn't," I say just loud enough so she can hear. She grunts, her hand appearing on the root as she hauls herself back up next to me.

"What is it?" she asks, wiping her hands on her pants.

"How should I know? This is only my second time here." I turn on my light and shine it in the direction of the scream. It was a deep scream, like that of a man. I hear the skittering of many legs and the grinding of... stone?

"Oh... We don't want to stick around," Anna says, pulling on my arm. "Come on, Peter, let's get out of here."

"What's wrong?"

"That sound."

"What is it? What if that scream was Joel?" I watch as Anna's face goes white then red then white again in my flashlight glow. It's obvious she has feelings for my best friend, but there's no way I'm discussing that with her right now.

"I told you this place is dangerous. That sound... if it is what I think it is, belongs to strange creatures called Reachers. Though I've never seen one in person, I know enough about them to keep my distance."

"Anna, this is all real, so real that I believe you. Hold nothing back. I'll protect you, if only you'll tell me. If that scream was Joel, I'm willing to save him. Just tell me what to do."

Anna swallows and nods. I swing my flashlight towards the trees. The lumens on my phone light hardly spread wide enough to get a good view of the treeline, but it's all I have. I keep the phone pointed down but high enough that I can still see Anna's face.

"The creatures are called Reachers. They are told to have been born from stone, precious gems, and metals, but their initial birth is unknown. They have four back legs and two fronts with spines of stone and teeth of iron. They have the body of a wolf but the armor of a porcupine. They cannot be killed with anything unless it is tipped with a diamond. However, they are drawn to precious metals and must eat them to stay alive."

"My phone has lithium in it. Will that attract them?"

"Maybe. Darn it!" Anna pats her pockets and finds her phone. I remember that I still have Joel's.

"We are never supposed to bring electronics in here, aside from Reachers. I didn't even think about it." She slides a hand down her face in frustration.

"We were kinda in a hurry," I say, darting my eyes to the side as the sound of stone against stone ripples through the treeline. Something is prowling the forest, and it's close.

"Reachers are protective, overly so, and regardless of who is in possession of a precious metal or gem, they will kill to claim it," Anna begins again, rubbing her hands together. Cold nips at my nose, and I tuck my chin in against the collar of my jacket.

"So they don't eat us, just the metals?" Anna frowns at my question.

"I don't know for sure." I'm not comforted in the least by Anna's knowledge or lack thereof. Had I known this world was inhabited by strange beasts lured by precious metals and gems, I might have thought twice about entering. But it is too late now...

"How about to be safe, we stash the phones within the cliffside? They will be very difficult for the Reachers to obtain. I'm not sure how sensitive they are to the phones, if at all, but I'd rather our information not be crunched in this realm. Think you can hold me by my legs so I can dig?"

"You want me to lean you off the cliff so you can dig a cache for our stuff?"

"Do you have a better idea?" Anna looks left as another ripple of stone against stone echoes from the woods.

"Not currently."

"Hand me your stuff." She pulls out her phone, and I hand her mine and Joel's devices. "Grab my ankles and I'll do this as quick as I can." Anna shoves all three phones into her coat sleeves and squeezes the end shut in a fist. With one free hand, she inches to the edge of the cliff on her stomach.

I do as she instructs, grateful that my strength training in Colorado is doing its job. I brace my feet against the root and allow her to hang over the cliffside. I grip her ankles firmly, thankful that I'm not holding all her weight as her lower half is still level with me.

"Almost there," she grunts. "All right, pull me up." Anna shakes her head from side to side then wipes a dirty hand on her pant leg. "I found a soft spot in the cliffside and stashed the phones there. Unless they happen to dig in this spot for a long time, they shouldn't find them."

"So, now what?" All I want is to find Joel and Briar and get out of here.

"We don't have anything that should attract them so... We should be able to go check on the portal?"

Another yell erupts from the forest. It's much less distressed, weaker. Anna steps towards the woods.

"Let me go first," I say, stepping in front of Anna. I'm not going to let anything happen to her. I promised Dad I would protect her. I promised myself that I would. She shivers, her lower lip trembling. Realizing just how cold it is, I grab her hand and lead her away from the cliff. The trees seem to reach out with long, black fingers, and chilly air swirls around us as we duck into bark and foliage. I pick up the pace, praying that these creatures Anna spoke of will leave us alone.

A cry of pain and a low coo of distress warble in the distance. We are almost to the clearing where the portal is. A patch of moonlight outside the trees illuminates a dark shape on the ground. Brilliant white feathers catch my eye, and Anna gasps.

"Auriol?" She breaks away from my hand and rushes to the clearing.

"Anna!" I trip, my foot catching on a bush, but I regain my balance and am at her side in a moment. A man, wounded and weak, is on his side. An enormous owl stands off to his right, blinking and cooing in concern. In the faint moonlight, I see the man is dressed in strange medieval forester garb, like something out of a fantasy book. My mouth hangs open, studying the scene before me, but it's hard to stay surprised for long in the presence of an emergency.

"Wystan! What are you doing beyond the border?" Anna cries, dropping to her knees. The man groans and opens his eyes just enough to see who addresses him.

"I... had to save her," he wheezes. My pulse races. If he's seriously wounded, how can we help him out here?

"Her? Who is her?" Anna speaks quickly but calmly. She assesses the man called Wystan for injuries.

"Briar," Wystan says through gritted teeth. My blood runs cold at the way he says her name. Is she okay? Is she hurt? I watch as the owl cocks his head and coos twice, stretching out his wings then refolding them.

"Briar was here? Where is she now? Oh, goodness... You *are* hurt." Anna casts a look at me, face pinched in worry. Blood oozes lazily from a wound on Wystan's leg, and there are cuts on his hands and a nasty gash on his arm. He needs medical attention, stat.

"She was here, but she made it through the gate. I made sure of it." His words sound as if they are painful to say. "Reachers attacked us. The king gave her a truth pearl, knowing full well she would be targeted. He probably believes she is dead."

"You had no weapons?"

"They dissolved them, taking the diamonds and leaving me for dead. I thought they would finish me off but—" Wystan swallows. "They scattered once I ran out of bolts in my crossbow. I don't know what scared them off."

"When did Briar get here? Where did you find her?" Anna asks.

Wystan is about to answer but I cut in. "Anna, he needs a hospital, someone to give him stitches and to clean his wounds."

"We can't take him to our world Peter. Wystan will be outcast from his people if we do that, and what would the people at our hospital think of someone like him?"

"Anything is better than him suffering in pain like this!" I say. Wystan opens his eyes into slits to scan me, then he closes them again, swallowing, each breath slow and labored.

"Don't worry about me... Just get me onto Auriol," Wystan wheezes.

Anna places a hand on Wystan's shoulder and says, "We will too be worrying about you. Peter, help me get him onto Auriol." She stands and circles to Wystan's feet, grabbing his ankles as best as she can. I look towards the owl again, understanding that *it* is Auriol.

"How are we going to get him onto—"

"Auriol knows what must be done. Lift Wystan's shoulders." Anna cuts me off. Her tone is filled with stress. Auriol coos and steps closer to us. He's an enormous bird and incredibly beautiful, his snowy feathers catching the moonlight with a pearlescent radiance. I already thought owls were cool, so this is only increasing my appreciation for them. Auriol begins to crouch and nestles close to the ground, his height now level with our waists. I hadn't noticed it before, but now I catch the intricate shape of a saddle on the owl's back. Loops of leather hang for a foot and hand to grasp. What medieval time has enormous owls to ride? Not to mention creatures of stone who eat metal and gems to stay alive? Only this one I suppose. Or are there more worlds beyond ours?

"All right, now lift!" Anna grunts, lifting Wystan in sync with me. I didn't expect him to be so heavy, but I notice it has nothing to do with his physique and all to do with his armor. It's some sort of stone for crying out loud. We manage to lift him high enough and close enough to pin him to Auriol's side. The owl coos again, and Wystan groans in pain.

"I'll be all right. Just move me closer to the loop." He grunts and reaches with his unmarred hand to one of the loops. Slowly, we lop him into the saddle. He arches his back and winces. His other hand and arm is limp at his side. I eye the wound on his leg and grimace.

"Where is he going to go to get that sewn up?"

"To... Tara."

"Tara?" I look at Anna who shrugs.

"If you go back to Breezewood Castle tonight, won't the king know you tried to help Briar based on your wounds?"

"He won't know I helped her. Not if I tell him I saw more Worlders in our woods and was attacked by Reachers upon confronting them."

"Reachers don't just attack for no reason though, right?" I ask, still confused about all this kingdom stuff. Whose side is Wystan on anyway?

"Reachers target anyone with precious gems. Breezewood patrols and guards carry diamond-tipped spears, swords, crossbow bolts, etcetera. Since Reachers can only be killed with such things, it makes sense that guards would have those weapons." Anna says.

"I guess, yeah." I nod, wanting more answers. Wystan moves his left heel, and Auriol spreads his wings and stands. Wystan's voice is clearer now, as if mounting the owl gave him some relief, and he turns to look us both in the eyes.

"I thank you both for helping me. I am indebted to you. But you both should leave. Once the king finds out that more of you are coming through, he won't hesitate to up the patrols. I can't keep coming up empty-handed. He'll be onto our plans."

"I understand, but we are still looking for our friend, Joel."

"Joel? He's... he's in Breezewood Castle. If he's still alive, I'll do my best to free him." Anna's face goes pale and Wystan lowers his eyes. I raise my voice.

"What do you mean, *if* he's still alive? If he's in the castle, doesn't that mean he's safe from the Reachers?" I look at Anna, waiting for her response.

"Breezewood Castle is no place for a Worlder, especially one such as Joel." Anna's voice is barely audible, and I know I see a tear forming, the droplet catching the moonlight like a precious gem. Wystan sighs then lifts his head to look at us both again. Despite the shadows of night all around us, I catch the frown and glimmer of tears at the corners of his eyes.

"I would advise you both to go back home and only come through if absolutely necessary. If Joel is alive, I will do my best to send him back. If he is not, I will find some way to get word to you. Can you both promise me you'll go home?"

"We can't promise anything," I say, looking from Anna's face to Wystan's.

"Fine. Then just promise me that Briar will never come back here, that you will do your best to keep her from returning. If she does, then she will be hunted like never before. She has a truth pearl, and Reachers find them irresistible. And the king, well, he won't hesitate to use her to gain information on your world."

The way Wystan says Briar's name sets my mind racing. I'm almost positive he just struggled to ask us to keep her away from this place, as if he's sorry to do it. Can he have already formed some attachment to her after only just meeting her?

"We can try, but we can't promise. We'll tell her, but there's no guarantee she'll listen."

"That's all I ask," he says. Auriol flaps his wings, eyes blinking.

"I should go. You both should, too."

"We were going to head to the meeting place, but if Joel isn't there..." Anna wipes under her eyes with the edge of her sleeve, a shiver shaking her body.

"He won't be. In fact, no one is right now. It's Harvest Eve."

"Oh..." Anna hugs her arms tight against herself then looks at me. What's harvest eve? Despite all my questions, I look to Wystan. "I don't know who you are or how exactly you know Briar and my sister, or Joel, but thank you for protecting them. And I hope you find someone to help with your wounds."

It's all I can think of to say in the moment. Anna doesn't jab me in the ribs so I take that as a good sign that I said something right.

"Don't worry, I'll be alright," Wystan tips his head to us both. "Remember, don't come back unless absolutely necessary!" Auriol spreads his wings to their full length and begins to trot towards the cliff. As if they weigh nothing, the owl's wings lift them into the sky. The moonlight, the stars, the dark trees, everything, is like a movie. I watch them until they dip below the cliff edge, out of view. Anna sniffs.

"I don't want to go home, not without Joel. We can't just leave him."

"You heard Wystan—we can do nothing here. We need to go home, to keep Briar from coming back in."

"But our phones."

"Oh, yeah..." I turn back in the direction we came from. I don't want to tread back through the dark trees for them, but I know we should get them back.

"Peter, did you—"

"Huh?" I swing around, the familiar whooshing sound of the portal snagging my attention. Light erupts from the trees, and then it softens as the portal liquefies at the edge of the clearing.

"You didn't ask it to open, did you?" Anna asks.

"I didn't, but I'm seeing it now, thinking about it."

"Then someone else opened it." Anna loops her arm through mine. She's trembling and if I'm being honest, I'm trembling too but I'm trying to hide it. All I can see through the opening is darkness, but something is moving through it. Something tall and humanoid. I crane my neck and squint my eyes, holding as still as possible as the being emerges from the liquid gate.

Fifteen

I stand before the front door, spine tingling with unease. Is someone leaving another note or is it entirely unrelated to all this portal stuff? Another knock sounds. I can't tell if it is echoing through the house or just in my mind. I swallow, opening the front door with a shaky, clammy hand.

Instead of some shady visitor, Jen stands at the threshold, beaming from ear to ear. Relief claims me. If it hadn't been her, I don't know what I would have done.

"Hey! I hope I didn't interrupt anything, but you weren't answering your phone. Figured I'd come check on you." Good ol' Jen, always looking out for me. She stands on her tiptoes then lowers herself down, frosty breath rising around her face. I want to bring her inside and offer her a cup of tea, but I'm still reeling from this morning's unexpected happenings.

"Jen, hi. Yes, I'm okay." My heart begins to slow down but instantly picks up as I remember the pearl beneath my tongue. I clamp my lips shut. She'll notice it if I'm not careful.

"You sure? Your dad was actually the one who told me to come check on you. I think he and your mom have been worried about you since you called them last. I'll let him know you're okay."

"I am doing well enough. Can I call you later today? I have company over right now." I keep my tongue as flat as I can while attempting to keep it from hindering my speech. I want to invite Jen in, to reveal the rest of the mystery, to tell her about my crazy life, but I refrain. Still some things to confirm.

"Sure thing. Glad you're okay." Jen smiles, turning to leave with a wave. I close the door, relieved, though still a little startled. My phone didn't go off?

I pat my pockets, sure that I'd feel it on me, but then I remember the book bag and all my stuff. I sigh. It must be on silent. I head back into the living room where whispering flits back and forth. They stop as I enter.

"No threat?" Cedric asks.

"If there was, she wouldn't be walking back calmly," Sam says, his voice dripping with sarcasm.

"No," I reach for my phone in the book bag and click the side button, but nothing happens. It's dead. *That explains it.* "Apparently my dad called and didn't get an answer so he sent my cousin to come check on me. All is well, for now," I say, searching for my charge cord.

"Well, in that case, can you spend the day with us?" Naomi asks again, hands resting primly in her lap.

"If I can somehow explain to Andrew where I went, then sure, you all can spend the day with *me.* I have work in fifteen minutes." I glance at the kitchen clock across the room as I plug in my phone.

"You gotta sign the paper though," Cedric says, looking from me to Naomi.

"Briar doesn't have to tell Andrew any details about her disappearance yesterday. An emergency is all that needs to be mentioned. And she can say that it has been sorted out. Please, sign the paper, Briar. If you really are on our team, that is."

I take in the entire situation. Everything that has happened to me in the past few days reminds me of the *Nutcracker* story—when Clara falls asleep and dreams of a wild adventure only to awaken and realize that it was all real... It resonates within me deeply. Only my story hasn't ended happily ever after yet.

With my classmates reinforcing this new reality, I know this decision is serious. Do I want to sign this paper? What can they do to me if I do tell the world about this magical portal and the world beyond? Sue me? For what? It's not like any of them own the portal or Breezewood. Technically, Andrew does as the book is in his shop and so is the gateway. Is that world in his shop, too?

"If I can openly discuss this with my cousin, Jen, and possibly my parents if they ask, I'll sign this paper. I have no reason to share it with anyone else. They'll think I'm crazy otherwise. You all only believe me because you've been there." I tuck a strand of hair behind my ear and cross my arms. They'll have to agree to my terms.

"We can't..." Cedric protests, but Naomi puts up a hand. Her styled hair and pink, glossy lips give off the same air they did in high school: put together. But she isn't conceited. Rather, her demeanor and overall appearance make her like a best friend. She's kind and handles tough situations with ease, taking the lead when needed. I can tell she's the head organizer of this group and second in command.

"Look, I trust you, Briar. This document is really to keep a record of those that know about this place and have been there. It really doesn't stop you from telling anyone. But we plead with you to keep this to yourself. Jen will need to sign the paper as well if we go through with this, even your parents."

Cedric clears his throat, then spills forth his thoughts.

"If enough information about this place gets out, imagine the flocks of people who would come to investigate and seek ways to harm and or make money off something like this. It would turn into an amusement park, one that wouldn't stay amusing for long."

"This isn't *Assassin's Creed* or *Skyrim*, no matter how much Breezewood feels like it. There are real people in there," Orin adds, speaking up for what seems to be the first time in a long while.

I consider their views. They're right. This broken world is full of people who would exploit this childhood wonder of an experience into something twisted for their own gain, perhaps even harming innocents in the process. It needs to be protected and kept a secret, despite how beautiful and wonderful it is.

"In essence, this place is still a mystery to us. We are unsure how it all even came about, though we strongly believe it has something to do with you and that book you discovered. The one that is still in the store. Whoever wrote that story about Breezewood somehow tied it to the shop with what we would call magic, and now there's a portal to that very world." Samuel goes back to tapping on his watch, squinting as the screen produces a readout of numbers and letters.

"And don't bother looking for the author. We searched the pages cover to cover. There's no publication date, no author, no publisher, nothing. Only the story," Naomi says, answering a question I had. If the author were still around, or at least family members of the author, maybe they knew something about all this? An unfortunate dead end. Sam looks from Naomi to me and adds his own thoughts.

"The thing is, Breezewood is just as curious about our world as we are about theirs. Though some mock us for our technology, they are curious, and the king of Breezewood Castle is smarter than we give him credit for. He may have sent spies through based on rumors, spies tailing us for information. We believe the person responsible for the riddles and strange messages of help we've been getting are from a homeless guy wandering around Homer." I wrinkle my brow at these observations and theories. So many things are weird.

"How do the Breezewood people know about our technology?" I ask, recalling how Sam had been so distraught about phones disappearing into the portal.

"Others have entered Breezewood long before us and decided to stay, most not even knowing how to return home, let alone even how they entered. What they know of technology was shared with some of the people, and information has circulated. Not to mention the time Sam accidentally brought his watch in." Naomi says the last part with gritted teeth.

"Hey, that was before we knew about the Reachers. Now that we know, we are better about it. Very careful. At least, Anna was supposed to be."

"Have you seen the Reachers?" I sit on the sofa, leaning in as Naomi opens her mouth then closes it. Sam looks at his watch.

"No time now. Gotta get you to work. We can talk in the car."

I stand, everyone falling suit. Soon, we are piled tightly into Sam's Xterra on the way to the bookstore. Orin sits up front while Naomi, Cedric and I take up the back middle seats. I make sure my belongings are on my person this time, book bag left at home. I make the mental note to call my dad and Jen to let them know I'm doing all right, as soon as I explain to Andrew yesterday's mess. Or rather, an incredibly un-detailed version of it.

With the car rolling out onto the highway, I lean back into my questions.

"Reachers. You've seen them? Because, I have. In fact, another man from Breezewood and I were chased by them." No one seems surprised by my statement, but there are a few eye glances between Sam and Orin in the front seat.

"Sam and I are the only ones of our group that have seen Reacher's in person. We never want to again. They are like something out of a science fiction novel if you ask me," Naomi says, pausing then looking at me. "Who did you meet in Breezewood?"

"He said his name is Wystan? He's some guard from Breezewood but he didn't seem to agree entirely with the king and his ways." I remember how he brought me into the castle and showed me around and how hesitant he was to show me to the king. He was obviously breaking some rules.

"So Wystan is alive? We didn't know for sure. It has been a long while since we've seen and heard from him. That's good news," Sam says, catching my eyes in the rear view mirror.

"You know him?" They continue to surprise me. Just how familiar are they with Breezewood? And how long have they been traveling into the portal?

"He's our informant on particular Breezewood news. When we are in Breezewood ourselves, Wystan risks his life to meet with us and discuss plans of action and defense in a hideout in the forest."

"So, Wystan is a double agent?" He seems the type. Strong, sure of himself, a rebel, but loyal in some regard. He risked his life for mine, and I don't even know him. What kind of person does that?

"Of sorts. He has to play the part." Naomi frowns, tipping her head to look at me. "Is there something we don't know?"

"How loyal to the king is he? Like, if he was asked to harm a friend of his on behalf of the king, would he do it?" I remember the pain in Wystan's eyes when he believed Joel to be a goner. Was Joel even still alive? I don't know why I have this sickening feeling that there were things Wystan wasn't telling me about Joel and his fate.

If Wystan had been willing and able to save my life, what stopped him from helping Joel?

"I don't know..." Naomi trails off, looking to Cedric who shrugs.

"We don't know him that well, but he hasn't lied to us yet. We've been able to verify almost all his information so far."

"It's just that he didn't think Joel would live long. Yesterday, he had little hope when we spoke. The king said Joel was going to be fed to the wolves. Are these wolves the same as Reachers?" I'm concerned that something more dangerous is at work in Breezewood, something Wystan was too afraid to tell me about and had little hope of competing against. Reachers apparently he could handle, but these wolves?

"Joel is smart. He'll get out of this mess, right?" Naomi says for everyone in the car. She's rather quiet now, the clipboard in her lap. Sam watches the road, letting silence permeate the vehicle, then he starts talking, skipping over Naomi's question and answering mine.

"Wolves are not the same as Reachers. In fact, they look nothing like wolves." He makes eye contact with me again.

"What are they?" I ask.

"Shadow creatures. I won't go into details. Don't want to give you nightmares," Sam answers, taking the turn down Main Street. Finally, I'm getting answers.

"If knowing the details will help us figure out a rescue plan, I want to know." Though, I second guess my stomach for anything remotely disturbing. I never was one to listen to scary stories and come out without being creeped out, but I want to know what Joel is facing, or faced. I swallow, preparing myself for the grim details.

"No one knows for sure exactly, but they have been said to have the shape of a human though there are no features. Only sometimes, eyes that glow. They call them wolves because they are always hungry, always lurking. In my opinion, the names should have been flipped for the different creatures, but what I think doesn't matter. The Breezewood king is known to keep a few inside the castle from reports given by Wystan. It's said they cannot be contained, only invited."

"Sounds like something we should be staying far away from," I say, thinking back to things my parents had taught me. Darkness was to be conquered, not invited or played with. Even so, I shiver. If the Breezewood king is playing with darkness, then Joel and Wystan, everyone adverse to the darkness needs to get far away from it. All in all, the king needs to be stopped. Such a task seems too daunting for a group of young adults from the small Alaskan seaside town of Homer.

"What about Reachers? Why are they called that?"

"Reachers got their name from their uncanny ability to reach for their next meal. Wystan told us that the name arose after a comrade of his was escaping a pack of them in a patrol years ago and one reached out its long neck and pulled him from his owl. The man did not survive. Ever since then, they've been dubbed Reachers." I shiver at the story. No wonder Wystan's hate for the creatures was strong. They'd killed one of his own.

"Briar, you can't go back through the portal with the pearl. It's too dangerous," Naomi says as soon as Sam stops the car in front of the bookstore. All talk of Wolves and Reachers comes to a complete halt.

"That's what you've said, but the only way to get it taken off is to go to the king again, right?"

Naomi's eyes waver. She's probably still processing the reality of my predicament.

"We'll find another way." Naomi unlatches the door, stepping out of the car before I can ask if it needs to come off. What happens if I never remove it? I don't like the thought of having it stay. I imagine pretending that it is some kind of piercing, and with me not being that kind of girl, my parents would be so confused.

Cedric exits the car on his side and holds the door open for me as I scramble out of the middle. I feel like I'm back in high school, nearly all my closest classmates walking up to the bookstore door like we are on some sort of field trip. It is such a weird feeling, but if I'm honest, it is a feeling I've missed.

"There are two cars here that I don't recognize. And neither of them are Andrew's subaru," I say, looking between the group. They don't say anything, and Naomi shrugs. As soon as we enter the store, I expect Andrew to greet us, but there is no one at the front counter. Come to think of it, the OPEN sign wasn't even on. *Is he even here?*

I start to pace the hallways and check behind the shelves. "Andrew?" I call out, tentatively. I even press my face against the glass of the private book room entrance. This door is always locked, keeping the rarest books out of view of customers before being properly priced and picked over. I scan the room to be sure he isn't inside sorting. Nothing. I step back, frowning.

"Let's check upstairs." When we reach the upper room, there is still nothing. Light from the frosty morning streams in through the windows, creating golden shafts of swirling dust.

"Whose cars are those if no one is here?" Orin says, taking in the room. A good number of books in the center of the room have been removed, though there are a few empty shelves waiting to be filled with the piles I never finished.

Instantly, everyone's phones go off except for mine, each with different text tones. My classmates reach for them.

"Well that explains one of the cars. Peter and Anna left their keys with the book," Sam says, beginning to search the room. "The texts must have still been swirling in cyberspace up here. Who knows what the magic does to texts when the sender's phones are in a different world."

Naomi shows me her phone. A text bubble populates the screen sent in a group chat with all my classmates' names. Even Peter's.

> Anna: We are going through. Please get our car away from the shop and hide it somewhere safe. The car keys are with the book. Our hypotheses were right. That homeless guy is from Breezewood.

"Then who does the other car belong to?" I ask as Naomi tucks the phone back into her pocket.

"No idea."

"But Anna said *we*. Peter is with her, so isn't one his car?" I recall the first day I saw him back from Colorado at the coffee shop. Memories of him staring at the paintings while waiting for his drinks linger in the forefront of my mind. I hope wherever he is in Breezewood, no harm has come to him.

"Peter doesn't have a car in Homer. He rode with Anna," Naomi says. I'm not sure how she knows all that, but considering there's a group chat I'm not a part of, there's a lot I don't know.

"Got the keys. Let's go," Sam says.

"Wait..." I have a thought, whether it is relevant to the situation now doesn't matter but I have to get it off my chest before I forget. Plus, it is a reasonable question. "Supposing Joel, Anna, and Peter make it back home safe, and this book is connected to Breezewood somehow, wouldn't destroying the book protect both our worlds?"

The question lingers in the air, and my classmates' faces wrinkle. Naomi raises a finger, tapping it on her lips in thought.

"We have thought of that, but there are several reasons why destroying the book would not be a good idea. First off, we have no idea what that would do to either of our worlds."

Fair enough. But the question is still valid.

"What we do know is that, one, removing the book from the shop keeps people in Breezewood from coming here and us from going in. Taking the book into Breezewood keeps us on this side from going into it as well. If it is in the middle, however, in this shop, it allows both sides to pass through freely, granted they know the key phrase," Orin adds.

"How long did it take you all to figure this out?" I ask.

I wonder why the book has never been bought before, effectively removing it from the shop. What would happen if someone bought it and never returned it? Would Breezewood never be heard from again? What sort of precautions are they taking to make sure the book never leaves the shop? Surely hiding it behind other books isn't secure enough. If there are ever any other book lovers like me shopping here, then you always look behind books. People stash good books there all the time.

Something isn't adding up. Either they don't know it or they are keeping something from me. I'm leaning towards the fact that they don't know.

"Not long. I ran some calculations through some software and we did some physical tests," Sam says passively, as if this is a normal everyday thing for him. I don't doubt it is.

"What did your calculations say would happen if you destroyed the book?" I'm trying to come up with ideas on what might happen myself. Would Breezewood simply cease to exist?

"It didn't say definitively. It pumped out so many predictions, none of them exactly pleasant, so we have been afraid to try." Sam frowns. I turn over his words, dusting them off with a mental archaeology brush. How can a machine predict magic?

"There are also several poor souls, names given to us by Wystan, who have wandered into Breezewood years ago and are unable to return because they don't know how. We feel the need to at least give them the chance, the choice to return," Naomi says.

I believe her. I would be one of those poor souls had Wystan not been to my rescue. And Joel.

"Not that this is related, but Alaska does have the highest missing person percentage based on our sparse population. I can't help but draw parallels. Blame my analytical brain," Sam says, hitting himself in the side of the head jokingly. Naomi waves him off with a playful eye roll.

"There are obviously some tests we still need to run, but first and foremost, we need to rescue Joel and protect Breezewood."

"Don't forget protecting our world too. There's at least one spy around or more. The best thing is to keep them in our world for the time being."

"The only way to do that is by removing the book from the shop, right? Why don't you just carry it around? Wouldn't that keep everyone safe?"

"Theoretically, yes, but, I don't know. With all the weird note stuff, we just thought it best to stay here. Someone is following and watching us, and so far, they haven't put the pieces together about the book. I mean, really, if they take it to Breezewood, we can't get there. Wystan is trying to help individuals through. If the book is out of the shop, he can't send them through. It is all so complicated. Time works differently there, and we can't have people just showing up when the shop is closed."

"Have individuals ever returned before?"

"Not that we know of since we've discovered the portal. We've only just been working on a plan to facilitate the return of people as well as their backstories for reentering society. Can you imagine what a shock wave it will create to our community when missing people just start showing up? The media will be all over it."

"I'm sorry to say it, but before we understood what had truly happened to you, Briar, back when your incident happened, some of us kinda believed all the theories surrounding your disappearance. We wanted to believe them because it was exciting, and in doing so, they painted a bad picture of you for us."

"As soon as we knew the truth, however, we discarded all that. But the point in saying this is those blogs and theories are still out there. If and when people start showing up from the portal, those theories will resurface and your name might get smeared again. We want to have a plan for when we begin bringing missing people through." Naomi looks at me sympathetically.

"And, I personally want to say I'm sorry. I treated you unfairly and even pulled Joel and Peter a little into our circle, turning them slightly against you in high school after the incident. Will you forgive me at least for being a part of it?" Sam says, reaching out a hand.

"Same here. We should have known better than to believe strangers on the internet. We could have asked you," Naomi adds. Orin and Cedric nod in agreement. I'm surprised by their sudden openness and humility. Why would they lie if they are apologizing to me now?

"I forgive you guys. I never held a grudge, honestly. I was hurt, yes, but I thought it was merely because I didn't fit in or something." I shake Sam's hand, and there's a glimmer of understanding that passes between us. This guy is going to be like a big brother to me. All of them are. Naomi, being the sister of course.

"If all is well between us, then we need to lay down some ground rules. No lies. No keeping secrets about Breezewood," Naomi says.

I begin walking towards the stairs, my phone now in my hands. "I have no secrets to keep." I take one last look around the room. "We technically shouldn't be here if the shop isn't open. Let me call Andrew really quick." I pull up Andrew's contact. I need to still call my dad and Jen, but first, solve this small mystery.

"Cedric, Orin, you go take Anna's car and the Xterra somewhere, then meet us back here in the Xterra. Hopefully we'll sort all this out by the time you get back."

Andrew's phone rings but he doesn't pick up. I try again. Naomi and Sam stand by, waiting. When the call drops again, going to Andrew's voicemail, I leave one.

"Hey, Andrew, this is Briar. Sorry about yesterday. I had an emergency, but it's all good right now. I'm available to work if you still need me. Just let me know. Thanks, bye."

With Orin and Cedric still gone, Naomi walks over to where Sam pulls out Anna's keys.

"I really should have Peter make some sort of secret shelf compartment for the book so it never gets taken from the shop."

"That or frame it on the wall," I say. "Sometimes, things in plain sight get overlooked."

"We can talk about it when Peter and Anna get back." Naomi brushes her hair over her shoulder and wrinkles her nose at the dust flying through the air.

With little warning, the room brightens, and it isn't from the sun. All three of us go rigid. The portal is opening.

We step out of the way, the strange watery sound filling the air. As the light peels back, revealing the forest glade beyond, a humanoid shape approaches. Temporarily blocking our view of the landscape behind, they inch forward to walk through.

Sam steps in front of Naomi and me as the figure glides a hand and foot through the barrier. As soon as their face is visible, the pearl beneath my tongue begins to grow as cold as ice. No one was prepared for who and what just stepped through the portal.

Sixteen

PETER

The portal widens, and Anna and I take a step back. My heart feels like it is about to beat out of my chest, my gut coiling with fear. I hold Anna's arm even tighter as the person, or thing, steps through the opening. Ever since returning to Homer, Alaska, I've been continually surprised, but this nearly tops them all.

It is indeed a person. A person I know quite well. Someone I never thought I would see stepping through this portal. Why on earth is *he* here?

There's no doubt in my mind that August Heaverly has just stepped foot in Breezewood.

Anna loosens on my arm then immediately squeezes harder. I know she has never seen him before. How could she? He's been working at my side in Colorado for the past few years and has no connection to Homer. At least that I'm aware of.

August doesn't notice us yet. He stands just inches from the portal, looking left, right, and center before advancing farther into the clearing. I try to hold Anna still, shivers wracking us both, hoping he doesn't see. If August is here, what sort of secrets has he kept from me? Can I even trust him anymore? Was his entire method of sending me to Alaska to build and escape room just for this? How would he know I would pick the bookstore? Unless he influenced Andrew to reach out to me. I remember the recent phone call I had with August. His questions about my timeline had caught me off guard a little. I didn't realize I was on a strict timeline for the room to be secured before construction happened. What else didn't I know about that was time sensitive?

August turns to the left, melting into the trees in the direction of the cliff. I pull Anna deeper into the forest, away from the clearing. We both settle to a crouch, trying to control our breathing as best we can, shivering increasingly.

"Peter, I don't know who that-t-t was, but did you see how confident-t-t-ly he walked through? He's been here b-b-before and I didn't know about it." Her chattering words send spikes of alert through me. We aren't going back for the phones today.

"I saw. And Anna, I know him. That's my boss back in Colorado." I look towards the portal area, contemplating when to walk across and open it.

"What?" Her eyes widen at my remark and her fingers dig into my sleeve a little more. I'm still trying to sort out how this could be happening and why. I still haven't shaken off the feeling of unbelief about this place, but at this moment, whether I'm mad or sane, Anna needs to get warm.

"We're going back through. Hold on." I roll the sentence over in my mind, waiting exactly sixteen seconds. "Get ready to run," I say. Anna doesn't argue, and both of us are poised for action. As soon as the portal extends, we break through the treeline and rush to the gateway. While I'm mildly still aware that the homeless man we tried to escape from earlier could be on the other side, I don't care. Anna is more important at the moment.

We step through the portal, the other end bright, airy, and warm. Relief floods my muscles as we practically collapse in the upper room of the bookstore. In a stoic circle are my classmates, and lo and behold, Briar is among them. My heart leaps in my chest, my fears of Briar being lost in Breezewood dissolving like sugar in hot tea. "Good grief you guys!" Naomi says, kneeling to reach for Anna. Anna, face beginning to gain color and warmth, unclasps my arm. I'm on my knees, a hand on the floor. I rise up, brushing fingers across my face, then stand. The sun, dusty books, my friends, and everything about the room is thoroughly familiar. It's good to be out of the cold and darkness of the unknown.

Sam breaks through my thoughts. "Your phones... Where are your phones?"

"Give them a moment, Sam," Naomi's mom-voice coos as she holds Anna's cold hands in hers. "Are you guys okay? What happened there?"

"Give them a moment indeed," Sam mutters.

"Our phones are buried in the cliffside, away from Reachers for now. We had to come back through. It was too cold."

"Too cold?" Naomi looks from Anna to me, then back to Anna. "I'll say."

I avoid locking eyes with Briar, but I can tell she's watching me, her stare leaving a warm trail up the side of my face. Is she upset? Does she remember the past? Our past? I hope that any flush that comes into my cheeks will be thought of as the return of warmth into my bones, not because the girl I like is standing feet away from me. I swallow, forcing myself to be confident and answer all the questions while demanding some of my own.

"Tell us everything. Orin and Cedric will be here shortly, and we'll take you back to your car," Sam says, eyes diverting to his watch to punch in whatever it is he does.

"Oh! We never got to tell you but, Briar made it back in the night," Naomi says, animatedly gesturing to the girl that I'm fully aware of. I bravely look at her, trying my best to do it as non-awkwardly as possible. When our eyes meet, warmth radiates off her and I'm glued in place, not wanting to leave. It's been a long time since I've looked her in the face like this. I've missed seeing her bright eyes and rusty hair and the overwhelming sense that she's about to say something that will make me smile. She continues to look at me, a blush of her own creeping across the bridge of her nose. She looks quickly away, avoiding my eyes. No, she hasn't forgotten me. While there's no animosity in her face, I can't help but see sadness there. I did this to her and she's embarrassed to be next to me. All because I believed some made up stories and lies about her. And to cap it off, I friendzoned her. Despite the magic that has plainly presented itself before us, I wonder if she believes I think of her as the girl all those crazy conspiracies made her out to be. I need to bring her to the light and tell her that I believe her.

"It's good to see you. I'm glad you and Anna are all right," she finally says, breaking the awkward four seconds that have passed between us. I can see Sam grinning out of the corner of my eye, so I follow up as smoothly as possible.

"I'm glad you're alright. The way Anna and Joel described Breezewood, I had to worry a little." I throw in a genuine smile. To my delight, she returns it with a small innocent smirk but it quickly falls and she looks away, almost determined to ignore me. Dare I hope to believe she'll learn to trust me again like she did in school? I swear I can hear Sam groan, but he's in fact, ignoring us, squinting at his watch. Naomi fidgets with a jeweled bracelet on her wrist.

"Tell us about your time in Breezewood. What happened?"

"It seemed only a max of fifteen to twenty minutes, but hours have passed," Anna says, nodding to the sun's refraction through the window panes. I follow her gaze and nod, then look at Naomi.

"In short form, we entered Breezewood, walked to the cliff in order to make our way down, and upon attempting the descent, we heard a yell."

"Wystan was injured by Reachers. He's the one who helped Briar through," Anna adds, looking to Briar. A flash of soreness crosses Anna's eyes. She's still blaming part of Joel's disappearance on

Briar. Even if she never says anything in front of the rest of the classmates, she can't hide it from me.

"That's right. He was fighting them off when I stepped through," Briar answers, a concerned look sweeping over her features. "Was he badly injured?"

"Fairly, but we got him onto Auriol, and he said not to worry," Anna says quickly, avoiding Briar's look. I'll have to talk to Anna again in private. Briar can't be blamed for what happened to Joel. He made the choice to look for her.

Aside from everything else going on, this whole adventure is causing a strange pull on my emotions, and I hate that my thoughts are veering towards jealousy. The last thing I want is some sort of love triangle or love square between Joel, me, and this Wystan guy. I won't let that happen, though. I have no claim on Briar as her choices are her own. Jealousy has no place in our relationship. I made my choices long ago, and whatever happens, happens. But I won't back out from telling Briar the truth. In fact, I will soon find the guts to tell her my mind, even how I feel.

"So Joel is still missing?" Naomi asks, a crease in her forehead. There's a pause. Anna drops her head.

"Wystan says he's not confident..." Anna tries to repeat Wystan's words but fumbles.

I rescue her from tears about to spill by speaking up. "Joel isn't in a great spot considering what this Wystan character explained. But if he is still alive, Wystan said he would do his best in trying to free him." I hope it's true for the sake of Anna's heart and for

Joel's life. He is my best friend, or used to be, and I hope we can still repair our friendship.

"There's no way. The king doesn't just release people that he sends to the Wolves." Anna's voice drips in hopelessness, her shoulders crumpling.

Naomi puts a hand on her back. "Joel is smart. He's not one to give up easily. Not to mention, if he went in to help save Briar, he had a plan."

"He said he was going to trade his life for mine," Briar adds. I wish she hadn't spoken.

Tears well in Anna's eyes and she turns away. Naomi looks to me for help. I look at Briar whose face is now full of mixed emotions. Tears glisten at the edges of her own eyes and she casts them to her feet, pink still washing her face.

"Sam, can we go to the lighthouse? We need to debrief everything in safety." Naomi glances between us while rubbing Anna's shoulder gently.

"Yeah, Joel made sure to hide an extra key."

"Good. Let's all go and make plans," I say, nodding to Naomi. She catches my look and begins to guide Anna down the stairs.

"But wait. What about your phones?" Sam throws his hands out to the side as if he can't believe I'm about to walk away.

Briar steps past us. "I'll be downstairs, waiting," she says before exiting the upper room.

I keep my eyes focused on Sam, trying to ignore the fact that Briar is no longer in the room. I already miss her, and I'm not afraid to dwell on it. "They aren't a priority at the moment."

"Look, if you want, I'll go grab them. Just tell me where they are," he suggests. He's completely serious, already in the action of removing his smart watch.

"Sam, It would be faster if I went since I know right where they are."

"Then come with me." He taps his watch. "Already sent a text telling them that we are grabbing the phones really quick. You with me?"

I hesitate, and for good reason. I really don't want to go back into Breezewood right now. The darkness and cold, the strange creatures and wounded owl-riding men, the recent sighting of August. It's literally the last thing I want to do.

"I know I sound like a baby, but it's the truth. I'd rather not."

"But Joel's phone is in there, isn't it?" Sam asks. He sets his smart watch behind some books and crosses his arms.

"Yeah..."

"Well, we need that. Joel has some of my latest tech design project files on there, and I don't want them falling into Breezewood hands, regardless of how much they despise technology."

"Don't you have copies?"

"Of course. What good designer wouldn't? But the purpose is copyright and safety. I haven't put a patent on them yet!"

I'm about to come up with another excuse as to why going into Breezewood just isn't a great idea right now, but I don't. I'm just remembering all those phone calls and interviews I conducted earlier with businesses this week. My phone number is kind of essential in case some decide early to provide support. While I had told them I didn't need to hear back from them till the end of the week, it is likely some could offer support sooner. Unfortunately, I need my phone. I look at Sam.

"Fine. But we are going in then out. No exploring."

"I don't want to explore. I have enough fear already of Reachers chasing us towards the portal as soon as we grab the phones."

"I did not need that voiced out loud," I say. The portal begins to open with the watery sound of whatever it is that holds back the fabric of space and time. Magic? Or is it something else entirely?

"Lead me to the place," Sam says, urging me to go first. I force myself to step through, expecting the cold air of that unknown world to take my breath away. But it doesn't. As soon as we're through, we're greeted by a tingling sensation all around, as if particles of cold are fleeing at our entrance. Then, faint tinges of pink begin blushing across the sky. The portal recedes behind us, and instead of me continuing towards the cliff with swiftness, I'm nearly forced to stand still and witness the masterpiece of a sunrise. The pink increases and is met with peach and gold, intensifying with such grandeur that awe is the only thing that escapes my lips.

"Wow." There's no other word for it. I could never describe it accurately to anyone. Sam is nodding next to me, a contented smile on his face, eyes full of sunrise. We just stand there, continuing to soak in the beauty. Then, in the most magical way possible, the sun's rays break the horizon and spill over the cliff and through the trees. Elongated shadows stretch from the trunks that are now edged in brilliant gold and cherubic rose. My breath no longer billows in frosty clouds like it did when Anna and I were in Breezewood last. It's as if the sun is holding this world in its hands, the air absent of any icy kiss.

A few moments more and Sam nudges me. "We'll have to be quick. Time works differently in this place. A few moments here could be hours on the other side," he says.

"They are over here." I lead him through the trees, retracing mine and Anna's steps to the cliff edge. With little trouble, I find the root that we used as a handhold and the disturbance in the dirt from where I braced myself holding Anna. "I'll have to hold you over the edge. Anna buried it in the side."

"On it, just don't let go," Sam says, dropping to his knees then sprawling to his chest, leaning over the side, exactly like Anna. I grasp his ankles and wait for the call to pull him back up. When I hear his signal and haul him back to the top, he's holding three phones in one hand.

"Never bring them in here again," he says, brushing off his shirt that is now smeared generously in dirt. "Now, back to the portal!" He takes off first this time. I keep up with him as we race to the clearing. My mind almost goes to thinking about Reachers, but I force myself to begin thinking about opening the portal, the key phrase rolling over my tongue without me having to say a word. When we reach the clearing, nearly twenty feet away from the portal location, I'm counting, and it expands after sixteen seconds on the dot. Our feet kick up dirt as we plunge one at a time into its opening.

Breath and blood racing, Sam and I turn as the portal recedes again. We made it back in one piece.

"See? What'd I tell you? Phones are back and the girls should hopefully be waiting for us." Sam slaps his watch back on, and I'm surprised to hear a snap as it fits to his wrist instantly. Magnets. Actually I'm not surprised. This kid is such a nerd, and I love it. "Ehh it's been a little over half an hour here and we were in there for like six minutes tops. Hopefully they didn't ditch us for coffee or something."

"Let's hope they are still waiting for us." I look out the window, and thankfully, I spot a cluster of familiar faces, some leaning up against a black Xterra. Sam and I exit the bookstore and walk out to the crew all waiting patiently. Well, mostly.

"What took you so long? I thought it was only going to be—"

"It took us six minutes and it's been over thirty here. Chill out," Sam says, quickly tapping the on buttons to our phones. "Hmm. They are dead. Probably due to the cold. I have charge cords in my car. Everyone hop in." He hands me all three phones. Orin offers Briar shotgun, but she kindly denies it, following Naomi into the back.

Cedric and I look at each other, and Sam grins at us from the window. "Looks like we gotta gently break the law to drop Peter and Anna off at their car. It's just down the way. Hop in the back." Sam nods to the hatch. Cedric and I pile into the cargo area then balance while crouched, Sam putting the truck in drive.

When we finally reach where Anna's car is parked, just down the street tucked near the bakery, Anna and I exit the Xterra. No one says anything to us as we round the front of the vehicle. Anna grabs the keys from Cedric, and Naomi pops her head out the passenger window from the back.

"Lighthouse?"

"We'll be there," I say with a nod. Before Naomi rolls up the window, I catch Briar's eyes. A spark shoots through me as she quickly looks away. Turning before anyone can see the flush creeping up my neck, Anna and I head for her car.

Once in the car, she doesn't speak to me. She's slumped in her seat, eyes staring off into nothingness. When the Xterra rumbles past us, I start the car and turn to look at her, initiating the conversation I know needs to happen.

"Anna, we are going to try and save Joel. We will make a plan," I say it as confidently as I can, trying to convince myself that we will solve all the mysteries and save our friend.

"There's just so much we have to do... and so much stuff we can't do." She folds and unfolds her hands in her lap, not making eye contact with me. I'm willing to bring up the obvious feelings she has for Joel now, all for the sake of getting it out in the open. I want my sister to be able to trust me, and this might be the ticket.

"Anna, you like Joel don't you?" I don't have to specify what I mean. She catches my meaning and closes her eyes, a large tear sliding out from under her lashes.

"I never want you to tell him. Never, okay?" she asks, eyes red with pent-up emotions. Emotions like hers are understandable. I've been out of the picture for three years, and she's been an only child since then. If Joel was in the picture while I was gone, it would make sense that she would look up to him and maybe even develop feelings for him.

"I won't tell a soul. These are your feelings." I'm serious about that. I won't break her trust, but I hope these feelings have been discussed with Mom and Dad. If not, I'll do whatever I can to urge her to have a conversation with them. I haven't talked heart-to-heart with Joel in a while and neither have my parents. He could have changed since high school, and I don't want Anna mixed up with someone I don't know like the back of my hand. I'm protective of her, and it's only natural. She's my built-in best friend and only sibling.

"We are just friends. He doesn't want a relationship like that with me." She wipes her tears away, trying not to smear her make-up. I doubt her words, but again, I don't know what has transpired between them.

"I won't tell him. I'll leave that up to you." I put the car in reverse. "Joel is nice. It's no wonder you like him."

"He's nice. I'm just... He's just pining for Briar and I'm fading into the background. She doesn't even care for him."

I don't know why she thinks that but I'm putting a stop to it immediately. "Hold on, let's not assume things."

"It's true. Why else would Joel risk his life for her?"

"Until you ask him directly, I don't want any more assumptions. People get their feelings hurt more often than not by simply as-suming. Okay?"

"Okay." Anna sits farther in her seat and sniffs. It isn't a pouty sniff, though. She wants to believe me, and I want to believe myself.

There's deep concern in her features, as if she's been caring for Joel for such a long time, and with him in danger, it's all finally being revealed.

"We'll talk about this later. Let's get to the lighthouse."

We leave all our devices downstairs, even Sam's smart watch, just in case any are compromised somehow. With that out of the way, I know the beginning of this top secret meeting is gonna be a doozy.

When we are all finally seated in the upper room of the lighthouse, doors locked and shades closed, Sam and Naomi stand. I catch Briar's eyes from across the table, and she holds mine for point two seconds then looks away. There's no telling what she's thinking now.

"Secrecy. Secrecy is key. If any of this portal news gets out to the public, Breezewood is doomed," Sam says in the bossiest voice he can muster.

Naomi glares at him then begins her own introduction. "Sam's right, but apart from secrecy, we also need safety and security. There are spies in our world that at some point will try to get back to Breezewood to report to the king. What they will tell and what he wants, I'm not entirely sure."

With the mention of spies, I catch most of the crew up on our spotting of August in Breezewood. Anna recounts the run-in with the homeless man and the strange riddles along with her observation of his eyes, a clear sign of being from Breezewood.

Everyone is silent for a few moments before, to my surprise, Briar speaks up. "That explains the other car then. Do you think August has something to do with this escape room you are going to build? The location I mean, as he obviously knows the portal is there."

"I'm suspicious they are somehow connected. If it is alright with you all, I'm going to try and call him as soon as we are finished here."

"Speaking of calling, Briar, ever find out where Andrew went?"

"He won't answer his phone. It's weird for him to just up and abandon the shop in the middle of hours. He normally puts a sign up and locks the doors if it ever happens."

"Wait, I remember him saying something earlier this morning about running errands and closing up the shop. Something about returning after eleven. It's past that time now. But why was the door unlocked?" Anna says, elbows on the table.

Cedric scratches the bridge of his nose, brows furrowed. "Don't know. And if that car is this August guy's, how did he get through the portal? Does he know Andrew? How did he even know about Breezewood?"

"I should be able to resolve most of this today," I say, looking between Sam and Naomi.

"We need to keep the portal open until we get Joel out. But we also need to keep people from going in."

"This book—it seems to be the key to Breezewood. Is that what I'm hearing?" I ask, cross-checking between everybody.

"More or less," Naomi says, "But we don't fully understand it. All we know is that once it is taken out of the bookstore, no one can go in or out, even if you know the sentence."

"So, as soon as we get Joel back, we remove it from the shop to keep Breezewood safe?" Briar says.

"That's a method. There's only one problem, one we never talked about yet." Naomi looks at Sam who just studies the table and shakes his head.

"We should have told them a while ago," he mutters. I'm alert at his tone, staring holes into Naomi's eyes. She looks at Briar and me hesitantly then begins to speak.

"In our tests we conducted several months ago, the book only stays within our possession outside of the bookstore for three days. Then, it disappears, reappearing back on a shelf somewhere in the store. In random places. In order to keep it from jumping to random shelf locations, we have tried to hide it in the store to keep it safe. We're afraid of it getting bought by someone and accidentally destroyed."

"Why didn't you tell us this a while ago?" I ask, frowning at Sam who just points accusingly at Naomi.

"And whatever happened to no secrets and lies?" Briar says, looking equally hurt. I swivel to Anna who just shrugs. Of course she knew, too.

"We are telling them now. Anything you want to know, we'll tell you. These were all things we kept to ourselves simply because it is odd and connected to Breezewood," Naomi says quickly.

"Under Joel's leadership, we have kept them hidden. Now, since you are a part of the group, we'll tell you all we can." Anna turns to me and folds her hands under her chin. Sam nods and begins swinging a hand in the air as he talks.

"We are a team, and in order to save Breezewood and protect our world from whatever the king has planned, we need to know our assets." I lean back in my chair, still not convinced that they are telling the entirety of their knowledge.

Anna stands next and addresses the room. "We've been keeping secrets for a long time and trying to appear like normal young adults living in a small Alaskan town, but the truth is, we are tired of keeping secrets. We wish the world could know that another world besides ours exists and that there are people there like us but different. But the secrets have to stay between us. It's too risky to let the world know."

"There's a whole other culture, a whole different nature system and, dare I say, magic system. We don't know a lot about Breezewood, but we do know that something is desperately wrong with it. Wystan told us that the nights are getting colder and darker this winter but it has yet to snow. Harvest should have been yesterday according to what he told us, and that is when the king provides food for his people since they are unable to grow their own." Naomi glances down at a small notebook.

Orin's chair squeaks. "Wystan said the food is getting scarcer in the castle storeroom. They rely entirely on the king to provide them with a bounty for the coming year. He never detailed to me why they can't grow or hunt their own food, but for some reason, it is a problem."

"So we are trying to solve this other world's problems, too?" I ask, looking over the group but avoiding Briar. Her nearness sends ripples of heat up my arms.

"We feel obligated to help, especially when we've grown attached to the place. We've made friends there, and well, the culture there is entirely different. More relationship-focused. It's something our culture in our own world lacks." Naomi slides her notebook across the table to me. I reach for it, scanning the neat handwriting taking up nearly every line on the page. I turn the page and see it is just as crowded as the first one. It's packed full of observations on Breezewood wildlife, flora, and culture. I want to dive in and read through it all right now, but I know there are other things we all need to discuss.

"I hear what you all are saying, and while I don't fully agree and understand yet, I am willing to work with you. For now, we need a plan of action."

"First off, no one goes into Breezewood until we figure out how to rescue Joel and secure this homeless man spy."

"And figure out what August is up to as well as what Andrew knows," I add, looking at Briar.

She has been silent most of this time but finally speaks up. "And figure out how to get this truth pearl removed." She looks at me for a moment, then her eyes are on Naomi who sighs.

"Yes, and that," Naomi walks around the table and reaches for her notebook. I watch as she turns several pages then points with a finger to one of the sections. "Read this. It explains what we know about what truth pearls are and what they do. Briar got one while she was in Breezewood and is now stuck with it."

I skim the section and nod, a bit weirded out, but what else is new with my life?

Truth Pearl

Magic imbued precious stone harnessing the power of truth to the creator. Truth pearls are attached beneath a person's tongue by unknown means and can absorb any information the host learns. Whoever has one attached to their tongue is forced to tell the truth while touched by the creator. Case, the king of Breezewood.
Side effects, unknown. Complete origin, unknown. Permanence, unknown.

Sam leans in. "We should all get home before our families and friends outside of this circle start to worry about us. We'll construct a plan tomorrow via encrypted chat. We can't risk any high-level tech companies getting wind of Breezewood, so right now, all our messages need to be worded in such a way that it sounds like a bunch of teenagers playing *Dungeons and Dragons* in their parents' basement."

"Our normal group chat already sounds like that and we don't even participate in the game," Cedric says.

"Good, then it shouldn't be hard." Sam looks us all in the face. "So, adjourn?"

"Adjourn," Naomi agrees, and we all rise from our seats and shuffle towards the door. After we descend the spiral staircase that wraps down the bookcase walls of the lighthouse, we go to pick up our phones. Mine, Anna's, and Joel's are now charged thanks to Sam's plethora of tech gear and extra cords. As soon as I pick up mine, I see that there are three missed calls and a text from August. I show the screen to Anna who looks at me with wide eyes.

"Call him back?"

"I'm going to. Everyone be quiet." I hit the call button and immediately put it on speaker. If he has anything to say, I want the rest of my classmates, or *team*, to hear it. The call dials, and we wait in anticipation for the other end to answer. Just as the last ring is in sequence, the call clicks and muffled sounds come from the other end.

"Hello? Peter? Peter, are you there?"

"Yes, hi," I say, a serious tone to my voice.

"I gotta tell you something. You aren't going to believe me, but I need you to listen closely." I can practically feel the anticipation growing in my classmates as the silence between August's words and my own stretch for a few seconds.

"Try me."

"If you see someone that looks like me in Homer, I need you to disregard it."

"What?" I'm taken aback. Anna looks at Sam whose eyebrows knit together. He quickly whips out his phone and begins recording the rest of our call.

"That bookstore gig you got to build the escape room in? I need you to begin construction right away. I'll pay for it regardless of whatever sponsors you get. Whatever you do, don't engage me. I just need you to build the escape room."

"But wha—" The phone call drops, and I'm left with a sinking feeling in my gut. August didn't sound like himself. In fact, he sounded afraid. If he was the one in Breezewood, would he be able to call me?

And if he wasn't, then who was it that looked exactly like him?

Seventeen

BRIAR

I thought for certain that when Peter and Anna were coming through the portal, they were someone else. I was sure I saw the outline of the king and a Reacher at his right. But instead, sweet relief took hold of me and the pearl beneath my tongue grew warm again as soon as friends emerged. I blink. Did it grow cold when the portal opened? Did it somehow know when the portal opened and want to go back to Breezewood? Did it make me see things that weren't actually there?

Now, seated back at home, still no call from Andrew, I give Libby a scratch under the chin.

The air of Homer has turned from a drizzly wet into an icy cold. The roads are slick, and frost is beginning to fringe the trees like lace. With my coastal town heading into winter and the days till Thanksgiving nearing, I decide to clean the house to pass the time.

It's something that I find particular joy in doing when nobody is home.

I put on some calming piano music, grab the broom, and begin working on the floors. Earlier this morning, I made a batch of sourdough cinnamon rolls. The yeasty cinnamon smell still lingers in the kitchen. I glance at the recipe card that I'd sandwiched with a magnet to the fridge and pause to pull it down.

Sourdough Cinnamon Rolls

- 1/2 sourdough starter, bubbly and active

- 1/2 cup water

- 4 cups all-purpose flour

- 1/2 cup melted coconut oil

- 1/2 cup honey

- 2 eggs

- 1 teaspoon baking soda

- 1 teaspoon baking powder

- 1/2 teaspoon salt

Cinnamon Sugar Filling

- 1/2 cup softened butter

- 1 cup brown sugar

- 2 tablespoons cinnamon

Cream Cheese Topping:
- 6 ounces cream cheese

- 1/2 cup heavy cream

- 1/2 cup maple syrup or honey

- 2 teaspoons vanilla extract

I gently tuck it into Mom's recipe card box, immediately pinching a sweet section of roll into my mouth before continuing my sweeping.

My family should get home fairly soon. They are scheduled to fly in next week, two days before Thanksgiving. Already, so much has happened since their departure, and I still don't know how I'm going to explain the craziness when they return. The pearl beneath my tongue is only part of the problem.

A million things fill my mind—Peter, *the* book in the bookstore, Wystan's injuries, Joel's life, the homeless riddle man, my classmates, family, Thanksgiving. The list goes on. How will I ever return to normal life after all that I've experienced? *And still have yet to experience...*

My phone buzzes with the special notification I gave to the encrypted group chat: an owl hoot. It reminds me of Auriol.

Already, the chat has been blowing up with hypothetical ideas disguised as a game to cover up what's really going on.

Sam: I hereby call to order the league of adventurers. Cast your characters and choose your weapons.

Naomi: I'll be a cleric. I'll bring a scroll detailing the map of our destination, a dagger, and a vial of sleeping powder.

Cedric: Myself. My bare fists and a pocket knife.

Naomi: *eye roll emoji*

Orin: I'll be an elf ranger. I'll have a bow and will escort our company to the destination.

Cedric: Cue the Christmas music.

Orin: Not that kind of elf.

Anna: I'll be a Cleric as well. I'm still thinking about the weapon part.

Peter: I'll be a monk. I'm with Cedric on the pocket knife thing. How do you even play this game?

Briar: I guess I'll be a bard with a mandolin. Can that be a weapon if need be? I'm so lost.

Cedric: Anything can be a weapon.

Sam: If the adventurers are ready, we need to discuss who will be going first. Then, I'll narrate the first scene.

Naomi: Briar shouldn't go first. The bard needs to be kept alive to keep up morale.

Peter: I second this.

Sam: Noted.

Cedric: Orin should go first and clear the way for the rest of us.

Orin: I volunteer.

*Cedric: *Mocking jay gif**

*Naomi: *unamused face emoji**

No one has any true plans yet on how to get the pearl removed, rescue Joel, and keep our world safe, but they are trying, despite how chaotic it is becoming. Talking in code via text is challenging with a group of people.

The whole team has discussed going into Breezewood on a covert mission to rescue Joel and return, but I'm not allowed in. My pearl attracts Reachers, and if I'm found alive there, the king would want me in his presence so he might extract information from me about our world. And I don't have a key to give him. Either way, I'm dead. The king sent me out of the castle as a death sentence, Wystan stating that he knew Reachers would run me down. Whatever grudge the ruler of Breezewood has against us, he's not against getting rid of us on account of it.

But we really don't have time to spare on making a decision about Breezewood. Joel's life is at stake and maybe mine. We don't know what this pearl will do to me long-term. Will it erase my memories? Disappear? Anything is probable at this point. If you found a literal portal of creatures and magic in your town's local bookstore, I think we'd both agree that anything could happen.

My phone dings, pulling me from my thoughts. Instead of the group chat owl hoot, it's a default text tone. I pause in my sweeping and pull my phone out of my pocket. Stunned, I hover my finger over a text bubble from Peter's number. He texted only me, not the group chat. I set the broom aside and slump to a chair at the table.

> Peter: Hey, can we talk? And no, it's not about the 'game'. I know we haven't in a while. I wanted to talk in person at the lighthouse but didn't want to embarass you in front of everyone.

I blink. He wants to talk? About what? I set a hand on my face, scrunching my fingers into my hair. My heart is beating wildly while my mind is telling me to ignore his message. He lost his chance at being friends or something more by simply never contacting me after graduation. If we were truly 'just friends' then we would have been friends. Friends hang out and share hard life stuff together. I'm not sure what hurt worse, the rejection of my feelings or his three years of silence.

I type up a message, hovering my finger over the screen. Then, I hit send,

> Briar: I'm not sure there's anything to talk about besides the 'game.'

A text bubble from him pops up showing that he's typing. Then it disappears. Then it reappears. What's he over thinking about?

> Peter: For starters, we could talk about old times.

I'm so confused. Why now? I'd resolved to move on, to turn the page and live my life instead of waiting and hoping something like this would happen. Now that something is happening, I don't know what to do.

> Briar: I'm surprised you'd want to talk about the far ago past and not the exciting present and future.

> Peter: Three plus years isn't what I would call a long time into the past. And we'll have plenty of time to discuss the present and future. I want to know what you've been up to since graduation.

> *Briar: Not much. I went to college for a bit then came home. Mostly been reading and writing to pass the time.*

> *Peter: Sounds peaceful. What do you write about?*

> *Briar: Mainly fiction. Nothing is published yet but someday, I'll hold one of my own books in my hands.*

> *Peter: I have no doubt you'll reach that goal.*

I don't give another reply. I'm not sure what I want to do about Peter right now. I pickup the broom again, my phone now in my back pocket.

When I finish sweeping the kitchen, I grab a rag from under the kitchen sink, shooing Herbert out of the way as he tries to nestle into the towels. Rag in hand, I head to the living room to dust. The house isn't particularly dirty—it just needs to be shined up a bit.

I begin pulling books off of my family's living room shelf and feel a sneeze as dust spins into the air at my touch. Apparently, this area of the living room hasn't been disturbed for a while. I run the rag over the shelf and replace books in the clean areas. As I pass the rag over the last section and start to replace the book, I stop. In my hands is a small leather notebook that floods my mind with nostalgia. My old writing notebook. Why is it on the living room shelf?

I set the rag down and step to the sofa where I sit and open the cover. Inconsistent handwriting, a mix between print and cursive, sprawls across delicately lined pages. I hold in a groan as I scan my tween writing of magic, horses, and dramatic medieval fight scenes.

They galloped fiercely across the fields, sunshine and starlight and moonlight tossing their manes. Neigh! Neigh! They called and ran faster and faster. They were the fastest horses in whole wide world.

I stick out my tongue in embarrassment. Half of me really despises the writing, but the other half knows that this is evidence of my craft's beginnings, proof that I started somewhere and have something to show for improvement. Come to think of it, I have more of these writing notebooks in my room. This one should be with them, not down here where any visitor can pluck it from the shelf and be forever scarred by talking horses and their riders.

I tuck it under my arm and head to my room. Somewhere on my own bookshelf are six other journals filled to the brim with stories. I scan my own collection and find the journals. I pull them all off, curious as to their exact contents. It's been years since I read through them.

I want to see if I can remember which order they go in. Some have dates written in the page corners in curly letters with heart dots while others don't. I start with the first one off my shelf, scanning through it, sure that if anyone saw my face right now that they would laugh. My eyebrows raise at the end of most sentences and my mouth pulls into a cringey smile then a frown.

As I continue to read, I'm given pause by some of my sentences. Several things begin to set my face into one of curiosity and disbelief. There, printed in clear letters with the year I turned nine at the top of the page, is the word *Breezewood*. My blood goes a little cold at that.

I wrote this story, if you can call it that. This story was drafted long before any of this crazy stuff ever happened. Before I even set foot in the bookstore.

I read faster, my mouth in a straight line. A plot thread that mentions a portal sticks out to me and I turn the page. Tiny plot points are sprinkled in the pages, many of which I'm incredibly familiar with. I reach the end of the journal after skimming and open another, this one without a date at the top. With one glance, I know that this is a later journal, maybe when I was twelve? I skim some more and find another mention of portals, a bookstore, and Breezewood. Each journal, however, is a completely different story or filled with many short stories that, if I'm remembering correctly, are in no way supposed to be connected to each other. Each story has their own plot, but in every single one, I'm finding things that remind me of what I've experienced recently. Traveling through a portal, talking with strangers, jumping off cliffs, and characters wearing long green princess dresses. My eyes slide over to the gown on my dresser. It's still there, the constant reminder of my sanity.

I lay out all seven of my journals and order them from oldest to newest across my bed, determined to find something, anything, that explains what is going on. The book in the bookstore is strangely similar to my writings. Not word for word or even prose-related, but the plot threads and some specific details are so similar.

I scan the first page of each journal and find on all of them something significant that is connected to my current life. A bookstore. A portal. The name Breezewood. Wolves. Owls. Strange men with armor. And of course, an evil king. Why are my writings so close to the actual fairy tale book, the myths about Breezewood, the book that we try to keep secret? Why am *I* so connected to all of this?

The thing that strikes me the most is a short paragraph I wrote in one of my journals. I reread it again just to make sure I'm not imagining things.

Of all the places where love and fairy tale magic could be found, a bookstore is probably one of the best. The fair heroine sighs dreamily, her thoughts wholly on her true love. She whispers softly, just enough that the wind can hear her. What if we met in a bookstore?

That last sentence, what if we met in a bookstore, is the phrase used to open the portal.

I may not have the exact answer, but it's close enough. That fairy tale book in the shop is not written by me but somehow, it's connected to my writing by magic. It has to be. Nothing else makes sense. If that's the case, then I'm probably responsible for creating the portal to Breezewood. Not Breezewood itself, just the portal. Breezewood is far too real and complicated for that.

I might be crazy, but I have another thought. One that Peter and the rest of the group might just kill me for.

I get off my bed and run my fingers over the green fabric of the Breezewood dress, an ache forming in my heart. I can't explain it, but I want to go back.

If no one will go to rescue Joel or Wystan, who might be sentenced to death for helping me, what will happen to them? To Breezewood? To our world?

My crazy thought springs to my mind again, and I can't help but ponder it a moment more. Since the myth book is connected to the portal, what happens if I rip the sentence page out of the book and bring the entire book into Breezewood? Will tearing the page and bringing the book seal me inside Breezewood and block anyone from entering or exiting? There's only one way to find out.

I quickly grab a sheet of lined paper and scribble my thoughts down onto it. All of my thoughts. What happened to me years ago, the existence of my classmates' secret group, the confidentiality signature, my journey through the portal, and what I plan to do. On another paper, I do my best to write a confessional note to Peter. I tell him how I felt about him during school, at graduation, and the hurt he caused me. At the end, I manage to write that I forgive him and mention that if things had worked out differently, we might have been better friends. On another page, I write a goodbye note to my family. Just in case I'm never seen again.

I carefully seal the notes in an envelope, write Jen's name on it, and nestle it on my bed among the journals. Immediately, I type her a text.

> *Jen, can you check on the cats tonight and tomorrow? I'm not exactly sure how long I'll be gone. I had something come up and I need your help. There are cinnamon rolls on the counter. Leaving my phone at home. Check my bedroom.*

My text sounds a bit eerie, but I don't have the heart to rewrite it. Any more time alone with my thoughts and I'll psych myself out of this plan. I have to see if it will work.

Jen will speed over here as soon as she gets my text and my chance will be gone. I set my phone on the bed, the text bubble still waiting for me to hit send.

Deftly, I stuff a bag with the green dress and heave a large sigh. I don't know if this is goodbye, but in case it is, I give each of the cats a warm hug and pet over the ears. My stomach coils with uncertainty and emotion as I hit the send button. Leaving my phone behind, I make my way down the stairs. I throw on a warm jacket and slip on some boots. With the dress bag under my arm, I leave the house. The front door is locked. I know Jen has her own spare key for my family's home. She'll let herself in and everything will be fine.

Cold air wafts into my lungs. I hurry away from the house, feeling the anticipation that Jen will arrive any moment and stop me in my tracks.

All it would take is Andrew being at the bookstore for my plan to fail. Since he never called me, I highly doubt he is there. Sure enough, his car is nowhere in sight. Instead, the same unknown car from yesterday is parked in front of the store. If it belongs to the August guy who called Peter yesterday, I'd be willing to believe he's still in Breezewood since the car is still here. Whatever is going on, I plan to unearth all of it.

I try the handle to the front of the store. It's still unlocked. I step inside and call out.

"Hello? Is anyone here?" No answer. I know this is unwise, walking into work without permission and with an unknown car parked in front. All of my friends and family would persuade me to forgo this mission, but the pearl beneath my tongue and the lives of other friends drive me forward. Even still, I grab a medium weighted book from a shelf as a weapon and walk carefully towards the stairs. The wooden floor creaks like bones beneath my weight and the dusty air makes my throat constrict for a sneeze.

When I reach the upper room, I lower the book in my hands. Silence. Only the sound of my own shoes. I drop my guard and cross the room to where the hidden book is. I withdraw it from behind the shelf and trade it for the one I'd picked up downstairs. I begin to thumb through it, this book that is so similar to my journals. Without even trying, the portal key words cross my mind, and I count to sixteen seconds. The portal expands on the dot, and

I've already found the page in the tome I want. I hesitate, the page firmly in my hands. Dare I do it? I let the hum of the portal spur me on. How do I know what will happen if I don't try? I do it, the paper ripping from the spine with ease. The sensation of tearing the page nearly causes physical pain to my bookish heart. I never want to have to do that again.

I read the sentence on the page one more time just to be sure, then I crumple the page in my fist, my dress bag still slung over one shoulder. I grab the entire book and slip it into my bag. As I make the plunge into the portal, the hairs on the back of my neck raise up like spikes, and the meaty closure of a hand circles my arm. I squeal and leap forward, farther into the portal, and wrench my arm free from the grasp as if poison has touched me. But it's too late, for whatever held me momentarily has successfully followed me in. I hit the ground running as soon as I'm free from the grip. I risk a glance backwards, my feet still moving at a lightning pace. A man in a long brown robe clasps his hands gleefully together then pauses to fix me with a stare that turns my head back in the direction I'm running. I brave one last look. He hasn't moved, but I'm positive something else has. Someone else is behind him, coming through the portal. When the man turns, he begins to fight with the figure just outside the portal. I don't want to stick around to get in the middle of it. I weave into the trees and leave it all behind.

My heart races. The pearl beneath my tongue is warm, but there is a strange pulsing sensation to it, as if my heartbeat is causing it to move, but they aren't in sync. My fingers and knees shake but I keep running. It is full daylight here, though white and gray clouds dilute the light. Not a hint of blue sky can be seen.

I need to get to the cliff and find a way down. I need to find Breezewood Castle and see if Joel is okay. I need to get this pearl taken from me.

When my feet finally reach the end of the tree line and the cliff edge looms before me, I stop to catch my breath. The air and landscape look and feel different since my last visit. I scan the forest and horizon beyond. It is colder, and far in the distance, a fringe of white has begun to creep over the trees. Winter? It isn't quite cold enough now that I need a full blown winter coat, but the air could be described as thinner and cooler since my last visit.

Before I even have a chance to contemplate an escape route down, I hear the yaps and snarls of creatures I've seen before. Stone against stone. Metal against metal. I've heard it once in the dark, moments before I was lifted into the sky by Wystan and Auriol and during the last scene before I made it home through the portal.

As the sounds grow stronger, an intense cold consumes my hand that holds the crumpled paper. Then, my dress bag becomes lighter. I slide it off my shoulder and find that the book has disappeared. No, not disappeared, *disintegrated*. I dump out the bag, and the dress flops to the ground followed by a swirl of torn paper. I open my other hand, the cold fading as I retract my fingers. To my astonishment, the crumpled page has turned to white ash and in its place are tiny, faint letters of ink. The book and page are gone, and all that's left is the important part, the keyword sentence now permanently tattooed to my palm. I don't know what this means, but I know it isn't good.

In the fear of my new discovery, the Reachers breach the treeline at a dead run. There are five, six-legged wolf-like creatures coming at me from several angles. The only way of escape is down, or rather, *off*, then down. I have no choice but to slide over the edge. I contemplate a dramatic leap, but I don't have to think long to make it happen. I step off the edge and release a scream. There isn't a ledge to catch me, and I'm falling, my world in slow motion. It's a real fear this time. My previous adventure here, I had thought this all a dream, but now I know it's real. With the last few hundred feet approaching quickly, I catch my breath enough to let loose the only name I can associate with saving me from a fall like this: *"Wystan!"*

Eighteen

PETER

I run my hands over the many pages of notes and diagrams I've set aside for building the escape room. Musical puzzles, Alaskan-themed word and picture riddles, and intricate drawings of things I'd like to insert into the room—secret compartments, codes, and timed release capsules for clues. With August's latest phone call, I'm on the edge of my seat. What could possibly be wrong? He knows something I don't, and I'm hesitant to go through with the escape room because of all the strangeness, but he hasn't steered me wrong before. Even more concrete, I found several thousand dollars directly deposited into my account this morning. He really did what he said he was going to do. He wants me to get this escape room built.

Upon waking, I had two sponsors reach out to me to let me know that they would donate some building supplies to the project, and another offered a few hundred dollars in support. Not bad, especially with August's generous advance. I'd be able to get all the supplies I needed for construction to begin.

There has been zero word from Andrew, the owner of the bookstore. I, Briar, or any of the other classmates haven't seen him or his car since yesterday. It's worrisome, even though I am suspicious of the guy. He must be somehow connected to August.

I slide the stack of notes and plans into a folder and tuck it beneath my arm, my mind ticking with thoughts about the short conversation Briar and I had over text recently. While I highly dislike texting about emotionally charged subjects, it seemed the only good communication option in the moment. I guess I could have called, but I wasn't brave enough. Why didn't I just call her? Briar didn't seem too excited to talk with me based on her responses. I can't help but believe that she's moved on from me. If that's true, then I need to call her and talk with her in person. I need to know if she's truly out of my life. Grabbing a jacket from the back of my room door, I sling it over my shoulder.

Anna and I made it home last night after the lighthouse, telling Mom and Dad that we decided to hold off on camping. It had frosted overnight, and paired with the uncertainty involving the bookstore, we decided it was best to wait. Joel in trouble or not, we really didn't have a solid plan yet. And none of us, well, except maybe Anna, were willing to take a suicide mission unless absolutely necessary.

I make my way downstairs to the kitchen and find Dad, Mom, and Anna talking cordially over coffee and toast.

"I'll do extra butter..." Anna stops and looks up at me. "Just in time. We were just now discussing our Thanksgiving plans. The cousins have the contest already planned out."

"You mean they know they are going to lose?" I say with a smirk, walking to the coffee maker.

"Hey now, they might have a chance. When was the last time you baked anything?" my dad says, taking a swig from his cup. My mom just smiles, holding her mug in both hands, soaking in the warmth of the morning.

"Like... a year ago. But I've done way more important things than baking pies." I look to Anna who gives me a wry smile. I pour myself a cup, the caffeinated steam sending a jolt of energy through my body as I tip the mug to my lips.

"Filling pages and pages with chicken scratch is hardly important. Not unless you plan to actually bring it into fruition," Anna says sarcastically.

"As a matter of fact, that's where I'm headed to today. Andrew hasn't answered his phone, but I have supplies to buy regardless. I'm starting construction."

"Can I come?" Anna sits straight up in her chair as if perfect posture will persuade me to say yes.

"Later. I'll let you know when it's time to test it out. For now, I need quiet to concentrate." I give her a nod, hoping she understands. The squint of her eyes says she's disappointed, but I know she'll respect me. She might text me later and ask if it's done yet, but she'll let me be. Her posture droops and she resigns to take a sip of her own coffee.

"Text me if you need anything," she quips into her cup.

"If I need anything, I'll be sure to let you know."

I set my mug down on the edge of the counter and double check my papers. Everything is in order. Now to buy the supplies.

The back of Dad's work truck is filled with plywood, paint, chains, rope, brackets, screws, and all kinds of tools as I pull into the book-shop parking lot. A successful supply trip sets me in a good mood, and I hop out of the truck, eager to begin. I've been dreaming of this moment for so long. All my ideas will finally be reality, and if it turns out, I might just get to do this for a living.

With no sign of Andrew still, I shake my head and begin unload-ing the boxes of screws. When I make it through the front door, I hear a shuffle upstairs, as if someone is sliding a heavy foot across the wooden floor. No one, except the same car from yesterday, is here. I set the screws and screwdriver down and run up the stairs. As soon as I breach the upper room, I gasp. The portal is open, and I catch the long brown robe of a familiar figure slide into the portal. Heart pounding, I make the split second decision to reach for my phone and text the chat. As soon as I lift it from my pocket, it rings with Briar's caller ID. I set it to my ear in a flash. The female voice on the other end is not familiar but what she says is.

"Peter? Is this Peter?"

"Yes, yes, it is."

"Oh good. Please, you have to help. I'm Briar's cousin, Jen. Briar said she's going into a place called Breezewood? You have to help. Her cryptic note makes me afraid for her life!" The panic in Jen's voice speeds up my heart.

My throat goes dry and my eyes get a little blurry. Briar is in Breezewood? Or she's going to? Why is her phone not with her? I can't take the risk of not going in after her. She shouldn't be there.

"Are you there?" Jen asks.

"Yes, please let my friends know what's going on. Tell them... I'm going through." I don't waste any time and hang up, sliding my phone across the floor. I enter the portal just as it begins to collapse. My escape room is going to have to wait.

On the other side, I find the man in the robe standing several feet away from the portal. The man who scared Anna and I. He's distracted, watching something in the distance. He hasn't seen or heard me yet, so I move to the side and my eyes find what he's watching—a figure with rusty-colored hair running from the clearing and dodging trees. Briar. My heart quickens, and I take a step back. A dry twig snaps beneath my feet and I freeze. The man turns in a flash, and his face changes from one of relief to a reddening fury.

"Worlders don't belong in Breezewood."

I don't know what to say, my throat dry with shock. I back up farther. The man lifts a fist into the air. It shakes violently as if he's having trouble controlling his limbs, and his anger for that matter. He's not elderly, but he's at least in his fifties. I shake my head.

"Please, I mean no harm."

"Worlders bow before the king." He's out of his mind. I dodge the first blow, tripping to the ground in my dash of speed. Before I can scramble to my feet, the man has my coat in one hand, his grip like iron. I try to free myself, but he twists the coat tighter in his fist.

"I don't...want...to hurt...you." His voice sounds forced and he's short of breath. He raises a fist and I throw my hands in front of my face. I release a kick to his leg and he stumbles, but his hand still grips my coat. Before I can kick again, the man over me releases his grip as another arm is wound tight around his neck. I leap to my feet and put some space between us.

"Atlas, you've had your fun. No more!" I hear August say. He's got an arm around the robed man's neck, the other steadying him so he doesn't fall over.

Atlas grunts. August releases the man and waits till he's calm. August folds his arms across his chest. The two men stare each other down as if they have a score to settle but are choosing to not do it in front of me. If this Atlas guy is a spy for the king, how on earth does he know August?

"August..." I say, pleased he's come to my rescue but utterly confused.

"Peter, you shouldn't be here." August's voice is thick with authority, but I hear a familiar panic in his words. Is this the August who called me on the phone yesterday? Or is this the August I was told not to trust?

"I know I shouldn't be, but Briar... She's here! And she has a truth pearl. The king wants her dead." I look in the direction I saw her running. She must have reached the cliff edge by now.

"She's been marked by the king." Atlas says, face settling into a stony sneer. He continues to give me a dark look after August's tells him to leave me alone again.

A scream breaks through all my thoughts.

It's Briar. I shake my head towards August and Atlas, words failing me as I dash towards the cliff. A sickening feeling creeps into my gut, knowing just how much danger she is in. What horror will I see when I reach the cliff edge?

The pounding of feet echoes from behind me.

"Peter! Stop!" August yells. I break the tree line and skid to a halt at the sight of wolf-like creatures teeming on the cliff edge. Stone against stone, metal against metal. Six-legged beasts, four back legs and two fronts. Their bodies are covered with spines like that of porcupines, only made entirely of stone.

"Reachers!" Atlas shrieks.

August grabs my arm. "Peter, get away from here. Atlas also has a truth pearl. He'll attract the beasts just as much as Briar."

I obey, and separate from them. August pulls Atlas back the way we'd come. Slowly, Reachers begin turning around. One by one, their pawing and staring over the cliff edge is instead turned on August and Atlas. I edge away from them all, adrenaline coursing through me. I'm afraid to look over the cliff edge, afraid to see

Briar. But I'm also afraid for August and Atlas. They have no weapons, no way of escape. There's no chance they'll make it back to the portal in time. Seven Reachers, now with folded back ears, release snarls.

"Brother... Don't let them kill me!" Atlas yells. August stands in front of him, continuing to push him away from the beasts. I keep creeping towards the cliff's edge, and when I reach it, I look down. Trees. Rocks. No sign of Briar.

Thwack! Thwack!

Howls of pain erupt from two of the creatures. I snap my head up to catch a glimpse of arrow bolts protruding from the hearts of two Reachers. They stumble to their haunches.

August swivels his head, searching the surroundings like a hawk. I follow his example, looking for a source to the bolts. The Reachers grow tense at the sight of their fallen kind. Some perk their ears and noses in one direction, snarl towards August and Atlas, then edge backwards. I swallow a lump forming in my throat, hands and knees shaking with adrenaline.

Another bolt cuts through the air and slams into the Reacher closest to August. The creature yelps and falls like the others. A male voice booms from the shivering woods, the air echoing with his warning.

"Leave this place! Go back from whence you came!"

I hold my ground, looking for the assassin and any sign of Briar.

The last few remaining Reachers turn to their fallen comrades and wrench out the diamond-tipped arrows, eating the arrowheads with one snap. A jolt of energy washes through their bodies, lighting up the stone spikes in a vein-like blue grid. Then they race off into the forest with renewed vigor, away from the portal. Another arrow whizzes through the air and slams into the ground near August and Atlas. They jerk back in surprise. The voice booms again.

"I said, leave this place!'

August locks eyes with me, nods once, then turns, pulling a muttering Atlas with him in a half-jog. I don't know what to make of it. I can't leave Briar here, but I don't feel like getting stuck with an arrow. My choice is made when another slices through the topsoil near my foot. I stagger away from it, whipping my head towards the cliff for one last look. No Briar. I want to yell out her name, ask if she's okay. When another arrow zings over my head, I hurtle myself towards the trees in the direction of the portal. Before I'm out of range of the cliff, I turn and release my pent-up panic. I yell her name. It spills over the cliff edge and cascades to the forest below, bouncing over the treetops. I turn and run to the portal.

I have no weapons and no plan. Already, the squeezing pain of loss and fear is wrapping its hold on my heart. I never got to tell her how I feel; what I've been thinking about for years is on the tip of my tongue. If I could see her one more time, I'd confess all the things on my heart and mind. I'll call her. *Just let her be alive.*

When the portal site appears, I slow my pace. August and Atlas are circling around where the portal should open. I recite the sentence over in my mind, waiting the sixteen seconds. Nothing. What has happened? I rush forward, reciting the sentence over and over, willing it to work. Nothing.

"August? What's going on?"

"It won't open. Finally, for the first time since I could remember, a gateway is untethered." August just stares at the place, the cutout in the trees where the portal should be, unmoving.

"You mean... It isn't going to open?" Surely this is temporary?

"Not by us," he says grimly, finally turning to look me in the eye. The laughter and twinkle I remember from working with him is distant.

Atlas melts into a stony slump, gripping his arms tightly about himself. He darts his eyes to the trees all around us, obviously watching for Reachers. I've never seen a grown man so helpless.

August paces back and forth, hands on his hips. Then he crosses his arms. "I can't say I'm mad. I wanted this to happen. Breezewood needed the gateway closed. Your escape room was going to be the cover we needed to keep the entry a secret until we could close it off. Seems it is closed for the time being."

"Wait... You knew about Breezewood? Before I came back to Homer?"

"I've known about Breezewood since I was born. I'm from here." August holds onto my shocked eyes before looking away and continuing to pace.

"But the phone call..."

"It was the real me. I didn't know if you knew about Breezewood and wanted to make you believe this was all fake, just in case you were suspicious. Now, seeing you here, I know you are in on the secret." I want to believe August's words, but he's a puzzle master.

He's smarter than this. Or maybe, this secret is too far out of his hands. I know it is out of mine and my classmates'.

"Hardly. I've only been here three times before. This is my fourth, and I haven't even made it past the cliff."

"Most don't." He says it so matter-of-factly that I falter in my next words.

"Tell me, who are you really? And him?" I point to Atlas who avoids any eye contact.

August sighs. "We can't stay here. Unfed Reachers will smell the pearl on Atlas and find us."

"We can't go back to the cliff edge either. Are we just going to ignore that someone tried to kill us?" I say, holding back sharp words. My chest and head simmer with unreleased heat. I want to yell at August for keeping secrets, but I can't blame him entirely. Yet I'm still furious that he didn't let me know about this place sooner. I could have protected Briar from coming here. She could be the one with an arrow through the chest right now or a Reacher at her throat or...

"I'm fairly certain I know who was responsible. Breezewood has night patrols who skirt the cliff and hunt Reachers, as well as try and dissuade other people from coming onto our lands. Not to mention, Breezewood is known for using diamond-tipped arrows. The assailant is undoubtedly from Breezewood Castle."

"Do you think they've gone?"

"They won't stay long. Patrols typically pass through an area. They look mostly for Reachers. Since they were able to disperse a few, they'll probably move along to find the ones that escaped. As far as we understand, Reachers do not travel beyond the great river that separates Breezewood's territory from the rest of the realms' kingdoms. Night patrols will stay within Breezewood's boundary and hunt for the night then return to the castle."

My brain perks up at the mention of other kingdoms and at the words *our lands*. Breezewood isn't the only people group here? I swivel to take in Atlas's features. There isn't anything striking about him. No pointed ears or enormously obvious alien-like features. Same with August. They look normal.

"To answer one of your other questions, Atlas is my brother. He's been banished from Breezewood for the past twelve years for befriending a Worlder. He was in line for the throne before our other brother, Alder, banished him. I only realized just recently that Atlas somehow made it to the modern world." August lets the words drop like hot stones. Finally, some answers.

"You are all brothers?" The edges of my voice are hoarse with surprise. Pieces of the puzzle begin to fall into place. The Breezewood king we heard so much about had a name: Alder.

"Unfortunately, yes." August nods, sliding a hand to his jaw and running it over dark stubble. Cold, cloudy light filters in through the trees, and I wipe a stray hair off my forehead. No sign of Reachers yet, but the thought of them sneaking up on us lingers in the back of my mind.

"He isn't a spy for the king, right?" Everything my classmates told me is swirling around in my brain. A spy meant danger for our realm.

"No, he's not a spy. At least, not by choice. Everyone who is banished is given a truth pearl, that which can only be removed by the king. The pearl is a spy device of sorts, whether the wearer wants it to be or not. I don't think Alder realized Atlas found his way into the modern realm."

"I have so many questions, but what happened to you guys? Why is Alder, the Breezewood king, against Worlders? And what is with the portals?"

August takes a deep breath and looks towards Atlas, then he spears me with a stare of icy blue. I hold it, eager for whatever information he's about to tell me.

"Ever since Alder took the throne, Breezewood has been placed under a shadow. We cannot grow food. We can't hunt. Nothing will grow for us period and nothing can be gathered or be stored for the future. It all turns to ash in our hands. Alder however is gifted with magic, or, so it would seem. The people have become fully reliant on him to keep them alive. He used a dark magic in order to gain power, placing a curse on the land to bring himself more control." August pauses to scan the perimeter, then continues. "One night out of each year, we have Harvest. Every Harvest, Alder turns the precious stones inside the mountain mines into food. The miners bring the stones to the treasury store room and Alder goes in alone, reemerging with the news that we have food to last the year until the next harvest. But every year since Alder's crowning, the food stores have been less. Only his closest advisors and myself know."

"So you are saying, Alder, the Breezewood king, isn't providing for his people on purpose? Or that he simply can't provide at all?"

"His magic is drying up and the stones within the mountain are dwindling. He can no longer provide. Reachers began to appear when Alder was made king. They come from the deep cave places. Some are able to squeeze through abandoned mine shafts and live in the mountains. They are formed from the stone of the mountain every time Alder uses his magic. They are wholly connected to whatever dark power Alder has been dabbling with."

"When did the Reachers start roaming outside of the caves?"

"As soon as precious gems from the cave walls were mined or satisfied, Reachers could smell the Worlders and traders from other lands carrying valuables. The Reachers learned that valuables sometimes cross into our land so they have chosen to roam the upper Breezewood grounds, seeking life sources."

"And with the gems and magic dwindling..."

"It's only a matter of time before Alder can't perform Harvest at all," August says with a heavy sigh. His broad shoulders are inside a woolen suit coat that is neatly buttoned in the front. If I saw him in my world right now, I'd say he was dressed up for a Sherlock Holmes themed escape room act.

"The Breezewood people will starve then." I let my gaze fall to the earth. This place was so weird yet so *real*.

"Without a cure for his magic or a break to the curse, yes." I let his words seep deep into my ears. Breezewood is in danger and it affects all who live here. Maybe even the Worlders who'd passed in by accident and had to stay. It is affecting me. It affects Joel. My friends. Breezewood matters.

But how had the king not found and gotten rid of the apparent missing Worlders who wandered into Breezewood already? More questions arise the deeper I think about it. Regardless of those questions, one remains the clearest in my mind.

How does August know so much?

Nineteen

BRIAR

My breath leaves my body in one swift jolt. The scream of Wystan's name is but an echo at the edges of my consciousness. My vision is blurry with tears spurred on by the cold air and the panic of my daring leap. I can't tell if I'm still falling or if I've hit the forest floor. I wheeze, air once more within me. Moving my hands, my fingers collide with warmth and softness. I've fallen onto something, that's for certain. Pain radiates across my shoulders and legs, reality finally setting in. I'm alive. I hear the whoosh of air past my ears, but my vision is too blurry to tell what direction I'm going. Then, I hear the familiar coo of a great bird. Auriol. I comprehend the feel of his soft feathers against my fingers and the beating of his heart against my palms. My vision clears enough to see that I'm alone on the back of the great owl. I turn to find the cliff disappearing as we fly farther away, gliding beneath the canopy of the trees. Auriol coos again, and I face forward, hugging the bird tighter. I would have surely died from a leap of that height had he not come to my rescue. I grimace, remembering my fearlessness the first time I'd neared the cliff edge. But even now, the thought of a quick death by leaping is more favorable than the teeth of animals.

"You saved me. But, where is Wystan?" I run a shaky hand across the pearly, white feathers. What have I done?

Auriol coos in response, but I don't speak owl. I look behind again, this time searching the forest floor. What if I knocked Wystan off when I landed on Auriol? A blush of embarrassment and mortification creeps up my face. But with no concrete answers, I settle lower onto Auriol's back and lean forward.

"Where are we going?" Grateful that I am far above any Reachers or other creatures bent on destroying me for a precious stone, I let my worries subside. For the moment. I move my shoulders; nothing is broken, but I'm positive there will be bruises.

Auriol continues to maneuver around the trees, the whoosh of cool air swirling around my ears. In the trailing distance, my name echoes over the majestic forest. It reverberates over the land like a memory. Part of me wants to turn back, sure that Wystan is close to death on the ground somewhere, my name escaping his lips as a final cry for help, but Auriol doesn't seem to be concerned. I'm probably being over dramatic. In my fear, I'm hearing things.

I must confess, I am incredibly afraid. Afraid of failing my mission in rescuing Joel and getting the pearl removed. Afraid of Reachers clawing their way to my throat. Afraid of the Breezewood king denying me any help. I have many things to fear. Despite the list of worries, the longer I cling to the back of Auriol, the more relaxed I become. Slowly, I slump farther into the feathers. With no cues to give Auriol to make him turn back, I settle to comply. Wherever he's taking me, I'm confident it's somewhere safe.

Still zipping through the forest just below the canopy, I nestle closer into Auriol's feathers. The air is much cooler the deeper we fly into the realm. It smells of winter and mystery, the kind like Narnia, only this one is a bit darker. The farther we cross into Breezewood, the heavier my mission weighs on me, but for the moment, I feel like I'm riding on a cloud.

Auriol takes a sharp turn and begins to ascend. We break the canopy and climb higher, just below the stretching gray sky. It is the farthest I've ever been above Breezewood.Wystan never took me this high. Ever so gently, Auriol tips his beak down towards the trees and we coast on a draft of wind.

Green foliage of aspen, birch, spruce, and alder stretch for miles. Towering mountains and rolling hills make up most of the landscape. Here and there, dots of purple and blue tell of meadows of flowers edged by glimmering streams or shining ponds. But on the horizon, the land is turning to winter. Not with snow, but with a silvery, gray frost. There are no hints of red and yellow leaves or the browning of autumn; it's either green or frozen. This wasn't here the last time that I can remember. Wystan did say Breezewood was heading into the winter months. And what was it he had mentioned about there being a Harvest in order to provide food?

Auriol turns his head back to look at me, and I stare into his big unblinking eyes. Then he dives. Even with my coat on, the wind cuts through my jacket as we descend. My hair streams out behind me, and I can't help but gasp. The rush of almost falling while still in the safety of warm feathers is unlike anything I've ever experienced. Auriol flies through a break in the tree canopy then slows to land on a large birch branch. A tree, possibly hundreds of years old, holds up our weight. Its trunk is covered in green and black fungus, the breadth of it as many as twenty young trees fused together. Still high above the ground, I do a quick scan of our surroundings. Moss and ferns carpet the forest along with the occasional fallen tree or bush. Even from this height, I spy clusters of white mushrooms at the bases of trees.

Auriol cocks his head to the side and looks up. I follow his gaze farther into the branches. My mouth goes wide. I missed it before, but there, secure in the clutches of wide limbs, is a treehouse. And not just any treehouse, one that is expertly camouflaged through detailed branch layering and woven leaves. Auriol turns in a circle, his back now facing the thickest part of the tree. A stairway of woven branches circles up towards the opening of the house, and I take it as a sign that it's time to dismount.

"Thank you, Auriol," I say, sliding off his back and finding firm footing on the branch. I give the great bird a gentle stroke on the wing. He ruffles his feathers, beginning to preen. I balance as best I can, stepping close to the trunk searching for a hand hold. I reach for the closest makeshift railing and put my trust in the stairway leading up into the treehouse. Each step is cut into a branch, circling up the tree. Woven willow and alder are securely lashed to the thicker branches using braided grass and bark. Broken-off birch branches poke through the railing to give off the illusion that the stairway is a part of the canopy, the result being a sturdy and cleverly camouflaged bridge in the treetops. I ascend it while marveling at the artistry. This is unlike anything I ever read in the *Magic Treehouse* books. This is more akin to *Rivendell* or *Lothlorien* architecture from Tolkien's works, the *Lord of the Rings,* but far less stately.

I'm almost to the opening of the treehouse when Auriol spreads his wings and dives off the branch, soaring back into the forest. While I'm watching his graceful dive, there's a blur of motion and I'm pulled inside the house by my right arm. As my eyes adjust to the new lighting, I'm confronted with a question.

"Briar, is it?" a woman asks. She stands before me after securing the door, arms crossed. Her eyebrows are raised in a quizzical expression. I recognize her from my last visit to Breezewood.

"Yes. But what are you doing here?" I can't remember her name. She was the girl who gave me the green dress. The dress I brought back with me in my bag.

"I should ask you the same." She steps past and walks farther inside the house. I follow her, taking in the insides of the secret hideout. Woodsy smells with touches of beeswax and mint fill my nose, along with the undeniable hint of warm bread. Light filters in from around the edges of the closed door, and on every wall, are shelves filled with glass bottles, parchments, dried herbs, books, pottery, and cloth material in varying colors. There's only one window to the home which is positioned to get a view of the outer stairway.

"I'm here to drop off supplies and make sure the stock is in order. Wystan was out on patrol and it was my turn to keep watch on the hideout tonight while he's away. Why did you show up on Auriol in his place?" She looks at me as if I've done something terribly wrong.

"Really, I have no idea. Auriol saved me from a fall I made trying to escape Reachers. He brought me here." She frowns, clearly frustrated that I'm in Breezewood at all. What have I done?

"If Auriol saved you, it's because he's taken a liking to you. Breezewood owls don't just help random people. Wystan was probably looking out for you too. I imagine he was back patrolling the portal. Why he let you continue on into Breezewood without sending you back, I don't know." I heave an internal sigh of relief at her words, delighted to hear Wystan survived his injuries after the run in with Reachers Anna and Peter had mentioned. And, most likely, unharmed from anything I've done.

"I ran the moment I stepped through. I never saw him. He probably didn't have a chance to confront me." I try to recall the first few moments entering, but all I clearly remember is being panicked. I glance down at my palm again. The ink letters are still there. I clench my fist tightly.

"You'll wait here until Wystan gets back. He told me you have a truth pearl, so you won't be going anywhere near the ground. Reachers can't get up here; at least, they haven't figured out a way yet."

Her name resurfaces in my memory. Tara. I had first believed her to be a maid, but her clothes had given me the impression that she was of some noble descent. Maids in the stories I grew up with didn't typically wear clothes embroidered with gold and silver threads. But today, she stands before me in something less grand yet not anything resembling a maid's outfit. Tight, brown leather boots that nearly reach her knees with a half-length mouse-brown skirt. Her upper tunic, a darker brown, is bunched tastefully into a belt on which two crossbow bolts and a pair of scissors hang. Behind her, I catch sight of a crossbow. Is Tara some sort of night guard?

"I didn't know you worked outside of the castle."

"I don't work outside the castle. At least, not officially. I'm on break, and in my spare time, I train." Tara brushes a dark curl from out of her face, placing one hand on her hip. She's got a fierce look about her, and I finally realize who she reminds me of. Her demeanor is much like Naomi's though their sense of fashion is entirely the opposite.

"So you're a maid?" I dart my eyes to catch the flickering of candles about the room. A loaf of bread and a pot of steaming tea are positioned on a wooden counter clustered heavily with candles. A bolt of moss-green fabric is draped over a chair, and I spy a pin cushion full of needles.

"Of sorts. I'm the head seamstress of Breezewood. I sew the king's clothes along with the other nobles'. I also train others to sew. In my spare time, I train with Wystan and the other night patrols and when I'm not doing that, I learn about medicine and herbology."

I recall the workroom I entered back in Breezewood when I received my dress. Putting two and two together, her descriptions about being a seamstress make sense. There's a long, awkward pause as I try to think of something else to say. Tara shifts from one foot to another.

I break the silence with the first thing that comes to mind. "I suppose you will want this back. I didn't exactly mean to take it with me." I quickly pull the forest-green dress from my book bag and lay it across my arms. Tara's mouth opens then closes, surprised. I hold it out, again admiring its beauty.

"You didn't have to bring it back, but..." Her eyes close in a thought, then she opens them, her features relaxing. "Thank you. Won't you join me for tea? We can wait for Wystan to come back."

"Tea sounds lovely." I can't say no to tea.

Tara nods then takes the dress from me and lays it across the closest chair. I watch as she prepares our tea with careful hands. Pouring and stirring, there's an art to her assembling. To my delight, she pulls out a pitcher of cream and layers it in my cup along with a spoonful of honey. A delicate white tea set painted with blueberries and ferns is arranged onto a tray and placed on a smaller table next to three chairs farther in the house. I watch as Tara slices the bread and lathers on a generous helping of butter, transferring it to a plate.

"I hope you like peppermint tea. It's all I have steeped at the moment. Did you know peppermint has healing properties? In my herbology studies, peppermint does wonders for the mind and body." She finishes several more bread slices then carries them to the table in the sitting area.

"I didn't know that, but peppermint is a favorite of mine," I say and take a seat in one of the three chairs. I lift a cup and saucer from the tray, allowing the aroma to seep deep into my senses. I didn't expect to have tea in such a place, yet I'm not entirely surprised nor displeased. Tea is a welcome addition to any situation. There's just something about a cup of steeped dried herbs that gives one the peaceful frame of mind to talk.

I take a sip, closing my eyes at the sweet and minty flavor. I have to be honest, it is probably the best cup of peppermint tea I've ever had. And I'm having it in a treehouse in a magical realm inhabited by a large owl, strange beasts, and an evil king. Do those things have anything at all to do with the excellence and flavor of the tea? Very possibly, but I'm trying not to be biased.

"As soon as he returns, he's going to try and take you back to the portal," Tara says after her first sip. I set my cup firmly on my saucer.

"I'm not going back to the portal. At least, not right away. I need to get the pearl removed by the king." I scrunch my toes up tightly in my boots.

There's a pause as Tara takes another sip. Then her face twists in thought. "Pearl or not, Wystan isn't going to let you go anywhere near the castle, let alone the king. Just you being here is putting Wystan, me, and others at risk."

I take in her words. This was a stupid idea. How am I supposed to get the king to remove the pearl anyway? If I get near enough for him to touch me, he'll force me to tell him the truth on whatever he wants to know. And after that, he'll turn me over to the Reachers, or worse, these Wolves Sam and the others were talking about. I take another sip of my tea and contemplate my choices.

Going back home means resigning to leave Joel, if he's still alive, to a certain death in Breezewood. And me, being forever chained to a magic item that had no place in my world. And what about the portal? Had my destruction of the page and book sealed me inside Breezewood forever? I grip my teacup handle tighter.

Staying forces me to try and save Joel and help myself. And if what I did sealed the portal, then I'll also keep Breezewood and my world safe.

"I have to stay. Besides removing the pearl, my friend, Joel, was taken captive by the king. I have to see if he's alive."

Tara takes a hesitant sip of her tea. "Wystan will have final say," she says decidedly, setting her cup and saucer down in the tray with a clink.

As we wait, the treehouse sways gently in a gust of wind. The woven walls and floor creak with each bend. Tara grabs the moss-green cloth from the chair by the counter and begins to stitch tiny white star flowers into the fabric. I hold my teacup close, nibbling on buttered bread in between sips. What is there to say? Tara, though trying to be kind, obviously doesn't like me. Besides that, she doesn't have the answers I need. Or does she?

"Do you know where Joel is? The Worlder who was taken captive the day you gave me the dress?" She does several stitches before answering.

"I never met him, but there were rumors that the king had taken in another Worlder. They don't come through Breezewood often, so when we hear news of one, it is talked about rather extensively in the castle."

"Do you know if he is still alive?"

"I can't say that I know. The king does as he pleases, regardless if we agree or not."

"But don't you think someone should put a stop to cruelty? Where is the line? When will Breezewood stand up to tyranny?"

"The king protects us and provides for us. We haven't been able to store or grow food in Breezewood for over twelve years, but the king has fed us and kept us from the Reachers. The least we can do is leave him to his form of justice."

I can't believe what I'm hearing. Is Tara truly loyal to the king?

"Are you saying that you will do nothing to defy the king?"

"I don't agree with the king on everything and I certainly don't approve of what he is doing to Worlders, but there is nothing I can do to stop him. As of right now, I'm training to be a night patrol. That's a step in the direction of rebellion. I need to know how to defend myself first."

What can I say to that?

There's a rustling noise outside the treehouse and Tara looks up from her stitching. Two hoots and a creak of wood bring us both to our feet.

"Wystan in here." Tara sets down her sewing and opens the front door. Wystan dips inside, removing his crossbow from his back and shutting the door. When he catches sight of me, he stiffens.

"Briar." His voice is dry and pained as if he didn't expect to find me here.

"Wystan." I nod, finding it difficult to make eye contact. He's staring at me like I'm a ghost. Tara looks between us, raising her voice in alarm.

"I thought you knew she was here."

"I didn't. At last, not for sure. Auriol ditched me when I was in the middle of hunting Reachers."

"What exactly were you patrolling?"

"I was keeping Worlders at bay. There were three I found at the cliff edge. Reachers were hunting them. Not sure what they had that was drawing the beasts, but they went back to the portal. One called Briar by name." he says, flicking his eyes to mine.

I look into his face, surprised at the coolness there. He doesn't want me here.

"Do you know who?"

"Someone I told to never let you come back here," Wystan's eyes flash and dart away. "Why did you come back here, Briar? Only danger waits for you."

"I had to return. To find out why the portal exists and to save Joel. I have to remove this pearl. All while trying to keep my world from invading Breezewood."

"Is that a possibility?" Tara asks. Wystan sighs.

"Joel and the others on the team gave me every reason to believe that it's possible. In their modern world of technology and powerful men, Breezewood would be an easy target."

"Then if you all care about us, why do you keep coming back here?" Tara looks at me as if this is all my fault.

"I don't know all the things Wystan and my friends talked about. All I know is they have been in several times before me and have developed relationships with some of the people here and even made plans to help trapped Worlders get home. I know they are trying everything in their power to find a way to seal off the portal to keep you all safe."

Tara blinks then looks at Wystan. "Is this true?"

"Aye, it is. Joel was head of the team. I'm sorry you never got to meet them all. I've met the rest, and what Briar says is what I know."

Tara backs down at his words, grabbing her sewing and sitting down. Wystan directs me to a chair and we both sit. There's silence between us all but Tara pipes up, setting her sewing in her lap. "Briar, I hear what you are saying about staying, but there's no need to try and save us. There's nothing you can do. Joel, if he is still alive, will be under strict guard and none of us are anywhere near the level of clearance to be able to get close to him. It's best if you return home to your world and let us fight our own battle. You are in danger the longer you stay."

Wystan rubs his jaw in thought then puts both hands together on his knees.

"Wystan, please, I have to try."

"Briar, even if you stayed to try and help, Breezewood probably won't be around much longer."

"What do you mean?"

"What?" Tara snaps, whipping to look at Wystan.

"I haven't told anyone yet, but Harvest never happened. The king's magic is dead."

"Dead?" Tara stands, her project dropping to the floor.

"I overheard the guards talking, and it sounds like the room where the miners bring the stones and gems has been barred off and that the king has forbidden anyone from entering it. I know I'm not the only one but I saw the room before it was closed off. There isn't enough food to last the winter."

I twist in my seat. "Breezewood is going to starve?"

"Without the king's ability to turn precious gems and metals from the mines into food, the people within our lands will die."

"How do you know his magic is gone? Isn't tonight the Harvest masquerade ball? If there is a shortage of food, wouldn't the ball be canceled and food rationed?" Tara asks.

"If the king is worried about his kingdom panicking due to his loss of power, he won't cancel the ball. Any rumors that circulate about Harvest failing will be hushed if not put to rest if the ball goes as planned," Wystan says. Tara sits back down, eyes full of shock and disbelief.

"Why can't Breezewood grow food in the first place? Why can't you store the food you collect in the forests?"

"Breezewood fell beneath a dark shadow shortly before Alder, king of Breezewood, began to reign. Reachers started appearing, and the crops and food stores of our people turned to ash. There are stories that say Alder brought it upon Breezewood, and then there are others that claim his banished brother is responsible. No one seems to know what really happened. Regardless, Alder, with his magic, has kept us fed and safe since the start of his reign."

"I'm inclined to believe that Alder, the king, is responsible for such a terrible turn of events, but I have zero proof to back up my opinion." I cross my arms. Now what am I to do? Have I destined myself, Joel, and the rest of Breezewood to die of starvation by sealing up the portal?

"Neither do we. But it still stands; Breezewood will starve without a cure to Alder's magic or a restoration to Breezewood's lands."

"Why didn't you tell me about this earlier?" Tara directs at Wystan.

"I only just heard about it yesterday. Besides, rumors are rumors. We don't know for sure. But I am leaning towards it being true since the king has been asking less and less owl patrols to go out lately. We've always done our rounds day and night, keeping Reachers away from the castle's mountain entries and warding off invaders. A halting of exterior patrols means something is seriously wrong."

"Or that something is very right. Less exterior patrols means the lands are becoming safer. What if he's giving more of the men extra time with their families? What if it is nothing at all?" Tara says. She's trying to keep hope alive, her fierce and strong-willed personality resisting the urge to crumple. The way her lip quivers and eyes shine as Wystan speaks tells me that she's been living with her own doubts too. Wystan, the person she trusts, is simply bringing them to light. She bites her lip and keeps the tears from welling over.

"I wish that were true, but if that was the case, the guards would not be doubled at the vault of stores and neither in the dungeons. Breezewood has a big problem, and it starts with the king." Wystan's voice is firm.

"I don't believe you."

"Suit yourself, Tara. But if you, who is actively training to be a night guard, discover the truth and find you can't trust your king, you might be locked into a position to be used against your people. If we do begin to starve, food will be rationed and you will have to enforce whatever rules the king makes."

Tara bows her head in silence, staring a hole into her skirt. I listen closely to the whole conversation, taking in as many details as I can. This side of Wystan sounds like a rebel, yet he's still loyal to his people as a father is to his son. Tara sounds like she doesn't know what to believe yet. Why is she even working with Wystan? If she's training to be a night guard and has problems disobeying the king, why would Wystan trust her? She hasn't even met Joel and the others.

"Wystan, I guess I don't quite understand, but you said Breezewood has been under shadow since *before* Alder began to reign? And he has a brother who was banished? I want to help Breezewood if I can, so if you can tell me any more details, maybe we can think of a solution."

"I don't know much, but I do know that Alder has two brothers, one named August and one other who I don't know the name of. The mystery brother was banished twelve years ago for befriending a Worlder, and August disappeared from Breezewood the year after. No one has seen either of them since. Rumor has it August left to search for his banished brother and to look for a cure for Breezewoods lands, but he hasn't returned since."

August? Like Peter's boss August? I file this away. This can't be a coincidence.

"So no one truly knows why the darkness is over Breezewood and why you can't store or grow food aside from what Alder provides?"

"Correct."

"Then might I make a rather ridiculous suggestion?" I fold my hands neatly in my lap, trying my best to be diplomatic. I need Wystan on my side if I'm going to accomplish any of my missions here. I only just thought of this hypothetical solution because in all my time reading fairy tales and histories of the world, the king is always responsible for his people. When a king makes a choice, whether good or bad, there are consequences for his actions. And when the choice is made out of greed or lust, the consequences are always painful. Remove the king and some of the problems will go away; at the very least, the problems can be dealt with without interference from said king.

"I'll hear any thoughts," Wystan says, sitting straighter in his chair.

"If Alder is somehow responsible for this darkness, whether it be by his own hand or by the manipulation of another, would removing Alder from the throne solve Breezewood's food problem?"

"There's only one way to know. We'd have to get him out of Breezewood."

Twenty

PETER

The barrage of questions in my mind demands answers. August keeps darting his eyes and checking on Atlas. I can't help but think he's concerned about Reachers returning, but there's nowhere I know for us to go. With the portal shut, we have to wait for one of us to think of a plan. In the meantime, I need to know what my boss has been up to and who he really is. I cross my arms and pull my coat tighter against my body.

"So, how did you get to our world if you are from Breezewood?" August takes a moment to evaluate my question then dives in.

"When my brother Alder became king, I knew I could not stay at his side for long. His selfish decisions and lust for power enraged me. I was furious for his lack of self-control and how without consent or concern for his people, had invited darkness to live in our land and help him rule. When I began to notice a lack of food as a result of his choices, along with the sudden appearance and ever increasing number of Reachers, I discovered that he was desperate to find a cure. Without revealing to him that I knew of his despair, I organized a quest for myself. He agreed for me to leave, probably glad to be rid of me. He made the mistake of not asking the true nature of my quest. If he had pressed further, he might have discovered my determination to dethrone him, break the curse, and seek out my banished brother."

"So, how did you find a portal to the modern realm?"

"I left Breezewood and sought beyond our lands for something that could help me dethrone my brother and break the curse. In my journey, I went by land and then by sea and discovered the opening of a portal upon the waves. I saw it open and close from a distance, and old tales that my grandfather had told me about came to my mind. My grandfather and father had seen Worlders before, but none of them knew how they exactly came to our world. When my father died and Alder took the throne, the mystery of them became even greater. Alder began to develop a hatred for them and some of the technology they brought and talked about. I believe he was afraid that they would try and take his throne. All the ones he crossed paths with disappeared by his hand."

I didn't need to ask what he meant by that. Alder was a cruel sort of king. Perhaps he had good intentions, but he was obviously prideful and arrogant and had little mercy. Such traits did not make the good kings in history. I could think of only one Worlder who had made it past the king without losing her life, and the thought of her out in this cold, alone, screams at me to do something. Any moment now and I will brave the unknown to find her.

"Were portals something your people sought after normally?"

"No. We hardly ever saw such things if ever. We only rarely found the people who came through them. But for me, that one glimpse of magic revealed that the tales had been true, to some extent. I wondered what this magic portal could do. If I could go through it, what might I find on the other side? The cure?"

"And you found our world?"

"Yes. I sailed towards the place where the portal had opened and waited there for several days. Then, miraculously, the portal reopened. I leapt from the ship and swam through the gateway. What awaited me on the other side was chaos. A shipwreck of the worst kind, only they weren't ships I had ever seen the likes of before. Made of metal and other materials. All a part of the strange magic I assumed. I was rescued shortly after by strangers and was taken to a hospital. They believed I was the only remaining survivor of the wreck, but only I knew the truth."

"So you made it to the modern world. What then? What led you to become a puzzle master and find your way back here?" My head was reeling with the oddity of all this. My boss, August Heaverly, was from Breezewood. And not only from here, but some kind of prince!

"I learned to live in the modern world, accepting the culture with the mind of one seeking a cure. But I tell you truly, there wasn't a clue for a cure for a long time. I found my place working with escape rooms after befriending one of the search and rescue men who helped me from the wreck. He found me a place to stay and eventually a job which required a move to Colorado. Let me save you the long story of adjusting to the modern world by just saying that it was a challenge."

He lets loose a small chuckle then clears his throat, seriousness washing over him once more. "I got into puzzles when helping one of the chaps who rescued me. He was friends with the owners of a local escape room company. We got to talking and I ended up going to one with him. Together, we beat the escape room record by twenty minutes."

"That is impressive."

"From there, I got asked to develop puzzles. Invented some new ones and tweaked old ones to make them better. For eleven years, I've been working in that escape room company and because of that, I've trained my mind to think about things in different ways."

"No wonder everyone likes you. You're a natural."

"I just like challenges."

"All this time, you haven't even been from the modern world. You've been living a double life."

"It hasn't been so hard when you get paid cash under the table and get to rent from a friend and don't need to drive anywhere because your work is a few blocks down the street," August says.

"So technically, you don't even exist. The government doesn't even know about you."

"I suppose you can put it like that."

"You haven't had to pay taxes in eleven years?" I'm trying to imagine the look on Sam's face when he finds out. That techy kid is going to have a meltdown when he finds out that my boss has been avoiding the IRS for eleven years.

"When you get paid in cash and you pay for everything in cash, you don't need an ID. No one asks and no one knows. It's better that way."

"I know it's illegal, but I'm impressed and kinda jealous. Not sure how you would even get around to getting an ID in the first place though. No birth certificate, social security number. You are literally off grid."

"In a manner of speaking," August says with a grin.

"How'd you get a car then? You need a license and insurance for that." I remember the unfamiliar car parked out in front of the bookstore. It had to be August's.

"I don't own it. A friend does."

"Andrew?"

"Yes."

"Where is he? The car is still parked out front at the bookstore."

"I'm not sure right now. Calling doesn't work in Breezewood, and I left my phone in the store."

I note the way he sidesteps my question, but time is passing us by. Before I can protest about braving the forest in search of Briar and safety, August says something that makes me believe he's been thinking about it for a long time.

"Peter, the gateway we now stand before is not the only one. In my research for a cure, a portal is created each time a creative, a writer, or really any artist gets close to what is completely and utterly real, aka, Breezewood. It creates a torn seam between our worlds and lets the creator and sometimes those who figure out the special key to that creator's work to access the realm. Think of Tolkien and C.S. Lewis. Their writings and craft brought them so close they nearly touched the true reality. They are responsible for several gateways. I personally believe both men got a look at Breezewood at least once. But even if they didn't, their work is probably connected to several portals. True beauty is tethered to the true reality."

"But what does all this mean? Why Breezewood? Why not another world? Are there other worlds?"

How many portals are there or have there been? What does all this mean for the safety of our world and Breezewood?

"To answer them all, yes and no. Breezewood is an extension of reality. It is the reminder that not all we can see with the naked eye is all that is there. There is more to life than what you purely see. Think of the world you live in. Breezewood is connected to it. But I think it has been barred off for a specific purpose."

"What on earth could that purpose be?"

"I believe that purpose is to allow mystery and discovery for both realms. Me, for example, finding your world and you finding ours. Already my worldview has been shattered like glass a million times. No, I don't think there are multiverses, if you will. Breezewood seems to be the only realm the gateways go to, or the modern world if you reverse it. But I think there is a place outside of our mortal worlds. A place that is like our world, except it is perfect."

"Heaven?" I surmise.

"Yes, I suppose it could be heaven. Yes... heaven. Except, it isn't at all like what people have made it out to be. It's much better. It is all the good and pure things we love here, like tea, laughter, light and dancing, only amplified beyond our imagination."

August has really been thinking about this for a while. Whether it is all true, I don't know, but hearing him speak passionately about something is bringing me back to the August I remember from Colorado. He loves puzzles and discussing history, and all the unknowns and what ifs. I always enjoyed talking with him, even if it was about the things that some people determine a waste of time. Talking about those things seemed to bring us closer as friends and helped us look at the world differently. All in all, it was never wholly a waste of time.

"What do you think these portals are from?"

"More like a who. There's someone who put it all here who is outside space, time, and matter. Someone who created all of us and the portals, everything. I can't prove it to you in mere words. You just have to look and discover the truth for yourself."

I never thought about it before, but the deeper I think about it, the more it makes sense, even if it does make my brain hurt a little. My mind wants to dwell on it, to delve into the unknown and take in the deeper meanings of reality and life. Why are we here? Where do we go when we die? Where did the world come from? You know, all those questions. But instead, I'm contemplating how the air is growing colder with each moment that passes and that danger lurks in the growing twilight, further cementing my fear for Briar's life as well as my own.

"If the portal is closed, where will we go for the night?" I rub hands up and down my shoulders, trying to bring some more warmth into them.

August steps over to Atlas and places an arm on his shoulder. "I'll call upon my brother, Alder, for his hospitality in exchange for bringing Atlas home safely. He's served his time outside Breezewood long enough. It's time to go home," he says while looking at his brother. Atlas stands, giving me a side glance that tells of dislike and untold secrets. What is he hiding?

"You mean, we are going to Breezewood Castle?" Fear creeps up my spine at the thought of King Alder telling his guards to do away with me.

"It's our only chance at safety," August says.

All I can do is nod and follow as the two brothers lead me through the forest, away from the portal. Some things aren't adding up, but I'm not entirely sure what. I have no choice but to follow and hope August knows what he's doing. But one thing is certain: I don't trust either August or Atlas completely.

I slipped Andrew's name into our conversation and August fell for it. As far as I know, Andrew hasn't been back to the bookstore. He didn't drop August off if that other car is his. How would August know who Andrew is anyway? The portal in the bookstore isn't the one August says he came through initially eleven years ago. How did he know there was a portal in the bookstore at all? Unless Atlas told him. They must've been communicating prior to all this. Both August and Atlas are holding something back. I just hope I'm not the one who'll reap the negative consequences.

Twenty-One

BRIAR

"Getting Alder out of Breezewood isn't going to be easy. He hates Worlders and hasn't left the castle for a very long time. I don't know how we could convince him to leave," Wystan says.

"He hasn't left the castle at all?" I'm shocked. Normally a king went out to fight battles with his knights or to hunt. However, all of Breezewood lives in a mountain. So not leaving the place meant he never saw the sun. Was being in darkness a source of his power? Maybe not if it is dying.

"Not that I am aware of. He was crowned in the mountain and has never left. But not a lot of the people have left either. There's no need to when all our food and water and supplies are here and the outside is dangerous. But the occasional brave few will leave for fresh air and the like," Wystan answers, looking briefly at Tara.

"Hmmm." I stand from my chair and pace the room.

Tara stays sitting, blinking at both of us like we are crazy. "The king doesn't leave because he doesn't need to. And we don't even know if what you're saying is even true," she says, hands splayed over her knees. Wystan addresses her gently.

"Tara, trust me on this. You know as well as I what the rumors have been."

"But that's just it. They are rumors. I just don't think we should do anything crazy. Give it time to really know what is going on." Her tone is even and controlled, but her narrowed eyes and tilt of her head tells me she doesn't trust me. I'm an alien in her life, and I'm uprooting all she's ever known. Not to mention, the guy who's supposed to be teaching her night patrol stuff is talking to me instead. No wonder she dislikes me. She's tolerating me, but that's about it.

"But we don't have time. I would like to go home to my family, if I could. I would also like to return to normal life and see my friends safe. Despite how incredible this place is." I say and let my eyes follow the intricately woven walls. I know that Breezewood, despite how foreign and scary it feels right now, will be missed. It's not every day you find a portal in your local bookstore that takes you to a magical realm. But I won't miss the stress of it, that's for certain. "What could we possibly say to him that would get him to leave? If his magic is dying, he needs a cure." I get us back on track. We have to keep thinking about this. I won't just sit idly by and let my friends worry about me for nothing. I want to do something big, something worth my time and energy. Something that will mean a great deal to people in the years to come. Saving lives seems like a good start.

"We don't have a cure," Wystan says, disheartened.

"Well, Alder wouldn't know that. What if we made the claim... that I have one!" I whirl around, the edge of an idea leaving my lips. It leapt into my mind like a spark leaving a fire. Ideas do that with me sometimes. When I'm writing stories, I have no problem coming up with ideas. In fact, I have a problem with coming up with too many ideas. I want to use them all and often find myself with an overcomplicated story that is difficult to finish writing. I hope this idea isn't too difficult to accomplish.

"You aren't going into Breezewood Castle, Briar. I won't let you." Wystan stares at me like I'm made of glass and will break at a moment's notice. I stand straighter, ignoring Tara's disapproving look she's giving him. I don't know what's going on between them, but I don't want to get in the middle of it.

"I wouldn't have to go. You could tell the king that you found someone who has a cure. In exchange for the removal of a truth pearl perhaps?" I might as well try to kill two birds with one stone.

"He'll know it's you the moment anyone mentions the pearl."

"All the better. He'd be more willing to leave the castle and meet up if he hates my guts, right?"

"We have no idea if it will work."

"It's our only chance. Do you have a better idea?"

"I'm still thinking." Wystan scratches his chin then wipes a hand down his face.

"While you're thinking, I'll develop my idea." I pace some more, thinking about all the ways this plan could go wrong. If I were to get a note or verbal message to the king detailing my terms, then we'd be giving away that I was most likely in Breezewood. There'd be nothing I could do to get him to leave the castle and come to the portal if he decided not to come. If, however, the king did come, we'd have to find a way to force him through the portal.

Only problem is, if this pearl makes me tell the truth when the king is near enough to touch me, then he could simply ask if I truly had a cure. I'd be forced to tell him I didn't have one. He could ask other questions and figure out the entire plan and everything would be a fail. I swallow. What if I went through the portal first and had Wystan open it and push the king through instead? Then, I could be at a distance from the king and he couldn't find out the truth unless he went through. If he came through, I could force the king to remove the pearl in order for me to let him back into Breezewood. Or maybe I wouldn't have to force him to do anything. If he leaves Breezewood, maybe the dark magic he brought to the kingdom would disappear and leave the pearl too, freeing me. So many what ifs and maybes.

But there's one last what if I need to make sure of before we try any plan. What if the portal is sealed? Have I doomed us all?

"I think I need to go back to the portal," I say, pausing in my pacing.

"That solves that then," Tara says, standing. I wrinkle my brow. Does she think I'm just giving up?

"I'm not leaving. I simply need to see if it will open again. I think I may have sealed it from the inside. No one can come in or go right now. If that's the case, then I might be the only one who can open it." I glance down at my palm again, eyebrows furrowed.

"I can take you, but it will have to be lightning fast. There were Reachers on the cliff."

"I'll just need to get close to it. I don't think I'll even have to be on the ground. Can you fly Auriol over the location?"

"That I can do, but I'll need to do it without being spotted by any other night patrols. There are at least two others hunting Reachers from the air. If they spot me flying past the border, they'll report me, and our game is up."

"Just get me close. If the portal opens, then we move on with the plan."

"What plan?" Tara looks at Wystan, clearly perturbed that I am the focus of all his attention. I haven't done anything to encourage his focus on me. Simply conversing can't be a crime, can it? But I don't know Tara that well, and right now, me just existing is punishable enough.

"Tara, can you stay here and keep watch? We'll be back. Briar needs to stay above ground," Wystan says, adjusting his crossbow on his back.

"Why can't I come, too? I'm just as good with a crossbow as you." Her eyes hover over me, jealousy oozing from her. She pats the bolts on her belt and looks back at Wystan, hands on her hips.

"I can go alone. That way you won't get in trouble if I get seen. Auriol will take care of me," I say quickly before Wystan can answer her.

"But if the riders see you..."

"I'll take my chances. Besides, you need to discuss more of the plan with Tara," I add, giving her a quick wink. Her mouth drops, stunned.

I'm not here to make more enemies. I'm here to help people.

"Okay. Since you are with Auriol, I'll allow it. Under no circumstances are you to have Auriol land on the ground."

"I wouldn't dream of it," I say, double checking that my coat is fully zipped. Time to fly.

The flight back to the portal is uneventful. With a plan brewing at the back of my mind, hope begins to kindle. If the portal opens when I recite the key, phase one of the plan can be set into motion.

Auriol takes me lower, nearly skimming the treetops. Neither of us have seen any other night patrols. Wystan said they would be armed aboard their own owls. His last words as Auriol and I left the treehouse replay in my ears: "The king suggests we shoot first and ask questions later. I have been one of the few night patrols who doesn't listen to all the instructions, so watch your back."

The cliff edge appears, and Auriol makes an adjustment, climbing higher to account for the rise in elevation. The sky begins to dim, evening nearing with the first tinges of purple and gold glowing on the clouds behind us. Already, the forests beyond the mountain of Breezewood Castle are turning silver, the frost creeping closer and closer. The air has plunged into a much colder temperature, along with the wind driving a cutting chill. Without having to experience it fully, I know staying out at night with no shelter would be devastating.

We cross the Breezewood border and crest the cliff edge, the portal clearing is now visible from our height. Auriol circles low over the clearing, giving me plenty of safety from any beast that might want to make a meal of me yet close enough that I can see if the portal opens. I look down at my hand and recite the words imprinted there. *What if we met in a bookstore.*

A flash of light in the trees at the edge of the clearing tells me it's working. Excitement rises in my stomach, and I almost let out a whoop but hold my tongue at the last minute. No need to draw anymore attention to myself.

The portal gleams with that watery substance, rippling and twisting. Auriol circles a few times more before I tell him we can go back to the treehouse. As we drift away from the gate, I look back and think of all my friends and family at home. I think of the bookstore and its impending closure if Peter's escape room doesn't happen. I think of Jen and wonder if she called Peter and gave him my note. Heat flushes up my face as I think of him reading it, my thoughts laid bare. He already rejected me once; would he do the same a second time? I don't know what he'll do, especially now with how he wanted to talk about our past. I shake those thoughts away. It was time for saving Joel, saving Breezewood, and protecting my world.

⹈⹈⹈⹈⹈ ⹈⹈⹈⹈⹈

"I've got it." Wystan says after I relay the success of my mission. He holds out a scrap of cream paper, slightly wrinkled and lined with writing. "We'll attempt your plan this way. It's the safest option which leaves room for failure. If the king rejects the note, then you are still safe and have time to think of another plan before he sends people out to find you." As Tara walks past and hands me another cup of steaming tea, I take Wystan's note and read every line with careful eyes.

For His Majesty, the king and ruler of Breezewood, a compromise is enclosed.

Meet me at the top of the cliff this evening to remove my truth pearl. In exchange, I'll give you the cure to your dying magic. Heal me, and I'll heal you.

"Safe is good." I add, handing him the note back. I take a sip of the sweet peppermint tea, the temperature rushing through my bones and all the way to my fingertips.

"I'll slip the note into the king's pocket or into one of his advisors' pockets tonight at the masquerade Harvest ball. That way you aren't anywhere near the king when he reads it."

"From there, we can get him to meet us at the portal, pull him through and see if the darkness leaves Breezewood. Then we can have him remove the pearl once on the other side." I finish reading the note and Wystan folds it and tucks it in a pocket. I try to work out some of the details in my mind, attempting to see past the fact that Wystan is in danger at every turn. The king would suspect Wystan was the one who delivered the note or at least was responsible for part of it. But this is the only way for this to work. He won't let me in the castle, and I have no one else willing to deliver the note. It has to be him.

"Exactly. When I send Auriol back to the treehouse with Tara, that's your signal that the note has been delivered, and you are to ride Auriol to the portal with her. Send him back and I will arrive shortly after, hopefully with the king alone or with very few men. Tara will protect you."

"The king doesn't know where the portal is, does he?" I ask.

"He has never left the castle to see it, but he will be suspicious."

"It's all we have." I hold up my teacup like it's a toasting glass. "To Breezewood."

"To Breezewood," Wystan says. Tara doesn't raise her glass. Instead, she stares into her drink then flickers her eyes to a candle on a far table.

"I have to get back. There are several touch-ups I have to make to my dress, and I need to be available in case any of the nobles need last minute stitching done." She sets her teacup down and heads to gather things around the room.

"I'll take you back," Wystan says, downing the rest of his tea.

"I'll be ready for when Tara and Auriol return," I hold my warm teacup close to my face like it's my only source of heat.

"I'd bring him myself, but I should be present at the ball for a while to ward off suspicion. In the meantime, I can try to find your friend Joel." I mull on Wystan's words. What leverage did I have to even get the king to do what I want quickly? Was there anything I had that could persuade him to act this very night? Maybe there was.

"Do you have the pen?" I ask, setting my cup down. "I have one more thing to add to the note."

"Sure. Here. I have yet to seal it anyhow." Wystan snatches the quill pen up off his chair and hands it over, unfolding the note from his pocket in a swift manner.

"Thank you." I set the edge of the note down on the sitting room table and begin to scribble an amendment to my terms, dipping the pen in ink every few letters. "Just something extra in case he decides I'm not worth the trouble." I lift the paper up and blow on it to dry. I tried to write it in my neatest writing, even adding a swirl at the ends of my serifs.

If you don't agree to my terms, I'll tell your whole kingdom the truth about your magic and the failed Harvest. Be there tonight.

"You're threatening to blackmail him?" Wystan says, reading my additions with a raised brow.

"Why of course. He's got to know I'm serious." I pick up my tea again and wait for him to fold the letter.

"By saying you'll tell his whole kingdom that he's lying to them and that everyone will know he's failed."

"Effective, yes?"

"Maybe. But Breezewood will be tumultuous if that happens." Wystan takes the folded note and reaches off one of the shelves and pulls down a green envelope.

"Let's hope it doesn't have to come to that. If the king agrees to our plan and it actually works, then the rest of Breezewood might be past the worst of it."

"Aye, I hope." Wystan slides the note into the envelope and carries it near a candle. He grabs a stick of silver wax off the table and proceeds to melt the wax onto the envelope. In a deft motion, he seals it with a wooden handled stamp. "Finished. It looks more official this way. They'll be more likely to read it and won't mistaken it for trash. This is Breezewoods official seal."

I catch a glimpse of the letter and gasp. The seal, a floral letter B stamped in silver, is identical to the one I found on my porch and matches the envelopes that my classmates found.

"That seal, the envelope. You sent the letters?"

"Letters?" Wystan looks at the envelope then back to me, eyebrows pinched.

"I found a letter on my porch a couple days ago. Something about asking for help because of danger. You sent them didn't you? How?"

Wystan's eyes widen.

"You got the letters? I gave them to Auriol to deliver to other kingdoms outside of Breezewood lands. I sent them months ago though and you got them in your world?" Wystan's mention of Auriol reminds me of the white feather I saw blowing across my porch when I first received the envelope. Auriol must have delivered the letters.

"I don't know how but yes, my classmates and I got some of your letters though we never could make them out entirely. The one I got was wet and the ink had bled." I remember the notes in the book I found in the bookstore, one note mentioned someone named Peter. I wonder if Wystan's comrade, the one who died by a Reacher, had been named Peter.

"I was asking for help. I figured since our realm has magic, that maybe someone in the other kingdoms might have pity on us and try to use magic to help us. Apparently, Auriol didn't take my instructions very clearly and instead found his way to you and your friends. How he made it to your realm I'll never know."

"Did you have a friend named Peter?" I ask carefully. Wystan's eyes sadden.

"Once. He was one of my best patrols."

"Reachers?"

"Yeah. How did you know?"

"I think I got one of your letters. You mentioned it briefly." Wystan sighs.

"It seems Auriol decided to take every single letter I wrote to your realm instead of where I had intended. The problem with that is no one in your realm should have reference for the Breezewood seal, while kingdoms in my realm do. Not to mention, the words you read were only a fraction of what it actually says. Other kingdoms know that in order to get the whole context of letters sent from one faction to another, they need to send a confirmation note back with a piece of their identity. Each letter is imbued with conceal magic so they can't read it all until I receive and approve their identity." Wystan looks at me, his expression pondering as if making sure I'm not lost. I smile.

"Please, continue."

"It's a method of keeping important correspondences secure. In order for a recipient to get the entirety of the letter, they have to send a piece of their identity. Usually this involves a fingerprint in wax. The conceal magic in my letter will relent and disappear, revealing the rest of the message as soon as I receive and approve their identity. I do that by resealing the letter they send me with new wax."

"What does having their identity do for you and how do they know where to send the letter back to?" There's so much about Breezewood and magic that I don't understand. Does everyone have magic here?

"By having their identity, I am able to store it. It will forever be ingrained in my mind and I can recognize them as the reader and receiver of my note if I happened to meet them in person. I don't need to have seen them before to know it's them. Plus, since I was asking for help, I wasn't really caring who found my letter. I just needed to know that someone had and wanted to read it. Having knowledge of who might be coming to help would give me time to prepare for their arrival. Oh, and the magic of my letter will be with their seal and will guide their messenger who is usually a bird of some kind." I understand for the most part. Some letters can be concealed with magic if the sender wants them to be. Neat. Makes a little more sense why the notes my friends and I got seemed incomplete and strange.

"Since Auriol found my house, that explains a little why he likes me and rescued me. Maybe it's a sign that my friends and I are meant to save Breezewood."

"Maybe." Wystan says, eyes glowing at my words. He glances at Tara as she approaches from the other end of the room. She's got her crossbow strapped to her back and a bag stuffed with fabric and ribbons.

"Ready," she says, meeting him at the door.

"Leave the crossbow, Tara," Wystan says. Tara, stunned, unslings the weapon from her back. "You'll need it when you get back, and if Briar had want of it, it would be here."

Tara nods slowly and releases the bolts on her belt, setting them on the table in the kitchen area.

"The trigger is sensitive," she says before opening the door and leading the way out. Wystan gives me a pained smile.

"Tara will be back, and that'll be your sign that the plan is in motion." His eyes are drawn to a candle on the table. He points to it and says, "When that candle is burned down to the table, Tara should be here."

"And if she isn't?"

"Then I would suggest you stay put. There's no use attempting a nighttime walk in this cold. Stay inside and keep warm. There's plenty of kindling for the small stove for a fire and items for tea. Help yourself."

With that, he's gone, and I'm all alone in a treehouse far above the ground. I step to the window and watch Wystan mount Auriol first then reach down to give Tara a hand up. I don't need eyes to see that she's determined to be noticed by him. The way her dark hair is catching the sun's last rays as she tilts her chin to look up at him gives me the clearest look at her expression. She's pining but he's oblivious. I can't help but feel sorry for her because I know what it feels like. Peter may not have been around other girls in a situation like this, but he certainly didn't notice me the way I noticed him. I sigh, nearly turning away from the window as Tara's eyes catch mine, watching her. The tree sways as Auriol's weight leaves the branch, and then they are off into the sunset.

As it should be. I watch out the window until the sun is gone and then I'm pressed in by darkness.

While waiting for Tara to return, I decide to explore the treehouse. Taking a candle stick off the table, I begin hovering it over the shelves. All kinds of herbs, teas, and powdered dyes fill the space. The candlelight reflection flickers over the array of glass bottles, and I find myself moving things to read labels. There's dried mint tea, dandelion roots, and rose petals ground into a fine, pink powder. Tara, or whoever is responsible for the collection, has it well organized.

I move on past the shelves and head to the left side of the room. Scanning the corner, I'm surprised to see that there is another door poking out behind a cloth that hangs from the wall. I pull on the handle and lift the light up higher so I can see. I find that the room is made into a storage area, but there is no food in here.

Instead, there are many different bolts of fabric on shelves with dresses already made up, hung by hooks on the rafters. Threads, needles and shiny ribbons are piled in baskets along one wall while several pairs of shoes for both men and women are stacked nearby. A dressmaker's workroom in the treetops? Tara must keep herself busy here while she keeps watch. Only, why is the tree house here? Is it a night patrol rest tower or some secret meeting hideout for Wystan and those who don't trust the king? I'm thinking the latter, but Tara doesn't seem fully invested. There's obviously something I don't know.

After exploring the farthest end of the workroom and finding nothing else but a pallet of blankets, I disappointingly make my way back to the main area to refill my tea. There is a small iron stove attached to a pipe chimney that is still glowing with a few coals. I open the front and add in a few more pieces of wood then spy around for the kettle. I discover running water right after finding the kettle on a shelf. A pipe sticks out of the side of the wall and over a basin, only this pipe is made of stone. It comes down from the roof where I'm positive a barrel is for collecting rainwater. Maybe not enough water for a bath, but certainly enough for tea and dishes. I slide a piece of stone out of the end of the pipe, and a gush of water fills the kettle. Before long, I have another brew on.

It feels like hours have gone by, and I check the candle on the table. It has burned down, the flame just about to go out. Soon, I'm bored enough and am rolling the warm, partially melted wax into small figurines to pass the time. Tara should be here at any moment.

When the candle finally snuffs out, I light a new one and decide to wait just a little longer. I tell myself that if Tara is reluctant to come back, she'll take her time. I find spare paper and write out another note, as close to the one Wystan wrote along with my previous addition. Just in case I need it. I browse again over Tara's large collection of herbs and spot a book I'd missed. I pull it off and open it, holding the pages closer to the candle to take in the detailed letters.

Drawings and labels of tea and herbs speckle the pages. Reading the neat tiny handwriting, I find portions of the book to differ extensively from modern herb and tea books in my realm. Instead of the general uses of herbs to cure a sore throat or soothe an upset stomach, there is the addition of magic to do other things. I trace my finger under the artful script. Chamomile and lavender tea imbued with magic gives one the ability to see farther than normal. A steeping of lemon grass and lemon balm allows one to walk for miles without tiring or growing sore, while peppermint tea absorbs toxins in the body and clears one's mind. Interesting. I wonder if the peppermint tea I drank was imbued with magic. I close the book and slide it back onto the shelf.

When the candle has melted far more than I'd like, I grow restless. If Tara or Wystan don't come at all, then something is wrong. Anything could have happened.

I pace the front room, straining my ears to hear the rustle of a branch or the rock of the tree when Auriol lands. There's no sign of any of them. My stomach churns with unease. It is pitch black outside now, the wind blowing clouds to cover both moon and stars. I'm grateful for the tea, warm fire, and the plethora of candles, but being alone in a strange place isn't my favorite.

I know Wystan said to stay put. We can resolve this in the morning, but what if something has happened and I'm stranded here for longer than tomorrow? There's only a little bread left and there's only so much tea I can drink to stay full. I stop by the edge of the table where the crossbow sits. Shadows from the candlelight wash over the weapon, moving like the groping fingers of some malevolent ghost. I hope I never have to use it.

With no backup plan and no desire to descend into the darkness alone, I busy myself with doing the only thing a girl ought to do when given the opportunity: try on dresses of course.

There are several hanging up in the workroom, and after bringing one into the brighter light of the main room, I take off my jacket. Slipping the dress on over my clothes, I twirl. While not practical in the slightest, this first dress is the epitome of my childhood dreams. Light, silky, and elegant with stitch work all down the bodice; it's made for dancing and parading across clean floors. I search the house for a mirror and settle upon a cracked handheld one. Frowning at the fit, I try again and take my sweater and jeans off. When I pull the dress back up, the fit is perfect. It's lovely. I remove my boots and socks and tip toe to look through the shoes. There's a pair of small, silver heels that catch my eye, and I put them on. Like the story of Cinderella, they fit just as well as the dress. I walk through the house, feeling the entirety of the outfit.

I remember that the Harvest masquerade ball is going on right now, and a small pang of disappointment comes over me. If

Breezewood was not in danger and my friends and I were all safe, I would love to go. Especially in this. But with so much at stake, dancing is the last thing to do. Still, one can't help but imagine being there, especially when there's time to kill. I twirl in the moss-green gown once more, making some of the candles on the table gasp for breath. I stop and stand alone, half-smiling, half-frowning. What I would give for Peter to see me in this just once and take me dancing. As soon as the thought enters my mind, I banish it.

The tree house begins to sway, and my ears pick up the distinct sound of crackling branches. I freeze, adrenaline rising. I glance at the crossbow then back at the door. Has Tara returned?

When the branches stop crackling, I wait. There's a long pause of silence, and I take the time to slip the heels off my feet and cross to the table. I lift the crossbow into my hands and feel for the bolts. I've never used a crossbow before, but I think I can figure it out. As soon as I load a bolt into it, I hear the crackling of branches again. Snap. Crack. The tree house sways. Someone or something is out there. I swallow, fear growing with each passing moment.

Twenty-Two

PETER

As I tread through the forest, my sixth sense goes off. It's especially acute in this forest, one within a world of creatures and magic that are all next to unknown. But right now, I don't know what is exactly setting it off.

August and Atlas lead the way, whispering to each other like conspirators. I can't even begin to describe the uneasy feelings I have the farther we press into the foliage and undergrowth. I don't trust them completely, but there's something else that's making me a little sick. Something that isn't them.

The evening fades into sunset, and the more we walk, the colder I get. The forest seems to be placed in some dark grip of fear, as if every step I take is sending a shudder through the land. I don't know what Anna and the others really liked about this place other than the fact that it is exciting beyond belief. Maybe they are all just suckers for excitement. Me? I like a good puzzle, but this? It's a bit much. I'm ready for a slow and less exciting life. More along the lines of solving fireside puzzles over espresso while listening to Vivaldi's *The Four Seasons*. The thought of that warms me for only a moment.

As I step over a bush, thoughts of Briar and the last time I saw her face fills my mind. Emotions begin swelling in my chest at the memory of her shy smile. Is she safe? Or is she wandering alone somewhere out in this darkness? I keep my ears open for any signs of Reachers, remembering their vivid sound of stone against stone and metal against metal.

As if on cue, a howl erupts through the forest and Atlas whispers harshly under his breath, "We won't make it to the castle in time. They'll track the scent of the pearl."

"We have time. I have a knife." August says.

I didn't realize he had a knife. Is it a diamond one that can kill a Reacher?

"How much farther to the castle?" I swivel in place, hearing the disturbance of moss and bush behind me. I strain my eyes, my breath exiting my mouth and nose like a dragon's. A small animal darts behind a tree. I relax, turning to August.

"Not far, but if I'm correct, the Harvest masquerade is tonight. The kingdom will be locked down for the celebration. We will have to show up and hope someone answers the door."

"And if no one does?"

"We find a high place and hope the scent of the king's finery within the castle keeps the beasts circling at the base of the mountain."

"Someone better open the door," Atlas growls. He looks at me, but I can't see his face clearly in the dimness. I swallow, a twinge of fear washing over me.

"August, Briar might be out here somewhere. We need to look for her," I say, not willing to take another step until I know we'll search for her.

"We don't have the time Peter," he says with a debated sigh.

"I'm not going any farther until we look for her." I'd rather die trying to find her than die while leaving her to the beasts.

"And I'm not going to stay out here to be Reacher food. Risk your own life," Atlas huffs.

Even without seeing August's full features, I know he's looking between us, trying to decide what to do. "Peter, we don't even know if Briar..."

In that moment, we all look up as a shadow passes over. While the light on the forest floor is minimal, the interruption across the sky is enough to catch our attention.

"What was that?" I ask.

"A night patrol. Probably the one that was shooting at us," August answers, bitterness in his voice.

"Can we not ask for help? Don't they work for your brother?"

"They do, but they are trained to shoot first and ask questions later. Better to knock on the door than to yell for assistance," Atlas says.

I wrinkle my brow. Whoever made up that rule needs to be fired. Another howl echoes in the distance. I rub my fingers under my arms, trying to get warm. Our breathing hangs in damp clouds around our faces. Knees shaky, I swallow.

"If no one is going with me to find Briar, I'm going alone." Part of me is afraid to meld into the trees, away from the only person with a weapon. I don't want to face the beasts, but knowing I don't have anything they want makes it only slightly better. Without any words, August reaches into his belt tucked beneath his overcoat and hands me his knife.

"It's diamond-tipped. They'll smell it on you, but you can kill them with it. If you find Briar, they'll be after her. Better a weapon than nothing."

I stiffen, the cold handle of the dagger incredibly heavy in my hands. "Thank you," I say, my words hollow and pinched. Though I've always wanted to hold a real dagger, this is not the situation I ever imagined when I'd get to.

"You gave him our only weapon?" Atlas scoffs.

"He needs it more than we do. Now, come on." August pushes Atlas in the direction of Breezewood, then he calls over his shoulder, "Good luck, son." And with that, they're gone.

Now alone, I'm frozen with fear and with cold. My fingers are starting to go numb, so I blow on them, willing them to become warm. When that doesn't work, I shove them one at a time into my armpits beneath my coat, pinching the dagger between my knees. While feeling returns, I check my bearings. The cliff is right behind me, and that was the last place I saw Briar. I'll have to go in that direction. I pick up the dagger tightly in my right hand, my heart thumping like a drum. I'm now a target. Soon those howling beasts, the Reachers, will be after me.

The wind picks up and cuts through my thin coat. I hunch forward, sucking in my gut, as if trying to draw all of my limbs as tight and close to my warm core as possible. Another shadow passes over the top of the trees. I look up and see that it is a bird, and from the angle I'm at, I see that there is a rider too. I want to call out, but fear keeps my voice contained. Instead, I follow it. Looking up, I watch their flight path as they zoom in a straight line. Then they veer off to the right towards the cliff. I slow as they go out of view.

Quickening my pace, I decide to follow them into the last known direction. Soon, they return and loop around heading left, away from the cliff. I'm hesitant to follow now, but at this new angle, I catch the perfect outline of the rider. Sharp chin, hair streaming behind, and slender torso. Hope wells in me. If that's Briar, then she's safe for the moment. I prepare to call out to her, every fiber of my being desiring to be away from the darkness and cold of the forest and with her. Before my breath leaves my throat, a growl erupts from the surrounding trees. My heart drops, and my knees lock. I almost drop the dagger as my arms become jelly-like, but I hold my ground. When another growl sounds farther off, I find the courage to yell Briar's name, but it comes out like a croak, my lips trembling with little feeling. I'm shivering now, my toes starting to go numb. I force my feet to move, teeth chattering. It takes all my strength and will to move my feet and run. I recall dreaming about times like this. It's in those dreams that in the height of the action, right when I need to run, that I find my limbs move in slow motion. Delayed and slow, I panic and am often overtaken by whatever is chasing me.

Now, as those dreams seem to solidify into reality, I'm thankfully able to run faster, without the slow motion. My toes sting with every step which is probably a good thing. I need my blood to flow and keep the feeling in my feet. As I flee, the stone paws of six-legged beasts pound along the forest floor behind me. I run, following in the direction of the great owl and the rider whom I hope is Briar.

They disappear from my view, but I keep the course, dodging branches and hoping I don't step in a hole or stumble over the den of a grumpy creature. In my escape, I have the inclination to toss the dagger from me. The blade is still heavy in my hands, the metal like ice. My lips are starting to lose all feeling and my nose is about as similar as an icicle. Just as I make the decision to throw the dagger, a Reacher howls. Sounds of stone against stone and metal against metal drifts through the undergrowth like snakes. A metallic bark snaps behind me.

I'm slowing and my body loses heat, unable to compete with the dropping temperature only worsening with wind chill. I fling the dagger behind me at the beasts, giving it as much power behind the hilt as I can. In that swift motion, a zing and a clang startle me as the dagger makes contact with something. A flash of blue light shoves through the icy air, sending out a small shock wave of steam. The light flickers, giving me the chance to catch the outline of the great beast. Blue, vein-like light travels through the beast's body, just like the one I'd seen before on the cliff. Only this Reacher is much bigger, twice the size of the others. In my running, I turn back again and see the dagger between the beast's teeth; it spits out the handle, the blade now transformed into energy. The beast and any others that follow don't continue to pursue.

Blind in the darkness, I struggle through spruce and willow trees, pushing branches back and out of my face. The deeper I go, the more I wonder if I'm heading to my death. With the little feeling I have left in my fingers, I push away one more branch and stumble into a clearing that feels like frozen moss humps. Rolling in odd shapes, the ground beneath my feet leaves a satisfying sponge-like crunch with each step. I'm out of breath, my gut tight with fear. I brush a hand over my chest, trying to still my racing heart.

Again, I plunge my fingers into my armpits, desiring any warmth my body has left to soak into my bones. As I do so, I spot a warm glow emitting from the treetops just ahead. It shines like a beacon for me in this dark frozen world that may soon be my grave. I edge towards it, my feet heavy. My breath becomes slow and labored, the act of breathing now tiresome. I continue towards the glow, the tree branches above me catching with the yellow light. When I'm finally below it, I look up and see the faint outlines of a house with a window and woven walls of bark. Light pours from the openings, inviting me to find respite in its arms. The only way there is up, and I have little strength to climb. But I'll try.

Finding a branch closest to me on the large foundation tree, I wrap my weak fingers around it and hold on. Using the momentum of my legs to bring me up, I get a knee on top of the branch and lean my body weight against the trunk. Out of breath again, I rest my head against the tree, my ears, knees and fingers screaming with cold. Dare I ask for help? What choice do I have left? Someone lives in the tree above.

Calling out, my voice parched and weak, I croak, "Is anyone there? Please, someone. Anyone." I want to sleep, my eyes growing heavy with exhaustion. Though lethargic and ready to drop, I force myself to keep my eyes open. I can't fall asleep. Sleeping now is death. I reach for the next branch, not caring for how loud I am in doing so. The dry, frozen wood, papery and covered in lichen, bites into my hands. There is still some feeling left. Brittle twigs break off the branches, and I groan as I lift myself up to the next foothold. All my weight is again against the tree, and I take a break. At this rate, I'll never make it to the top before freezing. I crackle more branches with my fingers, hoping their sound awakens whoever might be in the house above, but the wind threatens to drown out anything I do. Again, I call out.

"Please, I need help." My eyes close, resting for just a moment. I feel myself drifting off, but I force my eyes open, taking in the shape of the next branch. I reach out for it, my hand shaking. I miss it, disoriented. I can't climb up the rest of the way alone. I call out one last time, swallowing to wet my throat.

"Briar," is all I can manage to say, and though it is louder than my other pleas, it does little to shatter through the icy night air. I hug my arms close to my body and sink down with my back to the tree, knees to my chest. As I dip into the realm of frozen sleep, I faintly hear the rustling of branches and the touch of something rough against my nose. It slaps me awake, and I let my eyes open into slits. Light floods around me. I must be dead.

Twenty-Three

BRIAR

Clutching the crossbow, I open the front door. Cold air pours in, and I grit my teeth at the chill. Wind swirls across the floor and bites at my feet. The sound of crackling branches has stopped, and I wait on the deck of the house, light from the open door illuminating the tops of the nearby trees. I listen, watching for movement. Then, far below, a soft groan and a raspy, helpless voice calls my name. Something about it strikes panic into my heart.

I clutch the railing to the deck and lean over, scanning the array of tree branches that separate me from the forest floor. Setting the crossbow down, I turn inside and look for a lantern, anything I can use as a light to penetrate this cold darkness. Heart soaring, I find a glass lantern in the kitchen and shove three candles inside. Holding it above my head, I lean over the railing again and lower it. Something leans against the tree, up on the bottom few branches. Whatever it is doesn't move, and I turn back inside, searching for a rope. Finding one, I tie a tight loop in the end and attach the lantern to it. I lower it down, afraid of what I'll find. As the lantern descends, more of the tree lights up and I make out the distinct shape of a person slumped in a fetal position on a branch. Short, sandy hair and pale skin turning blue.

"Hold on! I'm going to help!" I accidentally bump the rope into their face and grimace. Quickly, I pull the lantern up and remove the light. With as much speed as I can, I tie a large loop, big enough for two feet to step through, at the end of the rope. I throw it down again, beneath the railing this time, making sure my end is secure. I find a sturdy tree trunk jutting up through the floor of the deck and wrap my end around it to take the brunt of the weight, using it like a pulley. I'm not strong enough to pull them up myself with brute force, but using the tree will aid me immensely if they can help navigate the branches.

"I'm dropping a rope to you! Step in the loop and I'll try to pull you up." My voice echoes wildly through the forest. I can't see them clearly, and I don't know if they even heard me. I shake the rope, making sure it is free and not caught on a branch. With my end secure, I wait. Just when I think this attempt is futile, the rope jerks downwards. My heart thumps wildly, and I grip tighter. The rope stretches and I strain, muscles beginning to burn.

"I'm going to pull now!" I call, beginning my attempt. While grunting and straining, the cold causes my fingers to fumble. I can't let go. I heave, the rope sliding on the smooth, papery bark of the birch tree I've anchored it to. Inch by inch, I haul up the mystery figure. Several points during my straining, the rope goes a little slack, then it tightens again. I keep pulling until I see the nearly blue fingers of the individual reach over the edge of the deck. Frantically, I wrap the end of my rope around and around the birch tree and cross it over itself until the tension keeps it from slipping. I'm free to help and immediately crouch and grip their wrists. When I pull them to the top, my eyes fill with tears and I collapse to my knees.

"Peter!" He doesn't answer me. His face is turning blue, and his hands... I don't know how he even made it up the tree. I drag him by his arms into the house, retrieving the lantern then latching the door. I pull him next to the fireplace and begin stoking it. I set the kettle on the stove and then crouch and pull off his shoes and socks, inspecting his feet for frostbite. "It's going to be all right." I rub his feet vigorously when I find they are free from damage—trying to warm them and get blood flowing is the only thing I remember to do. I recall the hypothermia class I took as a child during a wildlife refuge camp, and piece by piece, information comes to me. What to do, what not to do. Does hypothermia work the same in a fantasy realm? I do the next thing I know to do, and that is to keep Peter awake. I slap his face multiple times, gently but firmly. Panic rises in me when he doesn't respond right away. He stirs, lips opening and closing. He's half-frozen, but he's not unconscious.

"You have to stay awake. Please." Tears stream down my face, and I wipe them away, determined to keep him alive. I grab his hands and carefully unzip his jacket and remove it, inspecting for moisture. Thankfully, his clothes are dry, so I go and retrieve the blankets from the pallet in the back room. I begin piling them on and continue to rub his feet. When the tea water is warm, I fill a cup and edge to his upper body, lifting his head into my lap so he can drink. He's half-awake. When I bring the cup to his lips, he drinks. I breathe a sigh of relief. Just that sip alone will go a long way in helping revive his core temperature. The fire is roaring now, and the room is toasty and comfortable. I continue to feed him the tea, and when it's empty, I pour another cup. When I bring over the second brew, he speaks.

"I could get used to this," he says. I almost spill it all over myself when I see him smile. He opens his eyes and looks at me with a tired, contented expression. His face is pink and his fingers are holding onto a warm corner of the blanket. He'll live.

"You aren't in heaven if that's what you're thinking." Is he flirting with me? I look down at my dress and cringe. I look *real* mature in this. Though I'd secretly wanted him to see me in it, this wasn't how I'd planned for that to happen, if ever.

"I know that now. But I might as well be. I never thought you'd serve me tea in a million years, especially like this." His voice is soft, eyes sweeping over my dress. I swallow and crouch to my knees, still holding the cup. My dress puffs out behind me like a silky cloud as I settle to answer him.

"Why's that?"

"We aren't exactly friends anymore. At least, last I checked." He tilts his head in my direction, moving his hands to either side of his body. I stare into the tea, a blush creeping over my face. Even if I just saved his life and he may not be one-hundred percent conscious, he still makes my heart flutter and my cheeks bloom. I thought I was going to get over him and move on with my life. If he doesn't care for me, why is he acting like this?

"I guess not. I mean, not real friends. We haven't kept up," I squirm, watching the steam from the mug coil into the air. He had tried to text me. I hadn't been super talkative. I wonder if his sister told him I'd tried to call him and he was only texting me because of that. I want to believe that but the way he's acting now is entirely different to the Peter I used to know. We've both grown up.

"That's my fault. I should have—" He doesn't finish, and this time, it's his turn to blush. He tries to sit up, and I move backwards, steadying the sloshing cup. When he's fully upright, he rubs the back of his head then stops to look at me. I glance from him then quickly to the tea.

"Here, drink all of it." I hand it over.

"Thank you," he reaches for it, our fingers touching. My stomach leaps at the feel of them against mine, invisible fireworks sparking all over. I'm so confused right now. He's looking at me like I'm the only person he cares about. The crackling of the fire in the stove seems to resonate and sync up with the sparks flying over my skin. Blinking, I slowly break free from his side, and move to the stove and dampen the air flow before it overheats. Soon, I'm drinking my own cup and watching Peter stare silently into the fire. We don't say anything for a long time.

"How did you get here? Why are you here?" I finally ask. There's so much awkward tension between us that any conversation is life-saving. I move to sit across from him on the floor. Peter swallows then goes on to tell me everything that happened the moment he came to the bookshop this morning and all the events leading up to now. I tell him my side of the story, and soon, we've connected the dots. He knows why I came through and why I must stay. He doesn't scold me but instead taps his fingers on his now-empty cup.

"I won't let you execute this plan alone. If Wystan is in trouble, then the only way to deliver the note and begin the plan is by going to Breezewood ourselves." I contemplate his words, taking in the chivalrous gesture of help. He knows I'm independent and per-haps capable of completing the plan, but the tone of his voice tells me he doesn't want me to do it all by myself. If I'm being honest, I don't want to go alone. I want protection. I need someone who is stronger than me to watch out for us both. Two people are better than one.

"We'll have to dress up. It's a masquerade. Blending in is how we'll get close enough to the king to even have a chance at deliv-ering the note." I look down at the smooth fabric of my dress. My heart beats faster at the thought of him dressing up as well.

"You look ready enough," he says, eyebrows rising playfully. I blink quickly, flattered. I hide part of my face with my cup.

"Hardly. But you'll definitely need something. Thankfully Tara has a whole workshop here," I say, trying to ignore his subtle flirta-tion. I toss a look towards the back room. We'll need masquerade masks, and I'll need to darken my hair. Peter will need a suit of some kind, and then we'll have to walk all the way to Breezewood in the dark. Peter sets his cup on the floor then draws his knees up, his arms wrapped around them.

"I suppose we should match." His eyes graze the floor then they coast up to me, waiting for approval. I want to say a million things. I want to tell him that he lost his chance to talk to me like this years ago. But I also want to tell him that I've liked him since we met in school, and that I haven't stopped. The words from the confession note on my bed dry up in my throat as I remember our conversation from the night of graduation. I don't want to be told the same things from him again and feel the pain of rejection. Maybe it's better if I don't say anything at all. I avoid his eyes and set my cup in my lap, fidgeting with the handle.

"We can look through the supplies and find what we need." When I explain the rest of the plan, Peter nods, agreeing.

"Regardless of the method, masquerade or not, we have to be in close contact momentarily with the king. This seems to be our easiest option. When do we leave?"

As soon as preparations are made, both of us have done our very best in attempting a masquerade wardrobe with Tara's supplies. I carefully apply a powder that darkens my hair and takes the edge off my rusty coloring. Peter helps me pin some of it up, setting a floral accent near my part. He dons a gray suit and pins a matching floral accent to his front pocket. I've never seen him looking so handsome.

We outline our plan and make the decision to walk to Breeze-wood Castle. Peter, though mostly recovered, is still a little weak, and neither of us look forward to descending the tree. But upon further inspection of the tree house, I find a rope ladder that unfolds from the far end of the deck. After bundling up with blankets for shawls and doing our best to zip our coats over our fine clothes, we descend the ladder with the crossbow and lantern. The wind has died down and the distance to Breezewood Castle is not terribly far. I'm confident we'll keep from getting too chilled. When we reach the forest floor, I carefully check my book bag where I stashed our normal clothes, dress shoes, and intricate masks for the event. I have the crossbow on my back, and when I unsling it to check for any forgotten items, I catch Peter looking at me. He slowly sets the lantern at his feet and continues to stare at me with unblinking eyes, but I can't tell if it is from fear or curiosity. Just before I can look away from the intensity of his gaze, he steps towards me.

"Briar, I.." He falters, clenching and unclenching his fists. I can't tell a single thing he's thinking. In the soft light of the lantern, I make out a wateriness in his eyes. Is he crying? "I should have come to you and asked. I shouldn't have just taken what others said and believed it. It was wrong of me to deface your character based solely on what others said about you."

"I don't understand," I say truthfully. What could he possibly be talking to me about at a time like this?

"The time you disappeared. I didn't know what to think. I believed the lies and speculations that erupted after the incident. What you told the police, I should have believed that over what people at school told me. For years, I doubted you. I'm sorry."

"Peter, I'm not offended." Well, I was years ago, but I'm not anymore. I've had a lot of time to think about this. I never truly knew what he thought anyway but I had prepared myself for this. It didn't hurt like it could have.

"It doesn't matter. I was wrong to tell you a lie based on others' viewpoints."

"You lied to me?" I raise my eyebrows, curious as to what this lie could be.

"I once said I only ever thought of you as a friend. I didn't tell the whole truth." He presses his lips together tightly, a look of regret painted on his face.

My face burns at the hint of the conversation I had with him years ago over text. He remembers it just as clearly as I do.

"We should have talked about it in person. I should have told you what I really felt about you instead of pushing you away over a bunch of false claims over text. Briar, I'm sorry. Will you forgive me?" He reaches out a hand as if I am to shake it. I stare at him, disbelief flooding me. He'd lied to me? He'd actually cared for me? My assumptions had been true?

I stand, shocked. I examine my thoughts and find that I don't have any hard feelings towards him. If anything, I'm ready to make amends for something I partially instigated. If I'd never reached out and asked his true feelings, would he have been honest with me? Or would he have slowly stopped hanging out with me like he did after graduation? I know there's no use asking about what could have happened. What matters is what happens now. I truthfully miss the small bond we used to have and can't help but want it to be even more. Despite what I've told myself about getting over him and moving on, the truth is, I don't want to. I still care for him, and if he's wanting to renew our friendship, then who am I to say no?

Slowly, I extend my own hand. When our fingers touch, heat floods into my face and up my arm. The handshake he gives me is firm and gentle. My heart flutters at the small caress of his thumb. I don't want him to let go. He smiles, the corners of his eyes crinkling, pressed there by immense joy.

"I thought I had lost our friendship. The moment I found the portal, I realized just how stupid I was. I should have believed you."

"Even if you would have believed me, what I believed then wasn't the whole truth. But we can't change the past," I say.

"But we can learn from it, and I've learned all right. In fact, I've learned enough that I don't care how dumb I look and feel. Briar, I've wanted to ask you this for a long time." His words are fast and nervous. My stomach does a flip, and there's a brief moment where I think Peter is going to do something I'm not ready for. But he surprises me. Still holding my hand, he squeezes it and says, "Briar, if it is all right with you, I want to get to know you more. I realized that I didn't know you well enough then, and I certainly don't now, but I would like to pursue you. That is, if you want me to." He looks at me with a shivery, hopeful smile.

I melt. Almost laugh. Giddy with happiness, I smile, relieved and beyond ready to give him my answer. All I ever wanted from him was the truth. Even if this conversation had never come up, continuing to be friends would have been enough. But this is beyond what I'd hoped for, something I thought I knew would never happen. Obviously I was wrong.

"I would like that very much." My face is glowing. There are not enough words to describe all the things I'm feeling. The part of my heart that was bruised is now finally being healed. Peter moves his thumb over my hands again. I look up into his eyes, not caring for the awkward silence between us. If anything, I've craved this exact moment for as long as I can remember. No one has ever wanted this kind of romance more than me.

"Then as soon as this adventure is over, I'll make it right with you and your family. I want this. I want you," Peter says, lifting my hand up to his lips. His touch is soft against the back of my palm, and the gentlemanly gesture is more than I can bear. I suck in a breath, hardly believing the words I'm hearing. I only ever dreamed of these things, and now, just like the existence of the portal and Breezewood, they have finally come true.

I find my eyes brimming with tears of both happiness and relief, the longing of many years spilling like a cup overflowing. I step closer to him, and he releases my hand, pulling me in, accepting my embrace. In the dark of the forest, he pulls me close and surrounds my waist with his arms. I wrap my own around his neck and bury my face in the crook of his neck.

"I never want to be apart from you," I say, my voice muffled. Finally, something of my confession note bubbles to the surface.

He squeezes me tightly, whispering back, his breath tickling my skin, "Neither do I."

In the soft, glowing light of the lantern, he presses a warm and gentle kiss on my forehead. It's in this moment I feel the closest to anyone I've ever felt in my entire life. I want him to kiss me for real, but I know he won't. Not yet anyway. He's too much of a gentleman, and without getting to know me longer, he won't do it. He wants a clear conscience. Somehow, that just makes him all the more romantic.

"We need to get to Breezewood and stop Alder. We have to make this plan work," Peter says against my ear.

"I'm confident I know the way. I tracked the direction from when I flew to the portal and back. We'll just have to hurry. The party goes only until morning," I whisper, then slowly break from his embrace. I pick up my book bag, slinging it over my shoulder and re-wrap the borrowed blanket like a shawl. The cold does not seem so bad now.

"Then lead the way. I'll take the crossbow." He picks it up off the ground and shoulders it. I can't help but admire him. A guy willing to put their life on the line and be your protector is incredibly attractive. I turn away, smiling as he looks at me in my masquerade gown. I take the lantern and hold it out, stepping through the forest. My heart quickens as he slips a hand into mine. "It's cold out and you don't have gloves," he says. I could roll my eyes but I don't. I don't want to. He can be as sweet and cliche as he likes with me.

"What if my other hand gets cold?" I answer back sweetly, not meeting his eyes. I can almost hear him smile when he answers.

"We'll just have to switch hands."

When the mountain entrance of Breezewood finally greets us, my candle in the lantern is about to go out. Quickly, we don our dancing shoes and masks, the note secure in my dress pocket. Peter and I hide the crossbow and bag with our other shoes behind a bush, still taking the lantern. While thankful for no run-ins with Reachers, I knock on the door quickly, remembering foggily how Wystan had knocked. I plead that Finn will answer the door. When it creaks open, my face falls at the sight of another door guard that I do not know.

"Business?"

"The masquerade. We are late." I feel like I should curtsy or something but I don't, not sure of all the customs. The guard raises a brow.

"Very late. The height of the dancing has begun. You've missed all the introductions." The guard's voice is grave and stern. He probably thought he wouldn't have to open the heavy door tonight.

Peter steps in. "August and Atlas invited us. We were told we were welcome here. When celebrating the great Harvest, all in Breezewood are welcome."

The guard hesitates at Peter's words, but as he surveys our clothes and sees that we are dressed appropriately, he opens the door wide. "Then by all means, welcome to Breezewood Castle. The common room is this way."

The moment I step through the halls and into the Breezewood common room, my body goes numb with anxiety. Anyone here could remember me from my initial run in with the king. Anyone here could report me, and my mission will die. My hands rest on Peter's arm as we enter, and I can feel the eyes of many.

My hair would have been a dead giveaway had Tara not had a great deal of supplies at the treehouse. One look in a cracked mirror and I thought I might have done an excellent job in disguising it with powdered clay and woven flowers. But now, I'm not confident in my abilities underneath so much light.

My borrowed dainty, silver heels collide with the rich marble floor of the Breezewood common room, sending shivers of unease and excitement through me.

The tinkling of the waterfall combined with the soft hum of stringed instruments is all that is needed to break through my survey of my appearance, reminding me of where I am. The fluttering laughter of maidens near a food table and the swirl of sparkling dresses and metallic armor sends my nerves into overdrive. I don't know how to dance. The mask over my face feels hot and crowded. I press my tinted lips together. All I need to do is blend in and find out where Wystan went while successfully delivering a new note.

Peter whispers in my ear. "I'm going to try to find August. I'll stay in the room if you need me."

I nod and release his arm. He slips through the crowd, parting it without even touching anyone. He looks so regal and noble in the borrowed suit and black mask. I turn away and cross the floor, heading in the direction of the food table. Maybe grabbing a drink will dissuade anyone from trying to dance with me.

Before I reach the table, the music begins to swell. Sweet and sorrowful notes fill the room. The dancers on the floor briskly change their pace, and I'm left to watch as glittering figures glide over the gray marble as if propelled by invisible wings. Instead of fast twirling and weaving in and out, dancers couple up and begin a slow-motion choreography.

An unfamiliar hand slips into my own and pulls me out onto the dance floor. I stop watching the other dancers, my throat dry with fear. I've been discovered.

"Pardon me, but I believe you promised me a dance?" a familiar voice says. I turn my eyes up to see a crimson mask drawn back with black ribbon. I'm about to free my hand, but the soft smile and the shine of the eyes stops me. My heart leaps. Joel!

Joel pulls me farther onto the dance floor, and I forget about all my fears of not knowing how to dance. The music grows, each note more sorrowful and romantic than the last. Almost as if the players and music itself know the plight I and the rest of Breezewood are in.

My dress sways around my ankles as Joel leads me in a graceful waltz, twirling me and dipping me in a circle. I don't need to know how to dance. The music... It's almost as if it is guiding me. My feet need no direction. I feel the steps and then I take them. This is real dancing.

I'm lost in the moment as if time is in slow motion. Elegant chiffon, tulle, satin, and lace ripple over the dance floor while my own gown of moss-green silk almost floats. When at last the music turns in a different direction, Joel continues to dance with me, but we edge farther off the floor until we melt into a crowd of others too busy eating and drinking to pay us much notice. Joel leads me by the hand behind a column, then lets go.

Leaning to my ear, he whispers a string of chilling words. "Whatever you're planning, it's not going to work. The king may be mad but the people at his side are not." With that, he removes his mask.

Twenty-Four

PETER

As I mingle with the glittering guests of the masquerade ball, I marvel at the beauty and intricacy of the common room. The edges of the ceiling are decorated with royal crown molding, all made of stone. Each section of the trim works together to accentuate a spherical painting of stars and their constellations over the center of the room. Large ceramic vases are stationed around the common room filled with white birch branches and ferns. My eyes are drawn back up to the painted ceiling and an idea sparks. An escape room could do with something like this, something different and interesting. Maybe instead of constellations, a clue to aid or distract could be added into the room? Storing the idea away, I continue taking in the rest of the party.

I avert my eyes from several ladies who look my way, whispering. Though each attendee wears a mask, I'm certain people recognize peers and strangers. A simple mask isn't enough to hide your identity. Or is it? No one approaches me to ask what I'm doing here. No one pesters me for proof of invitation. At this type of event, everyone is determined to blend in and stand out at the same time. I just hope Briar and I aren't the ones winning.

I scan the room for August and Atlas. I have more questions, and it's imperative that I get answers. I need August to help with Briar's plan. As far as I'm aware, we both want the same things. But Atlas, I'm not so sure.

I see the dark overcoat of a man standing near a waterfall, talking with another shorter figure. I head that way, sure that it is August. When I circle the pair, they turn to look at me. I avoid them as soon as I realize that neither man is familiar. I walk past and continue my nonchalant perusal of the rest of the party. The dancing has taken a new turn, and I pause to scan the middle of the floor. It's flowing with skirts and soft-toed gentlemen, guiding their partners in an ethereal three-step. I accept a glass of something from a servant and hold it between clammy fingers. Staring briefly into its contents, I refrain from drinking the purple liquid and instead turn my eyes back to the dance floor. I spot Briar's green dress circling over the marble, and my mouth goes dry. She appears to have become one with the music. The lighting on her hair and dress is gauzy, while her flushed cheeks remind me of antique oil paintings of exceptional quality. Whoever is dancing with her is proficient in their skills, leading her like they've been doing it their entire lives. When the music slows, I watch as they twirl and waltz to the edge of the crowd. Slowly, Briar's partner pulls her behind a column and they are out of view. I grip the stem of my glass tightly then loosen my grip, afraid I'll snap it. I move in their direction, setting my untouched glass on the food table, my dress shoes clicking.

Before I reach the column, someone steps in front of me, and I'm forced to stop. They are taller than me, and by the sneer on their face, they know I don't belong.

"I heard you were formally invited by the majesty's brother. Is this true?" the man asks. He wears a long robe and his head is covered in thinning mouse-brown hair. His hands are neatly crossed in front like a butler's, and I'm inclined to believe he has some importance. He's also not wearing a mask.

"Undoubtedly. I was actually looking for him. Do you know where he is so I may speak with him?"

"Mmmm, indeed. Right this way," he says, uncrossing his hands and extending an arm towards a corridor that leads away from the party. I look past him, trying to spot Briar. Unable to see her, I hesitate.

"Might you tell him to meet me here? I have someone I'd like to dance with," I say, trying to avoid leaving the room. It isn't a lie. If I can, I'll ask Briar to dance at least once. She won't be wowed by any means, but I'll try my best.

"I'm afraid August is occupied currently, but I'll let him know your wishes," the man says with a short and stiff bow. I can't tell if he is a butler or someone of higher importance. The way he stares at me gives me the creeps. He has snake-like eyes and a sniveling, nasally voice. That uneasy feeling I'd felt in the forest earlier returns, and my stomach coils with distrust. The man steps away and hurries down the corridor he'd directed me to. I watch him leave then turn my back and look for Briar.

Quickly, the dancing stops. Men and women begin clapping as the musicians in the corner change the song from one of sweeping romance to a regal and powerful melody. Soon, all our eyes are drawn upwards as the stone ceiling begins to glow with hundreds of what looks like stars. Servants begin to extinguish candles and torches and little by little; the room grows dark except for the points of light above. The hum of amused guests and stringed instruments sends my senses into overdrive. I should never have left Briar's side. Anything and anyone could steal her away in this blackness.

As the starry ceiling twinkles, a larger glow begins to emit from the balcony above. Soon, torch-bearing maidens file along the balcony walkway, and then a man with a stiff countenance steps through and places both hands on the railing. He leans over partially, head held high. As the guests begin to raise their glasses and hands, the music quiets.

"To our king!" They say almost in unison, then they drink and clap. Alder lifts his hands to quiet the crowd.

"My people, we celebrate another successful Harvest. Again, our miners have filled our vault with precious gems and now, our storeroom is filled with good things. While the winter may be cold, our home here will be warm and merry. Dance the rest of the night and fill your plates. Talk of the good times and let this night warm you for the rest of the winter." The crowd cheers again, and the musicians begin to play a lively melody that brings many couples together into a large circle. Soon, the torches are relit one by one, and I see Alder accompanied by several robed men, similar to the man I met earlier, descend stairs onto the common room floor. When he is at our level, he takes a seat near the food table in an elevated chair. A servant brings him a goblet, and soon, he's watching the dancing with about as much enthusiasm as a snake would. I study him, every so often his eyes scanning the room, falling on couples here and there but ultimately not lingering long. I swallow, thankful he hasn't spotted me. With the room fully lit again, I continue my search for Briar. When I reach the column where she had been pulled to, she isn't there. Worried, I scan the dancers again. No sign of her green silk dress and no sign of her mystery partner. I turn my head and step backwards then forwards, looking for her. When my eyes dart towards the food table, I find the king looking me dead in the eyes, a goblet to his lips. Somehow, he knows.

A conversation I had with Anna resurfaces, and I remember her telling me she knew Atlas was from Breezewood because of his eyes. Did the king see something in my eyes that gave away that I was a Worlder? Did the others at the party see as well? I avoid the king's gaze and step behind a group of nobles who are gossiping about the latest dresses and taste of the wine. Before I know it, I am drawn into the conversation by an older woman in a dress that matches the contents of her glass.

"What say you? Doesn't this year's Harvest celebration seem grander than the last?" All five sets of eyes in the circle are on me. I open my mouth then close it, unsure of how to answer. One of the men raises a brow at my hesitation, taking a sip of his drink. I clear my throat and give it my best shot.

"To me, this masquerade is only a little above the rest. It seems quite grand, but I don't know. Something about it seems off. Doesn't the king look bored?" I risk offending them, but I want to know what they think. Do the people really love their king?

"Yes, he does. We were commenting on it last year. Every year the parties are grander and longer, and every year the king looks more bored," the woman in purple states, agreeing with me.

"I suppose that's what happens when you're used to such things. Me? I never get tired of it!" giggles a young woman in red. There seems to be no animosity in this group of guests. I resolve to forgo the subtle investigation and instead probe for other answers. *I need to find Briar.*

"I'm looking for my dance partner. Have you seen her? She's in a green, silk gown," I ask, changing the subject. Any direction at all will be helpful. I'm so lost in this place. Briar didn't give me a full debrief of the way around or much of an expectation. Not that she knew much herself.

"Oh, you mean the one who was dancing with the king's son? Oh, yes, of course. We've been watching them," the woman in purple says, taking a small sip. The king's son?

"I'm not sure where they've gone to, but they are beautiful to-gether. He's a fabulous dancer," the girl in red says.

I nod and dip my head. "Thank you." I excuse myself from the circle, keeping out of view of the king. Alder has a son? And he was dancing with Briar? Almost as soon as I decide to leave the common room down a side corridor, someone puts their hand on my shoulder.

"You made it," August says. His voice is low, but there's a twinkle in his eyes beneath his emerald-green mask. He's glad to see me, but I'm not entirely glad to see him.

"Barely, but I'm here. Briar is okay, too, but she's missing." I scan the room again, and August wraps his arm around my shoulder and pushes me into a stroll. I capitulate and walk with him.

"Alder is watching you quite closely. There's not much a Worlder has to do to draw his eye. Simply existing is enough. But he's becoming more curious about your kind. His power is nearly gone as well as the jewels in the mountain. With next to no food left, traversing into your realm is a possibility," he says in a low tone.

I stop walking and look at him.

"Are you saying he's considering uprooting Breezewood and crossing into our world?"

"I know my brother well enough to say it is his last resort. While he once felt threatened by Worlders and how they might come to take his kingdom from him, now there's a change in his thinking."

"You spoke with him?"

"As soon as we arrived. Atlas is with him now." August tips his head towards Alder's chair, and I see Atlas at his right.

"Does your brother not hate him? Wasn't he banished?"

"Alder is glad to see him again. Atlas's truth pearl has given him enough information, more than he ever thought possible."

"Alder didn't realize Atlas had gone through a portal into the modern world," I say with little inflection.

"Precisely. Now that he does, the information Atlas knows is at his fingertips."

"Why didn't you stop him?" My brow wrinkles. Surely this information should be kept from Alder. The less he knows about our world, the better, right?

"In my research in the modern world, the portals that open due to creatives simply crafting beauty that mimics or touches the true reality are categorized into two different types. Tethered portals and untethered. The portal in the bookstore was once a tethered portal, and now it is untethered. The person who made it closed it, and only they can go through at their will."

"What's the difference?" Shocked at the information so readily falling into my lap, I listen while August walks me to the edge of the circular common room. We lean against a wall beside a potted plant and keep our voices low.

"Tethered portals allow anyone to enter through it with the use of a word or phrase that is associated with the portal and its creation. The phrase is tethered to an object and that is the only thing standing between others entering the realm. The person who created the portal doesn't have to be alive or even present for it to work when a gate is tethered. As long as the word or phrase is known and spoken near the portal, it will open and allow that person to step through. There are also rare cases of portals not associated with a word at all and simply open at the creator's beck and call. Like the one I went through on the sea. I didn't open it. Someone else did before they died in the crash, and I was able to see it and pass through. But even if no one else did ask for it to open, there are times in history where portals opened and people passed through."

"And untethered portals?"

"An untethered portal is one that is closed off to everyone except for the creator. Only the creator can open it, and in order for others to pass through it, they must be present and touching the creator as they step through. I believe the bookstore portal is now untethered. Someone has closed it and drawn it to themself."

"Briar," I say.

"If Briar is responsible, you will need her to open it. If you don't have her open it, you'll be trapped here. The chances of stumbling across another portal, especially a tethered or rogue one, are very low. I was lucky all those years ago."

"What does Alder plan to do then? If Briar is able to keep the portal closed unless she wants it to open, is Alder going to try and find a new portal somewhere else?"

"That, or force Briar to do his bidding. He has you here. And your friends." I withdraw from the wall. The way August says 'your friends' puts me on edge. Why do I feel like he keeps subtly telling me to leave this place?

"Are you saying Alder wanted us to come here?"

"Alder may not have planned it, but those influencing him did."

"Then what are we to do?" I don't like what's being tossed around.

"Alder may be my brother, but he needs to be stopped. For the time being, he believes I am on his side."

"What about Atlas?"

"I don't know," August says with eyes that dart towards the dance floor. I follow him and see that the lively dance has continued into an intricate weaving pattern. I watch August's eyes flicker over the crowd then look away.

"What is it?" I ask.

He turns to me sharply. "Remember when I told you about the escape room and how you needed to build it quickly?"

"Yes?"

"It wasn't just to keep you distracted. I needed you to protect the portal from the modern world. But now that it is untethered, it isn't as dangerous. As long as you find out who it's who made it and get them to keep it a secret, the bookstore portal will remain under the nose of the modern realm."

"But how did you know about it? How did you know to come through?"

"Listen, Peter," August swallows, a spark of fear in his eyes. "I came back... because I'm the true king. Alder is a false placeholder. Any portals on my land that open up I know about. Even from Colorado, I sensed a portal in my lands."

I just stare at him dumbfounded. This is getting even more confusing. August is the true king of Breezewood?

"You have... powers?" I truly didn't know this guy. I thought I did, but nope. Absolutely not.

"Yes, the power to know when portals in Breezewood lands open and where they are. Since I was on the other side, I knew right where it was in the modern world. The bookstore. Right where you had decided to build your escape room. I came to make sure you were safe and to find a way to close it after I sensed a lot of opening and closing activity."

"How is this possible?"

"I am the heir to the throne. We brothers are triplets, but growing up, no one ever told us who was born first. However, Father told only me on his deathbed thirteen years ago. With that knowledge, he passed on his gift to me that I might reign in his place. But Alder, believing himself to be the firstborn and greedy for the throne, took up any power, even dark power, to assert his dominance and gain the kingdom. Atlas was banished shortly after."

"Why haven't you declared your kingship over him? Why haven't you stayed in Breezewood to protect your people?" I'm still struggling with the fact that magic and powers even exist. Where was this in science class?

"Alder had already called the darkness upon Breezewood, even before my father died. By the time I came into my power, Breezewood was under shadow. I did not know how to fix it and was afraid to speak out as the true king until I had a solution. I also wanted to find Atlas. But since being away from Breezewood and in my gifting, I have finally gained an understanding for the portals I can sense. And I found a cure."

"Truly?"

"If Alder and the darkness at his side can be tricked into reversing the curse, Breezewood can be saved."

"What does it look like? Where is it?"

"Can you not feel it? It's in the air of this place. When you walk the halls, a feeling of a shadow presses around you. Even the forests. When you look into my brother's eyes, you can see the hollowness and corruption of his soul. He's given himself entirely over to evil. The darkness manifests into what we call Wolves. They choose to show themselves when they please, and I have found some can shapeshift into beings."

"Like, people?"

"People, animals, or their own creation," August says with a shiver, voice in a harsh whisper. I think of the man with no mask I had encountered just before and of the Reachers in the forest.

"And how do you propose we fight it or trick it?" I watch as August opens his mouth then closes it, eyes looking away from mine. He's just as afraid as I am. He's been hiding sadness and fighting cowardice. Even more so, he's been afraid to speak the truth to me. I wonder if it was because Atlas was around?

"You can only fight darkness with light," he says, glancing again towards the dancers. There's a sadness pooling in his once-twinkling eyes. If he's the true king, then I must be seeing compassion and care for his people mixed with the fear of failure.

"Why didn't you tell me all this first thing?"

"Because. I didn't want to drag you into my problem. Breezewood is my responsibility, and your life didn't need to be in danger."

"What about earlier, at the portal? You don't trust Atlas do you?"

"He's not exactly in his right mind. His time being banished has caused his senses to become warped. Not to mention, the truth pearl he carries has slowly been leaking a poison to alter his thinking. He now believes Alder was right to banish him, yet he still treats and looks up to me as a brother. I don't trust him to keep his mouth shut, that's for certain, or what he might do on a whim."

"Then Alder does know I'm here," I say with a swallow. And if the pearl Atlas has is anything like Briar's, does that mean she's being fed poison, too? I shudder. I know now that I am exactly where I need to be.

"Yes, yes, he probably does. But he might not know if Briar is here yet." August scrunches his eyebrows. I clench my fists, mind racing. August is the puzzlemaster. He out of all people should know how to trick Alder and these shadow beings into reversing the curse. I think fast, laying out a plan.

"Is there anywhere more private we can talk?" I ask.

"The museum. Alder and his men shouldn't find us there." He leads me away from the party, and I follow, ready to detail to him Briar's plan and my new addition to it.

Twenty-Five

BRIAR

When Joel removes his mask, his face is tight with anxiety. The fact that he's alive is a balm to my hurting soul. Everyone at home will be relieved.

"What do you mean? What's wrong?" He doesn't answer me and instead puts a finger to his lips and pulls me outside the common room into a secluded hall, away from any ears.

"I needed you to see that it was truly me and not someone you didn't know. There are shapeshifters among us," he says, indicating the mask in his hands. I nod, only partially understanding.

"I was pretty sure it was you. Wait until Peter knows you're alive," I say. What exactly did he mean by shapeshifters?

"Peter's here?" His face contorts in worry.

"Yes, he's here to help bring you back and help save Breezewood."

"Briar, we all have to leave, and you have to get that pearl removed, now."

"I know. That's why I came back. I had to try to save you, keep the portal closed, and get the king to remove the pearl."

"He won't remove it, not without cause."

"I was going to give him one. Peter was helping me. How are you still alive?" I ask, not hiding the fact that I'm glad to see him well. I let it fall however, not wanting to confuse him. My heart belongs to Peter, so I hope he doesn't take my smiles and the dance that just happened as something more than friendship. Though, I remind myself, he was the one who asked me to dance.

"I'll get to that later. For now, you must know that the people of Breezewood have been temporarily drugged with deception magic during the course of the party. I think it is in the drinks."

"What?" I think back to how I had planned to get a drink to avoid being danced with. No wonder Joel had stolen me away before I had a chance to touch a glass. I might have been poisoned.

"The magic is playing with their minds. It relies on lies and weaves its way into their consciousnesses. Because of it, some think you are a princess of Breezewood. Some even believe that I am the king's son, though Alder isn't even married and has no son. They are severely confused and being lied to by whatever dark power Alder is working with," he says, looking over his shoulder then resting his eyes on me.

I blink. "Why would the king do that to his people?" Alder must be truly mad to send his own people into confusion by putting a deception magic in their drinks. However that works. All this new information is happening at once, and my head is beginning to ache. Shapeshifters, deception magic, and Joel being alive. Where will it end?

"Because he wants control. He doesn't want people questioning his methods in gaining more power. If his people are believing certain lies, it's because they are being fed them through the magic. If everyone is confused, they won't know who the enemy is and will accept whoever meets their needs."

"Why not turn them against us? What does he gain by keeping us alive?" I ask. All it would really take is one well-placed lie and enough belief behind it to send the people into becoming our enemies.

"Because he needs us for something. More specifically you."

"As if I have any role to play in this," I add, wondering what on earth the king could want with me. From what Peter told me in the treehouse, the king would have more than enough information from Atlas about our world because of his pearl. Mine seemed of little use in comparison. I take that moment to feel it with my tongue. Had it gotten smaller?

"There are people in the castle, however, who have been spreading rumors that are not acquainted with the deception magic. They say that Alder is growing increasingly corrupt and there are even some that deny his right to rule. Wystan is one of these."

I nod, understanding the motive for these rumors. Rumors I believe as all I've seen thus far shows that Alder is insane. "You mentioned earlier that my original plan won't work? How do you know what I was going to do?" I stiffen at the look that crosses his face. Despondency.

"Wystan and Tara have been questioned and detained. Whatever plan they were involved in has been found out."

I groan at his words. The plan is basically doomed. "What does Alder really want?" I ask, disappointment slipping through my teeth. We were so close!

"To bring our world's resources to Breezewood and to use you and any Worlder he can to do it. Not to mention, corrupting anyone with his deception magic to do what he wants."

"What can I do that would help him attempt this?" Whatever it is, I want to unlearn it quickly and leave this place with Joel and Peter. Maybe simply leaving and closing off any portal I can will keep him trapped here and away from my home and family and friends. But I think of Wystan and Tara and the others Naomi had mentioned that are trapped somewhere within this world. They will die unless we stop Alder completely.

"You can freely come and go through the portals. In fact, you are responsible for the one in the bookstore, are you not?"

"I don't know. I think so, but I don't understand it. How can Alder use me for that ability?"

"He'll use the truth pearl and deception magic to enslave you. He'll make you open portals for those in his service to travel through. Some might even bring Reachers through to use as servants to sniff out power sources. I've seen it done here. Alder and the ones he serves are responsible for the Reachers. They have been the ones mining for gems in the mountain, not any of the people. Over time, he has been releasing miners to be free of work in order to hide the fact that the gems are running out."

Interesting. Using Reachers to mine for gems.

"But Alder won't go through a portal himself?" I ask, putting pieces together. So Reachers were planned, and he controls them somehow. Were the ones on the surface just there to scare people? Why then did he have the night patrols fight them? Maybe to complete the ruse that Reachers are against them?

"If Alder goes through a portal and leaves Breezewood, the curse over the kingdom is broken, which means his power dies. Whatever pact he made with the dark power keeps him confined here. But he's trying to find a workaround."

"That's what I planned to do. I wanted to pull him through a portal." I think of Jadis, the white witch from Narnia and how she had accidentally traveled with Polly and Digory to the modern world and caused chaos. I think of her entrance into Narnia and ultimate wintry rule there. What would it have been like to have her in the modern realm with the power of winter and darkness at her fingertips? I compare her to Alder in Breezewood. Their motives are basically the same. I don't want any of my what ifs to come to fruition. No, I have to stay and help Breezewood.

"He won't go near a portal. He won't leave Breezewood for anything. The wolves at his side won't let him. I've seen it. Sometimes he breaks out of the darkness for a moment and I think I see the Alder that used to be, but then he's quickly enveloped in darkness again, the wolves surrounding him like dark vultures."

Joel's words make my stomach tighten into knots. Shivers slide over my arms like a million tiny spiders. I've heard many stories of people falling into darkness, their lives descending into varying stages of oppression. Alder's story sounds similar, if not exactly the same.

"What about a cure to his magic? If he is unable to feed his people anymore due to his magic dying, won't an antidote entice him to leave?"

"His magic isn't dying!" Joel says, eyes flying wide with surprise. "Who told you that?"

"Wystan and Peter."

"Wystan doesn't know it all. And if Peter learned it from someone else, then they don't know the whole truth. Briar, Alder is growing *more* powerful, not less. The only thing he lacks is resources. The mountain is dry of gems and metals. He only needs more."

Realization hits me like a wave. So Alder's power isn't dying—it is only being focused somewhere else. What Wystan had told me was based on the little that he saw and heard. Rumors. Therein lay the problem. The king probably let him find out that information, maybe even starting the rumor himself with deception magic. If people believed Alder to be weak, they would underestimate him. Mix that in with other confusion, and you pin the entire kingdom against each other and no one knows what to believe.

"So if Reachers are servants of Alder and Alder wants me alive, why was I given a truth pearl and sent out of the castle to die?" I ask the question before I forget it. I remember Wystan being adamant that me being sent outside the castle that one night with a truth pearl was to ultimately kill me.

"To test you. I don't actually believe the Reachers were going to kill you. I've seen some in this very castle, and they are quite docile when fed. My guess is he sent you out to see who was on his side. Some Wolves shapeshift into Reachers. If any who were seeking you the night you left and saw you rescued, then they could report back to the king."

"If they shapeshift, what shapes can they take?" I recall the two guards who walked me to the exit during my first time in the castle. Their necks and a part of their jaws had been reflective like glass or metal. Had they been wolves in disguise? Had they seen Finn's kindness to me and turned him in to the king?

"There are five wolves in the castle. Two are guards, one is an advisor, and one is attached to Alder. The fifth one is unknown. They can take the shape of most anything that gives them permission," Joel says. I shiver. I'm almost positive now that the two guards I saw were wolves. I remember being led down the corridors of the mountain by them. They had been so close. Had they morphed into Reachers and followed me, seeing Wystan come to my rescue?

"Were you almost fed to them?" I ask, pushing aside some of my racing thoughts.

"Nearly. But I was deemed useful to them. Also, partly because I would not let them have total control over me. Being fed to a wolf here isn't the same thing in our world."

I nod understanding what he meant by control, but he was deemed useful for what? I feel the note in my pocket, its contents seemingly weak now in the face of all this new information.

"I was kept alive for one purpose. I'm supposed to turn you and all my friends and any traitors over to the king and wolves in exchange for my life and the life of one of my friends," Joel says, eyes sad. His jaw twitches as if he's holding back more information that he wants to share. Before I can interrupt him in protest, he speaks again. "But I can't do that. I won't."

"Joel, stop. You are going to come back to Homer with me and Peter. Plus, all our other friends are safe. Worried about us, but safe."

"Briar, you don't understand, Alder is not the only bad guy. At least, he's not just in Breezewood all the time. He never leaves the castle, but he also has a root in our realm. One we are familiar with."

"What are you saying?" My stomach drops then fills with dread. My fingers and ears tingle and my head pulses with pain.

What Joel is saying now is the information he's been holding back. The way his hands clench at his sides and the way he keeps swallowing and looking over his shoulder. This is the information that has evaded us for too long.

"Alder isn't just Alder all the time. Sometimes when he's in Breezewood, he's someone else from our realm." Joel swallows. My vision swims, and the blood drains from my face. No. What he's saying can't be happening. "He's got two lives, and when he falls into the clutches of darkness, I think he's transported from our realm and into Breezewood."

"Who. Is. He." My words come out in quick sharp breaths.

"I think it's Andrew. The one who owns the book store."

I can't believe it. Andrew, the boss I loved working with? The one who brought me the best sandwich of my life and chai tea the day I stepped into Breezewood? The one who owns my favorite place in all of Homer?

"It can't be. No, that doesn't add up. He was still in Homer when I was in Breezewood and met with Alder. You came in after me, Peter said, and Andrew was working the counter. Andrew can't be in two places at once, can he?"

"Are you sure it was Andrew working the counter the day I went in after you? Were Peter and the others positive?" he asks. But his asking doesn't settle my nerves or clear anything up.

"I'm sure. They knew what they saw. I even saw him working the counter when I came back the next day. Are you telling me he's traveling from our world to Breezewood when we aren't around?" I'm not convinced. This is insane, and I don't want it to be real. I recall him going missing not too long ago. I hope and pray it isn't connected to this madness.

"Well, if the real Andrew is in the modern realm and is not connected to this, then it's a wolf parading to look like him in Breezewood. Alder is controlled by them and since they can shapeshift, maybe they change to confuse. Regardless, there's dangerous power at play. I just hope we can find a way to break it before it corrupts the best of us," Joel says, eyes brimming with near-hopelessness. I continue to deny the possibility. Andrew is a good guy. I don't want it to be any other way. Setting my thoughts on the present, I address the issue at hand.

"How do we get Alder out of Breezewood, if this isn't the way?" I feel around for my note in my dress pocket and then slowly hand it to Joel. He reads it quickly before answering.

"Even if the king was desperate for a cure, he would not have bought this. Nothing can convince him to leave, even the death of the kingdom. I've seen the greed he has."

"Not to be morbid, but wouldn't killing him be the easiest?"

"Not in the slightest. He's far stronger than a simple human with the wolf attached to him. A knife will barely cut his skin. If we can remove him from his place of power, then the wolf can be detached and Breezewood's ability to grow food and hunt will be restored. There will be no need for any precious gems or Alder."

"Then if the king won't leave the castle, that means we'll have to bring the portal to him," I say, bringing up a solution that answers my question.

Joel's eyes light up. "Yes. Do you know how to do that?"

"No, but if I accidentally created and opened the bookstore portal, it's possible I can do it again." I'm not even sure where to begin. I think back to all the journals I found in my room. Somehow, through my writing, I had opened a portal to a world I never knew existed. Could writing something similar yet entirely new create the same effect?

Joel must see thoughts spinning in my eyes because he quickly interjects. "What do you need to try and open one?"

"Pen and paper. A secluded place to work. And a distraction." I focus on his face. "Find Peter and tell him the plan."

Twenty-Six

PETER

The museum is exactly what you would expect: a place where interesting things are on display. Only it isn't at all like a normal museum that we have in our world. Instead of the ancient history of Breezewood I hoped to find, items I thought I'd never see decorate the room. Stone arches are inset into the mountain walls and covered with glass. Strategically lit with torches, the small alcoves bare artifacts from our realm. Modern tech. Smart phones, laptops, digital cameras, and one of those old portable DVD movie players. Some technology dating back into the 1920s is on display, all the way up to modern day. My eyes are wide, and I find August watching me.

"Strange, isn't it? Breezewood has long been fascinated with the modern world for years. Very few from Breezewood have ever been able to travel there. The few in your realm who made it here by accident or on purpose brought tech with them. Confiscated, it was studied and then placed on display here."

"Are you responsible for confiscating any of the items?" I ask.

"Some of it I found and brought here from the forest. Some was given to me off prisioners. I must confess I was just as interested in your world as any other."

"And what about now? Has twelve years in the modern realm been enough to satisfy?"

"I can say there are things I enjoy and appreciate about the modern world, but if I'm being honest, I prefer the quieter and more intentional way of living in Breezewood. People don't have to rely on devices to run their lives. People talk to each other more here. Friendships are deeper."

I nod, agreeing with him. Without the use of devices, people didn't have room to be nonchalant with contacting friends and loved ones. Every conversation could be more intentional and precious than simply always knowing you can send a message at any given time. Why do we forgo such intentionality when we have access to those we love most at our fingertips?

"The Worlders who came here before you, they no longer live, do they?" I ask, a great burden of sadness pressing down on my shoulders. How many missing people in our world ended up here but remained lost to even the inhabitants of this world?

"There are a few who survived and have traveled out of Breezewood's lands to the other kingdoms. But most never lived past Alder's throne. When Alder doesn't understand something, he often takes it as a threat to his power."

"And now that he's slowly understanding us, he's seeing the power he could gain," I add. If Alder is the ultimate threat to both our realms, then getting rid of him is what must be done. We must conquer evil.

"Precisely. He may be my brother, but I hardly recognize him anymore. It is time for his rule of darkness to end."

"Then hear me out." I relay my plan to August in low tones, telling him Briar's portion and my own additions. The worried lines on August's forehead slowly recede. Soon, he's smiling.

"This might just work, though I don't know how on earth you'll get Alder to leave the castle. Especially during the party."

"The party is the distraction and the best place for blackmail. Everyone will hear of Alder's failings much faster when they are in one place. Chaos will ensue. Alder's power is weakening, and if he wants more, he'll do what it takes to gain it."

"And the first order of the plan?"

"Find Briar, get the note delivered, and get back to the portal," I say.

August's eyebrows scrunch. "I don't know what Atlas will do, but we'll try it. Come on, the dancing will still be happening and it's best to mingle with the rest of the guests to avoid any more suspicion."

⁕ ⁕ ⁕

When August and I step back into the common room, the dance floor is flooded with whirling colors. The musicians are playing a quick and lively melody, dancers weaving with skill. I scan the room for Briar, this time trying to appear even more inconspicuous. August touches my elbow.

"As soon as we find Briar, I'll implement my portion of the plan. Stay in the common room," he says, heading towards the drink table close to where Alder sits. I walk among the guests, taking in the view of the ceiling and walls, admiring the intricacy of the decorations. In a world where magic seems to be as normal as our technology is to me, I wonder how different we are. Instead of electric lights, plugs, and cords, torches and floating orbs of energy light the room. Dazzled, I file the memory away.

A mask-less figure slips into the common room from a side doorway. He looks to the left then the right, surveying the room with a steady gaze. I blink, taken aback. *Joel*. He's alive. Heart pounding, relief like I've never known sends me in a brisk walk across the marble to meet him. When he sees me, his tight and steady features soften.

"Peter, I'm glad I found you."

"You're alive," I say in choked words. I'm not going to cry, but my throat is dry with emotion. He was and hopefully still is my best friend. I pray I can renew our friendship and pick up where we left off in high school.

"Only just. Come on, you need to speak with Briar." Joel motions for me to follow him back into the corridor.

I hesitate. "August said to stay in the common room."

Joel's eyes narrow. "Peter, August can't be trusted. He's a brother to the king," he says in a low voice. I stiffen, unsure of who to believe at this point.

"August wants Alder off the throne. We can trust him." I think.

"If you still think Alder has failing power, then you need to come with me. Briar has new information. Your plan won't work without it."

I study Joel's words. Who do I trust more? The friend I grew up with who's been missing in a magical realm for the past few days and who I lost touch with after high school, or the boss and friend I've had for the past few years who's actually the king of the magical realm? Oh, and he has powers. I look towards the drink table. August is there speaking with Alder, Atlas at his side. I feel that all three will glance our way at any moment. Joel pulls me out of view.

"Alder's magic isn't dying. In fact, he's been waiting to use it to gain even more power. You need to hear the rest from Briar. Peter, please. Breezewod depends on it."

I capitulate. If he's taking me to Briar, breaking August's wish can be done. I follow Joel, and he leads me to a small room adorned with a trickling waterfall, stone bench, table, and cushioned wood couch. Briar sits at the table and bench, her green silk dress pluming around her like a fern. I watch as she scribbles madly on a parchment. She looks up when we enter and her face lights up.

"He needs to know the new plan," Joel says.

Twenty-Seven

BRIAR

"See why we can't try your old plan?" I say as soon as I finish explaining to Peter what I know. Likewise, he had a chance to fill me in on what he learned from August.

Peter blinks, swallows, and slowly responds. "Yes, but how do we know this one will work?"

"Do you have a better plan?" Joel crosses his arms, looking between us. I'm certain I see a flicker of disappointment cross his face as he catches Peter looking at me with an admiring expression. I avoid both of their gazes, keeping my eyes on my paper.

"No," Peter says.

"We have to try. If you're willing?" I ask, still looking at my page. I stand from the bench and lean over my parchment, pen poised. I need the perfect ending, a glorious plot twist.

Joel and Peter continue to discuss in hushed tones the last few steps to our plan. I try to tune them out, focusing on each word I inscribe.

"You do realize that if this plan fails, we'll die here," Joel says.

"I'm aware," Peter responds dully. Joel inclines his head to me.

"Even if we somehow made it back home without saving Breeze-wood, our world is still in danger. Not to mention Briar's truth pearl will still be attached. From what I understand after listening to the Wolves, it is coated in deception magic. Over time, it will shrink and release a poison to cloud her mind."

I catch his words through my haze of story ideas and stop writing, a hand going to my throat. "What did you say?" Maybe this whole adventure was all about to be one big murder mystery, one no one would ever solve.

"The truth pearl will be poison if not used as intended. When it is not used to extract truth, it dissolves into lies. It needs to be removed," Joel says, eyes round and jaw firm. I wonder what he went through to find that out.

Peter puts a hand through his hair, mouth grim. "How long until it will poison her?" He catches my eyes. If I could read his thoughts, I think they would be somewhere along the lines of stress for my well-being. Not that I need to read his thoughts to know that.

"I don't know. Could be a few more weeks. Or just days. De-pends on how long Alder planned to keep you in his reach. Giving you a truth pearl keeps you from lying to him when he asks you questions, though he must have a hand on you."

I remember that information clearly. Though he hadn't forced me to tell the truth that day, he very well could have. I suppose if the Reachers had caught me just before Wystan rescued me, then there might have been a reason to. Maybe he wanted to see where the portal was. Did the Wolves already know where it was? Surely one that paraded as a Reacher had been among the group hunting me down the night of my escape. But how was I to know for sure?

"We need to implement the plan quickly then." I crinkle my brow in determination though it is still steeped in unease. Alder seems to know more about my abilities than I know of myself. I feel the pearl with my tongue, a shiver running down my spine. It is smaller. How long until it poisons my mind? Or has it already?

"August, we need to let him know," Peter says.

"I'll tell him," Joel confirms.

With the last stroke of my pen, I write the final words that I hope will save Breezewood. The parchment is filled with a story I made up, though parts of it are true. I tell the tale of a bunch of young adults finding a portal to a realm called Breezewood where they break the darkness by sending the evil king far away. I do my best to tie it to what I remember of the myths book in the bookstore—the one I accidentally, though willingly, destroyed. What Peter had quickly conveyed to me from August in the last few minutes, catching me up on the ability of tethering and untethering, I'm fairly confident that this idea is grounded somewhat in reality. If that's a thing anymore.

I was apparently the creator of the bookstore portal through my teen writing sessions, and my words were connected to the myths book. That portal had allowed others to walk through if they knew the phrase that was in that book. Peter said August had called it a tethered portal, meaning anyone could walk through as long as they knew the phrase. Now, since I destroyed the object that I had connected the portal to originally, the key phrase now forever inked into my palm, I made it untethered and drew the portal to me. I can only open it, walk through, and bring people with me by the hand. I am the key. Alder wants me.

With this information, I hope this new portal I plan to open will work. If I can connect my recent writings to a new portal and a new phrase, maybe speaking it out loud will open it where I need it to. I just hope opening a new one won't make me drop access to the portal in the store, barring us from a convenient escape back home. But this is the only plan. I tuck the parchment into my dress pocket, my only solution to Breezewood's pain. I just hope I'm strong enough to shove Alder through.

"Let's do it then," Joel says with a stiff sigh, leading the way.

Joel and Peter accompany me to the common room, the dancing now a slow and leisurely waltz. Joel touches Peter's shoulder as we skirt the crowd, telling him he'll begin the first phase of the plan. After he leaves, Peter quickly whisks me away by the hand into the flood of dancers.

"I promised myself I would try and dance with you at least once before the night is over. If something happens to me or you or both of us, I want this to be a good memory," he says. I feel the gentleness of his fingers in mine and the strong arm at my back and give in. We stand still for a moment, poised in the position of a waltz. I wait for him to lead, but he doesn't. Red floods his face, and he looks to the floor. "I must admit, I don't know how to dance."

I almost laugh at his declaration. Instead, I give him a soft smile, turning my chin up to stare straight into his eyes. Even though I'm afraid of all the many things happening right now, Peter brings a smile to my face.

"I don't care if you step on my feet or if we trip and tumble to the marble like children. You simply asking me to dance is enough," I say warmly. He shakes his head in amusement, eyes glittering with admiration.

"Then will you dance with me, Briar Verlice?"

"Certainly." I step away from him and give a graceful curtsy. I've been preparing for this moment my whole life, except for the obvious dancing part. Peter rejoins with my hand and, with an awkward step, guides me to the music. Slowly, the tension disappears and I'm once again floating over the marble like I had with Joel. Only this time, it is much more impressive. Peter doesn't know how to dance, but the more we move, the better it gets. Soon, I can't tell anymore that he doesn't know the steps. It's as if the music is brimming with magic and our feet are caught in the current of melodies, sound waves, and vibrations. Peter doesn't hesitate at this phenomenon, and I don't either.

He continues to twirl me and dip me, our bodies weaving around others. In one exhilarating rise of the music, he casts me out over the floor so that I slide, one hand still in his. As he passes his arm over his head to guide me around, my feet leave the floor and my dress rises with me. It's as if pixie dust has just been sprinkled over me. I begin to float in a circle around Peter, the twinkling lights overhead furthering this fairy tale experience. I feel as light as a feather. Whatever darkness fills this realm, there is still good here. There is still beauty. Just like our world, there are little pieces of it everywhere, sparking like gems catching sunlight. Despite the dark hold of evil, Breezewood has a beauty that needs rescuing and protection.

When the music begins to diminish, Peter pulls me back to the marble. I always wondered what it would be like to dance with Peter West. Now I know.

We glide for just a few more steps before hearing the crash of glass against the cold crust of stone. The sound shatters my dream-like haze and I whip around to see tje commotion. Joel has begun the distraction.

"I knew it! It was in the drinks. You have been poisoning us!" Joel yells, his voice echoing through the common room. His dramatic words are shocking, even though I know it's all a facade. Musicians freeze, guests gasp, and dancers slow.

From where Peter and I stand, we see Alder rise abruptly in his chair, eyes dark and brow lowered. His shoulders hunch forward as if pressed on by some invisible weight. A cruel look creeps over his face as he takes in Joel.

"Why have *you* come to disrupt the party?"

"Send him to the dungeons," an advisor says, stepping out from behind the chair. I spy two other men at Alder's side. I recognize the man in the coat from the portal entrance, the one who had followed me in. Atlas, Peter had called him. And August must be the man at his right. Both watch the scene unfold with tight lipped faces. Who's side are they on?

"Everyone here, if you took this drink, you have been poisoned by your king with dark magic. He's confusing you, to divide you. He is not the kind king you believe him to be. The Reachers who plague the outside lands? Breezewood's inability to grow crops? All of it is because of this man and the Wolves that control him." Joel's voice is raised so strongly that my pulse begins to race with anticipation. The parchment in my pocket is like fire as I shove a hand inside, ready to pull it out and say my part. Peter squeezes my free hand, knowing and reminding me that the time to break this darkness is soon.

"Guards!" Alder yells. The guests begin whispering, some openly questioning Joel's words and the sanity of the king. Some shake their heads in disagreement with Joel. Some take steps backwards from the king and hold their glasses of purple drink away from their bodies. Joel stays still, shards of glass glittering in the magic-induced light while varying shades of lavender pool on the floor.

Several guards approach Alder's chair, each brandishing a spear; August and Atlas straighten. Before Alder can make a command, Atlas speaks up.

"My lord and brother, this man may be out of his mind, but I think we should let him speak. You have nothing to hide."

Alder's mouth twitches at Atlas's words, and he fidgets with the edge of his robe. I watch the discontentment on his face settle briefly.

"But he's disrupting the Harvest celebration," Alder snaps.

"Maybe so, but he can't do anything to you. Let him speak his mind, however wild it may be." Atlas withdraws from the makeshift throne, and I watch him look over his shoulder. What is he looking at? August pulls on Atlas's arm, whispering something to him.

"No, seize this man," the advisor contradicts. He points to Joel, disgust in his face. I clench the parchment tighter, slowly withdrawing it. Joel begins the next phase.

"Atlas, how long were you banished from Breezewood? Why did your brother banish you from your home?" Joels words catch Atlas by surprise. Alder's eyes narrow.

"I did not banish him. He broke Breezewood law. My father banished him," Alder says, defending himself. Atlas holds up a hand.

"I was banished for many years..." Atlas doesn't answer the rest of Joel's question and instead trails off, as if unsure of what else to say. He shakes his head, his posture slumping. Soon, his hands go to his throat. Alder reaches out and touches Atlas's shoulder.

"Is that really the truth?" Alder asks. Atlas's hands drop from his throat and he gasps out his next words.

"I was never banished."

Joel and August frown. Alder was calling on Atlas's truth pearl.

"Sire, you guests are frightened. Show them your power and have this man sent away to be dealt with later," the advisor says cooly. I watch as Atlas sways, his stance hesitant. Alder removes his hand, face twisted in suspicion. August steps forward to stand next to Atlas.

"Are you all right, brother?"

"Don't touch me," he says, slapping August's hands away. Strangely violent, Atlas skitters away from the group. I watch him walk. A strange slide step. Slide step. Slide step. As if he's fighting to move forward, like something invisible is holding him back.

Joel stands straighter. Alder eyes move to track us, and I notice the muscles in his neck bulging. He looks moments from sending us all to the dungeon.

"What's going on?" I say. Peter puts hand on my shoulder.

"Just do it now."

In a flash, I pull out my parchment and select the phrase I want. The same one from the the portal at home: *What if we met in a bookstore*. As soon as I utter the words, I know something is wrong. Instead of a portal opening within the vicinity of where the king is as I'd hoped, I feel a rumble begin beneath my feet. It increases in intensity and many guests begin to cry out and press closely against the common room walls. Soon, the entire mountain is shaking. Some guests stand still, unphased, clearly under the influence of deception magic. Alder, several guards, and the advisor steady themselves and look around in bewilderment as the mountain kingdom continues to shake. Did I cause this? Or is it a result of something entirely unrelated?

Atlas wanders and stumbles to his knees just behind the king. August breaks away from the king's side and watches Atlas as the earthquake continues. Another jolt and the common room floor begins to crack down the center. I take a step backwards, dizzy. Peter swings around to steady me.

"I've got you," he says calmly.

"What's going on?" I ask in a harsh whisper. This wasn't a part of the plan. Peter doesn't answer; instead he squeezes my arm in reassurance. His nearness and calmness keeps my heart from exploding in fear.

We ride out earthquake, the marble floor near Alder cracking and popping like thin ice. At once, the two guards at Alder's side drop as if dead to the ground, but before they even hit the stone, their bodies begin to change. Each guard melts into a stream of black dust, reforming into the stone, wolf-like creatures I've grown to fear. Their weapons are absorbed into their bodies as they morph. In seconds, two snarling Reachers face me. I knew something was strange about them. Alder and the advisor hardly blink at the transformation. They've always known.

"You dare invade our home!" Alder yells, pointing across the room to Peter and me. "You dare use magic against Breezewood!" His eyes are wild. He's completely insane. The advisor narrows his eyes, and despite the trembling and cracking floor, he proceeds to head in our direction, the two Reachers at his side. Cold begins to creep along the floor and spread to the walls of the common room. Frost climbs from the cracks in the floor as if the core of the mountain itself has a heart of ice to match its king.

"We knew this time would come. Worlders have no place here. Every single one must be destroyed," the advisor says. His eyes are devoid of any goodness, and the two Reachers lick their chops. Peter clamps his hand down on my arm and moves me to the side.

"You will not harm her," he says in my defense.

The Reachers growl, and the advisor, clearly influenced by the Wolf in his skin, sneers. "You can't win this, Worlder. Breezewood and the realms beyond are mine!" The Wolf's words are like a punch to the gut of my courage. Peter's grip falters on my arm, and I squeeze my eyes shut, preparing for what is to come.

What does one even say to darkness when it's about to devour you? I recall the truth my family spoke to me during my younger years. Light has power over darkness. Light unveils the lies and pierces the shadows. Follow the light. Joel's words fly back to me, the day I was sent out of the castle to find my own way home. Though he had meant it for me to follow the moonlight, there was simply power in words like that. Following the light. Light is the truth revealing the lies.

What if light needed to be a part of my plan? What better way to fight darkness than with light. With this realization, I know what to try.

"Peter, I need a light," I whisper. He nods, looking for a solution. If I could just get a light, something bright enough to catch these shadows' attention, maybe they can be distracted. Maybe light is my weapon.

The vibrating of the common room hall has my brain rattling inside my skull, but I maintain just enough control to think.

Like the fairy tale *Inkheart*, maybe I can rewrite the ending to this story that I've been caught up in. Just when I thought my life back home would be forever simple and cozy, magic and the true reality had to overturn it all and prove that one can't simply enjoy adventures from the couch. Adventures demand you to be present. Am I mad about this adventure? No. Am I scared? Yes. Maybe reading books has prepared me for this moment. Writing my own stories certainly has, but will it be enough to get us out of this mess?

Before the advisor and the two Wolves disguised as Reachers descend upon us, there is a resounding yell. Atlas does the unthinkable, the unexpected, and I hear August scream in response. "Brother, no!"

Atlas withdraws a knife from his belt and holds it against Alder's throat. Alder, wide-eyed, freezes. But not for long. Alder kicks Atlas in the legs, and he crumples, losing his balance. Both men struggle over the knife, Atlas kicking it just out of reach. Alder's strength is inhuman by the way he grabs Atlas by the throat, lifting him from the ground. They are both around the same size, the feat of strength nearly impossible for the average man.

August stands nearby, unable to do anything without a weapon.

"August gave me his only knife." Peter says, words hoarse. I don't ask where it went but instead watch as Peter and August lock eyes with each other. August mouths something to Peter that I don't understand, but Peter's next words fill in what I missed.

"Briar, there's a portal right in the center of the floor. August says it's right there, growing in strength, about to open," Peter says loudly enough for only me to hear, eyes wide. We are almost on top of it. It could open at any moment. Maybe my idea worked after all and the birth of a new portal just took time.

The advisor and Reachers hesitate as Peter steps forward and removes his mask.

I take that moment to remove my own mask, letting it drop to the floor. They never did disguise us from the Wolves.

"Kill the boy, then take her alive," the advisor says, making eye contact with me.

Atlas gurgles beyond them, Alder squeezing.

"Brother, let him go!" August screams, running at the king. The advisor reaches out towards the two Reachers now beginning to circle us, signaling them to attack. Guests cry out in alarm. Peter shields me, and my heart drops as I see the odds.

A familiar sucking sound breaks through the rumbling. It stretches out over the floor like water rushing to fill in every crevice. I can't tell what is on the other side of the portal. All I know is I need to touch Alder. I have to be the one to push him in.

I must be the only one who can see it because no one reacts. I reach out and touch Peter, hoping it works. I feel him stiffen. He must see it now, too.

Just as the first Reacher pounces, a long-stemmed glass sails into the beast's face. The beast sidesteps to avoid it and misses Peter's leg by inches. The glass still manages to contact the beast but bounces and crashes to the floor, shards cascading over the hem of my dress. Joel stands by, another glass ready in his hand. Peter releases a kick in defense and the next Reacher takes its chance.

Peter grabs my hand and whispers, "Run." I follow, hiking up my dress to keep the skirt from trailing across the floor.

Joel throws the next glass, and it hits the closest Reacher on the nose, buying us just enough time to slip past their defense unscathed.

"Joel, your watch!" Peter yells. I don't know what he's thinking, but as we race towards Alder, Peter lets go of my hand and leaps, catching an object.

The Reachers are at our heels, the Wolf advisor close behind. Peter fumbles with the object and it begins to glow. He passes it back to me, and with one glance, I see that it is a fancy watch with a strong flashlight built in. Oh, genius Sam.

I immediately turn and shine the light into the Reacher's eyes. They recoil, as if the light is poison. It buys me just enough time to see August pummel Alder, and at the impact, the king releases Atlas to the floor. Alder stumbles as Peter launches himself at him, both Peter and August shoving him in the direction of the portal. I approach and quickly shine the bright light in the eyes of Alder, sending the king limp as he recoils in shock. I put a hand on him and all three of us begin to shove him over the edge of the portal. Before he disappears through the watery gateway, Alder swipes at my hand and Joel's watch rips from my grip. The king's strong hand clasps over the device as he descends into the unknown. Screams erupt from the Wolf advisor and the two Reachers. I turn and watch in horror as a dark human-like shadow becomes visible, clawing at Atlas's body with such ferocity as if its life depends on him. But it is dragged away, along with the other wolves the second Alder is through the portal.

The wolves vanish one by one into the portal, their masked forms melting away and stretching across the marble in long streaks of black as if being pulled into a fast-flowing whirlpool. They scream in anger, all transported through the gate and into the unknown. The portal closes with a sucking sound, and immediately, the kingdom stops its shaking. The ice protruding from the cracks in the floor begins to melt, and like a gust of wind, the oppressive weight of darkness exits the room. The pearl in my mouth loosens, and I spit it out, glad to be rid of the thing. It bounces to the floor, shriveled and black. I crush it with my heel, the precious but evil-imbued stone now a pile of dust. As soon as it is destroyed, a thought about peppermint tea enters my mind. Maybe the tea I'd drank in the treehouse had actually been magic and protected me from the pearl's dark poison. In any event, I'd escaped.

The guests of the party, some weeping and some in shock, ultimately begin to filter out of the room and back into the mountain. They owe us their lives. I wonder how long it will take for the truth to circulate among them and for life to return to normal.

Heart racing, I stand watching as Atlas does the same with his own pearl, August helping him stay steady. Peter steps beside me, and I look up at him.

"How did you know Joel had a light, especially on a watch?" I ask, still in shock.

"I took a chance on the light. I knew Sam made Joel a watch and figured there might be one."

If we tell Sam his gadget saved the day, he'll probably let it go to his head. I chuckle inside. Maybe we'll save this part of the truth for a rainy day story. Not to mention, if he found out the bad guys have his watch, he'll freak.

Hurried footsteps pound from a corridor and Wystan and Tara crash through swinging doors.

"The dungeons are cracked open. The guards are gone," Wystan says, breath coming in heavy gasps. Both of them freeze when they see us. Tara's face is red from running, and her brows rise as her eyes roam over our grand attire—all borrowed things from her collection.

"Alder is gone," I say triumphantly then turn and blush as Peter entwines his hand in mine, giving it a squeeze. Everything about today happened so fast. My mind is still spinning. I just want to go home.

"We need to check if the darkness and the Reachers have truly left. Can the people of Breezewood now hunt and collect food?" Peter asks.

Wystan sees our hands and blinks, looking away, then responds quickly. "We can check. I'll send out the owl patrol and we can try to bring home some game." Wystan looks dazed and relieved. We all are.

"Can I come too?" Tara asks. She sets a hand on his shoulder. Wystan turns to her, assessing her request.

"It's about time you lead the patrol. You can take charge this time," he says.

Tara's eyes light up and she steps back, removing her hand. "Do I get my own owl?" she asks in a low but hopeful tone.

"I think that can be arranged. You've completed the necessary training." Wystan looks towards the ceiling. Tara's eyes widen and crinkle joyfully. She looks like she's just been granted her drivers license. Freedom entering her veins as if for the first time.

"As soon as we know Breezewood is truly safe, we are going home," Joel says decidedly.

"I'll get my patrol to take you to the portal site as soon as possible," Wystan says. Tara takes that as her cue and leaves at a run.

"What about Breezewood's king? They'll need a new ruler." I add, looking to Peter for help. Peter turns to August who steps forward.

"I am the true king. It is time I stepped into my rightful role to lead Breezewood into a future of peace and prosperity."

"August, you can't be blamed for what your brother did. His actions affected all those around him. He was responsible for the darkness. He invited it."

"I know, but I could have tried to prevent it. I could have stayed here to fight him."

"You did. You came to the modern world to find someone to help, to protect your kingdom. Without you and Atlas, we might never have been able to save Breezewood," I say, reminding him of his role in this.

"I lied to you."

"You can't change the past. You can only change your role in the present," Peter says, trying to reason with him.

"You don't understand. I am responsible. Andrew is my real brother, not Atlas," August says. All of us look at eachother. How?

"I thought your brother wreas right there," I say. Atlas bows his head, acknowledging me.

"Andrew is my real brother. This here is my personal body-guard," August says without inflection.

"Body guard?" Disbelief taints Peter's voice.

"Yes, well, he's my advisor and bodyguard, but we got separated on a mission in your realm. Actually, trying to find Andrew. That's why I'm responsible. I lied to you. I ran away from Breezewood with Atlas to find Andrew. I ran from my people, afraid of failing them as a king, when in reality, my not staying was the ultimate failure. I could have stopped Alder from being king long ago and taken his place. But I didn't want the position, and I was afraid to take it. Seeking Andrew was only an excuse to escape the life and responsibility I didn't want."

"Why did you lie to us?" Peter asks, hints of hurt in his voice.

"I lied to protect myself and Andrew. I was afraid to tell you that Andrew was my brother, fearing that a wolf was following Atlas. I was right. Pretending that Atlas was my brother only gave the wolf that knowledge to report back to the king. And only the king can take information from the pearl, the truth that only Atlas and I knew. Alder believed our brother —Andrew—to be dead. I thought pretending that my bodyguard was my brother would make the wolf believe and it would convince Alder of it. His mind has been tricked so many times, I figured one more trick on top would stick. Atlas was sacrificing his life for me and Breezewood if need be while Andrew was safe and oblivious. I couldn't risk Alder deciding to get rid of Andrew out of jealousy."

"You came back, though. You didn't stay away," I say, seeing the emotion in August's eyes.

"Hold on, Andrew is from Breezewood? Why didn't we know this?" Peter cuts through, his tone determined for answers.

"He never told you because he's forgotten. Breezewood has a strange effect on people. The more you come here or the longer you stay, the more you become like this world. When you go back, people forget you, or it takes them longer to recognize you. And when you are back in the modern realm, as long as you remember Breezewood, you have a strong desire to return. Andrew however has been gone from Breezewood so long he's forgotten about it."

"So Andrew is your brother, a prince of Breezewood, who has forgotten where he's from. So is he currently in the dark about all this?"

"Not anymore. I told him just before coming here, but in order to protect him from Alder, I found him a place to stay away from the store and turned off his phone. I also gave him some materials to read through to help him remember his true home. He should return back to the shop soon with a renewed memory. This all happened at the last minute, you see," August says.

"So Atlas, your advisor-slash-bodyguard... Why was he banging on my sister's car window and walking oddly and staring us down? Oh, and not to mention, trying to kill me," Peter asks.

"None of that was on purpose or a part of the plan. Atlas's truth pearl had started to degrade heavily and I didn't realize it. It began affecting his mind. Not to mention a wolf was influencing him at times, trying to get back to Breezewood." August says, giving Atlas a curt nod.

"But why was Atlas separate from you?" I'm still confused.

"Atlas came through the original portal with me years ago. He has been at my side trying to help me find Andrew and he wandered the streets as a homeless man to avoid suspicion. I gave him instructions to find the portal that I knew had opened somewhere in Homer. This was several years ago. I had things to finish up in Colorado and couldn't make it to Homer at the time. He stowed away somehow and made it to Alaska to search for the portal. Peter, when you said you were from Homer when we first met, I couldn't believe it. The chances were insane. The more I learned about you and where you were from... then I learned about Briar." August nods to me. I blush. "You do realize he paced the workroom thinking about you? As a matter of fact, I told him to call you and he chickened out," August says.

I turn to Peter, surprised.

"Oh, you just had to say that," Peter says, now as red as me.

"That isn't half as gushy as what I did," I say. "I wrote a confession note to you at home before I came in here. Jen was instructed to give it to you if I never made it back." I say the last few words softly. I had believed I might not make it back. Peter catches on and responds in the same manner.

"Oh, I can't wait to read it."

"Unless I burn it first," I say quickly, changing the mood from somber to something more humorous.

"I'll be sure Jen makes a copy," he says and winks. August clears his throat.

"Anyways, Andrew knows now, and he'll be waiting for you back in Homer. One of these days, he'll come back to Breezewood.

If he wants to." Atlas steps forward, giving Peter and I a sheepish look.

"And I severely apologize for my behavior. The wolf's control over me was less than ideal. With August pretending that I was his brother, the wolf believed him and was eager for me to get back to Breezewood." I nod.

"You are forgiven." Peter scratches his head then looks Atlas square in the face.

"So, you were the one that visited my sister in the bakery and followed my friends around?"

"I don't remember clearly but it must have been. I frequented the book shop because I knew the portal was there from what August told me since he can sense portals. The wolf knew too, but couldn't find a way to open it. When I saw the eyes of you and your classmates, I knew you all had been going to Breezewood, but the pearl kept me from speaking normally, the poison confusing me and giving the wolf more control. I couldn't even ask for help when I was lucid. I was fighting for my own body and thoughts. While the wolf was influencing me, we waited at the shop earlier. When we saw Briar there, the wolf forced me to hold onto her. Somehow it figured out that doing that would make me go back to Breezewood. The wolf also wanted me to reveal to Alder who was responsible for opening the portal, thus sealing Briar as a slave to the wolves and Alder." I shiver at his confession. Had things not turned out the way they did, I might be the one letting even more darkness into my realm while sentencing another to starvation and slavery.

"And August was unaware of your altered behavior during his time?" Peter asks. August nods in agreement, turning to look at us.

"I didn't find out until I arrived. He had no way of contacting me so I didn't know. I suspected it when I saw him trying to beat up Peter. It was out of character."

I raise an eyebrow. Peter hadn't mentioned that when we were in the treehouse. Peter looks at me and shrugs. He fixes August with another question.

"How did you even get to Homer? On a plane?"

"Plane and fake I.D.," August pulls one out of his coat pocket.

"Why aren't you a spy?"

"Who says I'm not one?" August winks. Peter exhales.

"Are you all ready to go? I've got word that the winter is reversing!" Wystan yells, his tone dripping with excitement. Stepping over the cracked marble, our entire group follows Wystan from the common room. After winding through several stone halls, we find ourselves in a large domed space filled with cottonwood trees. Their gray branches twist in all directions, floating orbs of light filling the air with enough glow to mimic sun through a skylight. I catch the scent of wet moss and earth, my senses blooming. The room hums with the steady vibration of a waterfall and the unmistakable sound of birds. More specifically, owls. Their large forms perch in tree branches while some soar in graceful circles about the waterfall and tree tops.

"Welcome to the stables. Auriol should be here somewhere." Wystan whistles, and from high in the branches, a snowy owl glides down and alights next to him, towering over all of us.

Peter whispers in my ear, his breath warm and soft. "If I had my own owl, would you ride with me?"

I pull back, surprised, then incline my head to his. "Of course, but you have nothing to be jealous about. I want to go home." I squeeze his hand. It's like our own secret code. A squeeze here or there, just something to remind the other that we care, that these feelings are real and not just our imagination. I won't ever get tired of it.

Joel steps up to Wystan, a hand outstretched.

"Thank you for what you tried to do, for doing your best. We will be back at some point, considering all that remains unfinished."

"There are others still in this world that could be reunited with their family's in your realm. I have no doubt you will be back," Wystan says with a nod, turning to look at us all. He searches for me. "Briar, I wanted to let you know. Finn escaped from Breeze-wood shortly after you left from your first visit. I don't know where he went, only that Alder never got a hold of him." I nod, surprised and relieved to hear about the gentle door keeper. I hope he's found a place somewhere safe.

"Thank you for telling me." Wystan nods, straightening and pushing his shoulders back.

"Let's take you all home."

Twenty-Eight

Peter

After changing from our masquerade clothes and back into our modern attire, all three of us travel home. Hand in hand, Briar and I step through the portal and onto the familiar wooden slats of the bookstore floor. Joel is right behind us, his hand on my shoulder. When the portal seals, we all take a deep breath, grateful to be breathing the air of our world, even if it is a little dusty. I squeeze Briar's hand and look into her eyes.

"It's all over. Breezewood is safe."

"For now," she says, her features smooth with relief. "Wherever Alder and the wolves went, however devoid of power, they will try to find a way to regain some control where they are and create chaos."

"But we don't have to worry now. We can move on with our lives," I soothe, taking Briar with me towards the stairs. Joel follows close behind. If I could, I'd find a way right now to keep Alder and any Wolves from ever setting a foot near Homer or Breezewood again. But none of us have the power or the knowledge to make it happen. At least, not now.

When all three of us descend and file into the main entrance, I find Andrew behind the desk. He lifts his eyes from his book and gives us all a knowing smile.

"Find any good stories up there?" he asks, a teasing twinkle in his eye. How good it is to see him safe and well.

"Plenty," I say.

He nods and returns to his book, adjusting his glasses. We turn to leave, eager to be back in the familiar confines of our modern world. "You all enjoy the rest of your day. Peter, I'll see you first thing tomorrow morning."

As soon as all the phone calls to family are made and the group chat is updated on what exactly happened to us, especially the fact that Joel is alive, it is mandatory to have pizza night at the lighthouse and invite Jen to join us. As I settle onto one of the couches in the main room with a slice from the local pizza shop, the secrets we learned are all shared with the rest of the group. I even confess that I'd told my dad we went to another world. Joel and the rest of the group weren't happy with the revelation but no one was mad, especially after I mentioned that my Dad didn't seem to believe me. Briar reveals that Wystan was responsible for the strange riddle-like notes, Auriol the owl somehow finding a way to our realm to deliver them. None of us have any idea on how the owl got to our world and back but the matter is soon pushed aside as unimportant in the wake of everything else that happened to us. It's a mystery that will have to be solved in the future.

There's lots of crying and laughter and silence as we continue our confessions. Briar sits next to me, and we both listen as Joel tells everyone about his experience in the dungeons of Breezewood and the dangerous role he had to play. Jen takes a bite of her Hawaiian with wide eyes, nearly spilling the toppings in her lap as Joel describes the darkness he encountered. Naomi and Sam interject with questions while Orin and Cedric eat through pizza slices like it's their last meal on earth.

After finishing the recount of the final moments we spent breaking the darkness of Breezewood, Joel accepts his own slice of pizza from Anna who sits next him. I encouraged her to call him and tell him her feelings as soon as possible. It appears they worked out some misunderstandings by the way Joel smiles at her. I'm glad. Finally, we can all be friends and forgo any jealous thoughts. I accidentally drop a pepperoni onto my jeans, and Briar quickly snatches it, popping it into her mouth without skipping a beat. I gently tap her foot with my own, a teasing smirk spreading across her face.

"While I haven't fully forgiven you for going back into Breezewood without telling us first, I must say, that was a gutsy rescue mission," Sam says.

"I'd say it was more than just a rescue mission. More of an overall learning experience. Extreme character development," Joel adds between bites. Naomi chuckles.

"Peter, Sam's just upset he didn't get to invent a tracking device made from non-precious metals before you went in." Sam playfully nudges her.

"I'm just glad it is all over. While there's more to discover about Breezewood and the lands beyond, I say we leave it alone for a while. I've had enough adventure to last a few years," I say, finishing off my salty crust.

"You can't just talk about this place and not let me see it," Jen says, looking at Briar. "When I found out my cousin and her friends have been riding owls and going to masquerade balls and meeting crossbow-wielding men in another world, I sure want to be included." Her words are adamant. She really does want to go.

"You forgot the almost dying multiple times part and evil beasts," Cedric adds. Briar waves it off.

"Jen, one of these days, I'll take you to Breezewood. I'll show you the castle, and I'll try to convince August to throw another masquerade."

"I can't wait." Jen's eyes shine with the statement. "Oh, and by the way, your cinnamon rolls were amazing. I got there just in time because Libby was about to give one a taste."

Briar laughs. "That cat takes almost every opportunity to steal my food, even if it is poison to her." Both girls laugh again and take another bite of pizza.

Briar's phone dings, and I glance over as she checks the screen. A text from her dad.

> *Dad: Looks like our flights got canceled. Bad weather. I'm sorry but it looks like we won't make it back in time for Thanksgiving. Have any friends willing to host you this year?*

Briar turns off the phone, her features drawn in disappointment. I look away. Little does she know, but I'm the most willing friend in her vicinity.

"So, the secret of Breezewood is currently safe, but to keep it that way long-term, the escape room needs to be finished. I hear it is set to be built tomorrow?" Orin looks to me.

"I finally start construction tomorrow morning. I should have it finished in a couple days. August plans on retiring, and I'll take his position if I get it, and I can continue to live here."

"When do the inspectors come?" Joel asks.

"They are set to fly in this weekend. If all goes well, I should have this escape room fully open to the public after Thanksgiving." I grin. Building the escape room will be the easy part. The hard part will be making sure the room isn't too hard but also not too easy. I need to impress the inspectors and the rest of Homer. This project may save the bookstore.

Twenty-Nine

BRIAR

The escape room is finally finished. Peter texted the group chat and asked us if we wanted to test out the room before the inspectors arrived. Of course we said yes. I think he's wanting to identify any last minute changes before presenting it. Just thinking about the finished room makes my heart race. To be involved in something so dear to me is incredibly special. If this doesn't save the bookstore, nothing will.

After a hot breakfast of eggs, sausage, and apple butter over sourdough toast, I meet up with the rest of my classmates. We chat at the coffee shop while waiting in line for lattes and chais.

"Knowing Peter, this room is going to require some caffeine to get anywhere near solving the puzzles," Naomi says, sipping her latte. I smile in agreement, licking the froth off my spiced chai.

"His ideas are something else," I say, remembering the idea he had about the flashlight. Without his quick thinking, we might not have escaped the teeth of shapeshifting Wolves and the hatred of a tyrant king.

When we all crowd into the bookshop, Peter and Andrew greet us with smiles.

"Are you ready to test out the room?" Peter asks, looking at me longer than the rest of the group. He gives me a wink before settling his eyes on his sister.

"Umm, yeah. We've been waiting for what feels like weeks!" Anna says, grinning from ear to ear.

"If you will all follow me," Andrew says, stepping out from behind the counter and leading the way up the stairs. I wait behind as the group follows, then I join my hand with Peter's.

"I'll let you in on a little secret," he says, whispering into my ear as we walk towards the stairs.

Surprised, I look up at him. "What is it?"

"I called your dad and let him know my intentions. He said he'll talk to you later today, but he's already given me the green light to ask you something since your family's flights are canceled."

I raise my eyebrows at his declaration. He'd seen my text? "And what is it that you are going to ask me?" I squeeze his hand, pretty sure I already know, but anticipation and fear of the unknown gallop in my chest.

"Briar, will you join my family and I for thanksgiving dinner this weekend as our honored guest?" His eyes are hopeful, but we both know what my answer is.

"Yes, I would love that."

Without much warning, Peter takes my left hand and lifts it to his lips. His eyes don't leave mine as he kisses it. When he lowers it, my heart and stomach do flips and my cheeks bloom with color. This feeling is nearly equivalent to feeling while watching the 2005 *Pride and Prejudice* hand-flex scene.

"I'll pick you up at eleven-thirty on Thanksgiving Day?"

"That sounds perfect. I'll be ready."

He nods, smiling the biggest smile I've ever seen. I return it, equally as big. When we reach the top of the stairs, Andrew is giving our friends a rundown on what not to do in an escape room. When he sees Peter, he pauses then hands off the conversation.

"Since Peter is the one who designed it, I'll let him debrief you on the rest. I'll be downstairs manning the counter. Have fun," Andrew says, giving Peter a pat on the shoulder as he heads down the stairs.

"So, since Andrew gave you the rundown on what not to do, I'll just touch on a few things. Nearly everything in this room is allowed to be investigated. If it is a picture or a clue, you may carefully pull it off the wall or move it to a different location. You will not need to destroy anything. No tearing pages from books or prying open walls or using brute force to break down the door. This is a game for your mind and your ability to think outside the box. You can expect a myriad of clues, but beware, there are some clues designed to throw you off."

"So bogus hints? Got it," Sam says.

"How do I know this speech isn't a bogus hint?" Orin says while laughing. Cedric punches him lightly in the shoulder. Peter rolls his eyes playfully then looks to Joel and Anna.

"I have incorporated sea-themed clues and music clues, and you may need book knowledge. All the items and knowledge you need to solve the riddles and crack the codes are in this room. I will be locking this door, so if you need to use the bathroom before the room starts, now would be the best time."

"Good idea. I'll be back," Naomi says with a laugh after finishing the last of her coffee. When everyone is present again, Peter gives us the final instructions.

"You have an hour and a half to solve the clues and find the key and the code to unlock this door." Peter motions to it. It has a keypad with numbers along with a knob inset with a keyhole. "For a public event, I would come up with a fun story as to why you are all locked in here, but for now, pretend I locked you in maliciously." Peter pauses, looking us all in the eyes with anticipation. "Comprende?"

Cedric waves a hand in the air. "Ahoy, or whatever sea captains say when they mean yes." Orin chuckles and Sam crosses his arms. Naomi puts a hand on her hip, and Joel and Anna stand with their shoulders set and feet apart. Everyone looks ready to conquer anything.

"Any last words?" Peter begins to close the escape room door. He locks eyes with me, and I know he's looking for any sign of my approval. I give him an amusing smile, and he blinks his gaze away. We are sappy.

Sam looks at his watch and matches it to the clock on the wall.

"Your time starts now," Peter says, and locks the newly installed door at the top of the stairs. He descends, and all of us jump into action and begin searching the room for clues.

On the far wall in front of the window is an old, upright piano. I remember seeing it in Andrew's rare and private study room downstairs. In the last few days, it had been brought upstairs. It had to be here for a purpose. Naomi raises her voice, moving her hands to get our attention.

"We should look for as many clues as we can and then bring them all together. Then we can work in teams to solve the puzzles."

"Sounds good to me." Joel says then looks at the ceiling. I follow his eyes and my mouth widens. Peter has outdone himself. There's a beautiful mural on the ceiling of a halibut. White, silver, and purple paint make up the brush strokes. I wonder if he painted it. I'd have to ask him sometime.

"Peter said there would be music and sea-themed clues. I'll look through the shelves for any books with those themes," Anna volunteers. I step away from the group.

"I'll start on this side of the room." Scanning the wall closest to the locked door, I let my eyes graze the spines. The bookshelves on this wall, the ones I organized days ago, have stayed the same. My color coordination and arranging remains. But what's different are the sea-themed trinkets placed on shelves about the room. Metal anchors, chains, a miniature lighthouse statue, a buoy, shells, stones, glass lanterns, a miniature glass fishing boat figurine against a dock, and cork-filled bottles.

I begin running my fingers over objects on the shelf, scanning them for numbers, hidden keys or codes. I glance at the red buoy at my feet and notice it has a few words printed on it.

FIND MY SPINE, I'M BLANK.

I pick the buoy up off the floor, planning to carry it to the table, but as I continue to scan the books, my eyes rest on the second-lowest shelf. I see a red book with nothing on the spine. I pull it off, intrigued. As soon as I pull, I feel resistance. Pulling harder, I find a piece of twine glued to the interior of the book. It catches on the back of the shelf. As I yank, a compartment clicks open at the bottom. A piece of the baseboard trim has separated from the wall. Surprised, I put the buoy down and the book back and kneel to pull open the compartment.

"Guys, look at this!" I can't contain my excitement as I withdraw a metal box with no lock from the secret compartment. Everyone looks up and watches me unveil my discovery. I open the metal box and pull a slip of paper out and unfurl it. Typed letters reveal a hodge-podge chunk of ABC's and random words that have no particular meaning when read as a sentence.

A B C D E F G

Halibut

F C G D A E B

Seal

B E A D G C F

Boat

"This doesn't make any sense to me. Any ideas?" I hold up the paper to the classmates, and Naomi grabs it from me, brow furrowed. She reads it out loud.

"Nothing rings a bell. Maybe hold onto it and we'll find some connections to it after solving some of these other clues." She gestures to the table in the center of the room. A variety of sea-themed trinkets, keys, and slips of paper are laid out on the surface—all items we've found that may or may not connect to other clues.

From across the room, I hear Anna gasp.

"I found a key inside of a book about halibut!" she says. That was fast. I watch her go to the door and try it in the lock. It doesn't work.

"Let's look for more," Joel adds. "My guess is the key is to open something else in the room, not the door."

Anna agrees, and they continue to search.

The clock ticks above the door. We have an hour left.

"Okay, guys. Let's think about this strategically. We are looking for a key to get out of this room. It's hidden somewhere," Orin says.

"Duh," Cedric answers while turning over a small, silver key in his hand. The way he frowns in distaste at it tells me it is not the one to the escape room exit door.

Peter and Andrew are probably laughing at us and our chaotic search from downstairs. The small camera in the clock at the back of the room allows Peter to monitor us while we solve the clues and hopefully give him ideas on how to make the room better. I refrain from making a silly face at the clock and instead turn to watch what my classmates are doing.

"Hey, Sam, can you help us unscramble some words?" Orin calls from across the room. Anna and Joel are busy by the piano flipping through books, looking for any more possible key cutouts. I smile at their camaraderie, one that is budding with sweetness by the way Joel watches her.

"Just a minute," Sam says. I look over, and he's staring at a medium-sized painting on the wall. Intrigued, I walk to him.

"What's your hunch?" I ask, looking to him then back to the painting.

"I'm not sure. It seems like any typical Homer painting; Kachemak Bay set with halibut charters and green hills covered in fire weed. The odd thing is the figure in the corner looking out at the water. He's got a pickaxe over his shoulder. I don't get it. Maybe it's a clue, maybe it isn't."

I study it closer. Sam's right. The figure is on the shore, and he's more or less the subject of the painting. The boats are off in the distance but the sea and the man are front and center.

"Why is he holding a pickaxe, I wonder?"

"Beats me. But he kinda looks like an older miner. See? There's a gold pan on the ground next to his pack."

"Oh, I hadn't noticed that. So, he's a gold miner." I squint, taking in the painting from a different angle. Maybe Peter hid something else within the painting, like codes or words that can only be spotted by squinting. Seeing nothing else, I step close to the painting, running a hand along the frame.

"Knowing Peter, he would hide something in the frame," Sam adds, helping me look.

"I keep thinking that maybe there's something hidden on it that we can't see normally. I remember watching a YouTube video where number clues were hidden in the actual paint."

"Like black light paint or glow-in-the-dark paint?"

"Maybe."

"We should rule that out, though. Hey, Cedric, can you flip the lights and close the window shades?" Sam calls.

"Oh, I got it." Joel jogs to the light switch and turns it off. When the others close the shades, the room plunges into darkness. I scan the painting, looking for any signs of glow in the dark paint. Nothing.

"Do you have a flashlight and a black light?" I ask.

"Always." Sam hands me a flashlight from his pocket.

"Your watch doesn't have a light?" I raise an eyebrow at him, a smirk pulling at my lips.

"It does, but I figured you'd want your own. Why?"

"No reason." I turn on the light to check for glow or black light paint, doing my best to hide the smile on my lips. If only Sam knew one of his flashlights saved our lives. I draw it over the painting and when nothing stands out, I click it off.

"All right, false alarm. Thanks."

Sam calls for the lights and shades to be restored. Everyone resumes their original tasks. I give him back the light, and we continue to stare at the painting.

"I think we should divide and conquer. I'm going to go see if I can help the others unscramble some letters," he says, clearly bored of standing still.

"Okay," I say. After a few moments of staring at the painting, Cedric, Orin, and Sam begin to boisterously talk among themselves in the corner. Soon they move to the middle of the room. Joel and Anna are now back at the table, another key in their possession. Naomi is busy trying all the keys in the escape room door lock.

I'm probably just wasting time standing here.

"See, Joel? I told you there was another," Anna laughs.

"Hey, there's always a chance I'm wrong," Joel quips back. Their voices filter through my head, and all at once, my brain organizes their words in a different order. Their voices and words get applied to my thoughts about the painting. Miner. See. Sea. Sea miner. I turn to the table.

"You guys, have you gotten any music clues at all?"

"The book I found the key in was a book on piano composers," Anna says.

"We just unscrambled a code and it spelled out *piano*," Cedric adds.

"Wow. Peter is truly a puzzle master," I say, ready to burst with my hypothesis.

"What?" Naomi asks, pausing in her key-trying sequence.

"I'm going to try something." I walk to the piano, excitement flowing through me. I think I'm right. *Oh, Peter, what a neat idea.* When I reach the piano keys, I find middle C and play a C-minor scale carefully and evenly. As I press down each note, the keys stick into place. When I press the final note in the scale, the side of the piano clicks open.

"No way!" Sam says.

I lean towards the compartment and pull it open like a drawer. A key lies inside on seafoam green velvet. I snatch it out. This key is fancy and ornate, and after one look at the teeth, I'm confident it is *the* key.

"I took piano when I was younger and studied art, but I did not put all that together," Naomi says, watching me grin at my find. I'm still reeling from the thrill of solving it.

"Try it in the door!" Anna says gleefully. I cross to the door and push it into the keyhole. It fits perfectly, and I hear the satisfying click of the bolt sliding out of the door frame. Success.

"One lock down, one more to go," I say.

"I think we may have found enough clues already to solve this next puzzle," Orin says, pulling my slip of paper up off the table.

"It's just a bunch of random letters and words," Sam says.

"Not random. Well, I guess they are random to people who don't play music," Cedric indicates.

"Or those who don't understand Alaska and Homer," I add, looking at it again. The words *seal* and *boat* intrigue me the most. Orin hands it over, and I smooth out the wrinkles in the paper, scanning the letters and glancing up at the room before me.

"Find anything to do with seals and halibuts and boats," I say, giving everyone an immediate job.

"Like navy sales?" Sam says with a smirk.

"Not that kind," Orin says, waving Sam away. I roll my eyes and continue to puzzle away at the remaining words and letters. The group of letters 'abcdefg' refer to the musical alphabet. Music only uses those letters when naming notes along the staff to differentiate certain pitches. The others are in reference to the order of sharps and flats. Since there is a piano in the room, I wonder if it had any more secrets.

"I found something!" Sam says.

"A navy seal?" Orin jokes.

"No, a real seal. Or rather, a book about real seals. Look, inside there's a stiff cardboard bookmark. On it is this riddle." Sam spouts it off. He brings it to me and I look it over.

In Homer, she sails, a vessel worth the boast,
For anglers seeking halibut, she's the host.
A vessel sturdy, seekers aboard,
With fins and tails, my bounty stored.
Seek me where land meets sea's embrace,
Where vessels rest in a special place.

I read it out loud so everyone can hear it again.

"So, we are looking for a halibut fishing boat?" Anna asks. I watch her glance at the halibut book on the table where she found a key. Since Homer is the halibut fishing capital of the world, I'm not surprised Peter added something halibut-themed into the room.

"Maybe, but listen to the last line of the riddle. 'Seek me where land meets sea's embrace, where vessels rest in a special place,'" Joel says.

"Boats only rest in one place where the sea meets the land, " Orin says with a definitive crossing of his arms. "A dock."

"So we look for a dock somewhere in the room," I say, turning to look at the piano.

"Docks are made of wood. There's a lot of wood in this room," Cedric muses aloud, running his foot across the creaky floor.

"We can't get that deep into things. Surmising like this will lead us down trails that ultimately waste our time. We only have forty minutes left," I say, glancing at the clock.

"Scour the room for any books on dock building or anything that looks like a dock or boat," Joel says, taking charge. I keep the note securely in my hand, pacing in front of the shelves. The clock's ticking in the room is a constant rhythm to my moving feet, reminding me that we don't have much time left.

Naomi is the one who squeals this time. "Guys! I found a little boat statue attached to a dock on the shelf over there." She holds it up proudly. "And there's something hidden in it!" She tips it upside down, and we crowd around her. She pulls out a piece of paper, her long, painted nails clicking against the glass knickknack.

"What does it say?" Sam rubs his hands together in anticipation. Cedric has his hands on his head and woven into his hair, eagerly leaning over to read the paper.

"It's another riddle," Namoi says. We all take a step back and ponder the words.

I am the key to unlocking your escape,
But also the rhythm that makes you pace.
Can you solve me in this musical race?

I am found in rooms, both real and fake,
But I'm not a puzzle you can simply break.
I'm hidden in plain sight, yet hard to find,
But once you do, you'll leave the room behind.

"I'm not great at solving riddles. Anyone have any suggestions?" Cedric says.

"Hold on, I got this." Orin puts his hands to his temples as if he's willing the answer to fly into his mind.

"Anything yet?" Sam taps on Orin's head with a finger.

"Cut it out. It's slowly processing... Almost have an idea," Orin says, rubbing his head like it will make his brain work faster.

"I'm hidden in plain sight, yet hard to find?' That basically describes everything we've found."

"Not everything. Secret compartments aren't in plain sight," I explain.

"But the clues to find them were. Like the painting and the piano for example," Anna says.

"Okay, fine, maybe they were," I add with a shrug. What could the riddle mean? Was it just something designed to confuse us?

"Got it. What is the rhythm in this room that is making us pace?" Orin says, face alight with enthusiasm. We all pause, taking in his words.

"What rhythm, there isn't any—" Anna tries to say, but I cut her off.

"Time. Time is making us pace. The ticking of the clock is the rhythm!" The piece of paper in my hands slips to the floor and I forget all about it as we race to the wall where the clock hangs.

"I'm the key to unlocking your escape. It has to be something with the clock," Joel says.

"Can you get reach it?" Naomi asks. Joel reaches up and tries to remove it, but it is secured strongly. The camera in the top of it makes it so the entire clock is wired into the wall. It won't budge.

"No go," Joel says, retreating.

"Okay, so we can't take it down..." Cedric scratches his chin, supporting his elbow with one hand, clearly thinking.

"Is there anything on the clock face that could give us any more clues?"

"There are your typical numbers on the face. Nothing else strikes me," Joel says, squinting.

"What else did the riddle say? Something about a race?" I ask, counting

"Can you solve me in this musical race?" Naomi says.

"Music requires rhythm, so I think we got that part, and we are racing to beat the clock. Hmm." I'm out of ideas, but I know that we can beat it. We've made it this far. Already, we've done a great job of solving clues and finding things, even if it has been a bit chaotic.

"We know we need a number code to get out. The pad only has numbers on it. The clock also has numbers on it. What other clues do we have that relate to numbers?"

"Umm... not to waste any more time, but do you think Peter would screw with us and simply make the code the time we had to solve the room?" Sam says.

There's a long pause. Then Joel breaks the silence. "You're a genius, Sam. Or Peter is," Joel says while laughing. Sam walks to the keypad.

"An hour and a half is the exact time we were given to solve the room," Sam says, "which translated into numbers could be inputted as sixty-thirty. Sixty minutes plus thirty minutes. An hour and a half." We crowd around him, hands twitching, knees shaking, stomachs quivering. The beep of the door glows green, and Sam pushes it open.

"We did it," he says in disbelief.

"We did it!" Anna leaps into the air and gives Joel a big hug. Everyone is talking at once.

I stand still, the jubilant cries and stomps of my friends seemingly slow motion around me as I take in the moment. Soon they whisk past and pound down the stairs, hollering victory. I move to follow but not before looking back towards the place where the portal to Breezewood normally opens. Longing fills me, a deep desire to return. One of these days, I'll go back and bring Peter along. I'll probably bring Jen at some point, too. I glance down at my palm, reading the ink words that are forever a part of me. I trace them with my fingers and smile. If Peter ever asks me what I want to do for a future date, I'll just hold up my hand for him to read. I'm easy to please.

Thirty

BRIAR

I'm so proud of Peter. Of course he got the escape room contract and won the puzzle master position. The inspectors came as planned, but so did the owner of the escape room franchise in Colorado, which was a complete surprise. Peter was so nervous, but after one showing and test on the room, they all came out loving it.

They enjoyed Peter's room so much they commissioned him to draw up several more in similar fashion, ones that can be built in other locations. He was also given the position to manage the room here in Homer under their franchise. He accepted the job on the spot, and I watched the handshake and everything. I'm just as thrilled as he is, if not more. Means he'll be staying in Homer long-term. While we have yet to hear any official congratulations from August, I'm sure it won't be long before he makes an appearance or sends us an invitation to join him in Breezewood.

Already, Peter has started spreading the word about the escape room around town and across the whole Kenai Peninsula. There's even a large stack of reservations and a queue of phone calls to return as the room continues to get booked. There hasn't been anything like this in our town, and people are excited for something new and different. Even now, Peter is coming up with more ideas and puzzles to keep the room in the bookstore fresh and exciting. Hopefully twisty enough that no one ever suspects what happened here or what may happen in the future.

With the future of the bookstore leaning heavily into the positive, my original panic to keep it alive has waned considerably. Though, I'm still willing to give it my special touch. Andrew did say that he would let me come up with any more ideas that could help sell books.

After a few days of thinking, I think I found an idea that might just make this place even more exciting.

"Here. Take a look at this," I say, slapping down a folder at the front desk. Andrew lowers his glasses and pulls the folder open. With one glance, his eyebrows raise.

"You came up with this?" His voice is level, impressed, though it trails off into necessary skepticism.

"Of course. I've been giving it a lot of thought."

"It certainly is ambitious and will take time, but it might do the trick," Andrew says, setting the folder down, the graphic inside in full display. I trace the photo with my finger and continue my presentation.

"Homer is one of the most artistic towns I know. Combine that with books that have been in this building for years, and we get sales. People in the community could donate their time to help." I turn the folder in my direction and pull out a few more photos. The night before, I'd spent several hours laying out my ideas and creating graphics to showcase exactly what I had planned. Pictures of old, grungy, low-value books are pasted over with some brightly colored but new tasteful covers. It was necessary to showcase how a good cover increases the book's value, though Andrew would already know this.

"The bookstore is full of books with stories or random writings that will never be bought and read by anyone unless they catch their eye. We both know that everyone judges books by their covers, and one of the key selling points is beautiful art on the front. My idea is that we invite the community to pick a title from a stack we make in the store, get a look at the blurb, and then they paint or craft a pretty cover for the book. We can market it as a way people can support the store without buying anything. Their creativity will literally be infused into this place."

There's a thoughtful pause as Andrew studies my graphics. The whole building creaks with age, and the way sound moves in here is echo free. It is entirely and most permanently dense and dusty.

"If you work out all the logistics and kinks, I'll let you give this idea a try," Andrew says, eyes on the folder.

Relieved, I draw in a satisfied breath, beaming from ear to ear. I can just imagine artists from all over Homer and even farther, sitting at their desks in sunlit rooms, painting to bring no-name books to life. I try to imagine how many more books I would own if almost every book in the store was a work of art. I think we can all agree that there is a high number of books with unjust covers. Some books simply don't deserve the ugly ones they have.

The bookstore is empty of customers except for Peter and Joel who are upstairs putting things back in place after another trial escape room run. There's a cacophony of sliding feet just now. Their friendly, muffled talking through the floor tells me they are almost done. Andrew taps his fingers on the desk.

"We can address this idea in the next few weeks. But for now, I have something to show you. I've never done this for anyone before and never will, unless you agree," he says, breaking me out of my contented thoughts.

"Done what?"

"Brought someone into my private study and showed them my collection," he says, stepping out from behind the counter and walking towards the back room. "Would you like to see it?"

There's no question about it. It's an easy yes from me. "Of course. Who could turn down the opportunity?" I follow, eager to get a glimpse at the rare tomes never before seen on shelves outside this room. The door to the study is left cracked, and I grow giddy as I cross the threshold into the forbidden space. The room is octagonal with tall rectangular windows. Floor lamps fill the room with soft yellow light. Piles and piles of books cover every surface. Desks, shelves, and the place where the piano used to be is stacked with leather bound manuscripts. Most of these books are special enough that Andrew has no heart to sell them while some are simply not yet sorted into the rest of the shop. I spot a copy of *The Hobbit* in green leather and before I can check to see how old it is, Andrew has my attention.

"Since you carry the secret, I know you'll treat this with great care," he says, going to a glass cupboard. He pulls out a keychain and selects a small key, inserting it into the cupboard. Once it opens, he reaches in to withdraw two books. Each is bound in brown leather with gold trim, but the covers and spines are void of any author name. "These are my most prized books out of any in the whole bookstore."

"What are they?" I gasp. He hands them to me, and I run my fingers over their delicate covers. Yellow, deckled pages combined with cracked leather tell me they are at least a hundred years old, if not older.

"Histories of Breezewood. I'm sadly just missing the myths copy. It never ended up in this cupboard. I think it got mixed up with the other books upstairs years ago. You wouldn't happen to know where it is?" He turns to me with a knowing smile.

My eyebrows rise. The copy I accidentally destroyed. It was the myths of Breezewood.

"I'm sorry about your other copy." I cringe, remembering the way the book had disintegrated. Peter and I had told August all about it. He must have told Andrew.

"No matter. Without its destruction, you may not have gone and saved Breezewood."

"I just wish I had connected to something else and not that particular book."

"From what August has told me, one can't always control what they connect to. I can't blame you anymore than I can myself. What's done is done." he says. I nod, staring longingly at the books. Already, the desire to return to Breezewood has taken it's hold and I'm excited to begin planning another journey through. Thinking about it reminds me that all this time, Andrew has been from Breezewood. Was this partially why my portal opened here in the shop? Because it was near someone from the world it connected to? I'd probably never know. I turn to look at Andrew.

"So, Breezewood is your true home?"

"Yes. Though August told you I had forgotten that fact for many years. And even if I had remembered, there was no reason to share a secret so beautiful and dangerous with the world."

"You haven't been able to return to Breezewood since coming to the modern realm, have you?"

"Sadly, no. I was banished and had no need to return plus coupled with my memory loss, I never made it back. But now that my memory has returned, I recall how I used to travel around in Breezewood, searching for books. I spent most of my spare time reading or book hunting. When I was banished from Breezewood and accidentally came through a portal, I was carrying these books with me. They've been my only reminder of Breezewood, but alas, I slowly forgot about them, too. When August told me everything, I finally remembered, and here we are." I sigh, nodding in understanding. What an adventure this all has been. I flicker my eyes to the books again and remember my tattoo.

"You wouldn't happen to know the reason behind the words on my hand, would you?" I ask and move one of the books out of the way. I flatten my palm. Andrew leans over and squints.

"Curious, isn't it?" he shrugs, a small smile pulling at his mouth. He retrieves the books from me and tucks them back into the cupboard, locking it tight.

"It's almost like an invitation." I study the words, shaking my head. In delicate scroll are the words, *What If We Met In A Bookstore.*

"An invitation to adventure." Andrew says.

"I don't know if I'll ever understand it." I squeeze my fingers closed around the words, dropping my hand to my side.

"Perhaps not now, but who says you can't try and find out?"

"What do you mean?"

"Well, I'll need someone to show me the way back home, and Breezewood is full of secrets and answers. Besides, you haven't seen my library," Andrew winks.

Of course there's a library in the castle. I'm going to wallop Wystan on the head next time I see him for not showing me the library the first time. Looks like Jen won't be the only one who's excited to return to Breezewood.

Two weeks later...

Briar,

I have no idea if this will make it to your hands, but I have a feeling Auriol knows how to find you.

Good news, the Reachers seem to have left Breezewood. No sightings of them. Tara and several other patrols have only found small piles of gems in the forest. We can only assume they are the remains of Reachers. Breezewood is safe for now.

August, with Atlas as his advisor, has already turned the mountain kingdom into a new place. With dark magic at bay, the people are learning to seek and trust the truth again, all with August as the new king. I can breathe deeply now. I owe you a great deal.

Kind regards,

~Wystan

P.S. I can teach you more about Breezewood's magic when you come back. And I can show you the new portal I found in the forest.

Acknowledgements

Thank you to all my writing buddies, beta readers, and cheerleaders. This story was made possible by you; Rebecca Alexandru, (For hosting writing nights and critiquing my stories) Drew Taylor, (For recommending resources and hyping up my stories) BethAnne Henry, (for all your encouragement and the many late nights writing with me as a teenager) Ithaca Bergholtz, (For being willing to read my stories and getting excited about it.) Teague Tozier, (For giving me ideas for puzzles and working through writing walls) and to my husband, (For putting up with my late nights, many story ramblings, building me bookshelves, and supporting my bookish dreams.)

Huge thank you to my fantastic editor, Leah Taylor (@ltaylor_author) for going over my manuscript and getting excited for every plot twist.

To ALL my early draft substack readers. You really inspired me to keep writing. Without you, I don't think I would have published this so soon.

To my campers from summer camp. Finally, I have a book published. It took 600,000 words of drafting several other books to get here but I did it. I hope you enjoy Breezewood and the adventures to come.

To the Harden family. You guys gave me my first escape room experience. I loved it so much I had to write a book with an escape room in it.

To Homer, Alaska, and my favorite bookstore there. I hope anyone reading this gets a chance to visit and walk through the maze. You never know, maybe I found a portal there.

To anyone else I missed who was a part of this journey, just know that you were an integral part.

Most importantly, I thank and give all glory to Jesus! I pray this story causes others to think about what it means to be human, what they truly believe in and why they believe it. I pray my readers find Jesus and that their lives continue shine for Him till the end of time.

Author Page

Scan to connect with me!

Find me on Substack: @brynnthebooknymph

Instagram: @brynnthebooknymph

Goodreads: Callie McLay